2 A.M.

By Mark Wilder

The Cold War Returns

2 A.M.
The Cold War Returns

Mark Wilder

Wilder Creek Publishing

Wilder Creek Publishing
30 N Gould Street Suite 29208
Sheridan, WY 82801
ISBN: 978-1-970587-01-2 (Hard Cover)
ISBN: 978-1-970587-00-5 (Paperback)
ISBN: 978-1-970587-02-9 (ebook)
ISBN: 978-1-970587-62-3 (Collector's Edition)
Library of Congress Control Number: 2025924118
Cover design and illustration assembled using Canva Pro.
Final cover copyright © 2026 by Mark Wilder
Interior layout using Atticus
Edited by Roxana Coumans, ProofReadEbooks.com
Final Proofreading by Jane Wilder
Published by Wilder Creek Publishing
Sheridan, Wyoming
www.WilderCreekPublishing.com

MarkWilderAuthor.com
First Printed in Sheridan, Wyoming, United States of America
First Edition: January 2026
10 9 8 7 6 5 4 3 2 1

This book is dedicated to those who served in the original Cold War on Inner German Border traces, the DMZ of Korea, and other thankless, forgotten roles.

For the modern Cold War, it is for those families separated, lives lost and utter senseless destruction in the world as we know it.

How soon we forget genocide and aggression
NEVER AGAIN
PLUS JAMAIS
NIE WIEDER
НИКОГДА БОЛЬШЕ

Unofficial commemorative medal honoring Cold War service.

Acknowledgements

<u>My First Reader</u>:
Armando Ramirez *(Armando Reads)*
Thank you for your honest feedback and review.

During my military career, I served with some great people who influenced my life and definitely this story. They deserved to have their roles defined as characters in my story; or through our shared adventures:

<u>*In No Particular Order*</u>
Carl Martin
Lewis Jefferson
Mark Latimer
Larry Dotson
Anthony "Tony" Carpenter
Antonio Aguto
Colin McArthur
Jason Whitus
David Esparza

From The Author

With thanks to these artists who musically inspired the spirit of this story –
Golden Earring, Queen, Van Halen, Kiss, and Sammy Hagar.
Your sound still chases us down cold roads.

The inspiration for this novel was a teenage boy listening to the lyrics of:

"Twilight Zone" by Golden Earring
and
"Another One Bites the Dust" by Queen.
If you haven't already, play them both before diving in.
This book isn't just meant to be read. It's meant to be heard.

PROLOGUE:
ICE ABOVE – THE HUNT BELOW

Bering Strait — March 1988
USS Hawthorne (SSN-749)
688i-class Fast Attack Submarine
(688i Quiet Upgrade Variant)

The hull groaned — deep, low, and slow, not creaking, but bracing. A cold pressure pressed in from all sides. No alarms sounded, just a soft warping of the walls, like the ocean pressing a little harder. Twenty knots beneath shifting Arctic ice, the *USS Hawthorne* was punching through a narrow channel — black water beneath a jagged frozen crust. There was no room to surface. No margin for error.

Commander Jack Johnson leaned forward in the command chair, a surge of adrenaline simmering just beneath his carefully controlled calm. Fire control was lit up. The crew had been tracking Sierra One, a Soviet Akula, for nearly two hours. The cat-and-mouse had turned into something darker.

They hadn't been hunting her. The Akula had crossed their path just south of the Diomede Islands, threading the narrow corridor between U.S. and Russian waters in the Bering Strait. Per SUBPAC protocols, Johnson's orders were to shadow, log every movement, and report — not engage.

Each sonar sweep and propulsion cycle was fed into the growing intelligence bank in Pearl Harbor, where analysts mapped the behavioral fingerprints of every Russian sub in the Pacific. But this one wasn't simply transiting.

Sierra One was maneuvering with intent. She darted just close enough to paint a signature, then drifted back into the thermal layers like a ghost. It wasn't random. It was a probe. A warning. Or worse — a test.

"Contact bearing 185. Range four thousand meters. She's running quiet, but fast," said Petty Officer Ramirez from sonar. "She's pivoting. Just flooded her tubes."

"Battle stations," Jack ordered. Red lights swept through control. The quiet tension broke into urgent movement.

"She's forcing us to react," Jack muttered, observing its cautious maneuvering. "She wants to flank us off from this channel."

The *Hawthorne* dropped ten feet, banking starboard to mirror the Akula's arc. It was a brutal engagement in tight waters, the kind that only fools or dead men lingered in for too long.

"Match her angle. Get me a solution now," Jack barked. "Tubes one and two — load Mk 48 Mod 5 torpedoes. Don't wait for the first splash. We fire when we see the whites of her screws."

"Tracking steady," fire control reported. "Updated bearing — 352."

The Akula's trail flared hotter. "She's preparing to fire. We've got to — "

"Shit! New contact! Designate Sierra Two." Ramirez snapped. "Close. Inside our baffles. Range fifteen hundred and closing — Christ, I don't know how she got there!"

Jack stood, white-knuckled. "Where is she?"

"Bearing 183. Rising slow. Ultra-quiet. Not Akula. It's something else."

The room chilled. Jack thought, "Two Soviet predators and an ice ceiling. Hell of a trinity."

Jack's voice dropped. "It's the *Kolyma*."

The name hollowed the air. Officially, she didn't exist. But every sonar tech in the North Atlantic had a name for the undersea cemetery she dragged behind her.

The Gravewalker. Unconfirmed by ONI. Believed to be an off-books Severodvinsk testbed — an early prototype in the future Yasen lineage. Internal tubes, twin quiet drives, no shaft line.

She didn't stalk. She waited. Then she erased her prey from existence.

The Kolyma didn't belong here. She was *the* North Atlantic undersea apex predator — Johnson's gut locked.

If the Soviets had sent her to the Northern Pacific, the

Bering Strait — under this much ice, in tandem with an Akula — it wasn't a patrol.

It was a message. And she had already closed the distance.

"Sir..." the sonar operator whispered. "She's right on our six."

"Jesus," someone else breathed. "What the hell is she doing in the Bering?"

"She's aligning off our aft starboard," fire control reported. "We're in her envelope."

The hunter had become the hunted.

Jack's tone stayed level. "They weren't tracking us. They were channeling us."

A piercing *PING* ripped through the hull.

"Akula just lit us up!"

"Active sonar," sonar confirmed. "Both subs have firing solutions!"

"Sir — outer doors opening on both!"

"They set us up," Jack said. "The Akula was bait. The Kolyma flushed us into the trap."

"Torpedo in the water!" sonar screamed. "Kolyma fired — it's close!"

Another voice cracked. "Second contact — Akula just launched!"

"Two fish inbound!"

Jack didn't blink. "Launch countermeasures. Now."

The internal plates shrieked under pressure as the primary countermeasures fired aft. Decoys and noise pulses bloomed behind them in frantic hope.

Jack leaned into the next move with ice in his blood.

Commander Johnson's voice suddenly steadied, low and iron-edged. "Set targeting solution for Sierra One — bearing 352. Tubes one and two, fire on my mark."

He turned to aft weapons control. "Tubes five and six — snapshot solution, Kolyma. Launch aft torpedoes. Do it — before we lose the shot."

Two Mk 48s streaked forward. Two more fired blind into their wake.

"Deploy secondary suite — launch the MOSS!"

A mobile submarine simulator, shot from the hull, sprinted toward the depth where it would mimic the *Hawthorne* and began pinging faintly, broadcasting the *Hawthorne's* screw signature to confuse any hunter still chasing.

"Activate towed decoy. Cut main trail."

The towed device spun off its cradle and bloomed into formation. Behind them, it dragged a new acoustic echo for the Russians to follow.

"CRASH DIVE!" Jack roared. "All hands brace. Dive planes full forward. Emergency descent!"

The helmsman made the sign of the cross, kissed his Saint Christopher medal, and drove the yoke forward as hard as possible while working the rudder controls.

The *Hawthorne* pitched hard. Everything not bolted down jumped, coffee mugs shattered against bulkhead walls.

"Set screw speed to flank — get us through the channel

before it narrows!"

The hull bucked once, like something insulted by its own survival. Bulkheads groaned. Steam hissed through pressure valves as the sub wrenched starboard and down, scraping the ice crust and pitching it into blackness.

Behind them, the MOSS shrieked once — then vanished in a controlled implosion, a sound designed to fool death itself, timed to sound like a fatal hull breach.

Torpedoes tracked them. One detonated behind their tail, close enough to rattle the frame. Another veered wide, drawn by chaff.

"Akula's hit! Splash confirmed!" Ramirez shouted. "Big bloom. Debris field forming!"

"Kolyma's fish is still tracking — wait — "

Nothing. Sonar went blind in the maelstrom of their own screws as they dove through the ice pack.

Then —

A distant thud. A second. Then, a long groan. Metal giving way.

Something imploded in the dark, icy depths. Maybe *some things.*

"Unknown outcome," Ramirez said. "They may still be stalking us."

Jack just stared into the red-lit dark as the hull shivered... as if confirming they were now the prey.

A quick burst transmission was sent: "Confirmed Submarine Naval Buildup. Evading Now."

That night, in the stillness of his bunk, Jack wrote:

Two enemies. One exit. They drove us into the mouth and waited. We fired blind and vanished into the deep. I don't know if she let us live — or just didn't care.

If my son ever walks the surface free, it's because I buried my fear under Arctic silence.

He closed the logbook.

Before he put it away, he reflected on the christening of the vessel, then added one final line beneath the scrawled ink:

"May we be worthy of your blessing on this boat, Commander Helen Bradley, and the Silver Star you earned for actions in this very theater of operations."

Because silence isn't empty. It waits and listens. Not for sound — but for its own absence.

Yet far above, the ice cracked with a strong, distinct, and distant thunderous roar.

*** *** ***

Back To The Wall

Volgograd, Russia – A Lonely Hotel Room

The fear hit first. A thin pulse of panic, cold in his chest. Steve Johnson's finger hovered, but not for long. He had pulled the trigger, squeezing off the only shot that mattered tonight. The gun fired once. Just once.

The body slumped. He didn't blink.

Kill or be killed.

Steve Johnson stared through the smoke. Ten minutes. At best, he had ten minutes to vanish.

The fear was gone, leaving only cold clarity behind.

Across the table, the GRU counterintelligence agent lay slumped, his once impeccable Savile Row suit now soaked in blood.

The man's lifeless eyes stared at Steve, frozen in the final, futile question of a dying counterintelligence officer, "*Who did you see?*"

The air was heavy with the acrid stench of cigarette smoke,

still curling lazily from the ashtray near the dead agent's hand.

The gray tendrils coiled and drifted upward, merging with the dim light of the flickering overhead bulb.

The room itself seemed to exhale decay. The peeling wallpaper sagged in the corners, jagged strips that exposed patches of mold and flaking plaster beneath.

The heater ticked. Warm air brushed the blood on his sleeve like it wanted to forget.

"How did I end up here?" Steve reflected as he glanced at the clock by the bed.

It's 2 A.M.

It was Moscow in late July 2005. The streets of Moscow felt different the morning after.

Steve had been out in the city, wandering through Red Square, past St. Basil's Cathedral, across the cobblestone alleys of old Russia, yet the feeling never left him.

The same one that had been gnawing at him since he left the Rossiya's piano lounge the night before.

Someone was watching him.

Steve turned left at a side street, his boots crunching softly against the uneven pavement. A dimly lit alley stretched ahead, flanked by rows of rusted pipes and decades-old graffiti from the Soviet era. A perfect dead-end.

He counted to five.

Then ten.

Then twenty.

No one followed.

Still, something was off.

Maybe it was the taxi driver glancing at him too often in the rearview mirror.

Or maybe it was the three men loitering near the curb at the stoplight, smoking cheap Russian cigarettes and speaking in hushed tones, their eyes glancing toward him for just a second too long.

Or maybe it was just the paranoia of a U.S. Army Staff Sergeant on leave in Moscow, enjoying good scotch and bad decisions.

He palmed the car keys in his pocket. A weapon, if needed.

The taxi rolled to a stop, and Steve stepped out in front of the Rossiya Hotel, its grand Art Nouveau facade glowing in the twilight. He turned, paid the driver, and started toward the entrance.

He bent down, pretending to tie his boot.

Reflected in a cracked shop window, he caught the man across the street pausing at a kiosk, pretending to buy a newspaper.

The same man who had been smoking outside the café an hour ago.

The same man who had stood near the taxi queue when Steve left Red Square.

A professional. Or someone trying too hard to be one.

Steve casually adjusted his jacket, using the motion to palm a small folding knife from his pocket.

He took a sharp right toward the hotel. The man didn't follow.

Then, the man from last night stepped out from the hotel's shadowed entrance.

A gentleman. Early forties. Nondescript. Black trench coat. European, maybe British. He adjusted his cufflinks, stepped closer, and slipped a small, white business card into Steve's palm.

"If you need help." His accent was unmistakably Scottish.

Steve barely had time to react before the man turned, disappearing around the corner, lost in the river of people passing by.

Something definitely wasn't right. The doorman looked beyond Steve while holding the door wide open. He quickly stared at the ground.

Steve turned from the entrance, eyes scanning the street. That's when he saw the black delivery van pulling to the curb.

Two men stepped out. No, they wouldn't risk a confrontation. Not here.

Dressed in black. No hesitation. Professionals. Military precision.

Steve turned, moving quickly for the doors –

But two more men rushed out of the hotel before he could reach *safety.*

They moved fast, expertly. He barely had time to raise his hands before they grabbed him, spun him, and slammed his arms behind his back.

"What the hell — "

A sharp strike to the kidney.

A sudden, burning pain in his throat from a well-placed elbow.

The last thing he saw before the hood was pulled over his head was the doorman turning away.

Complicit.

Darkness.

A sharp, stinging chemical scent.

Chloroform.

Then — nothing.

Pain woke him first. A dull, throbbing ache in the back of his skull. His wrists were bound to the arms of a steel chair, his ankles lashed to the chair's legs.

The single overhead bulb blinked, casting shadows along the cracked cement walls.

Steve blinked and exhaled slowly. Inventory time.

Wrists bound with zip-ties. Not rope.

No immediate dislocations.

Left eye swollen. Lip split.

Aching ribs. Could be cracked.

This wasn't amateur work. They wanted him awake but compliant.

A door creaked open.

Footsteps. Slow, calculated.

Three men entered.

One was massive, a brutish wall of muscle with a scar running from his left temple to his jawline. His knuckles were swollen from years of breaking bone. The other looked like a Siberian bear.

The third was the real threat. Small. Wiry. Eyes sharp and patient. The kind of man who didn't need to hit you to break you.

The interrogator.

He pulled up a chair, placed it backward, and straddled it with a casual arrogance. His crisp black suit was almost too perfect. A man who played the part well.

He smiled. "Sergeant Johnson."

Steve exhaled, making a show of relaxing into the chair. "Sorry, do I know you?"

A sigh, "I was hoping you wouldn't start with that. I ask the questions here."

The interrogator motioned with two fingers.

A barely perceivable nod followed.

Steve knew what was coming, but couldn't resist. "How cliché."

The bruiser stepped forward and drove a fist into Steve's ribs.

A sickening crack. Sharp pain lanced through his side. "Yep, it could be cracked," Steve thought. "Could be worse."

He ground his teeth, swallowing the grunt that threatened to escape.

The interrogator leaned forward, folding his hands. "Now. Why are you in Moscow?"

Steve let his head loll slightly to the side, blinking slowly. "The Red Square. The borscht. The incredible service at your fine hotels."

The interrogator chuckled softly. "Humor. A defense mechanism. I like that."

He reached into his suit pocket and retrieved a cigarette case, popping it open. Inside were two cigarettes. He lit one, took a long drag, and exhaled lazily. Steve noted the pack of American Camels.

"Here's the problem, Sergeant Johnson." He tapped the cigarette against the metal table. "You believe this is about you. It's not."

He set the cigarette case down on the table with deliberate precision.

Steve eyed it. A test.

"Who did you see last night?" The interrogator's voice was gentle, almost inviting.

Steve shrugged, wincing at the pain in his side. "I saw a bartender who poured an excellent Balvenie, a pianist with soft hands, and a woman who — "

The bruiser struck again. Harder.

Steve's vision swam, white-hot pain ripping through his ribs.

"Let's try again," the interrogator said, his tone unchanged. "Who did you see?"

Steve spat blood onto the floor and smirked. "My reflection."

The interrogator leaned forward, his cigarette burning down to the filter. He exhaled slowly.

"Your unit deployed to Ukraine last year, didn't it, Sergeant?"

Steve didn't blink. "I was stationed in Germany."

The interrogator smiled, shaking his head as he plucked a file from his briefcase and tossed it onto the table. It slid across the worn steel surface, stopping just inches from Steve's fingers.

A photograph lay on top of the file. The image made Steve's heart rate spike, barely — but it did.

A grainy surveillance image. A blurred figure exiting a train station. The timestamp read March 14, 2004. Kyiv.

Bullshit. He had never been there.

The interrogator tapped the image. "That's you, isn't it?"

Steve's gaze flicked to the side — just for a fraction of a second — but the interrogator caught it.

"We already know you were there. Why lie?" His voice was soft and patient, like a parent disappointed in their child.

Steve let out a slow breath.

They were trying to insert false memories. He'd seen the playbook before — start with a lie just close enough to the truth to make you question everything. Keep you awake at night, wondering if your own brain is the traitor.

The interrogator tapped the papers. "Maybe you were in Kyiv.

Maybe you weren't."

Steve met his eyes. The bastard wasn't asking questions. He was rewriting history, one fabricated detail at a time.

"Soon," Steve thought, "even I won't know what's real — if I let them."

He leaned back and smirked. "You guys always go for the bad Photoshop first? Or do you usually plant the evidence, too?"

The interrogator nodded toward the bruiser.

The next punch landed harder.

Steve blinked through the blood trickling down his forehead, lips curling into a weak grin.

"You hit like a bureaucrat," he muttered.

The bruiser's fists clenched.

The interrogator chuckled. "That bravado won't last."

Steve licked the blood from his split lip. "Oh, you'd be surprised."

The bruiser cracked his knuckles. "We'll see."

"Sure. But can I get a drink first? Maybe a cigar? You guys used to have style in the KGB days. Now it's just fists and bad cologne."

The interrogator leaned forward. "This isn't a movie, Sergeant Johnson."

Steve smirked. "Could've fooled me. You guys even got the evil lighting just right."

The interrogator nodded to the bruiser. Another hit.

Steve groaned, but the smirk didn't leave his face.

"Okay," he rasped, coughing. "Now it's a movie." Steve was not

going to break from a beating. But it might weaken him.

A gleam of something in the interrogator's eyes. Amusement. Or maybe approval.

"Did she make you feel like she could love you?" he asked.

Steve's heartbeat skipped. Just enough.

The interrogator caught it. His smile widened. "I know who she is. Sergeant Anya Kuznetsova. GRU. Counterintelligence."

"Do you know what I think, Sergeant Johnson?" He let the words settle between them.

Steve forced a neutral expression. "I think you love the sound of your own voice."

The interrogator laughed — a soft, genuine chuckle. "Oh, but you're good. Trained, clearly. The problem, though?" His voice dropped to a whisper. "She set you up."

Nothing.

Steve blinked. Didn't move.

The interrogator tilted his head slightly, watching him. Measuring.

"She knew exactly where you would be, didn't she?" he continued. "The Rossiya. The bar. The pianist. The 'chance encounter.' The stolen glances. And you — like the pathetic, desperate little American you are — thought it was real."

The bruiser grabbed Steve's hair, wrenching his head back.

"You don't look so confident now, Sergeant." The interrogator leaned in so close that Steve could smell the cigarette smoke clinging to his suit. "You think Sergeant Kuznetsova didn't report every detail about your meeting? That she wasn't

watching you from the start? You're a toy to her. A means to an end."

He reached for the cigarette case, plucking the last one.

"Tell me," he murmured, rolling it between his fingers. "Does it sting? Knowing she's already moving on to her next mark?"

His jaw tensed, with fingers tightening into fists despite the zip ties. Momentarily confused, Steve suddenly realized these were not Russian military-grade zip ties.

The interrogator noticed.

"Ah," he breathed. "There it is. The seed of suspicion. The doubt. It only takes a little, you know. Just enough to fester."

Steve didn't flinch, but the words cut deeper than the bruises. He didn't know what Anya had told them — or what they'd made her say.

Hell, maybe she never had a choice. But whatever truth existed, it wouldn't come from this room, and it sure as hell wouldn't come from the bastard grinning at him now.

If there was one rule Steve trusted in any interrogation, it was to "Never believe the man offering you a story."

He leaned back, exhaling smoke toward the ceiling. "You sign the confession, Sergeant. Say what we want you to say, and I let you go. You return to your little NATO world with a good story to tell. Maybe she even meets you again someday. Pretends to care."

His grin widened. "Wouldn't that be nice?"

Steve exhaled through his nose. Slow. Controlled.

Steve's mind worked even as the pain in his ribs pulsed like a war drum.

Something was definitely wrong about all of this. The GRU would never risk an open abduction in Moscow unless they were covering something larger. A misdirect. He was meant to escape.

But why?

His eyes flicked to the interrogator's wrist.

Cufflinks. NATO blue.

Not Russian. Western-made. The American Camels.

His breath slowed.

They weren't GRU.

They were something else.

That changed everything.

Then he smiled.

"You almost had me."

The interrogator's grin froze.

And in that split second, Steve knew the truth. He had to play until he could escape.

They were lying. They would pay for this, whoever they are.

"You know what I love about you GRU guys?" Steve murmured, his voice rough but steady.

The interrogator's eyes narrowed.

"You think you know how to break someone," Steve smirked. "You're used to agents, intelligence officers, bureaucrats. But you don't know soldiers."

The interrogator's fingers twitched. A tell. Steve pressed.

"You don't know what it's like to crawl through six miles of mud and blood, waiting for the moment to die. You don't know the thrust of an Abrams engine at full speed or the feeling of your best friend's last breath on your cheek."

He shifted, feigning comfort in the chair. "You think a few well-placed punches and some mind games are enough?"

The interrogator remained silent, his hand visibly trembling.

Steve chuckled, spitting blood onto the floor. "Get in line."

For the first time, the interrogator lost his smile. He wasn't supposed to face defiance.

Then he nodded toward the bruiser.

The next hit was coming. Steve braced. Interrogation techniques shifted from a nearly Western-style approach to those of the old Soviet era.

Deep inside, he had already won.

They didn't break him. And they never would.

Eventually, Steve stopped answering the hits. His body slumped in the chair, feigning weakness.

Then, the interrogator sighed. "Fine. You sign the confession; we let you go."

Steve lifted his head. "What's the confession say?"

"That you are an agent of the CIA, gathering intelligence."

Steve snorted. "And if I don't sign?"

The interrogator's smile didn't reach his eyes. "Then we find other ways to make you sign."

Steve nods ever so slightly, looking defeated.

He untied Steve's wrists, nodding toward the restroom. "Clean yourself up. Then, we record."

Steve stood, hands unbound and legs shaky. A test of his strength.

He moved weakly toward the restroom. Splashing water on his face. Looking in the cracked mirror.

His reflection stared back. Bloodied and bruised. Furious was the only way to describe the look in his eyes.

Realization washed over him. GRU would never attempt to capture a confession from a CIA agent. They would try to turn him. Something is incredibly wrong.

The light bulb exploded in his head. He clenched his fists. Time to move.

Back in the room, the interrogator adjusted the camera. A guard stood by the door, arms crossed.

The interrogator held out a sheet of paper and a ballpoint pen. "Sign," he said.

Steve lunged.

All six feet two inches and 230 pounds of him lunged into motion.

He slammed the camera into the guard's face, sending him crashing to the floor.

Spinning, he wrenched the ballpoint pen from the

interrogator's hand — twisting the man's wrist until he howled.

Before the second guard could react, Steve grabbed him by the throat, shoving the pen against the bear's carotid artery.

"Which way is out?" Steve growled, pressing the pen to the point of breaking skin. The guard dropped his weapon.

The interrogator, now pale, pointed.

Steve backed toward the door, spotting a wedding ring on the guard's finger. Steve moved fast to stab the guard deep in his thigh with the pen instead of killing him. Quickly, he scooped up the Makarov.

One step.

Two.

The Makarov's steel frame was cold in Steve's grip.

One shot to the door lock.

Sparks. A sharp whine of metal. It was jammed.

He took two steps back, his mind racing. No time. They'd be regrouping.

His eyes flicked to the fire alarm.

A calculated risk.

Steve fired once into the sprinkler system.

Water exploded from the ceiling, drenching the room.

Then, he grabbed the nearest chair, snapping off a wooden leg — a crude club, but a weapon nonetheless.

Footsteps pounded down the corridor.

Steve flattened himself against the wall, the Makarov raised.

The first man through the door didn't even have time to breathe.

Steve's gun hand moved fast. One shot to the knee. The man crumpled, screaming.

The second hesitated.

Big mistake.

Steve swung the chair leg hard — catching him in the throat.

The man hit the floor, gagging.

Steve grabbed the first guy's belt, yanking free a knife — a Spetsnaz ballistic blade. "Now we're talking," Steve muttered.

Then, he drop-kicked the interrogator in the chest, sending him sprawling.

He slammed the door shut — one round from the Makarov through the electronic door lock mechanism.

"That should slow them down." But who were they? They spoke Russian... but didn't act like Russians."

They weren't amateurs, but they weren't GRU, either. Too clean. Only one locked door. Too controlled. Like they wanted me to escape."

Behind him, alarms blared.

Time to disappear.

Darting through alleyways, he moved like a shadow. Past old brick buildings. Through side streets. Toward the city center. "Safety in numbers," Steve thought.

The cold wind whispered through the narrow Moscow street, swirling eddies of snow and dust around Steve's boots as he slowed his pace.

An elderly woman stood hunched over a small wooden table, her gloved hands carefully arranging hand-painted matryoshka dolls. The bright reds and blues of the nested figures contrasted starkly against the gray, worn backdrop of the city.

Steve approached, slipping his hands into the pockets of his coat. His weak Russian was steady, softened just enough to sound familiar.

"Babushka, do you have a doll for my mother?"

The old woman looked up, her sharp, pale-blue eyes meeting him with the weight of someone who had seen too much of history pass her by.

She nodded, selecting a larger nesting doll, its smallest figure barely the size of a thimble.

"For a mother? Then it must be strong... but beautiful."

Steve smiled, accepting it carefully and placing a few extra rubles into her wrinkled palm.

As the babushka wrapped the doll in crinkling paper, Steve's gaze drifted to the reflection in the window behind her.

The glass, slightly warped by age, painted a distorted view of the street. A black Lada idled at the curb.

A man in a dark coat loitered by a newspaper stand, his cigarette burning too slow, his posture too still. Coincidence?

Being hunted was exhausting.

He clenched the small doll in his palm, feeling the smooth, lacquered surface beneath his fingertips.

Why couldn't he just be 16-year-old Steve Johnson again? A kid from Maine, standing barefoot on the rocky shores of Nova

Scotia in the summer, salt spray on his skin, his mother's voice laughing in the wind?

He remembered his father, Commander Jack Johnson, standing beside him, staring at the sea with an unreadable expression.

Even as a boy, Steve had sensed something in his father's gaze — a longing for something beneath the waves. A memory? A haunting memory from old battles fought in silent waters?

Now, Steve found himself doing the same — searching every window, every reflection, for shadows that stalked him.

The old woman wrapped the wooden doll with careful precision; her hands weathered from years of work.

"You are not safe, grandson," she murmured, eyes scanning the empty street.

Steve stiffened. This wasn't just paranoia — it was a lived experience that older generations had seen before.

The way Russia's power fractured, the way outsiders were used as pawns in games beyond their control.

He thought of Moldova, of Belarus. Russian loyalists tightening their grip while their own countrymen whispered about secret uprisings.

The Kremlin wanted control. But not everyone inside Russia wanted to be controlled.

Steve clenched his jaw. "Nyet, Babushka. But I will be. Spasibo."

The woman pressed the wrapped doll into his hand. "A gift for your mother."

He turned, slipping the nesting doll into his pocket. His mother would love it. If he made it home to give it to her.

He saw it across the street. A payphone.

He reached into his pocket.

A few coins. A business card.

He dialed the number.

A voice answered. "Congratulations on the escape, Sergeant Johnson."

A few minutes later, a car pulled up. The same man from before. The one who had given him the card.

"Nice work," the man said as Steve opened the car door.

Steve slides into the car, breathing hard, still on edge. "So, who the hell are you?"

Grinning, "The man who kept your hotel room open while you were getting acquainted with Russian hospitality."

Frustrated, Steve glares at him. "I don't remember signing up for that."

"No, but we knew you'd pass the test." The man looked straight ahead as he drove.

Steve, anxious and quite upset, "We? Test?"

The man just looked at him. "Sergeant, let's not pretend you're still just a tank commander on vacation. Welcome to ESID, Susi!"

Of course. The European Strategic Intelligence Directorate. Steve exhaled. "Again, who the hell are you?"

"Someone who can offer you assignments in Eastern Europe, Russian language training, and excitement." The man had a smirk this time.

"Excitement?" Steve muttered. "That's one way to put it."

After a moment's pause, "My name is Alistair MacRae, code name 'Nansen'."

"Like the polar explorer?"

"Yes. I find things in the coldest places. You were already scouted by ESID in Hungary and Poland for your combat performance, strategic mind, and ability to function autonomously. This vacation in Moscow presented an opportunity to see how you reacted under pressure. The abduction was a test. You are exactly the type of lone wolf agent we need."

"The abduction was by ESID? I'm glad I didn't kill anyone, then." Steve was wondering if that was true, though.

MacRae nodded ever so slightly, then continued. "You will have your own assignments. Full NATO support. No politics, just action. We will train you to be fluent in Russian."

Steve looked at him as if to say, "Keep going."

The man smirked. "Unlimited access to Russia. Paid vacations. Best whiskey in the world. ESID and NATO Intelligence."

Steve ran a tongue over his split lip. "Let me guess. I don't really have a choice?"

MacRae chuckled. "You always have a choice, Sergeant."

MacRae reached over to delay Steve from opening the door.

"Before you go. Nervously twisting cufflinks is an ESID warning signal. Your fallback safety points are Istanbul, Sofia, and Tbilisi. Get to any one of them, and someone will guide you to a safe house in one of these cities. But only if you find yourself in a no-win situation."

Steve's dark, stern look came back. "I never accepted, Nansen."

"You just did, Susi. Besides, life makes choices for us."

Steve reflected, "There is never a true 'no-win situation,' just opportunities."

Stepping into the Rossiya, the desk clerk greeted him with a smile. "Mr. Johnson, your room has been changed, and your stay has been extended. Your bill has been covered. Meals, bar tab. Everything."

Steve took the key, then hesitated at the elevator before turning.

He walked to the bar, took a seat, and ordered a Balvenie 14-Year Caribbean Cask.

As he raised the glass, he smirked. "Why should I get deeper involved in a world where they recruit you with lies? Tankers rely on truth and trust each other."

"Well, at least it's paid for." Glancing at the key sleeve, it is the penthouse suite.

A hand on his arm, well-manicured nails that he instantly

recognized. Her look changed to deep concern as he turned his face to Anya.

"Oh my. You had an interesting day. Let me clean you up." She put his scotch in his hand, took his room key, and led him to the lobby elevators. He easily followed her lead.

Steve's grip tightened around the cold steel of the TT-30 Tokarev, the recoil of the single 7.62x25mm bullet still echoing in his senses. The warm gun brought him back to reality.

The clock on the nightstand now blinked, "2:05 A.M.," each passing second stretching into a suffocating void.

Outside the hotel in Volgograd, the city remained oblivious to the storm that had erupted in this forgotten room.

Steve's mind raced, replaying the events that had led to this moment.

Colonel Ivan Petrov had become his contact, a disillusioned officer desperate to expose the truth. The Colonel's unit, the 9th Motorized Rifle Regiment, had been a key piece in a larger Russian strategy — misdirection on the Ukrainian border, as two full Russian Tank Armies amassed for a devastating strike.

But what Petrov had shared earlier in the evening revealed something far darker.

Steve hadn't known much about Colonel Ivan Petrov the first time they met, just that he was one of the few Russians who could still look you in the eye and mean it. Not out of kindness. Out of conviction.

Afghanistan had carved him. He didn't brag about it — he merely carried it in his posture. Clean uniform. Faint limp. The kind of man who remembered the names of the soldiers he buried and the weight of the soil on each shovel-load.

His only daughter had been killed during the shelling of Sevastopol. Wrong place. Wrong time. Right war. Petrov never blamed Ukraine. He placed full blame on the generals in Moscow who called it patriotism.

They say after that, something changed. He stopped drinking vodka and started drinking information. He started asking questions no one wanted answered.

That's when he made the first contact — through a Polish intermediary. NATO thought he was probing, vetting us. Turns out, he was already finished with Russia. He just hadn't left the room yet.

Petrov loved Russia too much to abandon her. But he hated what she'd become. Said it reminded him of a patient in a coma — still breathing but brain-dead and full of tubes pushing propaganda into her veins.

***

Just hours before the fatal gunshot in the hotel, the scent of fresh-brewed coffee had mingled with the crisp evening air as Steve and Petrov sat at a small table in a café overlooking the Volga River. The soft hum of conversation around them seemed innocuous, but Petrov's restless gaze betrayed the tension crackling in the air.

"They're going to come after me for this, you know," Petrov began, his voice low and tight. His hands shook slightly as he lit a cigarette, taking a long drag before exhaling sharply. "But I can't stand by while doing nothing any longer. I'm done serving men who see the world as nothing but a chessboard."

Steve stirred his coffee deliberately, masking his unease. "What are we talking about, Colonel?"

Petrov leaned in, his voice barely above a whisper. "Two full Russian Tank Armies," he said, his accent sharp against the silence between them. "They'll feint along the Ukrainian border — smoke and mirrors. But the real strike will come from the south. Poland, Slovakia, Hungary, Romania. All at once."

Steve kept his expression neutral, though his pulse quickened. "That's ambitious. Even for the Kremlin."

Immediately, the fear of Colonel Petrov being fed false information rose in Steve. He pondered whether Petrov had possibly been caught in a counterintelligence canary trap, determining which person was feeding state secrets.

"Ambitious?" Petrov scoffed bitterly. He took another drag, his eyes scanning the café's entrance. "It's suicidal. But they don't care. Army Group South will push through and conquer Moldova first — the Dniester River is the key."

He traced an invisible map on the table, his fingers trembling as they marked out the strategic points, "Secure the crossing, then drive into Europe. NATO will be too paralyzed to respond in time."

"They're gambling with everything," Steve said, his tone even.

"Gambling? No, they've rigged the game." Petrov's voice dropped, his tone sharp and urgent. "They've infiltrated everything — command structures, alliances, even your intelligence networks. The GRU isn't just anticipating NATO's moves; they're shaping them. Feeding disinformation, controlling the flow of intelligence, and steering the alliance into a reaction that suits Moscow's plans. By the time you realize what's real, it'll be too late."

Steve narrowed his eyes. "You're describing NATO's funeral."

Petrov gave a grim smile, hollow and devoid of hope. "Yes. And Moscow will deliver the eulogy."

He reached into his pocket and pulled out a small USB drive. "This is the proof. The battle plans, the disinformation playbook, and the agents they've placed within NATO. Everything you need to expose them."

When he handed Steve the USB, his hand shook. Just a little. Not from fear. From finality. Men like him didn't expect to live long after the truth changed hands.

"Don't waste this," he'd said.

Steve eyed the thumb drive warily. "That's a lot of trust for a coffee meeting."

"They know I'm here." Petrov's tone darkened, and his gaze settled on Steve. "There's no going back for me. Take this, expose them. Do something with it. Because if you don't, there won't be a Europe left to save. I did not dedicate my life to Russia just to see a few power-hungry men collapse her from within."

Steve immediately knew their dead drop had been compromised, and his situation was becoming precarious.

The memory of Petrov's warning now rang hollow in the hotel room. The Colonel hadn't been wrong. The GRU had sent an agent to silence him before the plans could change hands.

And now, in the overwhelming stillness of the night that followed the gunshot, Steve stared down at the cooling body of the GRU agent and wondered what scared Moscow more — that the files were out — or that someone like Ivan Petrov had believed Steve Johnson was the one worth handing them to.

Petrov's lifeless body was probably already being cleaned up elsewhere, the loose ends tied off. Steve had always pondered what could drive a man like Petrov to betray his country.

In the eyes of the Kremlin, Colonel Petrov was a traitor. But to those who know the truth, he was a man of honor, caught between duty and conscience, fighting not for a regime but for the soul of Russia itself.

Now, the GRU's eyes were on Steve.

The room compressed around him — not by size, but stillness. The smoke hanging in the air curled toward the dead man's face, obscuring his hollow eyes.

Steve needed to move. He stared down at the crumpled figure of the GRU agent one last time, his breath steady, his pulse unnervingly calm. The sharp report of the Tokarev had been absorbed into the aged walls of the hotel, then faded into a silence so heavy it seemed almost alive.

The stench of burnt gunpowder mingled with the cigarette smoke still hanging in the air, an eerie reminder of the confrontation that had just ended.

Steve's gaze shifted to the small wooden desk by the window, where the night had begun to unravel.

The laptop was still open; its screen was casting a pale glow across the room. Petrov's words from earlier at the café by the river echoed in his mind, low and deliberate, each one heavy with meaning.

"They are moving pieces you cannot see, Stefan Ivanovich. Not just on the borders but in the corridors of power. I have the proof you need," Petrov hinted as he set up the meeting in the café, "it is the beginning of understanding. It is everything you need to know about what is coming, and who is behind it."

The GRU agent had been good. Too good. Steve hadn't

heard him enter the room, only the subtle displacement of air as he moved.

But instinct had taken over, the years of training and missions sharpening his senses. He'd feigned ignorance, staying hunched over the laptop as though unaware of the danger creeping closer.

The agent's mistake was his arrogance. He had assumed the element of surprise was enough that Steve would be caught off guard.

But when the agent lunged, the glint of a knife flashing in the dim light, Steve was already moving.

The fight had been brief but brutal. Steve's chair toppled backward as he twisted away from the blade.

A punch landed against his jaw, sending stars across his vision, but he recovered quickly, grappling for control. The agent was stronger and faster, but Steve had the advantage of resolve.

In the chaos, his hand found the Tokarev beneath the pillow where he'd stashed it earlier — a habit formed through necessity, not paranoia.

One kick, center mass. The agent had staggered, clutching his stomach as he fell into the chair. Steve held him there at gunpoint, offering him a cigarette.

The man took a few drags off of it. "пошел на хуй (poshel na khuy — fuck you)," lunged forward, grabbing Steve by the shoulder; he had tried to force the upper hand with his final question.

"Who did you see?"

Steve crouched beside the lifeless form, searching the agent's pockets with methodical precision. A black leather wallet yielded a GRU identification card under a false name, along with a handful of euros.

A burner phone rested in an inner pocket, its screen locked. Steve pocketed both.

Standing, Steve glanced at the clock again — 2:08 A.M. He needed to move. The gunshot wouldn't go unnoticed forever, and whoever this agent had been working with might already be on their way.

But there was something he couldn't shake — the agent hadn't come to kill him outright. No, this was an interrogation. They knew he'd spoken with Petrov, and they wanted to know what he'd learned.

Steve returned to the desk, grabbing the USB drive and shoving it into his pocket before biometrically securing the laptop and stowing it in the bag.

Petrov had warned him on another occasion. "Trust no one, Stefan Ivanovich. Not even those who say they love. The harder you dig, the more you will find. And the more they will come for you."

He slung the laptop bag over his shoulder, taking one last look at the body before entering the vodka and sweat-stenched hallway and stepping out into the cold Volgograd night.

Whoever the agent had worked for had just declared war.

And Steve had no intention of losing.

His thoughts shifted to the car. The GTO. It was his only hope.

The ignition clicked, and the deep rumble of the 455 V8 engine came to life beneath the hood of the 1971 Pontiac GTO. Steve's hands tightened on the leather-wrapped steering wheel as the engine growled, sending a surge of power up his spine. The dash clock read 2:10 A.M.

The tires gripped the asphalt with determination as Steve slammed the accelerator. The car lurched forward, its power palpable in every vibration of the chassis.

The Cherry Bomb exhaust roared in the cool night air, defiant and primal, a warning to anyone daring to follow.

The GTO's expanded fuel capacity gave it a range of almost 500 kilometers. Steve calculated his route quickly — straight west toward the border. He'd need fuel eventually, but with luck, he'd be across the frontier before dawn.

Nearly 1,900 kilometers to NATO territory. Every second counted.

Petrov was gone.

He was more than just a source of information.

Steve had met Katya later in 2005 during his second vacation in Russia, following the whirlwind that was his first visit to Moscow. St. Petersburg felt like a different world — artistic, elegant, and steeped in history.

It was there, in a modest dacha on the outskirts of the city, that Steve first met Sergey Ivanovich Orlov, a retired Soviet tank commander and the father of his girlfriend, Katarina — Katya.

Sergey was a towering figure in every sense of the word — physically imposing, with a sharp mind honed by decades of service in the Soviet Tank Forces.

He carried the bearing of a man who had seen the worst of war but retained an intellectual curiosity that often surprised those who underestimated him.

Over a dinner of borscht, black bread, and vodka, Sergey grilled Steve about his service in the U.S. Army.

Steve, unflinchingly honest, described his role as an M1A2 Abrams tank commander, his respect for NATO's combined forces, and his admiration for Russian military engineering.

Sergey, impressed by Steve's sincerity and tactical acumen, found himself warming to the young American reluctantly.

"You know," Sergey said, gesturing with his glass, "if you had been born in my time, you and I might have served on opposite sides. But I think we would have respected each other."

On a warm summer day in 2012, Steve was surprised to find Sergey bustling around the house, preparing for a guest.

"An old comrade is coming to visit," Sergey explained. "You will like him. He's a good man, though the years have made him ... complicated."

When Colonel Ivan Petrov stepped into the dacha, Steve felt as though the room had immediately filled with the weight of history.

Petrov carried himself with the confidence of a seasoned officer, his uniform sharp despite his pending retirement. His piercing blue eyes scanned Steve with a mixture of suspicion and curiosity.

"Sergey Ivanovich, you didn't tell me there would be an Amerikanskiy here," Petrov said in Russian, his tone cautious but not hostile.

Sergey clapped Petrov on the shoulder and laughed. "This one's different, Ivan. He's family — or close enough."

Petrov raised an eyebrow but said nothing, taking a seat at the table.

As the evening progressed, the conversation turned to the Soviet-Afghan War, where Sergey and Petrov had served together in the 1980s.

Sergey had been a regimental commander, while Petrov — then a young captain — had led a motorized rifle company under his command.

Together, they had endured the harsh realities of Afghanistan — the ambushes in the mountain passes, the deadly IEDs, and the grinding attrition of an unwinnable war.

"Do you remember the pass at Kunar?" Sergey asked, pouring another round of vodka.

Petrov nodded grimly. "How could I forget? We were outnumbered, outgunned, and out of supplies. If you hadn't brought those T-62s up the ridge, we would have been overrun."

Steve listened intently, absorbing every word. When Petrov glanced at him, Steve took the opportunity to speak. "It sounds like you saved a lot of lives that day, Colonel."

Petrov studied him for a moment before replying. "And what would an American tank commander know about that?"

"Was the bazaar at Marawara there in 1980?" Petrov and Sergey both stopped and stared at Steve.

"If I recall, they sold silk, saffron, and Soviet rifle parts." Steve sensed he had caught Colonel Petrov off guard. "In 2002, I was forward deployed to Camp Resolute. It was 15 kilometers north of Kunar. Our war was young, the roads were as deadly as the Taliban mujahedeen, and the roar of my tank's turbine was often the only thing keeping the ghosts at bay."

The room fell silent. Petrov leaned back, his expression unreadable, then gave a barely perceptible nod. "Perhaps you're not as naive as I thought."

Over the next few days, Steve and Petrov found themselves talking more and more.

They compared notes on tank tactics, discussed the differences between the M1 Abrams and the T-72, and even debated the merits of NATO versus Soviet command structures.

Steve's genuine respect for Russian military history — and his refusal to condescend or boast — began to chip away at Petrov's initial skepticism.

It was Sergey who finally broke the ice completely. One evening, as the three men sat by the fire, Sergey turned to Petrov and said, "Ivan, you've always been a good judge of character. What would you think of this American marrying my daughter?"

Petrov smirked, his blue eyes glinting in the firelight. "He's got guts, I'll give him that. But I think he'll need more than that to survive marrying into this family."

Steve laughed, and for the first time, Petrov joined in. It was a small gesture, but it marked the beginning of an unlikely friendship.

In the years that followed, Steve and Petrov would cross paths several times, often at Sergey's insistence.

Petrov came to respect Steve not just as a soldier but as a man who shared his sense of duty and honor.

Despite their differing allegiances, they found common ground in their desire to protect the people they cared about and to uphold the ideals of military service.

When the world descended into chaos during the new Cold War, Petrov found himself questioning his loyalty to the Kremlin.

It was Steve who reminded him of Sergey's words: "A true soldier serves the people, not the politicians."

That bond — born of shared respect, forged by Sergey's influence, and tempered by the fires of war — would ultimately lead Petrov to make a choice that would change the course of history.

The city lights of Volgograd faded in his rearview mirror, replaced by an empty stretch of road.

The stars above seemed cold and distant, the night closing in around him. Every instinct screamed at him to stay alert. The GRU wouldn't let this go.

His mind flashed back to Petrov's final words: *"If you don't, there won't be a Europe left to save."* Steve clenched the wheel tighter, the USB drive heavy in his pocket.

The GTO roared, its engine growling like it knew the road. He rolled the window halfway down. The wind smelled of snow and smoke. A stark contrast to the inside of the car, where gas fumes and gunpowder still clung to his skin.

For now, the pavement was all that mattered.

No Other Sound

Moscow – Rossiya
Hotel

*S*teve lingered next to Anya in the elevator, still battered and bruised from the interrogation, watching the brass-lit numbers climb toward the penthouse suite. He exhaled through his nose, trying to drown out the hum of shifting Cold War alliances in his mind.

She effortlessly and lovingly slid her hand into his.

The world had rewritten its battle lines in the last five years. Moscow was no longer just Moscow.

It was the epicenter of a new geopolitical arms race — one fought with disinformation, economic blackmail, and strategic assassinations.

The GRU played the long game. Destabilize Ukraine. Weaponize the Arctic shipping routes. Bleed NATO with proxy wars in Africa and cyber sabotage in Brussels.

Every move was a page torn from the old Cold War playbook, updated with modern tools and tactics.

And Steve was just another cog in the machine, hunting an

enemy whose face was still a question mark.

The elevator doors whispered open, revealing a world apart from the cold streets of Moscow.

The penthouse suite at the Rossiya Hotel was a stark contrast to the damp alleys and interrogation rooms Steve had endured just hours earlier.

Gilded chandeliers cast a warm glow over plush leather furniture, and the scent of fresh linen and expensive cologne lingered in the air.

Anya Kuznetsova rushed to the panoramic window, looking out; her silhouette was caught in the city lights — intimate, deliberate.

She turned as Steve followed her in. Her gaze immediately locked onto the bruises that were darkening his face.

The lighting in the room showed the full extent of his rough treatment. Her expression alternated between deep concern and barely restrained fury.

"Bozhe moi, Stefan," she whispered, stepping toward him, fingers tracing over the cut on his cheek. "Who did this to you?"

Steve smirked, exhaling through his nose. "Room service was a little rough at breakfast."

Anya wasn't amused. She caught his wrist, pulling him toward the master bedroom. "Sit," she ordered, already disappearing into the bathroom.

Steve sank into the edge of the bed, watching her move with precision. The way she shifted from affectionate to clinical in an instant was something he had always admired in his mother —

and now feared in Anya.

When she returned, she knelt before him, dabbing a damp cloth across his cheek with practiced hands.

"Hold still," she murmured, voice softer now. "You need stitches, but I doubt you'd sit still for that."

Steve grinned. "You doubt correctly."

She sighed, shaking her head, but didn't argue. Instead, she pressed a cold compress against his ribs. The sharp sting made him wince.

She picked up the phone and rang the concierge. "Send someone up immediately. We need some clothes dry cleaned at the hotel. Instruct them to use the delicate laundering process for Western clothing."

She thought briefly before adding, "We need them sent back up when we order breakfast."

Steve ran a tongue over his split lip, watching Anya pick up the phone. One call. That's all it took.

Russia's newest war wasn't fought with tanks. It was fought in digital shadows, in the whispers of doctored images, in deepfake recordings of NATO generals "admitting" to war crimes that never happened.

One phone call from Anya could be twisted into a grainy recording, edited, and broadcast as proof of "CIA espionage." One misstep and Steve Johnson's name would be paraded on Russian news as a captured NATO saboteur.

His grip on the armrest tightened. The bullets and knives weren't what worried him anymore.

It was the lies.

Steve's grin told her everything he wanted her to believe, "Staying for breakfast?"

Then his smile faltered. A dry cleaner used by the GRU, no doubt. I'd like to know what the delicate laundering process consists of here.

She wasn't just tending to him — she was setting something in motion. He wasn't sure if she did it willingly or if it was simply a precaution built into her life.

Either way, it didn't change anything.

"You really know how to pamper a guy," he teased.

Anya arched an eyebrow. "Oh? Then perhaps you will appreciate the next part."

She disappeared into the en-suite, and a moment later, he heard the sound of running water. A bath. A hot bath. Steve couldn't remember the last time he'd had one that wasn't lukewarm and stolen between deployments.

"You spoil me," he muttered as he leaned against the doorframe, watching her test the water's temperature.

Anya glanced over her shoulder, her smirk carrying something dangerous. "I know."

As Steve climbed into the tub, Anya disrobed, poured two glasses of wine from the suite's bar, and joined him in the oversized tub.

Steve watched her silently get ready for dinner. The way she moved with effortless grace and precision.

Just as her hand had lingered just a fraction of a second too long on the phone receiver after hanging up.

He'd spent years learning how to read a battlefield, but he'd spent even longer learning how to read a room.

Was she being careful for his sake? Or hers?

He glanced toward the balcony doors. The faintest reflection of city lights reflected off the glass. A trick of the light... a camera lens... or a sniper scope at a kilometer's distance?

He needed to know more. About Anya. About who had sent her. Or if anyone had.

Paranoia was part of the job — usually a virtue.

But this felt different. The signs were real... weren't they?

He didn't want to be right. God, he wanted to be wrong.

But in this world, wanting something didn't make it true.

An hour later, bruises hidden beneath a fresh suit and tension dulled by hot water, Steve walked beside Anya down the grand staircase of the Rossiya. Her dress immediately had all eyes on her.

The restaurant glowed with golden light, the sound of cutlery and laughter filling the air as they entered.

A sommelier guided them to a private corner table, the kind reserved for diplomats and men who operated in shadows.

Steve noted the discreet exits, the placement of security, and the presence of men who belonged to no nation but held influence overall.

The dilemma of the path in front of him, the path he originally chose, and the path his father wanted are all profoundly different.

Especially at the point in time in which he suddenly finds himself.

The gnawing of guilt at spending taxpayer dollars is wiped away instantly as a sharp pain reminds him of his bruised ribcage. "Let's go all out, Anya. Price is not an issue."

Anya ordered for them both — an impeccable selection of Georgian wines, Ossetra caviar, and stroganoff so rich it made Steve momentarily forget the bruises beneath his suit.

She was performing, playing her role flawlessly. For the GRU? For herself? He wasn't sure.

"You are smiling," she noted between sips of wine. "Something amusing?"

Steve chuckled, shaking his head. He muttered to himself, "I didn't say 'yes.'"

Anya's glass paused at her lips, her gaze flicking to his.

But she only hummed in amusement, taking a slow sip before replying. "You always say yes to me, Stefan Ivanovich."

Then added seductively, "Always."

She had heard him. Now she is toying with him.

He definitely had not said yes to ESID. And yet, here he was.

Reality hits as the rising sun glares into Steve's eyes, reflecting off the rearview mirror. His second day with Anya had been life-changing, but primarily because of the morning with

ESID and MacRae.

He didn't want this. And yet, here he was. Again. "I was happy making 'Tank go Boom'."

The GTO rolled to a low growl as Steve eased it into the gas station, its headlights slicing through the early morning gloom.

The pump's metallic clunk echoed as he parked next to it, and he stepped out into the crisp air, pulling on his hat.

Lushank lay silent and still — just another sleepy village on his long, winding path west, just under 450 kilometers from Volgograd.

Steve removed the fuel cap, listening to the hiss while pausing for a moment to scan his surroundings.

A hunched figure emerged from the station's dimly lit doorway — a man in his sixties, clad in a thick wool sweater and a fur-lined ushanka.

His steps were unhurried, his face deeply lined from years of sun and wind.

"Morning," the man said in Russian, his voice gruff but not unfriendly. "Don't see many cars like that around here."

Steve gave a faint smile as he fitted the nozzle to the tank.

"Probably because there aren't many left. 1971 Pontiac GTO. American muscle." He patted the hood affectionately. "Runs like a dream."

The attendant snorted. "It sounds like a thunderstorm and smells like a refinery. What does it drink — vodka or petrol?"

Steve chuckled, appreciating the dry humor. "Good

old-fashioned 95 octane, but I wouldn't mind if it took vodka. Might be cheaper."

The attendant smirked and leaned against the pump. "What brings you to Lushank? You don't look like a local."

"Business," Steve replied, keeping his tone light. "Passing through, looking for quiet roads and good coffee."

The old man grunted, crossing his arms. "Quiet, we've got. Good coffee? You'll be lucky. There's a café down the road, though. Decent breakfast, too, if you don't mind the occasional fly in the soup."

"I've had worse," Steve said, pulling the nozzle free and twisting the fuel cap back on. "How far is the next big town?"

"Donetsk's a good haul southwest. Kharkiv's even further to the northwest. Why? Are you in a hurry?"

Steve glanced at the early morning sun; a faint smirk showed on his lips. "Not particularly. Sometimes, the car just drives herself."

The old man shook his head with a wry chuckle. "Well, good luck, young man. The roads out here can be tricky, especially if you're not paying attention."

Steve reached for his wallet, handing over a few crumpled bills. "Thank you for the warning. I'll keep an eye out."

As Steve climbed back into the GTO, the sound of tires crunching gravel pulled his attention to a GAZ-31029 police car pulling into the station.

The faded navy paint and rust patches on the car told a story of long service, and the two officers inside looked equally weary.

The older officer climbed out first, a stout man with a thick mustache and the air of someone who had seen too much to be impressed by anything.

His younger counterpart remained behind the wheel, yawning into his fist.

"Beautiful car," the older officer remarked, approaching the GTO. His tone carried curiosity, but there was an edge of caution in his gaze.

"Thanks," Steve replied, stepping out again and tipping his hat slightly. "Just giving it a stretch on these quiet roads."

The officer nodded, glancing over the car. "Is it American?"

"American-born, Russian-adopted," Steve said with a slight grin. "It's getting used to the cold."

The officer let out a dry laugh. "Good luck with that. What's your destination?"

"Wherever the road feels smoothest," Steve answered cryptically, pulling a cigarette from his jacket pocket but not lighting it. "Though the gas station attendant here mentioned a café down the road. Said the coffee's good enough. I might go there first."

The officer raised an eyebrow. "He's generous. The coffee's passable at best, but the sausage and potatoes aren't bad. Local specialty."

"Noted." Steve looked at the officer's partner, who was leaning out of the car window, squinting at him. "What's his deal? He looks like he's trying to place me."

The older officer glanced back at his partner, then shrugged. "Don't mind him. He just had the sausage and potatoes. You know how it is with rookies; he needs a nap now."

Steve chuckled. "They don't make them like they used to."

The officer's eyes lingered on Steve's face a moment longer. "You don't look like a tourist. Or a businessman."

Steve shrugged, leaning against the GTO. "And you don't look like you're getting enough sleep, but here we both are."

The officer snorted but didn't press further. "The café's about a kilometer up the road. You can't miss it. And drive slow — our roads aren't made for racing."

"Thanks for the tip," Steve said, his tone light but his gaze steady. "I'll try not to wake anyone up."

As the officer turned back to his car, Steve climbed into the GTO, the engine rumbling to life. He gave the officers a small wave as he pulled away, the police car shrinking in his rearview mirror as he made his way toward the café.

Steve parked and started to put his hat on to walk to the café. He stared at it for a moment. He hesitated — and just like that, he was back in Maine.

The air was crisp with the earthy scent of fallen leaves as Steve drove Katya through Maine's scenic byways, the road framed by fiery reds, vivid oranges, and golden yellows.

Katya's face lit up with awe at every bend, her eyes widening as she pointed out maple trees. Her smile made her glow.

Bundled in a cozy knit sweater, her brown hair danced with the early afternoon breeze when they stopped for photos. Her laughter was like a melody against the peaceful country backdrop.

Every moment with her was sensation-filled — her joy, her curiosity, her warmth.

Steve found himself falling deeper in love as they kissed beneath the kaleidoscope of autumn leaves; he knew these weeks would be etched in his memory forever.

Outside Presque Isle, they soared high above the landscape in a hot air balloon. Katya clutched Steve's arm as they ascended, her nervous giggles fading into gasps of wonder as the world opened below them.

"It's like a painting!" she whispered, her eyes brimming with tears of joy.

The balloon pilot pointed both hands to the north, then spread his arms until his hands extended to the east and west, "Everything you see in the distance is Canada, on all three sides."

She gasped in awe. Steve turned her towards him and then kissed her gently, his heart swelling at her raw emotion.

Their journey took them to Vermont, where she eagerly sampled real maple syrup outside White River Junction.

Dressed in a warm scarf and boots, Katya laughed as she tasted it straight from the tap, her lips sticky with sweetness.

"I'm never going back to store-bought," she declared with mock seriousness, making Steve chuckle. "No. Seriously. Now kiss my sticky lips, Stefan Ivanovich!"

In Salem, Katya marveled at the historic homes and shops, her fascination with the witch trials drawing them into forbidding museums and cobblestone alleys.

Beneath the full moon outside the infamous Witch House, she shivered in the brisk autumn air, and Steve wrapped her tightly in his arms, knowing she was exactly where he belonged.

"I feel like we've been walking through history," she spoke softly... though her voice could not conceal her being awestruck.

In Boston, they spent a week at the Providence Hotel, where Katya's excitement was uncontainable. She wore a sleek leather jacket and held Steve's hand tightly as they navigated the bustling streets around Boston University.

The highlight was the Foo Fighters concert across the street at Fenway Park. She danced with abandon with the light show, her laughter and cheers blending with the crowd's roar.

Back in the room, after the concert, she surprised Steve with a black Curtis Bailey wool felt fedora, placing it on his head with a playful grin.

"It makes you look like a spy," she teased, unaware of how close her joke was to the truth. He would rarely ever be seen not wearing it again.

Steve kissed her passionately, the weight of his secret momentarily forgotten. If only she knew how much she grounded him, even as his world spun in shadows.

The café was modest, with faded paint and wooden tables that gave it a rustic charm. The smell of frying potatoes, fresh bread, and coffee hung heavy in the air.

Steve removed his hat as he entered, choosing a table near the window. The waitress, a woman in her forties with tired eyes and a cold look, approached with a notepad in hand.

"Coffee and a traditional farmer's breakfast," Steve said in Russian, his accent deliberate but soft. "And maybe a smile if it's not extra."

The waitress chuckled, jotting down his order. "Smiles are extra. Just like coffee."

The café carried the sting of burnt coffee, and sounds from the kitchen.

Steve let the warmth of the room settle over him, the aromas stirring another memory he hadn't expected...

Katya had sat across from him, her dark eyes glinting with mischief as he brushed a strand of mahogany hair from her face.

The afternoon sunlight streamed through the windows of the small café, the scent of gardenias drifting through the open window, mingling with the aroma of freshly brewed tea and warm baklava... and Katya Belikova .

Steve felt nothing could make his life more complete.

Outside, the muted hum of St. Petersburg's old, cobbled streets created a rhythm of the movement, like a melody they alone could hear.

"Nyet, Stefan," she had teased, her voice rich with humor, her accent curling softly around the words. "Not 'spa-siba' like an American. It's 'spasibo.' Shorter. Softer. Like a whisper."

Her smile deepened as she demonstrated the word again, her lips moving deliberately, the lilt in her tone impossible to mimic but mesmerizing to hear.

He had laughed, shaking his head at his own clumsy attempts to replicate her precision. The sound of his laughter had made her smile widen, her fingers brushing his hand as she slid a plate of golden, butter-slick blini toward him.

The faint spark of her touch lingered, sending a welcoming warmth coursing through him, sharper and more potent than even the vodka they'd shared the night before.

The sunlight danced across her cheeks, illuminating a delicate constellation of freckles he hadn't really noticed before.

She had leaned slightly forward, her expression softening from playful to something more intimate.

"You are stubborn, Stefan Ivanovich," she had said, her voice lowering. "But I admire your persistence."

Unhurried, they had shared the simple meal, the world outside their bubble of conversation receding into insignificance.

The shadows of their separate lives — his clandestine missions and her quiet work as a curator at the art museum — had felt distant; their life burdens were momentarily unimportant in each other's presence.

She had looked at him then, a quiet intensity in her gaze that made him feel as though she saw past the layers of secrets he carried.

"Tell me something in French," she had blurted, breaking the silence, her voice carrying a note of curiosity.

He hesitated, searching for the right words, before finally leaning closer, his voice low and deliberate as he spoke.

Her laughter in response had been light and carefree, a sound he would later carry with him, replaying it in those dark and uncertain moments of his missions.

It wasn't just the sound of her laughter — it was the way it softened the edges of his world, grounding him in something real, something worth fighting for.

And as he sat in the café now, waiting for his breakfast, the memory felt so vivid that he could almost hear her voice and feel the faint brush of her hand against his.

It was a memory that lived in the spaces between his missions, a tether to something untainted by the chaos of his life.

Steve blinked, the memory dissolving as the waitress set his plate down with a quiet thud.

For a moment, he could almost smell the gardenias again, but it was gone as quickly as it came, replaced by the sharp bitterness of the coffee in front of him.

His breakfast soon followed, the plates steaming. Steve ate slowly, savoring the rich, hearty flavors. The coffee, dark and bitter, was a sharp contrast to the warmth of the food.

At a nearby table, a man in his mid-thirties sat alone, nursing a cup of tea.

His plain suit and stiff posture betrayed military discipline, and his frequent glances toward Steve were anything but casual. GRU.

Steve lingered at his table longer than he usually would, sipping the last of the bitter coffee and watching the village slowly come to life outside the café window.

His instincts told him to leave — too many minutes in one place always carried risk — but something held him back.

The man in the stiff suit hadn't stopped glancing in his direction, each glance sharper, more deliberate than the last.

Steve's peripheral vision caught the subtle signs — barely noticeable tension in the man's shoulders, a hand lingering near his jacket pocket as if it concealed something important.

The movements weren't conspicuous, but they weren't casual either. This wasn't a passerby, idly curious about a foreigner. It was the watchfulness of a hunter sizing up his prey.

The man finished his tea, his movements methodical as he stood and made his way toward the exit.

Steve watched his reflection in the window — a fleeting moment of hesitation as the man passed his table.

The man stopped, hesitating before leaving. As he turned back to look at Steve one more time, Steve noticed and gripped the knife and fork just a little tighter.

Then he was gone, stepping into the sunlight beyond the door.

The sight of the man triggered a memory. A different place, a different time. Moscow. Twelve years earlier. A weekend date with Katya and a very special lunch.

That lunch was with Colonel Petrov and had been a quiet affair, tucked away in an old Soviet-era restaurant with dark wood paneling and stiff-backed chairs.

They talked about history, politics, and war. But it was only as they finished their drinks that Petrov had smirked and leaned forward, his voice edged with amusement.

"My first name is Ivan, you know," he had said, tapping his glass. "And your Russian name — Stefan Ivanovich — means 'son of Ivan.' If people overhear us, they might start thinking you are my son."

Steve had warmly returned the grin. "I would be honored if

they did.”

Petrov had gone quiet for a moment, then nodded. “You would have been a good son.” His voice carried an unexpected weight. “The son I never had.”

Neither of them had known then how much those words would mean. How, less than a year later, Petrov’s only daughter would be killed in Sevastopol, collateral damage in a war she had nothing to do with. How Petrov would break, and how Steve would step into a role neither of them had foreseen.

However, that was the future — Steve’s present day. On a different day, in August 2013, when Steve was still just a soldier on leave, a man about to meet his girlfriend for dinner and a show.

Before that, he was unknowingly about to have some impromptu fun as he was about to encounter the GRU for the first time.

It had started when he rounded a corner about a block from the restaurant and spotted the man across the street from his GTO.

Tall, lean, with a sharp suit and a sharper gaze — GRU, or at least close enough. The way he loitered, trying too hard to look disinterested, set off every alarm in Steve’s head.

The man was watching him, curiously assessing him.

Steve grinned. Alright, let's play.

Tugging his black Curtis Bailey fedora a little lower over his eyes, he slid into his GTO, the black paint gleaming under the Moscow sun.

The big-block V8 rumbled to life, a deep, throaty growl that turned heads.

He inched up to the stoplight where the GRU man now stood on the curb.

Steve turned his head, met the man's gaze, and revved the engine. The cherry-bomb exhaust didn't disappoint.

The man's expression barely flickered. But Steve saw the muscle in his jaw tighten.

The light turned green.

Steve dropped the clutch.

The GTO's tires screamed against the asphalt, leaving a thick streak of rubber behind as the car rocketed forward.

The roar of the engine echoed between the buildings, drowning out the honking horns of startled drivers.

In his mirror, he saw the GRU man grab his radio and bark something into it.

Then came the chase.

A black Lada Priora — likely the first available unmarked car — lurched into traffic a few cars behind him, its driver fighting to keep up as Steve weaved effortlessly through the afternoon congestion.

The Lada was a decent car, a common sight in Russia, but against an American muscle car tuned for speed? No contest.

Steve pushed the GTO onto the outer ring road, letting the speedometer climb past 190 km/h. The GRU car was fast, but not fast enough.

Then he saw another Lada entering the outer ring road ahead of him. He had two choices: get stopped and interrogated or disappear.

He reached under the dash and flicked a hidden switch.

The small nitrous oxide system he had installed months earlier kicked in with a burst of raw power.

The GTO launched forward, the surge slamming him into the seat as he left both Ladas — and the GRU's questions — far behind.

A few hours later, he had slipped back into Moscow, taking a long way around to shake any lingering tails.

By the time he parked behind Katya's hotel, his pulse had settled, the adrenaline still humming beneath his skin.

She was waiting for him in the lobby, arms crossed, one brow arched.

"Having fun while I left you unsupervised?" she asked, her voice laced with suspicion.

Steve only grinned. "Always."

⬛

Back in the present, sitting in the café, he exhaled slowly, his fingers tightening around his cup. The game was still being played. Only now, the stakes were much higher.

Steve slid his chair back, stood up, tossed some rubles onto the table, and put his hat on, pulling the brim down low as he exited the café.

Outside, the morning had grown brighter, the hum of life gradually replacing the quiet stillness of earlier.

He noted the silence, broken only by the rhythm of his steps. He kept his steps steady, though his muscles were taut with readiness.

The GTO stood where he had left it, gleaming even under the faint layer of dust. But next to it, a Lada sat idling, its driver's side door open. The man in the suit stood by the GTO's door, scanning the interior.

Steve's pace slowed, his mind racing. The café's warmth was a distant memory now, replaced by a cold, calculated focus.

The man's jacket had shifted slightly, revealing the unmistakable outline of a sidearm beneath the fabric.

Steve stopped a few meters away, his voice calm but carrying an edge. "Looking for something?"

The GRU man froze, his hands slowly rising from his side. Slowly, he straightened, turning to face Steve. His expression was controlled, but the tension in his jaw betrayed him.

"Who are you?" the man asked in Russian, his tone casual but laced with authority. "Why are you here? Where are your papers?"

Steve didn't answer. He feigned, reaching for his papers, and moving in a blur, he grappled with the man, slamming him into the side of the Lada.

The only thought going through Steve's mind was, "Now it's truly going to be fists and bad cologne."

The GRU agent twisted, throwing a wild punch, but Steve ducked and countered, driving his knee into the man's stomach.

Seizing the moment, Steve reached into the Lada, grabbing the PPS-43C.

The GRU man lunged for him, but Steve swung the weapon, the butt striking his opponent's shoulder and sending him sprawling to the ground.

The distant wail of a siren cut through the air. Steve looked up to see the GAZ-31029 barreling toward them, its blue lights flashing.

He grabbed two spare 35-round magazines from the Lada's glovebox and slung them into his jacket.

The police car screeched to a halt. The older officer from earlier jumped out, his pistol drawn. "Drop the weapon!"

Steve exhaled, gripping the PPS-43C tightly. "Please, don't do this," he said firmly, in clear Russian.

The officer's resolve faltered, but he raised his weapon anyway.

Steve flicked the setting to full auto and fired first, the submachine gun spitting a burst that tore through the officer's chest. He fell backward, his pistol clattering to the ground.

"Another one down," Steve muttered, his voice low and bitter.

The younger officer froze, his hands trembling as he stared at the scene. Steve fired at the patrol car's tires, shredding the rubber and ensuring no pursuit.

The GRU agent had crawled to the open door and keyed the mike on his radio.

Steve let loose another quick burst. As the agent slowly released the microphone, the last words the dispatcher heard were in English, "And another one down."

The younger officer stumbled out of the car, his eyes wide with panic as he fumbled with his weapon.

Steve didn't hesitate. Another controlled burst sent him sprawling beside his fallen partner. "And another one."

Steve glanced down at the bodies, the blood pooling on the dirt road. The distant hum of life in the village hadn't yet caught up to the violence.

He had minutes at most before the sirens brought more trouble.

"Sorry, comrades," he murmured, slinging the PPS-43C over his shoulder. "But you were in the wrong place at the wrong time."

Steve moved quickly, tossing the PPS-43C onto the front seat of the GTO. He retrieved a small black case from under the driver's seat and popped it open.

Inside were forged documents, cash in multiple currencies, and a compact satellite phone. He slipped these essential items into his jacket, slammed shut the case, and pushed it back under the seat.

The GTO roared to life, its engine growling like a mythological beast. Steve shifted into gear, the tires chirping on the pavement as he sped away from the scene.

His heart pounded, his hands steady on the wheel. The clean exit he had hoped for had turned into a bloodbath.

The road stretched out before him, twisting and turning through the sleepy Russian countryside.

The sleepy village of Lushank quickly faded into the rearview mirror, but Steve knew this was far from over. His mind raced, calculating his next move.

The GRU wouldn't let him slip away easily, not after what just happened — they'd have names, descriptions, and a trail of bodies to follow.

The GRU agent's words lingered in his head: *"Who are you? Why are you here?"*

The question was rhetorical.

They knew enough to suspect him but not enough to catch him — yet.

That would change if he didn't stay ahead of them.

The Pontiac GTO thundered westward, devouring the road beneath its wide tires.

The speedometer hovered at 140 kph, but Steve hardly noticed.

His grip on the steering wheel was iron-tight, his knuckles white against the black leather.

The Russian police vehicle was long gone in his rearview mirror — burning and lifeless.

He exhaled sharply.

He hadn't planned on killing them. That moment outside the café had been about survival.

But now, the adrenaline had faded, and the weight of what he'd done settled in his gut like lead.

They hadn't been GRU. Just uniformed officers in the wrong place at the wrong time.

Maybe they were corrupt, perhaps they were under orders, but at the end of the day, they had just been men — men who probably had wives, kids, routines.

Men who might've spent their shift longing to be home instead of caught in a shootout with a foreign operative they never expected to face.

Steve ran a hand down his face, feeling the crust of dried blood on his lip.

Was there another way?

Maybe. Maybe he could've disarmed them, knocked them out, stolen their vehicle. But there hadn't been time. They had drawn on him first. He had reacted.

And now they were dead.

The thought gnawed at him, sharper than the bruises on his ribs, deeper than the gash on his shoulder.

It wasn't his first time killing outside a war zone. But soldiers were different. Soldiers signed up for it. These men? They had been thrown into a world they didn't even understand.

He glanced at the pistol resting on the passenger seat. It wasn't personal.

The words rang hollow.

Up ahead, the road stretched into darkness. No checkpoints yet. No sirens. Just the vast, empty Russian steppe and the hum of his engine.

A memory surfaced. Jack Johnson standing beside him on the Maine coast, staring at the Atlantic, the cold wind whipping through his old Navy-issued jacket.

Steve had been barely fifteen, watching the tide roll in, hearing his father's voice, low and steady, as they spoke of him teaching his son to shoot.

"A gun is easy to fire, son. Too easy. The hard part comes after. When you ask yourself if it was worth it."

Steve swallowed hard.

He had done what he had to do.

But was it worth it?

The GTO roared on, but the question lingered, unanswered, in the cold night air.

He reached for the secure satellite phone and dialed a number from memory. The line clicked, and a calm, professional voice answered on the other end.

"How may we direct your call?"

"It's Susi," Steve said, using his ESID codename. "Compromised near Lushank. GRU on my tail. Three down, possibly more incoming."

There was a pause, then the voice responded. "Understood. Route to fallback point Zeta. We'll redirect your extraction. Avoid major roads — local police may already be alerted."

"Negative. Heading for the nearest crossing point. I will advise." Steve replied, ending the call.

He tossed the phone across the front seat and tightened his grip on the wheel. His eyes flicked to the rearview mirror. No sign of pursuit yet, but it was only a matter of time.

As the GTO thundered westward, Steve's mind returned to the GRU agent and the café. The man had been watching him, but not with the precision of a seasoned operative.

In Brussels, a secure cell phone receives a message. "Castling on the Queen's side. Cypher, Out."

Susi was a pawn, someone sent to probe to test the waters. The real hunters wouldn't be far behind.

Steve's westward direction was being tracked by more than just ESID, and that means the GRU must know, too.

The road ahead forked, one path leading to a small village, the other winding into dense forest.

Steve didn't hesitate. He veered toward the trees, the GTO's tires biting into the dirt and gravel as he left the asphalt behind.

The dimply lit intelligence operations center at Supreme Headquarters Allied Powers Europe (SHAPE) hummed with quiet efficiency.

Rows of analysts sat before banks of screens, dissecting intercepted communications, satellite imagery, and electronic warfare signals.

Each station monitored a different sector of NATO's growing battlefield, tracking the intricate movements of Russian forces across Eastern Europe.

Norwegian Air Force Sersjant Erik Nygaard rubbed his eyes as he scrolled through yet another set of satellite images from Budyonnovsk, a strategic airfield nestled between the Black and Caspian Seas.

He had spent the better part of the night correlating electronic warfare signals with unusual air movements, but what he had just uncovered stopped his breathing.

Two full wings of Tupolev TU-106 "Yastreb" bombers were now staged at Budyonovsk.

Russian ground crews were hastily covering them with satellite-defeating camouflage nets. But it was too late.

This was new. And not good.

Nygaard frowned. The TU-106, Russia's latest strategic stealth bomber, was an anomaly in Russian deployment doctrine.

The Kremlin had never concentrated them this far south.

Most of Russia's strategic bombers — TU-22M3 "Backfires" and TU-95MS "Bears" — were forward-positioned along Belarus, covering the Smolensk and Kaliningrad corridors for what NATO expected to be the main thrust into Poland and the Baltic states.

Yet here they were — Russia's most advanced long-range, nuclear-capable bombers, parked just outside Georgia.

This wasn't standard force posturing. This was something else.

His pulse quickened as he dug deeper.

Reviewing the file on the TU-106, Nygaard's stomach clenched. It wasn't *just another bomber*.

It was Russia's answer to the B-21 Raider, a stealth-capable, long-range platform designed for deep penetration strikes.

Official specifications were hard to come by, but the NATO intelligence assessment in Nygaard's hands indicated:

Combat Range: Over 6,500 kilometers, meaning it could hit any target in Western Europe or the Middle East without refueling.

Payload: Up to 30 metric tons, configured for:

Hypersonic Kinzhal-2 missiles (Mach 9, nuclear and conventional variants).

Kh-101/102 cruise missiles, capable of low-altitude terrain-hugging flights.

Decoy drones and electronic warfare pods for SEAD (Suppression of Enemy Air Defenses).

Electronic Warfare Suite: Integrated L402 Himalayas jamming system capable of disrupting NATO's AWACS and Aegis systems.

Low Observability: Composite materials, radar-absorbent coatings, and a profile designed to evade Western air defense radars.

Its placement in Budyonnovsk was not defensive — it was offensive.

Nygaard chewed his lower lip, flipping through additional sensor readings from NATO's Cobra King ground-based radar arrays in Turkey.

His fingers danced across the keyboard, overlaying the heat signatures of the aircraft with recent electronic emission bursts.

The bombers were cycling up their power systems.

Preparing for something.

He felt a gnawing sense of unease. If these bombers were meant to support Russian ground operations, they should have been in Belarus or Western Russia — not near the Caucasus.

Russia designed the TU-106 specifically to counter NATO's IADS (Integrated Air Defense Systems) and missile shield systems.

This is definitely going to be a problem for someone.

A voice snapped him out of his thoughts.

"Sersjant Nygaard, you're staring at that screen like a lovesick conscript. Find something interesting?"

Nygaard turned to see Adjudant-Onderofficier Jasper van Dijk, a Dutch intelligence warrant officer with over two decades in NATO reconnaissance.

Van Dijk was known for seeing through Russian deception — and for his sharp, unsentimental approach to intelligence.

"Adjudant-Onderofficier. Could you look at this, please?" Nygaard gestured to the screen.

Van Dijk leaned in, his sharp, analytical eyes scanning the

data. A long pause.

Then, a quiet exhale.

"The TU-106s are wrong. This is wrong." His voice was calm, but Nygaard could see his mind working at a blistering pace.

"They should be positioned in Smolensk or Kaliningrad. Instead, they're sitting on the doorstep of the Caucasus with strike packages configured for offensive operations. And they've begun running electronic warfare tests." Nygaard tapped a file. "They are pulsing jamming signals that — if sustained — could blind the Turkish Kalkan radar net."

Van Dijk straightened. His hands tightened behind his back as he processed the implications.

"This doesn't sit right," he muttered. "TU-106s should definitely be staged in Smolensk, not Budyonnovsk."

Nygaard nodded. "It's an offensive setup, no doubt."

Van Dijk exhaled sharply. "Check the Black Sea Fleet's latest movements. Any signs of unexpected maneuvers — rerouted supply convoys, submarines repositioning, a spike in radio silence — anything that doesn't match their standard pattern."

Nygaard frowned, already pulling up satellite reconnaissance logs. "You think this is tied to a naval operation?"

"I think," Van Dijk said grimly, "that we're looking at only half the play."

"We need to firm up an assessment before getting this to Sentinel. The Russians are not playing the game everyone suspects they are." His tone carried weight.

Sentinel was the NATO Supreme Commander's call sign — information reaching Sentinel meant the highest levels of NATO command were about to react.

Nygaard exhaled. "You think they're using Budyonnovsk as a forward strike base? Against what?"

Van Dijk's eyes darkened. "Not Poland. Not Lithuania. This isn't about the Baltic offensive."

Van Dijk drew a quick circle 6,500 kilometers from Budyonovsk.

It went deep into Russia, the Chinese border, Iran, the Persian Gulf, the Mediterranean region, and... "Damn them ... this is about the southern borders of NATO."

Nygaard looked back at the satellite images, his stomach tightening.

Nygaard's brow furrowed as the naval database updated. "Strange. Two Kilo-class submarines slipped out of Sevastopol three days ago, but there's no record of their orders."

Van Dijk's gaze darkened. "Find them."

Nygaard typed rapidly, pulling up a secondary live feed of Russian fleet operations in the Black Sea.

His heart started racing when he spotted something even more unusual.

"Sir, I'm seeing patterns of consistent electronic warfare activity coming from the Kuznetsov's sister carrier, the RFS Pyotr Velikiy," Nygaard said, his voice suddenly more alert.

Van Dijk leaned in. "The Pyotr Velikiy? That ship's not

supposed to be in operation. It was supposedly docked for refits."

"Well, it's definitely operational now." Nygaard tapped a key, overlaying EW emissions on the Black Sea grid. "The ship is running continuous rotational jamming flights using modified Su-34R 'Fullback' aircraft. They're blanketing radar grids along the Turkish and Romanian coasts, right up to the NATO air defense perimeter."

Van Dijk stiffened. "They're actively testing NATO's response times."

"Not just that," Nygaard said, zooming in on the patrol rotation map. "They're mixing jamming flights into the fleet's regular Combat Air Patrols (CAP), masking them under normal flight operations."

Van Dijk exhaled sharply. "They're hiding their EW birds among their air defense fighters."

Nygaard's fingers danced over the keyboard. "They're targeting NATO's integrated air defenses along the Black Sea — jamming ground-based radar, testing gaps. This isn't routine. This is battle prep."

Van Dijk nodded grimly. "Write this up and send everything you've got to me. You'll brief Sentinel with me. This just became priority one."

The Russians weren't just setting up for a conventional war on the northern flanks of Eastern Europe.

They were preparing for something bigger.

And no one in NATO had seen it coming — until now.

Would Sentinel believe them?

Steve kept pushing through the night. The forest closed in around him, the shadows deepening as the sun climbed higher.

The GTO's engine echoed through the trees, its growl a defiant challenge to anyone daring to follow.

Steve allowed himself a moment of reflection, his grip on the wheel loosening slightly.

This wasn't the first time he'd been hunted, and it wouldn't be the last. But as long as he kept moving, he had a chance.

Steve thrived in chaos.

This war wasn't over. It was only just beginning.

Have I Gone Too Far

Southwest Russia – Desolate Highway

The Pontiac GTO thundered west along the P228 highway, its 455-cubic-inch V8 growling in defiance of the stillness in the open countryside.

The rising sun stretched long, golden fingers over the fields and forests, casting rays of light that shifted as Steve guided the car through the gently winding roads.

The crisp air of a mid-summer Russian morning rushed through the open window, mingling with the scent of pine and the faint tang of gasoline.

For the first time in 24 hours, there was no immediate danger, no lurking presence to track him or shadow of GRU agents.

But even in the calm, Steve felt the sirens in his head — echoes of his past mingling with the tension of the present.

Something was wrong. If someone was watching him, it should have been the FSB. The GRU handled military intelligence, not foreign spies.

So why the hell were they interested in him?

Steve had spent years in intelligence work, but habits formed long before that — back when he was just a tank commander who knew how to read a battlefield. This was a different battlefield.

Steve mulled the thought over, trying to piece it together. The FSB was supposed to be in charge of counterintelligence and domestic surveillance.

That meant if someone was tracking him, it should be one of their guys.

But FSB wasn't here. The GRU was.

Why?

That was the question that wouldn't let go.

Steve could not shake the feeling something was very wrong. It kept repeating in his head, "FSB handled spies, GRU handled war."

That meant whatever was happening wasn't just about one American on the run. It was about something much bigger.

Was Moscow losing its grip? Was GRU operating independently now? If they were ignoring FSB protocols, it meant internal fractures were forming inside Russia.

And then he remembered — this wasn't the first time he'd seen something that looked out of place...

Seven years ago. Brussels...

Steve had sat across from NATO'S intelligence Adjudant-Onderofficier Jasper van Dijk in an unassuming NATO bar, where intelligence officers gathered to talk off the record.

Steve still felt more comfortable around uniforms.

"You ever wonder why Russia hasn't invaded anywhere since the new President took over?" Steve had asked, watching Jasper swirl his beer.

Jasper had smirked, as if it were a joke. "The whole world is celebrating that fact."

"I think they're celebrating the wrong thing," Steve had countered. "What if it's not because he's strong enough to stop an invasion — but because he's too weak to start one?"

That got Jasper's attention. He loved exploring the opposing views and thoughts.

ESID never mentioned this in any briefings, and this would be important enough to mention.

Coincidence?

That was the moment The Flying Dutchman cell was officially born. An informal cooperation network.

It was merely two years ago when Russian General Markov stood at the head of the briefing room, staring down at a classified military assessment.

Russia's nuclear response time had slowed.

Certain missile bases were being decommissioned, replaced by hollow diplomatic agreements.

Western intelligence agencies had penetrated too deep.

"We are being dismantled." Markov's voice was measured, calm, but there was no mistaking the rage underneath. "We must choose a new course of action."

Colonel Petrenko, the GRU's top intelligence operative, leaned back in his chair, running a finger along the rim of his glass. "The FSB would never allow it."

Markov's lips barely moved. "Then the FSB will be removed."

The room went silent.

It was the first time Markov had spoken of eliminating the Kremlin's control.

Petrenko exhaled through his nose, considering the weight of what had just been said. He had spent years inside Russia's intelligence machine, and he knew one thing for certain:

Once you spoke about removing the FSB, there was no going back.

Markov didn't demand loyalty.

He simply showed them the truth.

He presented classified documents proving that the President had secretly considered nuclear disarmament talks with Washington.

He displayed FSB counterintelligence memos discussing how to limit the military's autonomy.

He revealed that NATO's infiltration of Russian assets was deeper than anyone had admitted.

By the end of the meeting, the first shift had happened.

Elements of the GRU had begun operating in secrecy, creating their own networks separate from the Kremlin.

It wasn't treason, not yet. But it was the beginning of something that could never be reversed.

The room waited for Markov to continue.

***

The rising sun triggered a cascade of memories, pulling him back to his childhood in Kittery, Maine.

Steve's father, Jack Johnson, had just returned from his final deployment aboard the USS Hawthorne (SSN-749), a Los Angeles-class fast-attack submarine. The Hawthorne had spent months prowling the icy waters of the Bering Strait, monitoring Soviet naval activity, intercepting encrypted signals, and tailing enemy submarines in cat-and-mouse games beneath the waves.

Jack would recount the tension of those patrols — the eerie quiet of the deep punctuated by the occasional ping of sonar or the muffled roar of an enemy sub's screws.

But back on land, Jack was a different man.

Steve fondly remembered the embers crackling in the firepit, sending small sparks spiraling into that crisp Maine night.

Jack nursed a Shipyard ale, the condensation beading along the bottle as he leaned back in his camp chair, boots resting on a flat rock warmed by the day's sun. A soft breeze rolled in from the lake, rustling the trees and carrying the scent of pine, damp earth, and woodsmoke.

His sisters, Rachel and Lynette, bundled in oversized sweatshirts, squabbled over the perfect marshmallow-roasting technique — Rachel insisting hers should be slow and golden-brown, while Lynette preferred to set hers ablaze, laughing as she waved the flaming marshmallow in the air before blowing it out.

Steve sat cross-legged, turning a stick absently in the fire, the heat licking at his fingers.

His mother, Lauren, had settled on a log beside Jack, her legs curled under her, a mug of tea wrapped in her hands.

The firelight danced across her features, making her look younger, though there was always a certain wild sharpness in her green eyes. The same look she had when she got behind the wheel on long road trips, the kind of confidence that made Jack tease, "You sure you weren't a rally driver in another life, love?"

Tonight, though, she was in storyteller mode, her Australian accent thickening as she spun tales of summers in Sydney and the Blue Mountains, of coastal roads and bushland, of a life that could have been.

"You'd have been surfing at Bondi Beach, not splashing around in a lake," Lauren said, nudging Jack's boot with her foot. "And these two," she nodded at the girls, "would be budding little lifesavers in red swimmers."

Jack chuckled, tipping his beer toward her. "And what about Steve? Would he be a surfer too?"

Lauren smirked, reaching over to ruffle Steve's hair. "Oh, he'd be a proper revhead by now. Probably tearing up the highways in some old Falcon, thinking he's Mad Max."

Jack grinned, shaking his head. "Nah. He'd still have found his way to an old GTO. Just would've been wrenching on it under a jacaranda tree instead of in a garage." He leaned forward, stoking the fire with a long stick. "Though I gotta say, wombats don't make good assistant mechanics."

Rachel giggled, her face smudged with melted chocolate. "What about kangaroos?"

"Ah, they're too busy boxing each other," Lauren quipped, winking. "They'd make rubbish apprentices."

Then she thought out loud, "Kangaroos! Why do Americans always go straight to the kangaroos?"

The laughter rolled over them, weaving into the gentle lapping of the lake water, the rustling leaves, and the distant hoot of an owl.

Steve could still taste the marshmallows, feel the stickiness on his fingers, and hear the soft hum of cicadas in the background.

Those moments felt like something untouchable now, a dream that had stayed intact long after he'd left home.

Steve turned the wheel with one hand, the warm morning breeze slipping through the open window, mixing with the growl of the GTO's engine. Memories of his father incessantly crept in again, uninvited.

Steve had been nine years old when he heard it for the first time. Not from a movie. Not from a story. But from his father's lungs, torn open in the dark.

A guttural shout ruptured the stillness of the house — raw, hoarse, nothing human in it. It wasn't his name. It was a command.

"Crash dive! Launch countermeasures! Kolyma's fired! Flank speed!"

Steve bolted upright in bed, heart jamming against his ribs. The walls trembled. Not from impact — but from Jack Johnson's voice, coming through a closed door like a depth charge breaking surface tension.

Lauren moved first. She always did. Not hurried, not alarmed — just deliberate. She slipped from the master bathroom and placed a calming hand on the doorframe before stepping inside.

Jack's voice kept firing in fractured shouts — bearing coordinates, sonar updates, breathless orders like he hadn't left the Bering Strait.

"She's in our baffles — we were channeled — 352, I said 352! Snap shot, snap shot — fire aft!"

Then absolute silence. A choking pause. Steve stood just outside the doorway, bare feet pressed to the carpet.

Inside, his father was kneeling at the foot of the bed, trembling, sweat slicking his undershirt, fists clenched like he still had fire control grips in his hands.

Lauren knelt with him, touching his face, grounding him.

"You're not under the ice, Jack," she whispered. "You're home. You're here. They're gone."

Jack didn't answer. Just stared past her, eyes locked on something miles away. Something steel and red-lit and closing fast.

He slowly saw Lauren and held her tighter.

The war, for the moment, faded.

Steve's grip on the gear shifter tightened as he blinked against the golden morning light. He was living his father's past, whether he wanted to admit it or not.

Jack had spent years seeing Russians as the enemy. Then he met Lauren. It took time, but she melted through the old defenses. Jack saw her, not just where her family was from.

Now Steve was doing the same. But this was different. Katya wasn't an Australian with Russian roots — she was

Russian, through and through. And in Cold War II, that meant something.

Perhaps he was more like his father than he cared to admit.

The storm in his head spun faster. He craved reminiscing about the good moments when the darkness had already crept back in.

Steve's memory quickly took a leap across time, across oceans, to another place where laughter had filled the air.

He could still see his sisters — five and seven years old — racing through the grand halls of the Hydro Majestic Hotel in the Blue Mountains, their tiny sneakers slapping against the polished wooden floors, their giggles echoing beneath the vaulted ceilings and chandeliers.

The Hydro Majestic was ornate and otherworldly, a relic of old-world luxury perched on the edge of a vast Australian bushland.

Inside, the Edwardian architecture felt like something out of a turn of the century film — dark mahogany paneling, elaborate gilded mirrors reflecting the golden glow of wall sconces, and towering windows that framed the mist-covered valleys beyond.

The Salon du Thé, where they had afternoon tea, was bathed in natural light from the Art Nouveau-style windows, the ceiling adorned with delicate cornices.

The rich scent of freshly brewed English Breakfast tea mingled with baked scones, clotted cream, and strawberry jam.

Rachel and Lynette, too young to care about tea etiquette, had been more interested in the intricate carpets and massive paintings of landscapes that looked like something out of a Victorian ghost story.

Steve had wandered the halls with them, trailing his fingers over the carved wooden railings, peering into rooms with velvet-upholstered chairs, ornate fireplaces, and walls lined with old books.

Every year his family visited his maternal grandparents in Australia.

"Feels a bit haunted, doesn't it?" he had murmured to Rachel, who immediately squealed and clutched his arm.

Lauren had rolled her eyes when she heard. "Steve, don't be a bloody galah. You'll give her nightmares."

His Nana, Margaret "Maggie" Lawson, had simply chuckled. "Oh, don't worry, love. It's just got a bit of history, that's all. Grand hotels always do."

Later that evening, they had driven from the grandeur of the Hydro Majestic to Lauren's childhood home, a weatherboard house in Katoomba, perched on the edge of a gum tree-filled gully where the calls of kookaburras echoed through the valley.

Inside, the kitchen smelled warm and familiar, the air thick with the scent of slow-cooked lamb roast, garlic, rosemary, and fresh damper bread baking in the oven.

Lauren and Maggie stood side by side at the cluttered kitchen bench, chopping pumpkin and sweet potatoes for roasting, the counter lined with bottles of olive oil, bunches of fresh thyme, and a bowl of bright red tomatoes.

His Granddad, Robert "Bob" Lawson, was outside on the back terrace, a stubby of Tooheys New in his hand, standing next to Jack, who was trying to work the barbecue while fending off a nosy blue heeler named Rusty.

"You Yanks never quite get the barbie right," Bob teased, taking a slow sip of his beer.

Jack smirked, flipping the tongs in his hand. "Oh, is that right?"

Bob grinned, his weathered face crinkling. "Bloody oath. You overcomplicate things. Just throw the snags on, give 'em a turn, and you're done. None of this precision flipping nonsense."

Jack raised his hands in mock surrender. "Alright, alright, I'll leave the snags to the expert."

From the kitchen window, Lauren called out, "Dad, stop stirring Jack up, will ya? We've got enough testosterone in this family already."

Bob just laughed, tipping his beer toward Jack in silent camaraderie.

Inside, Nana Maggie glanced at Steve, who was sneaking a piece of lamb fat from the cutting board.

"Oi, cheeky bugger," she said, playfully swatting his hand away. "You want a feed, you'll have to wait like everyone else."

Steve grinned, leaning against the counter. "Just making sure it's up to standard."

Maggie rolled her eyes. "It's been up to standard longer than you've been alive. Now go set the table before I put you to work peeling the veggies."

Steve took his marching orders, grabbing plates and heading outside, the cool Blue Mountains air crisp against his skin as the smell of eucalyptus mingled with the charred scent of the grill.

By the time dinner was served, the table was overflowing — roast lamb with mint sauce, crispy potatoes, grilled corn, steamed greens, and fresh-baked damper with golden syrup.

The family sat close, shoulders brushing, the easy banter flowing as Jack clinked bottles with Bob and the girls smeared butter on warm slices of damper.

Steve hadn't known then that these were the moments he'd long for most — the laughter, the teasing, the warmth of a home that felt like something more than a place. Especially when he was somewhere that felt out of place.

⚊

The GTO hummed along the road, and his thoughts shifted to Millinocket, where his teenage years were spent amidst the dense forests of central Maine.

It was there that Jack, retired from the Navy, taught him the finer points of car restoration.

Together, they'd bought and transformed a 1971 Pontiac GTO from a rusted-out relic to the beast that now carried

Steve across the Russian steppe.

"Compression ratio is everything, Steve," Jack had said one Saturday morning in the garage, his hands black with grease. "This 455 cubic inch V8 — 10.25:1 compression ratio. That's where your torque and power come from. But you've got to balance it. Timing, air-fuel mixture, ignition — all of it has to work together. Like a good chess team."

Steve had smiled at the analogy. By then, he was already captain of the high school chess team, leading them to nationals for the first time in school history. Jack's pride had been palpable.

"You've got a very tactical mind, Steve," Jack had said, tapping the quadrajet carburetor with a wrench for emphasis. "Whether it's on a chessboard or under the hood, you see the connections, you stay five moves ahead of everyone and everything. That's rare. It will take you far, especially next year as the soccer captain and as a naval officer, after the Academy."

Jack never stopped pushing Steve to be a sailor, a naval officer, and hopefully have his own boat one day; a career goal that Jack had lovingly attained and wanted Steve to follow in his footsteps.

Sebago Lake. The Blue Mountains. Millinocket High School. The smell of roasting lamb and engine grease.

Worlds away.

His mother's voice echoed in his mind.

"Trust your gut, Steve. But don't lose yourself in all of this. Home's always here, yeah?"

Steve kept his left hand on the wheel, the right resting on the shift knob as the GTO hummed along the road. For now, the only home he had was the road ahead.

His mind wandered, but his instincts remained razor-sharp. Even as he recalled the warmth of home, he couldn't escape the cold calculations of war.

This wasn't just about NATO, ESID, Moscow or the GRU. The entire landscape had changed.

Russia's strategic doctrine had shifted from overt annexation to asymmetric warfare, destabilizing Europe without a single conventional invasion.

The NATO intelligence briefings had made it clear this wasn't about land grabs anymore.

It was about economic blackmail, disinformation warfare, and shadow conflicts where alliances were malleable and truth was weaponized.

He had discovered a much larger game was being played out in Moscow.

He wasn't just being hunted.

Steve clenched the wheel tighter, blinking as the golden sunrise played tricks on his tired eyes.

His father's voice echoed in his mind, overlapping with Katya's.

"A gun is easy to fire, son. The hard part comes after."

"You ARE my home, Steve. You are my person."

He exhaled sharply. Home wasn't a place anymore. It was a memory, a voice in the past.

And then the distinctive thump from the sound of rotors shattered the morning calm.

Instinctively, Steve eased off the gas, guiding the GTO off the P228 and onto a narrow dirt track that disappeared into the woods in the Kamensky District.

The car's tires crunched over the uneven ground as he maneuvered deeper into the dense woods, where the canopy offered some cover.

He killed the engine, letting the stillness of the shadows envelop him.

The thudding rotors grew louder, and he slipped out of the car, moving carefully to a spot where he could see the sky through a break in the trees.

The helicopter appeared on the horizon, a sleek and menacing silhouette. Kamov Ka-60 "Kasatka", Steve identified immediately — a modern Russian scout helicopter used by the GRU for reconnaissance.

Its twin coaxial rotors made it highly maneuverable, and its composite airframe was built to evade radar detection. Armed with a pair of 12.7mm machine guns and capable of carrying anti-tank missiles, the Ka-60 was no ordinary patrol aircraft.

Steve's heart pounded as he watched the chopper hover for a moment, its nose dipping as if scanning the terrain.

The matte black finish of the fuselage reflected the morning sun, and for a brief second, he thought it might have spotted the GTO's gleaming paint.

But then the helicopter banked left, heading westward along the forest's edge.

The rotors faded, but silence didn't bring relief.

Steve crouched by the GTO, counting the minutes. Three. Five. Ten.

He scanned the ridgeline. Heat distortion shimmered in the morning sun. The dirt on the road behind him was undisturbed — but that didn't mean anything.

He had learned long ago that the best hunters never showed their tracks.

They might be running a search pattern. Or they might be waiting for him to move.

His gut told him to double back, take an unexpected route. But he was running out of time. He had to reach the border.

NATO and Russia had no idea they had been running out of time for years. "You have all seen the West encircle us," Markov continued his briefing calmly. "You have all witnessed the decay of our strength."

Sokolov, the economic advisor, shifted uncomfortably. "The President has worked hard to maintain stability. We cannot afford another economic collapse —"

Markov raised a hand, cutting him off without raising his voice.

"Stability is a fantasy the Americans sell us while they surround us." Markov paused. "What you call economic stability, I call surrender. What I am offering is a return to power. A return to our rightful place."

The words hung in the air, dangerous and electrifying.

Deputy Chairman of the Duma's Defense Committee Gorshkov leaned forward, intrigued. "And what exactly do you propose?"

Markov let a small smile form at the corner of his lips. "A gradual shift. Influence the President's decisions. Align the Duma's policies with our military's needs. Remove obstacles — quietly."

Markov poured a glass of vodka, setting it in front of Gorshkov. The Duma politician hesitated, then took it.

"What are you asking of me?" Gorshkov finally asked.

"Simple," Markov replied. "Influence the Defense Committee. Shape the budget to favor my forces. Ensure that no laws pass which interfere with my operations."

Gorshkov exhaled. "That's a tall order."

"You misunderstand," Markov said, smiling. "You are either with us, or you are an obstacle. And obstacles tend to disappear."

Gorshkov's hands clenched, the meaning clear. But then, a slow smile formed on his lips.

"And if I choose to stand with you?"

Markov raised his glass. "Then, Leonid, we drink to Russia's future."

Time to move. Steve flexed his grip as he turned the ignition key. If they weren't looking for him now, they would be soon. The weariness hit like a wave. His muscles ached from tension, his mind fogged by exhaustion. He couldn't remember the last time he'd slept — really slept — without danger clawing at the edge of consciousness.

Every move felt calculated. Every decision, a heartbeat from disaster.

Even now, deep in the forest, the pressure never eased.

It wasn't just lack of sleep. It was the kind of fatigue that seeped into the bones — a life lived too long in the shadows.

He hadn't thought about a "normal" life in years. Maybe he still could.

But what would it even look like now? A front porch and quiet mornings? Or just a new place to be hunted?

The weariness reminded Steve of a late fall morning in 2003, at the Hohenfels Training Area in Germany — Ponderosa Defensive Position.

Back then, he was just a tank driver in 1st Platoon B Team, 2nd Battalion, 61st Armor Regiment (attached to "The Triple Threes" — 3-33rd Infantry).

The Triple Threes were being evaluated for combat readiness. The battalion commander's future rode on every move they made.

It felt like everything mattered. But at least back then, the enemy was fake. And the war was still practice.

The cold morning air smelled of damp earth and exhaust fumes as Red Three, Steve's M1A2 Abrams, sat in a hull-down position among a series of freshly dug fighting positions. The tank's crew, worn thin from three days of near-continuous operations, huddled inside, their muscles stiff, their minds frayed.

Steve Johnson, the driver, fought to keep his eyes open.

In the past seventy-two hours, he had slept only nine. Tank tracks hummed constantly, distant explosions roared, diesel engines growled across the Hohenfels Training Area, and the endless demand to improve their fighting position left him restless.

They had spent two days fortifying Ponderosa, a key defensive position situated along a narrow ridgeline with limited avenues of approach.

An infantry platoon and a heavy combat engineer section had helped prepare textbook combined-arms fortifications.

Layered anti-tank minefields were placed at key chokepoints, ensuring enemy armor would be forced into pre-selected kill zones.

Anti-Tank ditches, carved out by M9 Armored Combat Earthmovers to funnel enemy armor into predictable lanes.

M8A1 Claymores and remotely-detonated demolitions were rigged to channel infantry into machine-gun crossfire.

Bradley IFVs positioned along the ridgeline were meant to provide overlapping suppressive fire, but the first artillery strike had neutralized them.

The problem wasn't the defenses. It was the speed of the opposition force's (OPFOR) assault — a coordinated strike using artillery masking, maneuver warfare, and precision infiltration.

It wasn't just a training exercise — it was a perfect simulation of how a real Russian tank division would dismantle NATO's front line in hours; and would be on top of them within minutes.

Steve's head had snapped up at the sudden burst of radio chatter. Adrenaline began pumping.

"Panther elements, this is Panther Actual OPFOR is massing! Estimated full regimental strength, coming at high speed from Phase Line Copper through Ponderosa! Prepare to repel!"

Then the attack began.

Through his driver's periscope, Steve saw the first M60A3 Pattons of OPFOR cresting the ridgeline in the distance, their 1,050-horsepower diesel engines screaming as they accelerated down the slopes toward the defenders.

The enemy didn't hesitate. They were coming in fast, engines wide open, hitting the tree line at over 40 kilometers per hour.

Smoke rounds burst across the battlefield as the OPFOR's smoke generators and smoke grenades created a fog of war to obscure their movement. The Multiple Integrated Laser Engagement System (MILES laser systems) flashed as the first simulated rounds impacted against the defenders.

"Incoming! OPFOR artillery just neutralized A Co's right flank! We're next!"

The MILES-equipped artillery simulating Russian 2S1 Gvozdika 122mm self-propelled howitzers had hammered the forward positions.

The defensive line buckled almost immediately. Orange whoopie lights lit up the early morning valley, reflecting off the smoke and fog.

White 1 and Black 5, the two other surviving tanks of B Company, tried to detach and shift positions to engage the enemy at range, but they were caught mid-movement by OPFOR's TOW missile-equipped HMMWVs, simulating Russian ATGM hunter-killer teams.

Their MILES sensors screamed "kill" tones, marking them as destroyed.

Ponderosa fell apart in mere minutes.

Switching to the Battalion frequency, Staff Sergeant Lewis tried to establish communications with any other unit. "Any Rampart unit this net, this is Panther Red Three, Over."

Radio traffic was confused and heavy. Steve heard bits and pieces. "This is Rhino 2! We're getting overrun! Infantry under heavy attack! We need help at VZ-7. Enemy tanks in the woods."

"Flash Flash Flash. Rampart Actual. Red Three, say again position."

"We are unassing Ponderosa and dropping back. VZ-7 is about 3 clicks from us, Over." Lewis was more excited than anyone had ever seen him.

"Red Three, you are a big boy, correct? Over."

"Roger Rampart. The last Panther standing."

"Red Three. Get to VZ-7 NOW. Hold the logging trail! You're now a sniper tank! The enemy has no idea you are coming. Over!"

Staff Sergeant Lewis chuckled over the intercom. "Sniper tank? Well, they are definitely improvising."

Steve pulled back on the accelerator, adjusted his t-bar steering controls, and started guiding Red Three through the uneven, muddy terrain of Hohenfels, skirting the wreckage of friendly Bradleys and Abrams as OPFOR units surged past.

The logging trails were narrow, winding paths through dense Bavarian pine forests — perfect for ambush tactics.

The battalion commander had cleared all radio traffic to communicate with Red Three.

"Hey Boss. Ever had the radio net cleared for you by a Lieutenant Colonel before?" Steve asked over the intercom.

Staff Sergeant Jeff Lewis, a seasoned tank commander, started to reply but instead called out a target through the CITV

(Commander's Independent Thermal Viewer):

"Gunner, sabot, tank! Traverse right! Range 1,800 meters!"

"Identified!"

"Fire!"

The Hoffman device main gun simulator exploded as the MILES laser system registered a hit. A simulated kill. One M60A3 down.

Steve kept Red Three moving as OPFOR tried to outflank them, infantry dismounting from simulated BMP-2s.

Red Three's .50-caliber M2 Browning ripped into the woods, "eliminating" dismounted OPFOR soldiers according to MILES sensors.

"Red Three, we have visual on you." Rampart 6 was sensing the tide would turn for him. "Be advised — enemy flankers moving towards you from VZ-6! They're using the ditches to sneak in!"

Steve threw the Abrams into a hard right pivot, grinding through the mud to reposition.

"Gunner, coax! Infantry in the ditch!"

"On the way!"

The M240 coaxial machine gun spewed simulated fire into the ditches, cutting down OPFOR infantry "advancing" on the defenders.

For the next thirty minutes, Red Three held the position, knocking out nine enemy M60s and several infantry elements.

But it was all for nothing. The battle had already been decided when the main defensive line collapsed.

Minutes later, a simulated Russian tank division at full strength had overwhelmed the defenders.

The radio crackled.

"EndEx, EndEx, EndEx. All elements return to assembly areas."

Steve slumped against the driver's seat, his head pounding. His hands were still clenched around the controls, fingers white with exhaustion.

He had barely survived, but Red Three had made it out, one of only ten tanks in Team Panther that hadn't been "destroyed."

Climbing out of the Abrams, his uniform soaked in sweat, he looked around at the "wreckage" of the battlefield.

OPFOR's M60A3s still smoked from MILES "kills". The remains of the infantry defense were scattered across the terrain.

Two days of preparation. Nine hours of sleep in three days. Destroyed in just minutes.

Staff Sergeant Lewis walked up beside him, slapping a tired hand on Steve's shoulder.

"Hell of a fight, Johnson. But damn, we never stood a chance. Great boogie boogie getting across the battlefield. And no, I never had anyone clear a radio net for me, or get assigned as a sniper tank. Interesting concept." Lewis paused, "Time to start training you to be a gunner."

Steve just nodded. He had never been so tired in his life. He didn't even care that Lewis was talking about a promotion.

Sliding back into the driver's seat of his GTO, he rested both hands on the wheel and just stared out into the trees. The constant vigilance was taking its toll, fraying the edges of his resolve. He had survived this encounter, but he couldn't shake the feeling that the storm wasn't over — not by a long shot.

The real storm had been growing for years. The Russians kept rattling sabers, backing down, flaring up again. It made no sense.

On many recent trips, Steve would see Reduced Strength Readiness divisions of Russian troops with outdated T-62 tanks and BTR-60s on patrol.

The Permanent Readiness divisions were on six month rotations in Siberia. Nothing made sense.

When he briefed a joint ESID/NATO intelligence group, only van Dijk took a deep interest.

In fact, the senior NATO intelligence officer shrugged it off as a non routine, routine training exercise. "Russia does what Russia does. Not everything has a reason."

The next night, they went back for another drink. This time Sersjant Nygaard and Major Jansen joined them. The Flying Dutchman crew was growing.

Nygaard had to disagree. "Russians never do anything without a reason. You are on the right track."

It was this moment when Jasper van Dijk realized something was forming around him. A network that could get the real answers.

A shadowy network that was operating within the

networks, just as the legendary Flying Dutchman had navigated the seas.

Steve felt a deep longing to be with Katya, the more he remembered. Ever since the Russian invasion of Ukraine, the increased tensions between Russia and NATO, the United States in particular, had closed the travel between the nations.

Each time ESID sent him back into Russia, the ache returned. Not just the fear of being caught, but the longing and feelings from the impossibility of seeing her.

Katya.

She hadn't asked him to fight this war, but he fought it for her all the same.

The world they once dreamed of — something simpler, something free — had been swallowed by geopolitics and shadows.

Yet he clung to it, quietly, stubbornly. He would see this through. For her.

Everything he did was for her. Not NATO, not peace. Katya.

If Sergey ever discovered the truth... that would be the deepest cut of all, if he ever learned of Steve's double life.

He was also the one person Steve wanted to ask for more reasons why there would be Reduced Strength Readiness troops on the Ukrainian border.

The one time he did get to ask, Sergey mentioned it would be to get them trained up again, or a deceptive tactic to appear weak.

⬤

Jasper Van Dijk didn't trust coincidences. Yesterday, Steve had finished his ESID debrief on the T-62s and the sudden deployment of Reduced Strength Readiness troops. Today, Jasper felt the whole setup reeked of misdirection.

Jasper spun his pen between his fingers, replaying Sergey's words that Steve had briefed — "Regular training would be regional, at their home bases." But why attempt to appear weak? For what purpose?

Jasper tapped an encrypted number into his secure line.

It rang once. Then a voice — smooth, unreadable.

"Claire Rousseau. How is my favorite Dutchman? It's been a while."

Many years ago — before Jasper joined SHAPE, when he was still with the Netherlands Army Intelligence, he had been swirling the whiskey in his glass, eyes drifting over the sleek, dimly lit bar of a high-end hotel bar off Independence Avenue in Windhoek, Namibia.

This wasn't a social stop.

Namibia's diamond trade was a world of its own — illicit, dangerous, and deeply tied to Russian oligarch money.

Jasper was here under the cover of a fact-finding mission for the Netherlands Army, officially evaluating mineral exports.

Unofficially?

He was here to confirm if Russia was using Africa's diamond smuggling networks to finance off-the-books operations.

And he wasn't the only one watching.

At the far end of the bar, a woman in a tailored black dress ran her finger idly along the rim of her glass. Her French accent was faint but unmistakable as she spoke to the bartender.

Jasper had read her file before coming.

Claire Rousseau.

Her reputation in intelligence circles was almost mythic. A French DGSE deep-cover operative, embedded in Africa's illicit diamond trade.

She posed as a high-end diamond broker, dealing with everyone from Nigerian syndicates to Russian oligarchs laundering billions.

Her real mission is tracking and financially mapping the secret money trails, with emphasis on those leading out of Moscow.

Her expertise is forensic finance and accounting — following the hidden transactions that intelligence agencies missed.

Claire had been aware of Jasper the moment he walked in.

She was fluent in patterns, movements and attention.

He wasn't a buyer. His clothes were too practical, his posture too alert.

He wasn't a tourist. The drink in his hand was untouched. He was observing, calculating.

But he recognized her. That much was clear.

Jasper took a sip of his whiskey, then stood and casually made his way over.

As he passed, he murmured something only she would understand.

"La Reine de Diamants." *(Queen of Diamonds.)*

She didn't react immediately. Didn't look up.

But Jasper caught it — the smallest pause in her breath, the glimpse of amusement in her eyes.

It was confirmation. He knew who she was. And she knew he wasn't just some passing intelligence officer.

That night, she didn't acknowledge him. But later, she joined him at the bar.

Claire sat down smoothly, crossing her legs as she studied him. No introduction.

"You must be very confident," she said at last. "Or very stupid."

Jasper smirked. "Why not both?"

She took a slow sip of her wine. "You're Dutch intelligence. But you're asking the wrong questions."

He raised an eyebrow. "Then enlighten me."

"Buy me another glass and I will tell you," she teased.

She told how Russian oligarchs were not just laundering money through diamonds. They were also routing these funds through unregistered cryptocurrency pools.

In addition, the GRU was using African diamond transactions to create black-market war chests.

Her forensic analysis had already linked these funds to several suspicious arms deals in Asia, but she wouldn't tell him how.

The real money wasn't in the diamonds themselves — it was in the financial networks behind them.

She swirled her new glass of wine. "The question isn't where the money is going, Jasper. It's who is pulling the strings."

Jasper leaned forward. "And you know who that is?"

Claire smiled slightly. "Not yet."

She tapped the table. "But when I do, you'll want to be the first to know."

Jasper watched her for a moment. Then nodded.

This would become the first of many meetings where he sought her insights.

From that moment on, when Jasper needed financial intelligence beyond NATO's bureaucratic red tape, he turned to one person.

The Queen of Diamonds.

And now, years later, she may have just cracked the case of Markov's hidden war chest. Before they were even aware Markov and the newly formed Perun Initiative existed.

"I need a financial pulse check on the GRU." van Dijk was all business at the moment.

There was a pause. A slow exhale.

"Funny you should ask." Claire continued, "Years ago,

GRU had purchased vast amounts of cryptocurrency when it was still in its infancy. It had since skyrocketed in value — now worth high billions in euros. Until recently, most of it sat untouched. Dormant. Hidden."

"That's interesting," Jasper mused. "But why move the money now?"

Claire's voice sharpened. "Because something just changed. Both financially and for an unknown reason. Crypto is being transferred into an unknown Moscow account. Just as you asked, 'Why now?'"

"I found an anomaly. The Moscow account is private. No state oversight. We're about to find out who owns it."

Jasper smirks slightly, shaking his head. "Took you long enough, Claire."

She mockingly flirted, "Jasper, you know I have to make you suffer a bit for any information."

He encrypted a request. "Send me everything. Just hit reply"

Time to see who inside Moscow was being funded by the GRU, and if there is a connection.

Steve missed St. Petersburg. It was home for him. Katya would remind him, *"Home is no longer a place, Stefan. It is a person. You ARE my home. You are my person."*

These were the last words Katya spoke to him in person.

At this moment he was so close to her, close to home. Yet so far away. Especially with war between their countries on the horizon.

For now, though, he chose to rest. His mind needed clarity, and his body needed to recover.

He shut his eyes for a moment, not daring to let himself fall too deeply, but enough to quiet the noise in his head. Steve exhaled.

The silence was worse than the noise.

They were already watching. And they weren't just coming.

Are We Ready For This

Southeast Russia — Kamensky Oblast

The GTO rested deep in the shadows of the woods of the Kamensky District, its black paint blending with the shadows of the pines. Beneath the interwoven branches, Steve had parked on a dirt track, his cautious nature guiding him off the highway.

Exhaustion finally caught up with him, and he allowed himself a few hours of rest. His head fell back against the seat, and for a fleeting moment, sleep claimed him.

The vibrations came first, faint and distant, like the pulse of a bass drum.

Steve stirred, blinking as the tremors grew stronger. By the time he was fully awake, the forest floor seemed to hum with life.

He slid out of the car, his hand instinctively brushing against the grip of his Tokarev.

Moving low, he picked his way through the undergrowth

until he reached a small ridge overlooking the P228 highway.

From his concealed position, he saw them.

The lead elements of the Russian 4th Guards Tank Brigade rumbled west, a column of T-90M Proryv-3 tanks moving with disciplined precision.

Their angular turrets glinted in the sunlight, Relikt reactive armor giving them an almost predatory appearance. Their 125mm smoothbore cannons remained fixed forward, an unspoken promise of destruction.

Behind them came the support vehicles, a column of BMP-3 infantry fighting vehicles, Msta-S self-propelled howitzers, and Pantsir-S1 air defense systems, their radars scanning the skies.

Logistics trucks, fuel tankers, and command vehicles brought up the rear.

Steve's mind raced as he counted the vehicles. This wasn't merely a battalion; it was an entire brigade, complete with artillery, air defense, and logistical support.

A full combat-ready formation.

Steve kept his breathing steady, crouching behind the remains of an abandoned guardrail.

The Russian column wasn't just moving — it was moving with purpose.

He narrowed his eyes, tracking the formations.

Infantry transports dispersed in a way that suggested they expected resistance. Not from NATO — no, this was an internal measure.

Someone in the Russian command structure was

anticipating partisan attacks.

The 4th Guards weren't just rolling in with confidence. They were moving like a unit preparing for urban engagements.

That meant Moldova wasn't just an objective — it was a staging ground.

The ground still trembled from the passing tanks, but Steve's thoughts raced faster than the armored column. Something about this didn't fit.

If Moldova was the real objective, why weren't NATO intelligence reports reflecting this movement?

And then it hit him — they weren't supposed to see it yet.

⬤

At the Kremlin's Security Council Chamber in December 2021, President Andrei Pavlovich's hand hovered over the USB drive, his mind struggling to process what he had just seen.

Mass graves. Executions. Entire villages wiped from existence.

"These are our people," General Sokolov said, his voice solemn. "And NATO does nothing."

Across the table, General Markov leaned forward, his expression carefully neutral. He had already won.

"Sir," Markov said smoothly, "we have intercepted NATO discussions. They are aware of this genocide. They are doing nothing."

Pavlovich's breath hitched. The words cut deeper than anything he had feared.

No significant threat to regional stability.

That was the phrase in NATO's own report.

A cold rage burned through him.

"They are ignoring the slaughter of Russians," Sokolov pressed. "Because they do not fear us."

Markov pressed the final piece of the deception forward — an edited NATO intelligence memo, planted carefully through false leaks.

The President didn't hesitate anymore.

"Prepare the operation."

The invasion of Ukraine was about to begin.

Steve's thoughts drifted to Hungary in 2007. Back then, he'd been a young tank commander with NATO's 10th Armored Strike Group, nicknamed "The Thunderwolves," a quick-reaction force stationed near the Hungarian-Romanian border.

Their mission was clear — counter any armored incursion from Russia's Western Military District. Equipped with M1A2 SEP V3 Abrams tanks, his unit had been trained to hold the line against elite Russian formations like the 4th Guards.

"They're not just tanks," Captain Rivera had told him during a briefing. "They're a trap. They'll exploit every weakness — your habits, your instincts, even the terrain you think you control."

Major Collier had been more direct. "Every officer in the 4th Guards is handpicked," he had warned. "Combat veterans from Chechnya, Georgia, Ukraine — they've seen it all. If you ever face them, it won't just be a fight. It'll be survival. *It will not be a war. It will be an annihilation.*"

Captain Donaldson added, "Staff Sergeant Johnson on Thunderwolves B-12 is our point tank. Johnson, I need you to study them in depth. If the shit hits the fan, I need your analytical mind to know exactly what they will do before Group S-2 tries to determine it. We need checkmate in seven moves."

In the barracks, rumors about the 4th Guards were as persistent as the hum of fluorescent lights.

They trained in near-total darkness, perfected night-fighting tactics, and had developed electronic warfare systems capable of blinding NATO's advanced sensors.

Steve had studied their maneuvers like a chessboard, preparing for a battle that had never come.

For Steve, the 4th Guards had become a specter — a shadow of Russian military power that loomed over every training exercise.

Even now, watching their tanks roll west, he could feel the weight of their reputation pressing on his chest.

Steve watched the last of the URAL-4320 trucks disappear westward. The vibrations faded, but the implications did not.

This wasn't a routine movement. The presence of the Kasatka earlier now made perfect sense — it had been an advanced reconnaissance element, clearing the way for the brigade.

Moldova — that was the key.

The Dniester River was the final obstacle before Russia could push into Romania. If the 4th Guards secured it, NATO would be locked out of Eastern Europe.

He traced the route mentally. Petrov's words echoed: *"Army Group South will push through to conquer Moldova first."*

Steve exhaled. He wasn't just watching a brigade move. He was watching the opening act of war.

⚊

In a dimly lit secure briefing room at Supreme Headquarters Allied Powers Europe (SHAPE), a group of intelligence officers huddled around a table strewn with satellite imagery, SIGINT intercepts, and UAV reconnaissance reports. The air was thick with tension.

A Canadian junior analyst, civilian contractor Michael Kern, adjusted his headset as he rewound thermal satellite footage captured six hours earlier.

The grainy image flashed onto the large monitor at the front of the room, showing dozens of heat signatures moving west — armored vehicles, heavy transports, tactical elements...

"This is not a small Russian unit maneuvering," Kern said, voice edged with urgency. He tapped the screen. "That's a full brigade. That large, it has to be the lost 4th Guards. They are moving west along the P228 highway, heading south. No prior intel suggested this movement. We need to escalate this."

Across the table, a young American 2nd Lieutenant, fresh from NATO's intelligence school in Germany, leaned back in his chair, shaking his head.

Lt. Markham, a by-the-book officer who still trusted doctrine over reality, smirked at the grainy footage.

"That's not the 4th Guards," Markham said, crossing his arms. "It can't be. All assessments place them in Belarus, preparing for a push toward Poland. You probably got a Category C Reserve Motorized Rifle Regiment doing routine maneuvers."

Kern's jaw tightened. "Then why the hell do I have SIGINT chatter confirming T-90M tanks refueling at a depot outside Tambov twelve hours ago? Why is this column covered by Pantsir-S1 air defense units and a reconnaissance Kasatka? The 4th Guards are a spearhead."

Markham sighed, flipping through outdated briefing notes printed before this satellite pass. "You're overreacting. The last estimated position of the 4th Guards was over 1,500 kilometers north, reinforcing Belarussian forces near Minsk."

"Then what the hell is this? A damn optical illusion?"

Kern snapped, zooming in on a heat signature. "Look at these chassis profiles. T-90Ms. BMP-3s. BTR-80s. This isn't some backwater reserve battalion doing training drills. They're deploying."

A more seasoned officer, Major Ross, leaned forward, rubbing his eyes. "Kern, your imagery is rough. If you want us to brief Sentinel with this, we need hard confirmation. Do we have boots on the ground that can corroborate?"

Kern hesitated. "No, sir. But —"

A communications officer suddenly turned in his chair. "Sir, we have a new intercepted transmission. Belarussian ground command coordinating fuel and resupply. Traffic patterns suggest they're moving fast and maintaining strict COMSEC. They are reporting to Moscow that the 4th Guards Tank Brigade just west of Minsk, refueled, rearmed, and prepared to reach Poland and Lithuania within 48 hours."

Ross's brow furrowed. "There you go. The 4th Guards are still at Minsk"

Kern nodded, seething in the moment. "Radio traffic is not solid intel. We need confirmation. Do we have any ISR assets on station? Drones?"

A drone operator on the other side of the room shook his head. "Negative. Our MQ-9 Reaper got spiked by Russian EW jamming over Bryansk. We lost telemetry."

Kern exhaled sharply, gripping the edge of the table. "Markham, if we're wrong, NATO loses nothing. If we're right, we're walking into a damn trap."

Major Ross shot him a warning glance. "Watch it, Kern."

Markham rolled his eyes. "And what do you expect us to do? Launch a preemptive strike based on grainy satellite images and a gut feeling?"

Kern's jaw tightened. "I expect us to not be goddamn blind when an entire armored brigade is missing from its last known position. Let's get a new drone out there."

Kern's hand tightened into a fist beneath the table. This wasn't just incompetence — it was willful ignorance.

Ross leaned forward, shaking his head. "Kern, if we took every missing armored unit at face value, we'd be launching false alarms every other day."

"This isn't an armored company. It's a goddamn brigade." Kern's voice was sharp. "And unless Minsk is suddenly able to hide hundreds of tanks, someone is lying."

Markham exhaled. "Even if they were moving, what would you have us do? We can't authorize a NATO response based on simple speculation."

"It's not speculation," Kern shot back. "It's intelligence."

The room fell silent.

Markham exhaled, still skeptical. "You need more than grainy thermal images and gut feeling to call this an armored brigade formation, preparing to attack. Go get a coffee in the caféteria."

Kern gets up to leave and grabs his folder with notes on the images.

"I bet that Dutch Adjudant-Onderofficier would take this

seriously. I might accidentally leave this whole file on his desk," Kern tells himself as he faces the struggle of following protocols versus doing what he knows is right.

Kern returned with two cups of coffee, handing one to Markham — who didn't notice Kern came back empty handed, minus the coffees.

* * *

The rumbling softened as the column reached an intersection west of the forest. Steve could barely make out the sound of tanks turning south, their engines fading into the distance. He stayed crouched, listening until the vibrations dissipated entirely.

Only then did he retreat to the GTO, his mind racing.

He restarted the engine, the GTO's growl subdued under the forest canopy.

Moving cautiously, he navigated the dirt track back toward the highway. The sun hung high in the sky as he eased onto the P228, heading west once more.

The countryside stretched out before him, a patchwork of fields and dense woodlands.

The GTO's tires hummed against the asphalt as Steve pushed westward, the events of the past hours replaying in his mind.

He couldn't shake the image of the Kasatka hovering

above the trees. Its presence now made perfect sense. The helicopter had been scouting ahead for the brigade, searching for obstacles and potential threats.

He thought back to his training in Hungary, to lectures from NATO officers about Russian doctrine.

Their combined-arms approach was systematic — reconnaissance units like the Kasatka identified weak points, and mechanized forces exploited them with overwhelming precision.

The 4th Guards weren't moving west on a whim; they were part of something larger, something dangerous.

As the miles rolled by, Steve's mind churned. He thought of Captain Donaldson and Major Collier, of the briefings and strategy sessions where they had dissected the 4th Guards' tactics.

He could almost hear Collier's voice: "If you see them, Johnson, you've got to stay five steps ahead. They'll play on your instincts, your habits. They're not just tanks — they're a trap waiting to be sprung."

Steve had only recently earned Major Collier's absolute respect. Sergeant Steve Johnson stood at attention in Major Collier's office, his uniform crisp despite the exhaustion pressing behind his eyes.

First Sergeant Gallagher and Captain Donaldson flanked

Collier, their expressions unreadable. The silence stretched for a long moment before Collier leaned forward, elbows resting on his desk.

"Sergeant Johnson," Collier began, "the tank commander for B-12 just went down. Broken collarbone. We roll out to Grafenwöhr in a week. Are you willing to step up?"

Steve didn't hesitate. "Yes, sir."

Collier gave him a sharp look, studying him. "Think you can get up to speed that fast?"

First Sergeant Gallagher, standing off to the side, cleared his throat. "Excuse me, sir, but Sergeant Johnson already asked me months ago if one gunner per platoon could receive after-hours training to step up as a tank commander. He also convinced me that one driver per platoon should train as a gunner." He turned toward Steve, nodding. "I personally operated as the IO in the Unit Conduct of Fire Trainer to make this happen. I have Sergeant Johnson's UCOFT certification printout in his company file."

Then it hit him. Gallagher exhaled. "Damn, sir. I'm gonna miss him."

Collier smirked. "First Sergeant, you're getting the gunner from B-12. He fired top tank last year. He's tank commander material. Get him up to speed."

Then he turned to Steve. "Johnson, the driver you trained as a gunner — he's now your gunner. What is his name? Specialist who?"

Steve blinked. "That would be Private First Class Anderson."

"I think I said SPECIALIST. If you two pull this off," Collier continued, *"I'm personally recommending you both for the promotion board."*

He glanced at Gallagher. "S-1 will cut orders for everyone within the hour."

As Steve turned to leave, Collier called after him. "Johnson, two things."

Steve grinned. "Yes, sir?"

"One. Don't screw the pooch. My ass is on the line too." Major Collier liked the cockiness he saw in front of him.

Steve saluted. "Wouldn't dream of it, sir."

Collier smirked. "Good. Second thing — if your mom sends more Tim Tams and Chicken Twisties, don't forget me."

Steve laughed. "Yes, sir."

That night, he found PFC Anderson in the barracks, still in a grease-stained uniform from a long day in the motor pool.

"Anderson," Steve said, arms crossed. "You're my gunner now. Get your uniform cleaned up for tonight's formation, and tomorrow, you better be standing tall for our first day in B Troop."

Anderson's eyes widened. "Wait, what?"

Steve smirked and winked. "Congratulations, Specialist Jerome Anderson. Now start acting like one."

"Yes, Sergeant!!!! Thank you. I will not let you down," and Specialist Anderson was last seen in a fast jog to the barracks, on his way to celebrate his promotion and posting to serve with the most well regarded noncommissioned officer in the unit.

The 17th Armored Cavalry Regiment (ACR) rolled into Grafenwöhr to qualify on their Abrams tanks, Strykers, and Bradleys.

The 10th Armored Strike Group had trained here many times before, but Steve wasn't leading a tank crew back then.

He was now.

The first week was a grind — classroom instruction, drills, rehearsals.

Steve pored over range cards, battle drills, and gunnery tactics every spare moment, pushing himself and Anderson to the limit. Anderson was green, but his instincts were solid.

But Tank Tables V, VI, and VII were a disaster.

They barely qualified V and VI.

But Tank Table VII was something else. Their combined score? A miserable 93 out of 1,000 points.

At the debrief, Collier looked ready to relieve Steve on the spot.

"I should bench you right now," he said, voice low and controlled. "I put my neck on the line, and you give me this? 93 points? That's a disgrace."

Steve exhaled, standing firm. "Sir, we just need a beer and a good night's sleep. We know what we did wrong. No disrespect, but we are NOT redoing Table VII... Sir."

Collier studied him for a long moment before sighing. "Still cocky. You'd better be right, Sergeant."

As Steve saluted and exited, Collier looked at the Master Gunner, Staff Sergeant Martin Crowley. "I like that kid."

Two days later, Tank Table VIII.

One by one, tanks started breaking down in the firing line. Engines overheated, weapons malfunctioned, hydraulic leaks. B-12 was last in the firing order.

Over the radio, the range tower OIC called:

"Any station this net that is REDCON 1, this is Charlie Niner-2."

Steve set down his thermos of coffee, keyed his mic. "C-92, this is B-12. We are REDCON 1. Where do you want us?"

As he released the transmission button, he turned toward his driver.

"PFC Simmons, start the engine."

The 1,500-horsepower AGT1500 turbine engine roared to life, the familiar vibration settling through the chassis. Steve adjusted his gloves and felt the past two days fade away.

They pulled into Battle Position One — left lane of the infamous Range 117.

Private Ortega nervously took down the green "weapons cleared" range flag down; and put up the red flag. It was his first Tank Table VIII.

They had forgotten the misery of Range 132.

And this time, they were ready.

The Grafenwöhr morning air was crisp, the faint smell of fuel and dust lingering inside the tank. Steve adjusted his gloves as the radio crackled inside his helmet.

The tower called, "B-12, this is Charlie 92, standby for engagement."

"All right team, this is it. Lock and load." PFC Simmons was

the only Tank Table VIII veteran of the crew still in the position he held previously.

The tower began the exercise. "B-12, this is Charlie 92. You will execute an assault on a fortified enemy defensive line."

"Objective: Eliminate forward positions and allow friendly forces to advance."

"Targets: Two enemy bunkers, one T-80, and dismounted troops."

"Battlecarry Sabot. You are cleared hot. Charlie 92, Out."

Steve felt the subtle shift in tension inside the tank. This wasn't about speed. It was about control.

Anderson sucked in a breath beside him, shifting in his gunner's seat. "This is it."

"Breathe, Andy," Steve said calmly. "We do it by the book."

"Driver, move out!" Simmons got them up to 30 kilometers an hour, holding steady. Ortega stared at his ammunition compartment door, memorizing where each round was."

"Gunner, Sabot, Tank." The crew came alive.

"Up!" As Ortega armed the gun and cleared the path of recoil.

"Identified."

"Fire."

The Gunner's Primary Sight (GPS) locked onto the target, its reticle a steady glow in Anderson's vision.

The laser rangefinder pulsed once, calculating the exact distance in milliseconds — 1,850 meters, T-80 frontal armor.

The fire control system adjusted for crosswind, barrel droop, and target velocity. Everything was set.

Anderson's grip tightened around the Cadillac G8 control handles. He exhaled.

"On the way!"

He squeezed both triggers.

A sharp electronic pulse shot through the fire control system, activating the breech actuator. In a fraction of a second, a high-voltage ignition charge set off the M829A4 APFSDS round's primer, sending a controlled detonation through the M14 propellant grains.

The turret rocked backward as the M256 smoothbore cannon unleashed 5,450 bar of pressure, launching the depleted uranium dart downrange at 1,750 meters per second — faster than a rifle bullet, faster than sound.

A violent shockwave rippled through the turret. Steve barely blinked.

"Target!"

The bore evacuator sucked the superheated gases forward, dumping them out of the gun tube's muzzle, preventing the turret from filling with choking smoke.

Before the loader even reacted, the breech block slammed downward, ejecting the charred remains of the combustible case into the spent cartridge bin with a metallic thud.

Load HEAT! Traverse RIGHT!!! Gunner, HEAT, PC."

"HEAT indexed. Identified."

"HEAT loaded." Ortega shouted, ramming a HEAT round into the breech with a practiced motion. "Up."

The round tore into the plywood BTR-30 target, right in the

turret ring, sending it back down.

"Target! Load HEAT! Traverse RIGHT!!! Gunner, HEAT, PC."

"HEAT indexed. Identified."

"HEAT loaded. Up."

"Fire."

"On the way"

Anderson already had it in his sights. "Identified."

"Fire."

Another thunderclap filled the turret, the tank bucking against the recoil. The BMP target exploded in the distance. "Target."

Simmons, steady behind the controls, exhaled. "Damn." Anderson smirked, adjusting the controls. "Next target."

Steve nodded, watching the battlefield through the CITV thermal display, already calling out the shots.

"Gunner scan."

"Gunner, HEAT, bunker, front."

Anderson had the target centered in the reticle. "Identified."

"Up."

"Fire."

"On the way"

The bunker exploded, sending chunks of reinforced concrete into the air.

"Target. Driver, punch through the smoke."

"Gunner, HEAT, second bunker."

"Identified."

"Up."

"Fire."

"On the way."

The second bunker exploded.

"Driver, push forward! Gunner, switch to guns and scan for troops."

Nervously, Anderson stammered, "Negative contact."

"Keep scanning, Gunner."

From the driver's compartment, "Troops, right side, 500 meters out.

"Gunner, coax, troops."

"Identified."

"Fire."

The coaxial machine gun raked the trench line, targets going down.

"Target, Cease Fire. B-12 REDCON 1."

The M1A2 was still in the fight.

Charlie 92 broadcast: "B-12, objective secured. Continue to Battle Position Two."

The day run continued flawlessly. 700 points. A perfect score. They had nailed all seven engagements.

Outstanding run. Clear and elevate, display the proper visual signals, return to baseline to be cleared by Safety."

Simmons cheered. Ortega pounded Anderson's helmet. Steve smiled. His team came together.

Anderson exhaled. "Weapons cleared. I love this job."

Steve smirked. "Welcome to being a tank crewman. Give us a green flag, Ortega."

"C92, B-12, Weapons cleared and elevated. REDCON 1. Returning to baseline."

The adrenaline was flowing through them as they grabbed lunch, cleaned the weapons, and checked the entire tank.

Collier walked by, after dinner chow, didn't say a word — just nodded as he moved them to the first tank in the firing order for the night run.

The sky darkened. The air cooled. The only light came from the faint glow of instrumentation inside the tank.

The long-range mover cost them two points on engagement time.

Final score: 998.

Superior Qualification.

The radios crackled. "B-12, stand by for debrief at the TOC."

As they climbed out of the tank, Steve clapped Anderson on the shoulder.

"You earned that Specialist rank today, Andy. Great job."

Anderson, still catching his breath, grinned. "Damn right WE did a great job."

Steve smirked. "By the way... I didn't tell you before, but Major Collier is sending you to the Sergeant promotion board if you scored at least 700 points."

Anderson blinked. "You serious?"

Steve nodded. "Congratulations. Now start acting like a Sergeant."

Back in the TOC, Collier leaned back in his chair, studying

Steve and Anderson.

"Not bad." He tapped the results sheet. "998 points. You made up for that embarrassing start."

Steve and Anderson stood at attention, silent. Simmons and Ortega were nervously quiet, by the door.

Collier took a deep breath, then leaned forward. "I'll be making those recommendations. But don't ever put me in that position again, Johnson."

Steve gave a crisp nod. "Yes, sir."

Collier smirked. "Good. Now get both of your arrogant asses the hell out of my TOC."

As they left, Steve could hear First Sergeant Gallagher chuckling behind them.

"Damn, Major. I really do miss that kid."

The afternoon sun was casting long shadows as it sank lower in the sky.

The GTO's fuel gauge hovered just above empty, the needle threatening to dip into the red. Steve tightened his grip on the wheel, scanning the horizon for any sign of civilization.

Petrov's words came back to him, *"Army Group South will push through to conquer Moldova first — the Dniester River is the key. Secure the crossing, then drive into Europe. NATO will be too paralyzed to respond in time." He traced an invisible map on the table, his fingers trembling as they marked out the strategic points ... there won't be a Europe left to save."*

As the 4th Tank Guards Brigade vanished without a trace, Steve was seething over the last time he saw them, in a briefing at the SHAPE Intelligence Center, Brussels — January 2022.

Susi leaned over the terminal, watching Jasper van Dijk scroll through encrypted GRU intercepts.

"This doesn't make sense," Jasper muttered. "NATO dismissed the possibility of Russia having full-strength reserves. They're treating this as a failed blitz."

Steve frowned. "So why are Category A armored divisions still in reserve? Why is Army Group South completely intact?"

Jasper's fingers froze on the keyboard. A satellite image loaded.

Steve's stomach twisted.

Thousands of tanks. 4th Guards Tank Brigade. Waiting.

"The invasion with Category C units is going to be a feint," Jasper whispered. "You were right, Johnson."

Steve sat back, exhaling slowly. The words "You were right" sound so hollow now.

Even now, he hated that he might have been right.

"NATO is falling for it." Steve realized that the Flying Dutchman is the only one taking this seriously.

Forcing himself to move, he retreated to the GTO. He eased it back onto the dirt road, careful to avoid leaving visible tracks, and merged onto the P228 once he was confident the brigade was well ahead.

The countryside unfolded around him, a mosaic of dense forests and empty fields. The GTO's tires hummed against the asphalt, the rhythmic sound a counterpoint to the thoughts churning in his mind.

The Kasatka's presence suddenly made sense. It had definitely been a scout, clearing the path for the armored column. No question about it.

Russian doctrine was methodical: recon units identified weak points, and mechanized forces exploited them.

The 4th Guard were elite, but they were still Russian.

"They'll play on your instincts," Rivera's voice echoed in his mind. *"You've got to stay five steps ahead."*

The GTO's fuel gauge dipped below red and dangerously close to empty as the sun began its descent.

The forest gave way to open farmland, and finally, to the outskirts of Dnipro.

The industrial city lay along the Dnipro River, its skyline dotted with smokestacks and drab shelled out buildings. But at least he was in Ukraine now, though still Russian controlled.

He rolled into a small service station on the edge of town, the lights flickering as a weary attendant emerged.

The GTO came to a halt, and Steve shut off the engine, exhaling deeply as stillness enveloped him.

"THE AMERICANS believe they have already won,“ Markov said, setting a classified intelligence file on the table. "They laugh at our hesitations. They see our President as weak. They expect us to retreat, to crumble."

Mikhailov's fingers drummed against the wood. "Because we have been weak."

Silence.

That was the truth no one wanted to say out loud, but here, in this room, they all knew it.

"Not anymore," Markov said.

In a secure penthouse overlooking Johannesburg, in dim lighting, sits the Queen of Diamonds with a laptop running multiple encrypted scripts, and a nearly untouched glass of wine.

Claire Rousseau sat at her desk, eyes fixed on the rapidly scrolling data on her screen. Something was off.

For the past two months, she had been tracking GRU-affiliated financial activity — off-the-books funding, black-market arms transactions, and deep-pocket oligarchs washing money through illicit diamonds.

But now, something new has emerged.

She opened a secure line to Jasper van Dijk. "Jasper, we've got a new problem. The GRU just funneled four massive crypto transfers — untraceable origins, but all landing in a missile radar software firm in China.

This isn't arms dealing. This is next-gen battlefield tech.

"If they're upgrading radar capabilities, they're preparing for something big. Maybe bigger than Ukraine. Thought you should know."

Jasper exhaled, rubbing his temple. This was bad.

He immediately pulled up an internal NATO radar assessment report. If Russia was advancing missile-tracking software, it meant one of two things:

They were reinforcing their own air defense systems.

Or, worse, they were about to deploy something that would require NATO's best pilots to counter.

He took a deep breath. "Understood. Thank you and keep digging. We need to understand why the GRU would be funding this, and why the secrecy."

Jasper reached for his phone, again.

The weight of the day settled on his shoulders. He had escaped detection and survived another close call, but he couldn't shake the feeling that the storm was far from over. For now, though, Steve needed fuel — both for the GTO and for himself.

Tomorrow would bring new challenges, but tonight, he'd

rest and regroup.

The 4th Guards were on the move, and their destination could mean only one thing: escalation.

Steve couldn't shake the feeling that their path — and his — would intersect again soon.

The 10th Armored Strike Group would undoubtedly face them, too.

The war hadn't started yet, but he had no intention of being its first casualty. His old unit at the 17th ACR will soon be deep in the midst of it all.

—

The Defense Minister looked at the folder Markov had thrown down. A software program had been developed to blind NATO anti missile defense and missile counter batteries.

It has been paid for, and installed on all mobile rockets belonging to the Army Group South.

The next pages listed FSB agents, by name. It was titled "Night Stalker Objectives."

But it wasn't just FSB agents.

The list contained Colonel Petrov, and his name was struck through. It also contained key members of the Duma, ministry officials, advisors to the President, and a few GRU agents.

Minister of Internal Affairs Viktor Malenkov showed concern. "FSB can be controlled. We can prevent them from slowing things down."

"They will not slow us down, anymore." Markov had a dark look behind his smile.

The list included top GRU counterintelligence officers. A few members of the Puren Initiative were listed under, "Pending." Viktor Malenkov was one of them.

At SHAPE, the analysts were still arguing over satellite images. The radio intercepts from Minsk insisted the 4th Guards were 1,500 kilometers away. But right here, right now, deep in the Russian steppe, Steve had seen them.

And soon, someone at NATO was going to pay the price for believing the lie. Major, now General Collier, would have taken the threat seriously.

Steve recognized the number on the secure sat phone. "Susi."

"We have a problem, Steve." Before Jasper could finish, Steve cut him off.

"Davy Jones, 4th Guards Tank Brigade is moving to the border of Ukraine. They are preparing to attack Moldova and follow on to Romania. Full report will follow." Steve had helped form the *Flying Dutchman*, and he was their man on the ground at ESID."

"Davy Jones acknowledges. "Susi, we've been tracking a

sudden spike in Russian defense contracts. You're telling me the 4th Guards are in motion?"

"Yeah. And I think SHAPE is blind to it."

"Then we need to move fast." Adjudant-Onderofficier van Dijk set the secure cell phone in his desk drawer.

Because while NATO planned for the wrong war –

The real war had already begun.

And Minister of Defense Viktor Mikhailov saw one last name as Markov took the folder.

Major Anya Kuznetsova — with € 2,000,000.00 next to her name.

Storms On The Horizon

Dnipro, Ukraine – A Quiet Restaurant

Traditional Ukranian folk music played softly in the background. A grandmother wiped down a table near the front, pausing to hand a sugar cube to a child in a patched coat. A man in a worn suit hunched over a chessboard, waiting for an opponent who might never come.

The world was still spinning — slowly, stubbornly — even here.

As he walked through, he acknowledged each person with the Slavic nod that was all too reminiscent of life in Ukraine.

Life continued — changed, yet still the same.

Steve chose a table in the far corner, his back firmly against the wall, with a clear view of the door and away from others.

He loosened his jacket slightly, keeping his Tokarev within easy reach, and scanned the room. Just another weary traveler looking for a meal.

A thousand kilometers away, another man committed to the

war — without ever leaving his chair.

At a hidden bunker outside of Bratislava, Cypher's off-grid operation is taking the silent war to an unthinkable realm, and he is watching it unfold on screen. The servers hummed in the background, casting a low vibration through the underground bunker.

Cypher leaned back in his chair, eyes flicking between six different monitors, watching the last line of code execute.

He had just done what no NATO intelligence team had ever pulled off.

There was no human mole inside GRU.

There didn't have to be.

He had just turned GRU's own encrypted networks into his informant.

The subroutine quietly embeds itself in all GRU and GRU-affiliated cloud and network systems.

It copies, encrypts, and reroutes intelligence into Cypher's isolated, off-grid server.

Every 30 minutes, the AI processes and summarizes fresh intelligence into "fact sheets." At night, it compiles these into a full digest while he sleeps.

The GRU won't see it because their own systems treat the data flow as part of their secured network.

The burst transmission is from a random GRU station.

Each burst transmission triggers the subroutine to move itself.

Every 12 seconds, the code rewrites itself to a new subroutine location.

Each system scan causes the subroutine to write itself in an already scanned line of code, before the scan reaches it.

Completely untraceable.

Their own technology had just become the traitor in their midst.

The first instance of merging HUMINT with ELINT.

Emil Kovács grew up in the shadow and memories of the Iron Curtain, born just before its collapse.

He was a quiet, intense child, preferring machines over people.

While other kids played soccer in the streets, Emil was hacking dial-up networks and cracking amateur encryption codes.

By 16, he had breached a Slovak government server — not to steal, but to see if he could.

Instead of being arrested, he was recruited.

By 18, he was studying under Slovakia's military cyber-intelligence division.

And by the age of 25, NATO had him on contract, feeding Slovakia's cyber operations into their Eastern European cyber unit.

But that was where his trust in the system began to crack.

The mission was supposed to be clean and surgical — penetrate a GRU-controlled communications hub in Ukraine and feed intelligence to NATO.

Emil was tasked with creating a backdoor into the system.

But his software worked too well. It unintentionally accessed deeper GRU systems than NATO anticipated.

NATO leadership panicked — instead of exploiting the breach, they burned the entire operation and blamed Slovakia's intelligence unit for "reckless infiltration."

Slovak agents on the ground were left exposed. Two of them were executed in a retaliatory strike by GRU operatives.

NATO wiped their hands clean, called it a "miscalculation", and buried the event.

Emil realized intelligence agencies didn't care about their assets — they cared about control; the system was broken.

Bureaucracy killed good people.

He was done working for any flag.

That night, he removed every electronic record that he ever existed, and vanished from the intelligence grid.

Using stolen black funds from a failed Russian cyber op — money no one could trace, purchased an abandoned Cold War-era nuclear bunker, originally built as a Soviet emergency fallback station.

Kovács reinforced it with independent satellite uplinks, an air-gapped decryption farm; a multi-layered security system, monitored 24/7 by AI-driven surveillance.

Exhaust vents were capped with wind turbine generators

and solar panels were erected in the back fence of the property.

A bank of lithium batteries could store 45 days of power, without a recharge. But it could reach full capacity faster than it used the power.

The bunker has no official record of existence. As far as the world is concerned, it's just another Cold War relic.

Now a rogue operative, he established his personal operating rules:

No government affiliations.

No personal meetings.

He doesn't sell intelligence — he trades it.

By 2015, he was one of the most sought-after cyber operatives in Europe.

During an early operation in Slovakia, Cypher had seen encrypted messages before. But this one was different.

The GRU's latest comms encryption wasn't following any known Russian cyberwarfare doctrine.

It was changing every 17 minutes, rotating through unknown ciphers, leaving SHAPE's best analysts scrambling to catch up.

Even Jasper was stumped.

"It's like someone's hiding a signal inside a signal," Jasper had muttered over a secure call.

"That's not how GRU works," Steve had replied. "They like brute force encryption, not... whatever this is."

The last ping from the encryption source came from a non-descript café in Bratislava.

So that's where Steve found himself — watching the door, waiting for someone to show up and claim the encrypted signal.

The café was quiet, just a few old men playing chess, a couple of students with laptops, and a lone man in the back, hood up, sipping coffee.

Steve ordered an espresso and took a seat near the chess players.

Then his phone vibrated.

> Unknown Number: *Nice try, soldier boy.*
> Unknown Number: *Did you really think you could track me with NATO's clunky old SIGINT?*
> Unknown Number: *You're not the only one who knows how to hunt.*

Steve's eyes narrowed. He looked around, then calmly took another sip of his coffee.

> Steve typed back: *So who am I talking to?*

A pause as three dots kept moving on the screen.

> Unknown Number: *Checkmate in three moves.*

Steve looked up. The old men's chess game was ending

exactly as predicted.

Then, the hooded man at the next table stood up, dropped a few euro notes, and walked past Steve's table — without looking at him.

A flash drive and set of two SIM cards landed next to Steve's espresso.

"You're going to need better encryption, soldier," the man muttered before walking out the door.

Steve picked up the drive, turning it over in his palm.

The name "Cypher" was etched on the side.

Back at his safe house, Steve plugged in the drive using a non-traceable laptop.

Inside was a decryption key. A perfect counter to the GRU's latest encrypted network.

A message popped up.

> Cypher: *One SIM for you, one for Davy Jones. You're about to owe me, Susi. Try not to get yourself killed before I collect.*

Steve exhaled.

Jasper had been right. *"The guy's a ghost in the machine."*

And now, The Flying Dutchman has its cyberwarfare specialist.

The first fact sheet spit out. The AI listed the items it felt was a priority. The first was the curious Night Stalker hit list targeting a GRU counterintelligence Major, putting a very substantial bounty put on her head.

It is a name he recognized from hacking Steve's records.

Time for old school spycraft. Major Anya Kuznetsova was being hunted for €2,000,000.00.

As Steve waited for a waiter, he noticed a young man in a heavy coat entered the café, glancing around nervously before passing a folded note to the barista. The barista didn't read it. She tucked it under the counter like it was routine.

Steve had seen that kind of exchange before. A message drop.

The resistance was alive in Dnipro.

The real question was, how long until the Russians crushed them?

A waiter approached, and Steve ordered.

Half an hour later, his meal arrived — a lavish spread of borsch with thick sour cream, vareniki stuffed with mushrooms and potatoes, and a perfectly roasted portion of holubtsi — cabbage rolls filled with rice, pork, and herbs.

A frothy pint of locally brewed Obolon beer completed the meal.

Steve savored each bite, his years vacationing in Ukraine, with Katya, on ESID's dime made him appreciate the regional flavors.

It was the first time in weeks he'd eaten something resembling a proper meal, and for a brief moment, he allowed himself to relax.

Then she walked in.

The blonde was striking — tall, poised, with high cheekbones and eyes the color of Siberian ice.

Her GRU uniform, immaculately pressed, clung to her athletic frame with an air of authority.

A major's insignia gleamed on her shoulder boards, catching the dim light. She scanned the room, her gaze locking onto Steve almost instantly.

Her lips curved into a smile.

Steve froze, every muscle tense, but he kept his expression neutral.

The warmth of his meal vanished, replaced by a chill that spread through his chest.

Anya Kuznetsova. He hadn't seen her since Moscow, since those three unforgettable days almost two decades ago.

Back then, she'd been a fiery, unpredictable intelligence analyst — equal parts charm and ruthlessness.

Even now, after all these years, the sight of her stirred emotions he didn't want to name.

Her smile widened as she walked toward him, the sharp staccato of her boots muffled by the carpet. Without hesitation, she leaned in and kissed him on the cheek, her perfume momentarily overwhelming the scents of the café.

"Stefan Ivanovich," she said softly, her voice carrying a faint trace of amusement. "It has been far too long."

Steve forced a grin, though his mind raced. The kiss wasn't an accident — it was a calculated move, a reminder of their history and her ability to disarm him.

She poured herself a shot of vodka and gestured toward Steve. "Beer, not your usual Johnnie Walker?"

As the memories flooded in, Steve merely replied, "You know damn well it is always a Balvenie..."

The Rossiya Hotel had stood as a silent witness to Russian history for over a century — its grand Art Nouveau facade overlooking Theatre Square, a relic of imperial opulence that had somehow survived revolutions, world wars, and the Cold War.

Steve had checked in earlier that day, still feeling the slow burn of jet lag, but the concierge had assured him the piano lounge was the best in the city — discreet, refined, with an unmatched selection of single malts.

It had been enough to convince him.

Dressed in a well-tailored charcoal blazer over a crisp white Oxford shirt, he took a seat at the mahogany bar, nodding in approval at the warm, low lighting that illuminated the room in shades of amber.

The tinkling of piano keys floated softly through the air, a jazz rendition of Rachmaninoff's "Vocalise."

When the bartender approached, Steve smiled. "You wouldn't happen to have a bottle of Balvenie 14-Year Caribbean Cask, would you?"

The bartender gave him a knowing look. "Ah, a gentleman with taste. Of course, sir."

"One ice ball, please." Steve exhaled and relaxed deeply.

A moment later, the golden liquid swirled in a crystal tumbler before him.

He took the glass, breathing in the rich, honeyed aroma, hints of vanilla and spice mixing with the faintest trace of rum cask sweetness.

Steve's smile said everything.

Steve was about to take his first sip when he noticed her.

She was seated near the grand piano, a vision in a deep emerald silk dress that clung in all the right places, her blonde hair cascading over one shoulder like a golden river.

But it was her eyes that caught him first — a striking, Siberian ice blue, watching him with an unmistakable glimmer of mischief.

He held her gaze for a second longer than necessary.

She tilted her head, her lips curving into a slow, knowing smile.

Steve raised his glass slightly in acknowledgment before taking a slow sip.

The game had begun. One Steve had not considered playing.

He wasn't surprised when, a few minutes later, she approached.

"Вы всегда пьёте в одиночестве?" she purred in flawless Russian. Do you always drink alone?

Steve turned, his expression amused, yet measured. "Only when the company isn't worth joining."

He deliberately answered in English, watching her reaction.

Anya's lips twitched in approval. "Ah. Not a tourist on business, then."

"Not exactly," Steve replied, taking another sip of his Balvenie. "Just a soldier enjoying his leave."

Her brow lifted slightly. "A soldier?"

Steve shrugged, playing it down. "Nothing glamorous. I drive a tank."

Her laugh was soft, rich, and just a little dangerous. "You must be very good at it. They don't just let anyone drive those beasts."

Steve smirked. "You'd be surprised. It's mostly about keeping it moving in the right direction and knowing when to stop."

She studied him over the rim of her vodka glass, amusement glinting in her gaze. "I somehow doubt you are just a simple tank driver. Or that you would know when to stop."

"You think I'm lying?"

"I think you're being... humble." She leaned slightly closer. "There is something about you, Stefan Ivanovich. You have the eyes of a man who notices things."

Steve's grip on his glass tightened slightly, but not noticeably.

That was an observation no ordinary woman would make. Steve's smile returned as he realized what the game truly was.

"You have me at a disadvantage," he admitted. "You know my name, but I don't know yours."

"Anya Kuznetsova," she said smoothly. "I work in — " she gave a small, teasing smile, " — government affairs."

Steve chuckled. "That sounds ... ominous."

"Only if you have something to hide." She took another sip, then set the glass down. "Tell me, Stefan, how do you find Moscow?"

Steve leaned back, feigning a casual air. "It has its charms. I like its history and architecture... the bars." He smirked slightly. "And I like that my French comes in handy here."

She arched a delicate brow. "Vous parlez français?"

Steve took another sip of his whiskey, letting the silence stretch just long enough to be intriguing before answering in fluent, unhurried French.

"Naturellement. J'aime les langues. Elles ouvrent des portes."

(Of course. I like languages. They open doors.)

Anya's smirk widened, but there was something else in her eyes now — genuine interest.

"Et vous êtes un homme qui aime ouvrir des portes?"

(And are you a man who likes to open doors?)

"Seulement si ce qui est derrière vaut la peine."

(Only if what's behind them is worth it.)

The air between them shifted, thickening with something

unspoken yet entirely understood.

Anya ran a single manicured finger along the rim of her glass, holding his gaze as if testing his nerve.

And then, just as effortlessly as she had walked over to him, she stood up.

"Come," she said, offering him her hand. "Let's see if Moscow is as charming as you say."

Walking towards the door, Steve made eye contact with a man sitting alone, reading a novel. The man gave a barely perceptible nod.

They walked through the heart of the city, past the glowing lights of Red Square, the grandeur of St. Basil's Cathedral, and the historic cobblestone paths near the Kremlin walls.

Steve wasn't sure when he first took her hand, but once he did, she didn't let go. She leaned into him.

They talked about art, history, music, and for a moment, Steve forgot that he was anything other than a man enjoying a night with a beautiful woman.

They stole kisses between shadowed alleyways, her lips warm and teasing against his.

"You're too good at this," Steve murmured against her mouth.

Anya smiled against his lips. "And you're too easily tempted."

"Not easily," he countered. "Just... willingly."

She laughed, wrapping her arms around his neck, pulling him closer. "I like you, Stefan Ivanovich."

And then, with a mischievous glint in her eye, she whispered,

"My apartment is not far from here."

They stumbled into her darkened apartment, still tangled together. The door clicked shut behind them, muffling the distant hum of the city.

Steve pressed her against the wall, hands trailing down her waist, feeling the heat radiating off her.

Anya's fingers worked the buttons of his shirt, slowly, deliberately, her breath warm against his skin.

"I don't usually do this," she murmured, her voice playful but deceptively honest.

Steve smirked. "That makes two of us."

Her lips curved against his jaw. "Liar."

And then — before the night could fully unravel in his mind — the scene snapped back to reality in the Dnipro café. She pulled out a chair across from him and, with a practiced motion, placed her Makarov pistol on the seat beside her. It was a gesture that spoke not of threat, but of truce.

"Major Kuznetsova," he replied, his tone carefully neutral. "To what do I owe the pleasure?"

"Relax," she said with a sly smile. "I'm not here to arrest you... Yet."

Anya flagged the waiter, ordering ukha — a traditional Russian fish soup — followed by beef stroganoff and a glass of chilled vodka.

She leaned back, studying Steve with a look that was equal parts playful and calculating.

"You've aged well," she said. "But then, I always knew you'd hold up better than most men."

Steve chuckled, keeping his tone light, though his shoulders remained tight. "You haven't changed much yourself, Anya. Still turning heads wherever you go."

They exchanged pleasantries while her meal arrived.

The ukha steamed as she sipped it slowly, her expression softening with a hint of nostalgia.

When the waiter placed her stroganoff before her, Anya was still watching Steve over the rim of her vodka glass, a small, knowing smile playing on her lips.

"You're thinking about that night, aren't you?"

Steve set down his beer. "I was wondering if you ever think about it."

She sighed dramatically, swirling her vodka. "Of course. But not for the reason you think."

Steve smirked. "And what reason would that be?"

Anya's gaze darkened slightly, the amusement giving way to something more serious.

"Because that was the night I realized who you really could become — and have become."

And just like that, Steve realized she had never just been a woman who caught his eye in a piano bar.

She had been watching him from the very beginning. It was

also the night before his recruitment into ESID began. He was torn in many directions by this memory.

"Za vstrechu," she said — to the meeting.

He raised his beer in response. "Za vstrechu."

The moment of calm passed as quickly as it had come. Anya set her fork down and fixed him with a serious look.

"Stefan," she began, switching to English to avoid eavesdroppers, "I've been following your career since Moscow. Your Russian has improved, by the way — nearly flawless now. I'm impressed."

Steve didn't respond, waiting for her to continue.

"I know who you are," she said bluntly, her voice soft but cutting. "I've known for years. You were reckless in maintaining your cover with your beloved car."

A cold evening mist had clung to the streets of Moscow's outer ring road, curling in the dim glow of sodium-vapor streetlights. The night was quiet now, but for a moment — just a moment — the silence had been shattered by the guttural, unmistakable roar of an American V8.

A black Pontiac GTO, its silhouette a relic of a bygone era, had thundered past Checkpoint K-17 before disappearing into the darkness, a ghostly comet streaking westward toward the unknown with an unmarked Lada losing its pursuit.

Inside a secure GRU field office, newly promoted Captain Anya Kuznetsova examined the grainy stills from a traffic camera — blurry, motion-streaked, but telling. The muscle car was an anomaly.

Not a stolen Lada, not an armored ZIL, not an unmarked FSB sedan.

No one in their right mind would drive an American classic car through Moscow unless they belonged here — or had been here long enough to know how to avoid getting caught.

A young intelligence officer, Lieutenant Viktor Mikhailov, sat stiffly across from her, his fingers drumming against a stack of reports. He looked eager — too eager.

"Captain," he said, nudging the images closer to her, "we're running facial recognition scans through all known American intelligence officers. The car's plates are Polish. Our working theory is Agencja Wywiadu — state espionage. They operate in silence, but we know they have deep cover assets in Moscow."

Anya's eyes flicked from the image of the GTO's Polish license plate to the grainy silhouette of its driver — impossible to identify at this angle, but the profile...

Too familiar.

She leaned back, swirling her vodka in its glass, watching the icy liquid catch the dim light.

Her fantasy lover had just run through Moscow like a predator on the hunt.

And the GRU had no idea who he was.

Yet.

Mikhailov flipped to another file, pulling up a red-marked intelligence report.

"There's a confirmed Agencja Wywiadu officer unaccounted for," he continued. "Polish intelligence has been operating here since the invasion of Chechnya, supporting Western agents where they can. I believe this is our man."

Anya remained silent, watching Mikhailov try to piece together a puzzle whose edges didn't quite fit.

"He doesn't operate like the Americans, or the Brits," Mikhailov muttered, eyes scanning the pages. "No known digital footprint. He moves quietly, deliberately. Doesn't leave trails."

Anya let him speak, but her mind had already made the connection.

Not Polish intelligence.

Not some rogue Western asset.

The GTO's driver wasn't just some intelligence officer slipping through Moscow. This was a hunter.

A wolf among sheep.

Anya tapped her finger against the image, her voice calm but edged with something Mikhailov couldn't place.

"Not just a hunter. A bear."

Mikhailov frowned. "A bear?"

Anya smirked slightly. "Wojtek."

Mikhailov looked even more confused. "The Polish Great War bear?"

Anya nodded, her ice-blue eyes narrowing as she leaned forward.

She lowered her voice, adding to her sinister tone. "Wojtek was a legend — a bear raised by Polish soldiers during the war. He carried ammunition, moved supplies. He was quiet, calm, even playful... until the enemy appeared."

She let the words sink in before adding, "Then he became a savage aggressor. Ruthless. Unstoppable."

Mikhailov blinked. "You're saying our target fights like a bear?"

Anya exhaled slowly. "No, Lieutenant. I'm saying he is a bear."

She tapped the Polish license plate on the still image. "And that plate will keep everyone else looking in the wrong direction."

Mikhailov still didn't understand. She could see it in his rigid, analytical expression — the kind of dangerous thinking that got people killed.

But Anya understood.

She had spent three nights with him, memorized his movements, traced the shape of his mind the same way she had traced the contours of his body.

Chills of a deeply passionate memory ran through her body.

And now, in some twisted cosmic irony, he had become her secret.

A mystery even to her own agency.

Anya leaned back in her chair, her fingers tightening slightly around the glass as she let out a quiet breath, looking him into his soul. His expression didn't falter, but a subtle tension gleamed behind his eyes.

Stefan Ivanovich... What game are you playing now?

Steve glanced around, noting nobody could hear them, let alone come to his aid if needed.

"You're Susi, the Wolf," she said, her voice barely above a whisper. "The elusive ESID agent NATO thinks is so clever. Who do you think gave you the codename 'Wojtek' all those years ago? I had to throw the others off your scent, make them believe you were Polish or Eastern European. And it worked — didn't it?"

Steve's hand tightened on his beer glass. "Why?"

"As you Americans say, it never hurts to have an ace up your sleeve." Anya's eyes gleamed with a mixture of pride and something else — something softer. "The GRU may be ruthless, and I had to keep something around for a career acceleration if something went wrong in the world. I do what I do for the people of Russia, not the people in power."

Steve leaned forward slightly, intrigued despite himself. "And now?"

"Now," she said, her tone sharp and urgent, "it has all gone wrong and we're forced to be on the same side. Whether you like it or not." Her deep, knowing look was in her eyes.

She reached across the table, taking his hand in hers, "But I know you like it."

She lowered her voice further, as she leaned forward, her tone remained sharp and urgent, sticking with English. "There's a rogue general. Russian Army General Grigorievich Markov, former Soviet Strategic Rocket Forces, now aligned with GRU hardliners. He's crossed into NATO territory, hiding in Budapest."

Steve frowned. "Markov? What's his game?"

"Complete destruction and annihilation." Her eyes darkened. "Markov misses the era of the entire world waiting for the day the Eagle would meet the Bear. It provided global balance and a tenuous peace. The East-West, Soviet-American standoff forced most of the world to pick a side. There is too much instability now. He wants to restore order through chaos."

Her Siberian ice blue eyes went even colder. "Markov has access to launch codes for mobile nuclear platforms — Iskander-M units. He plans to use them to strike major European capitals. Budapest puts him within range of Rome, Paris, London, and others. Millions will die, and NATO will be forced into surrender. The EU would collapse within days."

"How could he hide missiles around Budapest?" Steve pondered out loud.

"They are on mobile rocket launchers embedded with the Army Group South. You already know their objective, Stefan." Anya's face betrayed a sense of fear Steve never knew existed in her.

"NATO has missile defenses," Steve countered.

"Not against these." Anya's voice dropped to a whisper. "The newest NATO missiles have been compromised by a Russian hacked update. Our rockets emit a decoy frequency to bypass Western interceptors. Markov designed the software."

Steve sat back, his mind reeling. But as she spoke, Steve couldn't help but replay her earlier words in his mind. "How could General Markov bypass the two person launch code safeguard?"

"He contracted the developer to install the launch system software. He created the need for a bypass code, in the event of the two codes being compromised. He must be stopped," she continued. "I've pieced together everything. I know you have connections, resources, and the *'sisu'* to avoid this loss."

Steve tensed but didn't respond. Anya Kuznetsova, his one-time lover, had been watching him all along — protecting him, maybe even saving him, but only to use him when she needed him.

And now, she was asking him to trust her again.

Steve studied Anya's face. Cool. Measured. A practiced smile. She was good at this. Too good.

Was she telling the truth?

Markov was not existent — a phantom.

Half of NATO's analysts didn't even believe he was still operational, and yet Anya was handing him over like a gift.

Nothing in espionage came without a price.

He swirled the vodka in his glass. "And I suppose you're telling me this out of professional courtesy?"

Anya leaned closer, lowering her voice. "I'm telling you because it matters. This is something that I cannot stop by myself. Neither could you. Frankly, there is nobody else I would trust to go in with me."

Steve held her gaze. If Markov had gone rogue, it was the biggest intelligence failure of the war.

If Anya was lying, she was setting him up to chase shadows. Which one was it?

Anya smiled knowingly. "Meet me in Prague within 24 hours. We'll need each other to stop this."

As she stood to leave, she leaned in close, her breath warm against his ear.

"Something weighs heavy on your mind. Choose wisely, Stefan. Millions of lives depend on it. A bigger war is coming, and the politicians making it will not be fighting it. You and I serve our people, not the politicos."

With that, she disappeared into the night, leaving Steve alone with his thoughts — and the weight of the impossible choice ahead. "What in the hell just happened?"

As Steve sat there, drinking his third beer, the voices came back to haunt him.

Colonel Petrov's last words of wisdom as he handed Steve the encryption key, "*Take this, expose them. Do something with it. Because if you don't, there won't be a Europe left to save.*"

Major Collier's direct words, "*Every officer in the 4th Guards is handpicked... If you ever face them, it won't just be a fight. It'll be survival. It will not be a war. It will be an annihilation.*"

Anya's voice, *"Budapest puts him within range of Rome, Paris, London, and others. Millions will die, and NATO will be forced into surrender. The EU would collapse within days."*

His father Jack, *"You've got a very tactical mind, Steve. Whether it's on a chessboard or under the hood, you see the connections, you stay five moves ahead of everyone and everything. That's rare. It will take you far..."*

"Yeah, Dad. It may have taken me too far this time. It led me to the ultimate no win scenario." Steve reflected. "What would you have done, Commander Jack?"

Steve decided on one more beer and dessert before finding a bed for the night.

The waiter brought the bill. Steve unfolded it and the note from the underground agent fell out.

"Checkmate in one move." Cypher's most urgent code.

"A bigger war is coming, and the politicians making it will not be fighting it." What is she seeing from her end?

He needs to reach Cypher, before exhaustion kicks in. Then he can sleep safely tonight, knowing he is under Anya's protection. But for how long?

As Steve was preparing to contact Cypher, things were far from quiet at HQ SHAPE. The building wide emergency intercom beeped. The full staff sat up, listening.

"Lieutenant Markham and Mister Kern report to my office. *IMMEDIATELY!*"

It was the unmistakable voice of Adjudant-Onderofficier Jasper van Dijk. His thick Dutch accent accentuated his anger.

Sentinel knew better than to intervene when a Warrant Officer spoke, even if the emergency intercom system was being misused.

Standing On My Own

Dnipro, Ukraine – A Nondescript Hotel

The last words he heard last night were from Cypher. "There is a GRU assassination list. General Markov is plotting a reverse coup. He wants the Russian President to make mistakes, and be forced out of office by NATO action.

His *Night Stalkers* are targeting anyone who could get in the way. One of the names carries a bounty of €2,000,000.00."

Anya was now the most wanted person in Russia. Hunted by professionals.

Steve was trying to take all of this in. A reverse coup masterminded by General Markov.

General Markov is about to launch nuclear rockets and cripple the European Union.

The puzzle is piecing itself together. Anya's information is quickly validating itself.

"Susi. That high value target is Major Anya Kuznetsova." Cypher paused for a moment. "Steve, be careful out there."

"I know. I still owe you, Cypher."

"Now you owe me two. Three if you save Anya." Cypher swore he would never have allegiances. The Flying Dutchman hadn't changed him. But gave him purpose. That was enough.

⬤

The cold water hit Steve's skin like a slap, jolting him fully awake, while it was still dark outside. He leaned forward, bracing himself against the tiled wall of the cheap Dnipro hotel's shower, letting the freezing cascade dull the aches and bruises from days on the run.

It reminded him of the night in Volgograd, where he'd stared into the cold, dead eyes of a GRU operative, seconds before pulling the trigger.

His Tokarev had done its job, Sergey's old sidearm roaring to life after decades of dormancy.

Sergey had given it to him as a gift, a relic of his Cold War service and in Afghanistan — a symbol of respect. *"A weapon is only as good as the man holding it,"* Sergey had said as he handed Steve the worn leather holster.

That man, Steve thought, had once been a Soviet hero. Now that weapon was being used against Sergey's own countrymen — men who longed for a return to those days of unchecked power.

The irony wasn't lost on him.

Steve stepped out of the shower, drying himself with a threadbare towel.

He laid his Tokarev on the bed, meticulously wiping it down before holstering it.

His black leather jacket lay draped across the chair, and he slid it on, completing his look with a pair of dark sunglasses and his Curtis Bailey hat.

Regret had its place. Just not today.

There was no room for hesitation. Not with war seconds away; and his former lover to save.

All because he just wants to see his fiancée again.

The Pontiac GTO's engine rumbled to life, low like a tiger ready to pounce. Steve slid into the driver's seat, adjusting his grip on the wheel. The car's raw power had been his only companion through these hostile streets.

We need this to end.

As he navigated the checkpoints, the GTO's guttural growl blended with the chaos of occupied Ukraine — soldiers barking orders, civilians trudging through their days, and the ever-present sound of war hovering like a dark cloud.

As he left the city, Steve picked up his secure satellite phone and called ESID. The line crackled as his superior answered.

"Susi, where the hell are you?" The voice was sharp,

authoritative.

"Still in Ukraine," Steve replied flatly. "I need guidance."

"Your orders are clear," the superior snapped. "Get to the nearest NATO border and debrief. You're not authorized to continue."

Steve was not in the mood. "The clock's ticking. I need to get to Prague. The situation has developed and we have two major problems."

"Prague is out of the question," his superior barked. "You're to stand down. This isn't a solo mission."

Steve let the silence hang for a moment before hanging up without a goodbye. He tossed the phone onto the passenger seat, his mind racing.

"They don't get it," he thought.

He was out of time, and bureaucracy wouldn't stop Markov — or Anya.

He dialed a different number.

The voice on the other end was gruff but familiar, answering without pleasantries or following military protocol, simply saying, "Collier."

"Major Collier. Or should I say General Collier?" Steve said, forcing a smile.

"Steve? Hell, I haven't heard from you in years. What's

going on?"

"I need a favor, Nate." Steve said, his voice serious. "Can you meet me in Prague tonight? Late dinner."

There was a pause. Steve had never used Collier's first name before. "You're not calling just to catch up, are you?"

"Not exactly."

Collier sighed. "Alright. I'll clear my schedule and order my chopper. See you in Prague."

Steve hung up, glancing at the clock.

Sixteen hours until the meeting with Anya. But Prague was a 21-hour drive across hostile and friendly territory. He patted the GTO's dashboard. "Alright, girl. Time to boogie boogie."

As the Pontiac roared back to life, Steve's mind wandered to his days in the 10th Armored Strike Force. The memory of his driver, Specialist Meza, came flooding back. Meza had loved to hear Steve say those words — *boogie boogie.* It was the signal to push their M1A2 Abrams to its limits.

Steve could still hear the roar of the 1,500-horsepower Honeywell AGT1500 gas turbine engine as Meza maxed it out at 110 kilometers per hour on open roads.

Meza knew every road along the Polish and Slovakian borders with Ukraine. Those days were gone, but the spirit of the hunt remained.

The Ukrainian countryside blurred past as the GTO devoured the road.

When Steve reached the Polish border, things took a turn.

Steve spotted them the moment they appeared in his rearview mirror — a pair of black Audi Q7s, their factory LED daytime running lights gleaming in the mid-afternoon sun.

Their approach was methodical, their intent clear. ESID wasn't trying to shadow him anymore.

They were moving to intercept.

Steve flexed his fingers around the lacquered wood-rim steering wheel, feeling the familiar creak of the leather-wrapped grip.

The GTO's 455 HO engine rumbled under the hood, but he knew that brute force alone wouldn't shake off a pair of German-engineered pursuit vehicles designed for high-speed, high-stakes operations.

He exhaled, rolling his shoulders. Time to make this fun.

With one hand, he flipped open the RetroSound Hermosa head unit he'd custom-installed, scrolling through the list of playlists.

Hot Pursuit.

The opening riffs of Van Halen's "Panama" blasted through the JL Audio speakers, the deep bass vibrating through the GTO's cabin.

Steve smirked, cinching his five-point racing harness tight.

He pulled on a pair of Italian lambskin driving gloves, the soft, supple leather tightening around his knuckles.

With a flick, he dropped the shifter down a gear, the custom-built TREMEC TKO five-speed transmission humming in response.

The Audi Q7s weren't standard issue. These were the ABT Sportsline-modified variants — custom-tuned 4.0L V8 twin-turbos, 600 horsepower, Quattro all-wheel-drive, eight-speed automatic transmissions.

They could hit 175 mph without struggling.

But that was on the Autobahn.

This was open countryside, where raw muscle and a heavy right foot reigned supreme.

Steve's '71 Pontiac GTO Judge was a monster from a time before microchips and traction control. 6.6 liters of naturally aspirated, four-barrel carb-fed American fury.

A rolling war cry.

At full throttle, his restomod GTO could push 185 mph — but he wasn't running at full power yet. Not until he needed to.

The lyrics coincided with every curve in the road.

The ESID agents flanked both sides, one Q7 easing up along his driver's side, the other slipping in behind.

They weren't trying to force him off the road — not yet. They wanted to box him in, slow him down, long enough for air support to catch up.

Steve gritted his teeth, gripping the Hurst T-handle shifter, watching the highway ahead. Two lanes. Flat.

The afternoon sun gleamed off the golden fields stretching

endlessly in both directions. A few distant farmhouses, the occasional abandoned Soviet watchtower.

Then, up ahead — a curve leading into a valley.

Perfect.

He let the Q7 on his left inch closer, the driver wearing an earpiece, watching Steve through dark aviators. The Audi's V8 grumbled, trying to match his speed.

Steve acted first.

A quick flick of the wrist, and the GTO swung toward the Q7, faking an impact.

The ESID driver reacted instinctively — jerking the wheel left, then right.

That split-second reaction gave Steve the gap he needed.

He downshifted, redlining third gear, the 455 HO screaming with unchained power.

The Audi's Quattro system clawed for grip, but it had weight, electronics, and hesitation. Steve had instinct and torque.

The tempo increased, as if controlled by the accelerator.

The valley came fast.

Steve let the GTO's nose dip into the downhill grade, watching the tach climb past 6,000 RPM. The Q7s scrambled to keep up, their heavier chassis struggling on the descent.

Then came the long straightaway at the bottom.

Steve flipped the cover, then hit the nitrous switch.

The effect was instant.

A sudden whine from the injectors, the sharp, chemical hiss

of compressed liquid oxygen igniting.

The GTO lurched forward violently, the rear tires briefly chirping as raw horsepower surged through the drivetrain.

The hood scoops whistled, the entire frame quivering under the force of the additional 200 horsepower.

Blue flames spat from the side-exit exhaust.

The speedometer rocketed past 160, then 170.

"PANAMA!"

Steve's vision narrowed, the countryside blurring past like a fever dream of wheat and asphalt. The GTO's front end lifted slightly, the suspension flexing under the sheer force of speed.

The Q7s vanished in the mirror.

They had no chance.

The radio chatter inside the Audis would be frantic. The ESID agents knew they'd lost visual. But they still had one play left — air assets.

Steve grinned, still singing along.

Up ahead, a bridge crossing a dry riverbed appeared. A sign for a rural detour leading back into the hills.

His way out. "I bet Dad never dreamed the GTO we rebuilt would ever be used this way."

With one last flick of the wheel, he let the GTO slide sideways onto the unpaved road, sending a rooster tail of dust into the air, flipping off the nitrous as he straightened out.

By the time the helicopters were airborne, Steve would already be long gone.

Just a traveler on the open road.

And the ESID agents?

They'd have to explain how they let a lone man in a fifty-five-year-old muscle car outdrive NATO's best pursuit vehicles.

Steve eased back, watching the dust settle in the mirror.

"God, I love this car," he muttered.

Then he cranked the volume even higher, muttering under his breath, "Boogie boogie."

He cleared the 5 hour drive across Poland in just 3 1/2 hours.

The open border with Czechia loomed ahead, a chaotic scene of soldiers and an ESID checkpoint.

Steve didn't slow down.

He veered onto a dirt road, skirting the main crossing and plunging into the Czechian countryside.

The ESID agents wouldn't catch him tonight.

The GTO was more than just a car; it was his lifeline, his escape, his weapon.

Especially now that every country has become hostile territory.

At SHAPE HQ, Lieutenant Markham and Mister Kern had reported to the office of Adjudant-Onderofficier van Dijk who slammed a file onto the desk. "You ignored this? You ignored the goddamn 4th Guards Tank situation?"

Lieutenant Markham, a senior ranking officer to van Dijk, shrank in his seat. "It's unconfirmed and grainy images. There is nothing to confirm it."

With a finger deep in Markham's chest, stabbing with each syllable, "Your job is to forward ALL intelligence to MY office, with an estimate of the situation. Not to decide what I get to see. You WILL get ISR drone assets on the refuel depot within the hour."

Unable to decide how to respectfully address a subordinate who is in a much higher position by virtue of experience, Markham merely stammered, "Yes Adjudant-Onderofficier," as he turned to leave.

Mister Kern had been a quiet observer this entire time, now attempted to sneak out of the office.

"Not so fast, Mister Kern. I believe you are a Canadian Army Reservist."

"Yes, a Master Corporal." Kern did not like where this was going.

"Tomorrow morning, you report to my team, Master Corporal. You will work side by side with Sersjant Nygaard. Go get some rest. Your orders for active duty recall will be published tonight."

Jasper van Dijk needed everything to be pulled together before he took this to Sentinel.

It was going to be a long day tomorrow.

As the headlights cut through the early hours of darkness, Steve's mind was already on Prague. Anya, Collier, Night Stalkers, Markov — everything was converging. Just like the many sci-fi scenarios which had no solutions, Steve wasn't looking for one.

He was making his own, and nothing was going to stop him.

The headlights of Steve's black Pontiac GTO illuminated the cobblestone streets of Prague as the car growled its way into the city.

He checked his watch. Two hours to spare. Enough time to regroup before his rendezvous with Anya.

He parked outside a cozy restaurant with a warm glow emanating from its windows — "U Zlatého Válečníka" ("At the Golden Warrior"), a favorite spot from his days stationed nearby.

As he entered, he immediately spotted General Collier in a private backroom, seated at a small table.

The General was unmistakable with his broad shoulders and clean-shaven, square jaw.

A few obvious military men were scattered nearby– one at the bar nursing a drink, another pretending to read a newspaper, likely Collier's driver and pilot.

Not a single patron could find a seat within earshot of the

serious looking American. Most wouldn't have wanted to.

"Collier!" Steve said, his voice carrying through the warm din of the restaurant.

He strode over and embraced the General with a bear hug.

Collier chuckled, a rare sight for the no-nonsense officer.

"Still the same, Johnson. I could hear that damn GTO coming from three blocks away. Some things never change."

Steve smirked. "Yeah, but it's good to know some things don't."

They sat, and a waiter brought over the menu.

Collier raised a brow as he scanned the selection. "This is your kind of place, huh? A bit rustic, but I'll take it."

"I'd recommend the svíčková. It's a Czech specialty — beef in a creamy vegetable sauce with dumplings. And get a glass of their house pilsner if you're in the mood." Steve smiled, "Plus very few have private rooms and an excellent chef."

Collier waved it off. "I'll stick to scotch. Single malt?"

Steve grinned. "You remember me all too well. They've got one you'll like. 'Caldairn Reserve,' 14 years. It's as smooth as a moonlit night over Sebago Lake."

"Still waxing poetic, I see." Collier ordered the scotch, while Steve opted for the same.

The waiter returned with their drinks and took their orders — Collier went with steak, while Steve ordered svíčková. As they clinked glasses, Steve leaned forward.

"Nate, I didn't call you here to reminisce," Steve said. His tone grew serious. "I need to brief you on something.

Something big."

Collier's expression hardened. "I didn't expect it to be a social call. Go on." Quickly motioning to his men to keep an eye on the establishment.

Steve explained everything Colonel Petrov had told him — the movements he observed of the 4th Guards Tank Brigade, and the GRU's efforts to dismantle NATO's response capabilities, as well as the reverse coup and the assassination team.

Collier listened intently, his scotch untouched, his jaw tightening as the pieces fell into place.

The only sound at the table is the cracking ice balls as they melted in their scotch.

Their meals arrived, but as Steve took his first bite, he slid a small USB drive across the table. "This is the encryption key. Everything you need to verify what I'm telling you is on it."

Collier set his fork down, the weight of the moment settling in his gut like a lead ball. "Jesus, Steve. You're telling me the 4 Guards Tank Brigade really is poised to breach NATO's borders?"

With a deep breath, Steve knew he was believed. It's the truth itself that was questionable. "Exactly. With the entire Army Group South in support. NATO's spread too thin to respond effectively. You need to act, and fast."

Collier exhaled sharply, leaning back in his chair.

Collier began, his tone clipped, all business now. "I just came from a briefing. We're moving assets to the Polish and

Baltic borders with Belarus. NATO is repositioning assets to reinforce the Baltic flank."

"The 8th Armored Brigade Combat Team from Vilseck is already on the move, heading north through Poland to Estonia. We've got the 119th Airborne Brigade establishing rapid-response FOBs along the Lithuanian border." Collier paused to sip his whisky.

"But the truth is, we're stretched razor-thin. We're talking about two brigades trying to cover 1,200 kilometers of front. It's a goddamn logistical nightmare. We've got Norwegian and Danish battlegroups trying to bolster the Estonians, but they're light infantry — great for defense, not for counterattacks." Collier stared out the window before continuing. He had to take in his own reality first.

The NATO situation was proving the defense cuts had hurt. Nate continued, "Meanwhile, the Brits are stuck in Latvia trying to run recon with their Challenger 2s, but even they know they'll be outgunned if two Russian Tank Armies roll across the Suwalki Gap with the Belarus Army in support."

Collier took a longer sip of his scotch, his fingers drumming on the table. "We've got air cover, sure, but we're looking at Russian S-400s deployed across Kaliningrad and Belarus. If those bastards establish air dominance, they'll cut off our supply lines before we can even blink. It's not just tanks and troops, Johnson. It's the goddamn chessboard."

"But we are leaving less than ten percent of our forces near Bulgaria. We're exposed, Steve. If the 4th Guard pushes through the southern flanks..." Collier could not even finish the thought.

"When, Nate. When they push the Southern Flank. Not if," Steve interrupted.

"They will hit, and hit hard in the south. The Army Group South will hit Poland, Hungary, Slovakia, and Romania hard. When NATO tries to turn and respond, they will be trapped behind the Carpathian Mountains, and unable to bypass to the east without entering Ukraine. The 4th Guards Tanks will be flexed to cut west and north in order to encircle and hit the Thunderwolves in the flanks during the confusion." Steve knew Collier was the only man he could trust to stop Markov's advance. "You know this, General."

Collier cracked a grim smile. "You're not wrong. The problem is, Brussels is prioritizing defense. They're telling us to dig in and fortify, not go on the offensive. Hell, some of these politicians think we can sit this one out."

Steve remembered Anya's words last night, *"A bigger war is coming, and the politicians making it will not be fighting it."*

Collier rubbed his temples. His hands trembled as he picked up his scotch and drained it.

"I've lost my appetite." He signaled his team to pack up and prepare to leave.

Steve grabbed his arm. "Sit down, Collier. There's more."

Collier hesitated, his face pale. Slowly, he sat back down. His team exchanged confused glances but stayed put.

"A... close friend told me about General Markov. Not only

has he gone rogue, but he has the remote launch codes to the mobile nuclear rockets. They are going to target every major European Union city, including Brussels," Steve briefed General Collier, but could see reality was overwhelming him.

"Nate, he's looking to fracture NATO and force an EU-led surrender. If his plan works, NATO's political backing and resolve crumbles. He's in Budapest as we speak," Steve continued. "I'm going after him."

Nate needed another sip before he made the next statement. "You've got to stop them, push them back, Collier. No matter what. These launchers are embedded with the Army Group South, heading your way. Do the right thing and stop him." Steve watched Collier remaining impassive.

Collier's eyes widened. "You're asking me to disobey direct orders and take unilateral, unsanctioned action against the Russians?"

"Yes," Steve said firmly. "It's the only way. Hit their supply lines. If you can cripple their logistics, the 4th Guards tanks become nothing more than paperweights."

Steve took a deep breath, "What would General Patton do?"

Collier looked at him as if he'd grown a second head. "You've got some brass, Johnson. But damn it, you're right. I spent years teaching you Patton's doctrine and his strength through insubordination. Now you are throwing it all back at me."

Collier thought for a moment. "Even if we stop the entire Army Group South at NATO's borders, the rocket launchers will still be in range. If we can target them before Markov can launch... "

Steve nodded. "It's a gamble, but it's the only way to keep them from breaching our borders. The Russian Army Group South commander is betting on hesitation and surprise. Don't give it to him."

Collier stared at Steve, the weight of the decision pressing down on him.

Finally, he downed the rest of his scotch. "Alright. You've made your point. But I'll be damned if I'm going to like it."

He stood abruptly, dropping a stack of Euro notes on the table before turning to Steve and hugged him. "I'm proud of you, kid. You've become one hell of a man. But here you are, making it my job to save the world."

Steve stood and saluted. "You're the best man for it, General. Thank you for believing in me all those years ago."

"It's Tank Table VII all over again. I believe in you, even if I struggle to believe this could all be happening on our watch." Collier hurried out, his team falling in step behind him.

Steve walked to his GTO, its black exterior gleaming under the Prague streetlights. He drove aimlessly, the city's beauty contrasting with the chaos in his mind. Then he remembered where Anya might be — Žižkov Television Tower, a once-despised Soviet landmark turned modern attraction.

He arrived at the tower, combat parking, if they needed a fast getaway. And there she was. Anya.

Her slender figure leaned against the tower's base, clad in a form-fitting leather jacket and dark jeans.

The silver pendant she always wore glinted in the moonlight.

Her flowing blonde hair cascaded in soft waves, framing her sharp features.

She looked both modern and timeless, her beauty tempered with an edge of danger.

Steve approached, and Anya smiled, her blue eyes locking onto his. "You're late," she teased.

Steve looked her in the eyes, debating if he should bring up the Night Stalkers and the bounty.

"What if the information was intentionally leaked to make me trust her?" Steve thought hard. "But they had no idea Cypher was hacking them."

Steve and Anya sat at a quiet table in the corner of the dimly lit bar, its smoky ambiance casting shadows on the walls.

Steve sipped another scotch while Anya nursed a glass of red wine.

She was calm, her confidence unwavering, but her blue eyes betrayed a glimmer of concern.

"We need a plan," she said, her voice soft but firm.

Steve leaned back, watching her. "I've already put one in motion," he replied.

His tone is quite steady and reassuring. "But I need you,

Anya. You're the key to stopping General Markov."

Anya smiled, but there was a sharp edge to it. "And here I thought you were going to try to save the day, all by yourself."

Steve stared into her eyes. There were so many questions he wanted to ask, but every instinct warned him to stay silent. Push too hard, and she'd vanish. Lie too still, and he'd never know.

"I've been wondering, Anya. Why isn't Moscow stopping Markov?"

"The hardliners who know about this are supporting it. A rogue general acting on his own absolves Moscow of responsibility and accountability while Europe surrenders to Russia." She leaned in slightly, her eyes narrowing. "But that wasn't your real question, Stefan."

No. His real question was whether she already knew the answer he feared — and was testing him to see how much he knew.

She slid closer, the air between them pulling tight. Steve didn't flinch.

He brushed a strand of hair from her face, the gesture casual — too casual — and it made her pause.

The simple gesture made her pause, her eyes locking onto his.

For a brief moment, the chaos of the world outside seemed to fade, leaving only the two of them in the quiet intimacy of the bar.

Anya's lips curved into a seductive smile. "Careful, Steve.

You might make me think you still care."

Steve gave that knowing look he had perfected for Anya, "Still?"

She chuckled softly and full of mischief as she realized there was nothing emotional left there, if there ever really had been. "You always were good at doing the wrong thing at the right time."

Steve raised his glass. "To timing. Let's hope we get it right this time."

Anya clinked her glass against his, her eyes gleaming. "We'll make it work. We always do." Her heart was crushing. He never knew she had always loved him

Or did he?

Steve stood, knowing what he had to do. He couldn't be impeded and Anya needed to clear her head.

Pulling out his phone, he dialed ESID.

When his superior picked up, Steve simply said, "I'm acting on my own."

Before they could respond, he hung up. Anya raised an eyebrow.

Steve smiled. "Now, let's get to work."

Before they could walk toward the GTO, his phone rang again.

The Flying Dutchman already found out. "Susi, what did you just do?"

"You're thinking NATO is going to stop this," Steve said. "They're not."

Van Dijk sighed, adjusting his glasses. "No, Steve. NATO is planning to win the war they think they're fighting."

"And what if they're wrong?"

Van Dijk glanced at the encrypted report on his screen. His team was already mobilizing. "That's why you're here."

"That's why I did what I just did." Steve felt a deep worry in the pit of his stomach as he disconnected from the call.

His thoughts crept in. "What if Anya is wrong? What if I am being set up to take the fall?"

He remembered Anya and realized he truly believes that they are a team in this.

"I need to do this to end things and I can finally be Katya again," Steve reflected on how much he misses her.

He looked toward St. Petersburg, in barely a whisper, "I'm doing all of this for our future, Pchelka (little bee)."

His final thoughts are of losing everything important to him if he is wrong.

The office as dimply lit at NATO Eastern Europe Command HQ, Szeged, Hungary. A single desk lamp created a cone of light that spread across the maps and intelligence reports cluttering the workspace.

General Nathan Collier leaned back in his chair, cracking open a bottle of Hungarian Dreher beer.

He took a slow sip, staring at the USB drive Steve had handed him back in Prague.

Without hesitation, he plugged it into his secure NATO-issued laptop.

The screen flickered. A single folder appeared:

РАБОЧИЙ ПЛАН — ОПЕРАЦИЯ ЮГ
(*Operational Plan — Southern Strike*)

The encryption broke within seconds, tunneling into what had to be a Russian Army command cloud network — not a field-level operation, but General Staff level planning.

As the files loaded, Collier's breath hitched.

Everything Steve had told him was here.

The 4th Guards Tank Brigade's movements, the Northern offensive as a feint, and most damning of all — detailed minutes from Kremlin war councils.

One section stood out:

"Генерал Марков имеет полное одобрение от верховных лиц. Объединенные силы Юга должны действовать без ограничений."
(*"General Markov has full endorsement from high-ranking officials. Southern Group Forces are to operate without constraints."*)

A second line, just below it, turned Collier's stomach to ice.

He checked his watch.

The attack on Moldova would commence in 18 hours.

He exhaled sharply, gripping the edge of his desk.

This wasn't just an offensive into NATO's flanks.

This was a full-scale regional escalation — one that NATO command was utterly blind to.

Collier closed his eyes for a moment, the weight of history pressing down on him.

Then he reached for the landline.

"Jansen. My office. Now."

Kommandør Henrik "Hank" Jansen entered swiftly, his uniform slightly rumpled from long hours of analysis. A seasoned Dutch officer, he had seen his fair share of warzones and political backstabbing. He could tell from Collier's grim expression that this wasn't just another classified file dump.

"General?" Jansen asked, stepping toward the desk.

Collier turned the laptop screen toward him.

"Tell me I'm seeing things, Jansen."

The intelligence officer leaned in, scrolling through the Russian operational plans.

His expression barely changed — until he reached the direct Kremlin endorsement of Markov's nuclear contingency plans.

That was when Jansen visibly paled.

He straightened, jaw tightening. "This isn't a feint, sir. This is it. The playbook. The whole damn thing."

Collier took another sip of beer, rolling the bottle between his fingers. "And Moldova?"

Jansen's lips pressed into a thin line as he checked the time. "Overrun in less than 18 hours."

Silence.

Then Jansen exhaled and rubbed his face, his mind racing. "General... With your permission, I need to make a secure call. There's only one man I trust to verify this intelligence."

Collier studied him. "Van Dijk?"

Jansen nodded. "If anyone can tell me if this data matches what he's seeing, it's him."

Collier nodded once. "Make the call. Scramble it through SHAPE's encrypted relay. I don't want this traceable."

The secure line buzzed, before Adjudant-Onderofficier Jasper van Dijk picked up.

His voice was gruff, tired — but immediately alert. "Jansen? You better have a damn good reason for calling me at this hour."

Jansen didn't waste time. "You've seen the Russian movements. I just received high-level command documents confirming an attack on Moldova within 18 hours. Does this line up with your findings?"

There was a long pause.

Then Van Dijk exhaled sharply. "We were working up

exactly that scenario, and then some."

Jansen's stomach dropped.

Van Dijk continued, his tone grave. "Based on raw SIGINT intercepts and logistics tracking, I'd estimate an 85% probability that the attack is imminent. If they hit Moldova, we lose our last buffer. Romania is next. Then Hungary. Then the Danube Corridor is wide open. And NATO has nothing in place to stop it."

Jansen's grip on the phone tightened. "I'm here with General Collier. This confirms our worst fears."

Collier interrupted, "Jasper. Your analysis is never wrong, so I'm going to throw a few things at you. First, the validity of what we are seeing. Could this possibly be a complete charade to make us shift from the north? Second, this General Markov supposedly controls the ongoing operations, but nobody has heard of him before. Is he real, and is he behind this? Third, could small scale, tactical nuclear strikes be carried out against major EU nations?"

After taking this in, Adjudant-Onderofficier van Dijk started tapping away at his keyboard while answering. "Nate, only hours ago my team confirmed that the heat signatures which had been flagged earlier on thermal imaging. NATO reconnaissance has detected eight mobile rocket launchers concealed under camouflage netting — but until now, they were believed to be conventional missile systems." Jasper kept looking at his monitor.

Collier was gritting his teeth and looking at Jansen, "The

nuclear threshold has been crossed. This isn't a deterrent anymore. This is first-strike doctrine."

Jansen started checking the intercepted Russian war plans, his face darkening. "Sir, it's worse than that. These warheads aren't defensive. They're assigned to Army Group South. This is an offensive nuclear deployment. GRU notes 'radar interceptor upgrades completed'."

—

Jasper Van Dijk sat motionless, his fingers hovering over his console. Van Dijk muted his comms and made a call. Claire Rousseau picked up immediately.

"Claire, check my message, please. I need you to run something down. The name is Markov. General Markov. Hardliner, GRU. Whatever you can find." Jasper already knew this would cost a case of vintage Bordeaux.

Still tapping away at her keyboard, Rousseau asked, "Markov? You're certain?"

"Susi source ID'd him as the key figure behind the Russian tactical nukes. I want confirmation." Jasper waited

For two minutes, nothing but the soft click of her keystrokes.

Jasper switched over for a second. "General, please give me a moment. I'm chasing something down."

Jansen knew immediately that van Dijk had abandoned

the NATO intelligence reports and had activated the Flying Dutchman. "Sir, I can tell you beyond any shadow of doubt that whatever he tells us next is unconfirmed by SHAPE, but 100 percent accurate."

Collier had been in the game long enough to know when not to question things.

Rousseau was reading her findings, then exhaled sharply. "Oh, shit."

Rousseau urgently continued, "Jasper, I just ran blockchain analysis through secondary accounts linked to GRU crypto funds. He's the source. Markov is the financial architect of the Perun Initiative's funding network."

Markov had no history, no records, no direct state salary, no government pay records, no public expenditures.

Yet, "Perun" had appeared in an encrypted ledger — hidden inside GRU financial accounts.

The largest recorded payouts from these accounts were being directed to him. Nobody completely vanishes.

Markov wasn't on the payroll. He is the payroll.

Silence on the line.

Van Dijk was leaning forward, voice ice cold, "Tell me where his last payout was traced from."

Rousseau's fingers flew across her console.

The answer came in less than five seconds. She had his IP address. He got sloppy.

Rousseau's voice dropped, "He's in Hungary. Budapest"

Van Dijk sat back in his chair. The hunt was over.

Markov existed.

And now, they had his location.

"General, we just received external confirmation. Markov isn't just involved — he's the one funding the entire GRU operation." Jasper knew that his information told of something more powerful than ESID, or something NATO was watching. But he had to trust the General.

Sisu trusted Collier. That was good enough for him. "Markov's crypto disbursements are fueling the missile radar software in China, the mobile launchers my analyst Kern found, and every off-books payment tied to Perun's escalation."

Collier exhaled through his nose, absorbing the weight of the revelation.

Jansen, pale, checked the Russian General Staff war plans again.

Jansen, barely whispering, "Sir... it's all here. Word for word. The Russian plans we intercepted? They're exactly what's in your hands right now."

Before Collier could respond, Van Dijk's encrypted phone vibrated.

Cypher: *Davy Jones, check your secure link. You*

just got the full Russian war plans.

Van Dijk opened the document.

Cypher had hacked their systems. The exact same Russian General Staff plans sat in his hands.

The Flying Dutchman had just closed the loop. "Nate, my inside source has now just sent the exact encrypted key and Russian General Staff plans you have."

Now, it was time to make it a noose.

"You have someone inside the GRU?" Collier was shocked that SHAPE could do that.

"Nate," Jasper was the only subordinate in NATO that could address any officer by their first name. He did it this time for effect. "You would not believe it if I told you. Right now, you need to know. You have to stop this madman."

Jasper knew that under any other circumstances, nobody would believe what he was about to reveal to General Nathaniel Collier.

"The GRU network IS my inside information. Everything they do now, is reported. Right down to purchasing new pencils. I can have a full scale report of every GRU activity every 10 minutes. Now forget you ever heard this."

Van Dijk hesitated before continuing. "Hank. You tell

Collier ... if he's going to make a move, he better do it now. Before SHAPE ties his hands."

Collier exhaled, fingers pressing into his desk. "Van Dijk, I need to know — if I take this upstairs, what happens?"

The Dutch intelligence officer sighed. "The same thing that will happen if I take it upstairs. Nothing. Washington will demand further verification. Brussels will ask for another round of confirmations. By the time NATO even considers action, the war will be decided."

Collier's tolerance of bureaucracy was reaching the breaking point. "So that's it? No one's going to act?"

"They are acting," Van Dijk replied. "They're preparing for a war they think they understand."

Jansen hung up.

He turned to Collier. "It's real. Van Dijk puts the probability at 85% from SHAPE. That's more than enough certainty. The rest of the information, it's accurate. Do not doubt it"

Collier took a deep breath. He swirled the last bit of beer in his bottle before setting it down hard on the desk. "Tell me, Hank. Jasper has something going on. You are part of it?"

Kømmander Jansen was wary, but honest. Careers were being put on the line now. But more importantly, a war was coming. "Yes, Sir. I am."

The files on the screen put it at 95%. Steve bringing it to him puts this at 100%. The Flying Dutchman confirmed even more than was known.

Collier took another drink of his beer. "It's my career if I do; but it's the lives of millions if I don't make the decision."

He picked up the phone and called his Chief of Staff.

"Wake the battle staff. Full alert. Quiet recall of the forward elements. I want the 10th Armored Strike Group, including the 17th ACR, prepped for redeployment. No orders from SHAPE. Just contingency readiness. I need it finalized in 3 hours."

There was a moment of hesitation. "General, this will —"

Collier cut him off. "Do it. Now."

He turned back to Jansen.

"You're going to put a full brief together. Once we're in our battle positions, I'll contact Sentinel and tell them what I've done. Not before. We don't have time for Brussels to argue."

Jansen studied him for a long moment. Then, slowly, he nodded. For the first time in his career, he admired a commanding general.

Collier took one last look at the laptop screen.

The Russian war plans stared back at him, red and black markings carving up Eastern Europe.

Then he closed the lid with finality.

"I'm really going to do this."

Collier stared at the encrypted USB. No signatures. No official sources.

Just Steve Johnson's word.

He exhaled.

If he made this call and Steve was wrong, he'd be finished.

If he didn't and Steve was right, Europe would be ashes.

Nate looked at his coffee mug, *"What would Patton do?"* Another long pull off the beer, and self reflection, he knew what to do. Just like Patton, he would go with his gut instinct and consequences be damned.

He picked up the secure line. "Get me the 10th Armored Strike Group Commander."

Spinning Out Of Control

Hungarian Countryside

The GTO's V8 growled through the Hungarian countryside, headlights slicing the darkness as Steve Johnson tightened his grip on the wheel. Anya sat quietly beside him, her arms crossed, occasionally casting him wary glances. He could feel her unease; she didn't yet understand how far he'd gone or what stakes he was playing for.

She would soon enough.

If his plan failed, the line wouldn't hold — and his brothers and sisters in arms would be the first to pay the price.

His thoughts wandered back to simpler days — high school soccer, when every play felt like life or death.

That same thrill of outthinking an opponent now haunted him, knowing the stakes were infinitely higher.

He pushed those thoughts aside and focused. The NATO forces had already begun moving, and his next step had to count.

NATO's convoys rolled south under the cover of darkness. In southern Poland, Lt. Colonel Rebecca Carter of the 17th ACR led a column of Stryker reconnaissance vehicles toward forward observation posts. Her orders were clear — locate Russian movements and ensure the 14th Armored Brigade Combat Team had the intelligence it needed to engage.

Meanwhile, in Romania, Colonel Sarah Donovan's Iron Shield task force prepared for the coming storm.

Donovan's units — a mix of NATO's best — were spread across the Romanian-Moldovan border, their mission to stop the Russian 4th Guards Tank Brigade. From Abrams tanks to Leopard 2A7s, Challenger 3s, and CV90s, the task force bristled with firepower.

Every weapon system and vehicle was dug into defensive positions, camouflaged from satellite and drone reconnaissance. Yet Donovan couldn't shake her unease.

General Collier had personally ordered a focus on destroying enemy mobile rocket launchers, deviating from NATO's broader directives. *What did he know that Brussels didn't?*

The interior of the Stryker was quiet except for the steady hum of the eight-wheeled vehicle rolling over the uneven road.

Lt. Colonel Rebecca Carter sat in the commander's seat,

eyes fixed on the digital map display, though she barely registered the movements of the convoy.

The 17th Armored Cavalry Regiment was deploying forward, the battle line shifting, yet her mind was locked in place.

Collier's decision to bypass NATO directives had unsettled her, not because she thought he was wrong — but because she had sworn an oath to follow orders, and here she was, questioning them.

She had built a career on discipline, structure, and protocol — all of it drilled into her from the day she stepped into West Point. She had fought alongside men and women who trusted the system, who believed that even when things seemed uncertain, NATO's structure existed for a reason.

And yet...

The look in Collier's eyes when he made his decision.

The way Colonel Sarah Donovan had stood silent, wrestling with the same conflict.

Carter had never been one to hesitate on a battlefield.

But this was different.

She exhaled. This wasn't fear. This was conscience.

The makeshift command post was alive with activity.

Troopers from the 17th ACR moved with purpose, armored vehicles coming in and out, supplies being distributed.

Carter spotted Donovan standing near a tactical map, issuing orders to her operations team.

Carter stepped out of the Stryker, adjusting her plate carrier as she approached. Her boots felt heavier than usual.

Donovan turned as soon as she saw her. "Becky." The use of her first name was rare — too rare for this to be just another briefing.

Carter took a deep breath. "Sarah, I need to speak with you. Alone."

Donovan's expression shifted, a hint of understanding flashing behind her sharp gaze. She already knew what this was.

She gave a nod, motioning toward her command trailer. "Let's talk."

The inside of the trailer was dimly lit, a tactical operations board glowing against the far wall, marked with Russian unit positions, NATO force movements, and the creeping uncertainty of war. Carter took a second, trying to find the words.

"I can't command in violation of NATO orders." The words came out level, firm — a soldier's conviction, not an excuse.

Donovan didn't respond immediately. She studied Carter, arms crossed, then let out a slow breath. "I know."

Carter set her sidearm and unit patch on the small metal table. "I'm formally requesting that you accept my resignation as your squadron's commander. I won't compromise my beliefs — but I also won't compromise this unit by hesitating when they need leadership."

Donovan glanced at the patch, then back at Carter. "Denied."

Carter blinked. "Excuse me?"

Donovan picked up the patch, tossing it back into Carter's hands. "I won't let you resign. But I will reassign you."

Carter stiffened. "Reassign? To what?"

Donovan's tone softened just slightly. "The Strike Group Chaplain's office."

Carter's brow furrowed. "You want me to play preacher while my regiment goes to war?"

Donovan shook her head. "I want you to do what you do best — lead. You're not the only one struggling with this, Becky. There are good officers in this unit who are questioning everything, just like you."

"It is the duty of every commissioned officer to follow their conscience when they find orders questionable, immoral, or illegal. No officer in the 10th Armored Strike Group will be made to feel like they are less if they choose as you did." Colonel Donavan understood. "And I can't have my best people walking away when we need them most."

Carter swallowed. This wasn't a punishment. This was a lifeline.

"Sarah..."

"This isn't a blemish on your record," Donovan continued.

"This stays between you, me, and General Collier." She took a step closer, lowering her voice. "This is temporary, Becky. You are still a 17th ACR squadron commander. But right now, the regiment and Strike Group needs you in a different way. Help them find their footing. Be the leader they trust."

Carter's grip tightened around her unit patch. She looked at Donovan, seeing not just a commander, but a friend.

A moment passed. Then Carter exhaled.

"I'll do it."

Donovan gave a nod, the weight in the room settling into something quieter, something understood.

"Good. Now get out there and do what you do best."

At the southern edge of the Iron Shield's defenses, Colonel Donovan inspected Sector Alpha, her most vulnerable flank. The terrain — a mix of rugged hills and open plains along the Danube — was perfect for a Russian armored breakthrough. Holding the line were two key units — C Troop, 3/17th ACR, and the Royal Albion Armoured Guards Regiment.

C Troop, veterans of the Middle East and NATO's eastern flank, had their Abrams tanks expertly concealed in the northern treeline.

They were outnumbered but battle-tested, and Donovan

trusted them to delay the Russian advance.

The Royal Albion Armoured Guards Regiment, positioned to C Troop's right, brought a storied history to the fight.

From Cambrai to Normandy, their Challenger tanks had earned a reputation for resilience.

Lt. Colonel Gareth Pembroke, their commander, made it clear: "My regiment has never broken. We don't intend to start now."

Their crest — a lion rampant clutching a laurel wreath — adorned every Challenger in the sector, a symbol of their resolve.

Donovan keyed her radio. "Iron Shield Actual to Titan Six. Sectors Delta, Charlie, and Bravo at REDCON 1. Continuing mission. Over."

General Collier's calm voice came back through the static. "Acknowledged. What's the status of Alpha?"

Colonel Sarah Donovan, known across NATO forces as Iron Shield Actual, had built her reputation on an unyielding commitment to readiness and her ability to inspire confidence in her subordinates.

As she transmitted her situational report, her voice carried the weight of experience and authority:

"This is Iron Shield Actual. SITREP for Sector Alpha is REDCON 2, continuing defensive preparations. I am en route to verify readiness. What you expected happened here. I am establishing my command post, co-located in Alpha. Over."

Collier realized what happened. Lt. Colonel Carter is one of his best officers. "Understood. Charlie Mike."

Donovan dropped to her command frequency. "Alpha units, SITREP."

The replies came back in sharp, professional tones, each reflecting the discipline of their respective units.

"Alpha Two reporting REDCON 2. Standing ready. Over," Major Pembroke responded, his British accent precise and clipped.

From C Troop, Captain Morales added, "Alpha One is steady at REDCON 2. Holding firm. Over."

Donovan's acknowledgment was simple but deliberate, her jaw tightening as she set the mic down. Readiness was the first step.

What followed would test every ounce of preparation and resolve her forces could muster.

The Humvee rumbled to a stop at the forward outpost of C Troop, its checkpoint framed by a concertina-wire barrier and a watchful M3A3 Bradley Fighting Vehicle.

As Donovan stepped out, brushing the dust off her jacket, a young sentry approached, his M4 held at the low ready.

"Ma'am, I need to see your ID," he said, his voice steady but firm.

Donovan raised an eyebrow but didn't fault the trooper's professionalism. "Colonel Sarah Donovan, Commanding Officer of Iron Shield," she replied, pulling her ID from her chest pocket.

The sentry scrutinized the ID before stepping back and snapping a crisp salute. "Apologies, ma'am. Captain Morales is expecting you. I'll guide you to him."

"Carry on," Donovan said, returning the salute with a nod of approval.

As she followed the sentry through the camp, she assessed the troop's defenses with a practiced eye.

The layout was impressive: HESCO barriers reinforced with sandbags, firing positions commanding key chokepoints, and Bradleys concealed in defilade.

Every element spoke to preparation and an understanding of the terrain.

Captain Morales, standing by a map table with a tablet in hand, greeted her with a firm handshake.

"Colonel Donovan, welcome to C Troop," he said.

"Captain," she replied, her tone warm but businesslike. "Let's walk the line."

Their tour revealed a defensive network that was meticulous and pragmatic. Morales explained the overlapping fields of fire, mortars covering dead zones, and Javelin teams placed on elevated positions for maximum effect.

"We've got solid coverage, ma'am," Morales said, gesturing to a map's southern edge, "but if they push toward Bulgaria, they could flank us and bypass Alpha entirely."

Donovan considered this grimly. "I'll redirect Gray Eagles to patrol that sector. If they move, you'll see them before they become a threat."

Relief shown across Morales' face. "Thank you, ma'am. Any drones? Eyes in the sky could help."

As much as she hated being blind, Donovan agreed with General Collier on this point. "We are not supposed to be here. Titan does not want drones making the Russians wonder why they are being observed. As far as the Russians know, we are in Poland."

Turning to depart, she could feel the Captain's disappointment, but also his understanding.

Satisfied with the troop's readiness, Donovan moved to Major Pembroke and his Royal Albion Armoured Guards Regiment.

Their sector was a fortress, the terrain transformed by reverse-slope tank emplacements, interlocked fields of fire, and camouflaged defensive positions.

Even their logistics vehicles were optimally placed for rapid resupply under fire.

"Major Pembroke," Donovan greeted, her tone carrying equal parts admiration and curiosity.

Pembroke saluted sharply. "Colonel Donovan. Welcome to Alpha."

Donovan gestured to the formidable defense. "This is... impressive. Possibly the strongest hasty defense I've ever seen."

Pembroke allowed a measured smile. "Thank you, ma'am. We strive to uphold the standards of the Guards."

"But you're still at REDCON 2?" she asked, her tone skeptical.

"Our vehicles are offensive weapons, Colonel," Pembroke replied with the precision of someone stating a universal truth. "Until the routes of attack are cleared and camouflaged, we cannot consider ourselves fully prepared."

Donovan's eyebrow twitched. The Albions weren't just perfectionists; they were perfectionists armed with tanks.

Satisfied with Alpha Sector, Donovan keyed her mic. "Titan 6, this is Iron Shield Actual. Alpha Sector is at REDCON 1. Anchor set. Over."

From her perch at the heart of Iron Shield, Donovan knew the battle ahead would test not just their defenses but the cohesion and determination of every soldier under her command. In the quiet before the storm, she resolved to be the unshakable anchor they needed.

Donovan had no idea the importance of her role in Steve Johnson's plan.

Yet, as she stared at her map, her doubts lingered.

The Russians would come, and when they did, Sector Alpha would bear the brunt.

Collier's insistence on targeting mobile rocket launchers stuck in her mind. *Was he anticipating something even worse than what she could see on the horizon?*

In the TOC, General Collier set down his mic and leaned

back, a rare smile crossing his face.

He picked up his coffee mug, savoring the steam as he turned to face the sprawling battle map illuminated by harsh LED lights.

"Anchor set," he murmured to himself. His eyes traced the lines of his forces, visualizing the coming fight. Titan elements were ready. The Russians had no idea what they were walking into.

The TOC buzzed with life, its dim blue glow reflecting off maps and monitors as NATO officers coordinated movements across the region.

General Collier stood in the center, his presence calm yet commanding.

His coffee mug sat untouched on the edge of the table as he watched the deception plan unfold with surgical precision.

"All Titan elements, this is Titan 6," he said into his mic. "Phase One is a go. Execute the deception plan. I want the Russians convinced we're pulling north. Make it count."

"Titan 6, this is Titan 4-2. PsyOps elements are in position. Broadcasting false radio traffic suggesting redeployment to Suwałki. Drone swarms are currently simulating armor movements toward Grodno. Over."

"Copy, Titan 4-2. Ensure signals are clean and credible," Collier replied. Disobeying orders did not come easy to the General. Last night weighed heavy on his guilty mind, especially being this close to the borderline.

"Titan 6, this is Iron Hawk Actual. Combined arms team

is en route to the Visena region as a diversionary force. Additional vehicles are staged along the Lithuania-Belarus border to reinforce the deception. Over."

"Excellent, Iron Hawk. Maintain visual presence. I want them watching Kaunas and Grodno, not Giurgiuleşti," Collier said.

"Titan 6, this is Titan Shadow. Recon teams redeployed to Olsena and Byalka. Tracks have been laid to give the impression of a corps assembling in the area. Over."

"Outstanding work, Titan Shadow. Keep them guessing," Collier replied, his lips curling into a faint smile.

The ruse was coming together seamlessly. Collier's forces appeared to be withdrawing north, leaving the southern NATO borders seemingly exposed.

PsyOps teams flooded open radio channels with chatter about theoretical defensive setups near Poland's Masurian Lakes region.

Drones mimicked heat signatures of heavy armor maneuvering toward Lithuania.

Meanwhile, a combined arms tank-heavy team visibly rolled north, crossing bridges and small towns like Zalen and Rigova under the watchful eyes of Russian satellites.

"All Titan elements, this is Titan 6. Stay focused. The more believable this looks, the better our odds when they reach our real line," Collier commanded.

Back in the TOC, Collier picked up his coffee mug and took a deliberate sip, letting the moment sink in.

Around him, officers worked tirelessly, their focus on the maps, screens, and secure channels.

Every false and real movement on the map had purpose, weaving a narrative of NATO's "withdrawal" north that the Russians wouldn't dare to question.

He set the mug down and allowed himself a rare, satisfied smile. The pieces were falling into place, and the enemy was looking exactly where he wanted them to.

"They'll never see it coming," he murmured, turning back to the map as his brilliant deception began to take hold.

In the TOC, General Collier set down his mic, eyes locked on the battle map. Titan elements were in position, the deception plan unfolding with precision.

The war room in SHAPE's intelligence wing hummed with a quiet intensity, the kind that only came when pieces of a puzzle began falling into place — but too late to stop what was coming. Adjudant-Onderofficier Jasper van Dijk leaned against the metal frame of the situation table, studying the satellite feeds and intercepted Russian communications with narrowed eyes.

His sharp, analytical mind was known across SHAPE, but tonight, his gut told him something his brain refused to verify. "Close the loop."

Across the room, Master Corporal Kern — the freshly recalled Canadian Army Reservist — furiously typed on a secure terminal, cross-referencing real-time SIGINT, troop movements, satellite imagery, and newly decrypted Russian command messages. "I miss solid human intelligence on the ground."

Beside him, Sersjant Nygaard, the Norwegian electronic warfare specialist, muttered under his breath as he manipulated the latest ELINT feeds.

The enemy's digital footprint told a story, and tonight, that story was beginning to terrify him.

"This is madness," Nygaard finally muttered, his voice thick with disbelief. "We're tracking three separate Russian columns feinting north, yet every logistics route — every supply train — moves southward."

Kern looked up from his terminal, his brow furrowed. "You're sure?"

"I'm damn sure," Nygaard snapped, jabbing his screen. "Look. The 4th Guards Tank Brigade — more than 300 M90 tanks — was ordered north, but their fuel convoys are heading toward Army Group South. Same with ammunition resupplies, artillery, and mobile bridging units. The TU — 106 scare me, too."

Kern paled. "So they're feeding a lie."

Van Dijk exhaled sharply, turning to face them. His expression remained unreadable, but there was something in the very depths of his soul — something unsettled. Something only he could feel.

"This... confirms an unverifiable asset," he murmured.

Kern frowned. "What do you mean?"

Van Dijk tapped his fingers against the table, carefully choosing his words. "It means I know this to be true, but I cannot tell you how I know. And you will not ask."

Nygaard and Kern exchanged a look, both suddenly aware that van Dijk had knowledge far beyond their clearance level.

Kern pressed on anyway. "Sir, if you can't tell us the source, can you at least confirm how solid it is?"

Van Dijk's gaze drifted toward the satellite feed of Moldova's border — less than twenty minutes from erupting into chaos. He turned back to them, eyes cold, voice steady.

"The intelligence is absolute." His tone made it clear that he had put the pieces together.

Silence. A live feed broke in from airspace above Moldova.

Nygaard's hands clenched into fists. "We have to bring all of this to Sentinel. Right now."

Van Dijk nodded, pushing off the table and straightening his uniform. He motioned for both men to follow. "We are about to change the course of NATO's strategy. Pray we are not too late."

General Victor "Iron" Barrett — Sentinel 6, call sign for the

Supreme Commander of NATO Forces — was never in the mood for riddles. The room was alive with the hum of a war machine shifting into motion — briefing officers exchanging files, digital maps updating in real time, and muted discussions layering over one another.

The Suwałki Gap was the focus. It had to be. If Russia cut the corridor, the Baltics would be indefensible.

Standing at the head of the table, Sentinel, Supreme Commander of NATO Forces, adjusted his posture and cleared his throat. The murmurs quieted as officers settled in.

"We are now seeing final Russian staging operations for an armored thrust through the Suwałki Gap. We —"

The door burst open so violently it slammed against the wall, sending a coffee cup tumbling off a desk.

Jasper van Dijk stormed in, face pale, movements urgent.

"Stop the fucking briefing. Now."

A murmur of irritation rippled through the room. Sentinel's eyes narrowed.

"Van Dijk, what the hell is — "

Jasper didn't acknowledge him. He was already at the control panel, overriding the main display.

The crisp, color-coded battle map vanished.

The room fell into stunned, eerie silence.

The first images were grainy infrared feeds from Reaper drones circling at 50,000 feet.

Even in black and white, the devastation was unmistakable.

Moldova was dying.

The first explosion hit just as the feed transitioned to a wide-angle view over Chişinău.

A school vanished mid-evacuation — a direct missile strike snapping its concrete spine like chalk.

Children streamed into the street, backpacks still on, before fire consumed the courtyard.

Some were caught mid-step. Others never made it down the stairs.

A playground carousel spun lazily, pushed by the blast wave, while the screams bled through even the drone's high-altitude mic.

The camera caught a child's shoe next to a puddle of blood. The world froze.

Then the hospital.

A hypersonic missile struck the trauma wing first — the second hit ten seconds later, centered on the emergency intake bay.

The building's guts blew outward in a shockwave of glass, blood, and white-coated bodies.

An ICU gurney landed upside down in the middle of an intersection. A woman — maybe a nurse — crawled across the asphalt with half her face burned away before disappearing under falling debris.

Then the helicopters came.

Two Mi-28s thundered into view, their engines screaming, 30mm cannons spitting death across civilian roads.

A tram car lit up like kindling, scattering flaming silhouettes across the camera's field of view.

Homes, market stalls, parked cars — anything with a heat signature — was shredded.

One gunship hovered just long enough to track a group of people hiding behind a bakery wall, then fired. Nothing remained but dust and a crater rimmed with fire.

Another screen updated.

The city of Bălți blinked out — not just destroyed, *erased* — under a succession of precision warheads that turned an entire neighborhood to heat and light.

A maternity ward half a mile away shook apart.

Tiny forms were visible in the thermal feed — some limp, some crawling. All of them alone.

Bodies littered the road to Romania — not soldiers, but families.

A convoy of cars — clearly civilian — had been strafed.

One camera caught the moment a mother shielded her child and froze that way forever, arms still wrapped tight.

Then the radio cut in —

First static. Then screaming.

A new voice cut through the silence, raw with panic.

> *" — Moldova Defense Forces down to 30% combat effectiveness —"*

"— Taking massive losses — our air defense has collapsed — "

" — ANYONE OUT THERE? FOR THE LOVE OF GOD, WE ARE BEING EXTERMINATED!"

Jasper's jaw clenched so tightly it looked like his teeth might crack. His hands were shaking.

"This isn't an invasion."

His voice was hollow.

"This is erasure."

"General, the Russian northern feint is just that — a feint. Their true offensive is being staged in Army Group South. Moldova is their breakthrough point, and within six hours, Romania will be under direct threat." Van Dijk was animated.

Barrett leaned back in his chair, his jaw tightening. Sentinel would never dream to doubt Van Dijk. "That's a hell of a claim, Adjudant-Onderofficier. What's your intel assessment based on?"

Van Dijk hesitated, then made the call. "We have SIGINT, logistics traces, satellite imagery, and a separate source of the highest reliability."

Barrett's eyebrow twitched. "What source?"

Van Dijk met his gaze. "Unverifiable, but... I personally trust it. Completely."

The room was thick with tension. Barrett wasn't a man who accepted ghost stories. But van Dijk was known for one thing — he never gambled unless the odds were rigged in his favor.

But this is real time. Now.

A new satellite feed snapped onto the screen, displaying the entirety of Moldova in high resolution.

Jasper stepped forward and pointed at the swath of destruction — a clear, burnt path carved directly toward the Romanian border.

"Do you see this?" he growled, his voice shaking.

Sentinel exhaled sharply. His fingers curled into fists.

"They're clearing a corridor."

Jasper nodded grimly.

"Not just a corridor — an entire avenue of advance."

The footage updated again, and the realization crashed over the room.

It wasn't just a strategic path to Romania.

Every major city in Moldova was being wiped from existence.

One by one.

Barrett exhaled sharply. "Son of a bitc..."

The briefing room went absolutely silent. Sentinel's fists began to clench and unclench. The tendons began to show in his neck.

"I DON'T LIKE BEING MADE A FOOL!"

Van Dijk, Nygaard, and Kern stood frozen, knowing that everything they had just briefed had already come true.

Sentinel could not calm himself. He took one more deep breath.

But the images from Moldova had seared themselves in his mind.

Sentinel's fist slammed against the table.

"GET TITAN IN THE AIR! NOW!"

The operators scrambled, flipping controls, opening encrypted comms.

The monitors blinked.

The death toll in Moldova climbed by the second.

Sentinel's voice dropped to something dangerous.

"We are not watching another fucking Bosnia happen on our watch.

"GET ME COLL — " He caught himself. Not Collier. It was time. Time to use the name everyone feared.

He slammed his fist on the table, once more, for emphasis.

"GET ME TITAN. IMMEDIATELY! FLASH PRECEDENT! I WANT HIM IN MY BRIEFING ROOM — NOW!"

The war had begun.

The entire room scrambled into action. Across NATO's global command network, the highest-priority message NATO could send was issued.

FLASH PRECEDENT — EYES ONLY — IMMEDIATE CONTACT REQUIRED

To: TITAN 6 — NATO EASTERN EUROPEAN COMMANDER General Nathan Collier
Subject: Army Group South CONFIRMED. Moldova ATTACKED.
Directive: *Report to Sentinel IMMEDIATELY. NATO POSITION COMPROMISED.*

Barrett turned back to Van Dijk, breathing heavily. His voice was low, controlled, and lethal.

"If your source is right about this, what else are they right about?"

Van Dijk's throat went dry. He glanced at Nygaard and Kern before answering.

"The worst-case scenario."

Barrett stared at him. "There's something worse that you aren't telling me?"

Van Dijk simply nodded, turned, and walked out the door.

He stopped for a moment. "Sentinel. I am putting together the briefing, and I thank you for the trust you put in me. Please trust me on this. Titan will need every air asset you can get to him in the next 2 hours. Don't wait for my briefing."

"I need full air superiority over Southeastern NATO! Get every goddamn fighter on alert!" Barrett was livid.

And for the first time in decades, the Supreme Commander of NATO felt true fear. "Carry on Adjudant-Onderofficier." Barrett stood to offer Van Dijk a salute.

The ultimate respect a subordinate can receive.

"Sir, flash traffic from Moldova. Russian forces have launched a full-scale attack. Border defenses are overwhelmed." Collier's expression tightened. Moments later, another officer handed him a red folder. "Flash Traffic — SHAPE."

Collier exhaled sharply. "Damn it," he muttered, glancing at the map one last time before snapping into action. "No additional drones unless I order it. We are not supposed to be there."

"Get me transport. Closest and fastest air asset, I don't care what it is. Make it supersonic."

Within minutes, Collier was at the nearby air base. A two-seat Hungarian Gripen NG, its sleek gray form gleaming under the floodlights, was prepped for flight.

The pilot, a young Hungarian captain with a razor-sharp demeanor, saluted as Collier approached. "Captain Árpád

Tóth, call sign *Villám*."

"*Lightning!* Let's see if you live up to your call sign. This bird ready to go?" Collier asked.

"Yes, sir. Fully fueled, armed for air defense, and cleared for priority NATO movement," the pilot replied.

Collier saluted, climbed into the rear seat, strapping himself in as the canopy sealed.

The pilot's voice came through the intercom. "General, hold on tight. We're taking the direct route — full afterburners."

"*Villám,* you are cleared for immediate take off with Titan. All civilian air traffic has been cleared. Godspeed."

The Gripen roared down the runway, its General Electric F414-GE-39E turbofan delivering 22,000 pound force thrust with full afterburner, rattling the control tower windows.

As the fighter broke the sound barrier, Collier gripped the armrests, the g-forces pressing him into the seat.

The pilot expertly maneuvered through the dense NATO air corridors, their route cutting across Central Europe in a blazing streak of speed.

"Mach 2, Titan." *Villám* smiled behind his visor.

The soldiers of the 17th Armored Cavalry Regiment stood in a long, tense line, their eyes locked on the distant horizon. Even

30 kilometers out, they could see Moldova burning. The glow of flames turned the early morning sky into a sickening orange hue.

The low rumble of explosions carried across the open plains, shaking the earth beneath their boots.

Above them, a pair of Romanian F-16s circled — powerless to intervene.

A radio crackled. The command net was silent — men who had trained for war, now forced to stand by and watch genocide unfold.

A church erupted in flames, across the field.

Sergeant Walker swallowed hard, his fists clenched.

"Goddammit..."

Beside him, Captain Darren Cole stood with his jaw locked, his fingers twitching at his rifle sling.

His voice was barely above a whisper.

Less than twenty miles from forces that could stop this, people were being annihilated.

"If we break ranks and cross the border... what do they do? Court-martial us? Send us home?"

The XO didn't answer.

Because they both knew the truth.

The only thing worse than standing by and doing nothing... was knowing that they had to do nothing.

Sergeant Walker dropped to his knees, vomiting, knowing he had idly stood by while hundreds were killed.

Innocents.

Not a military target. No threat to the Russians.

Captain Cole turned back to his vehicle, but the rage was burning deep inside of him. Tears could not form.

The Gripen's comms panel flared to life. "Titan 6, SHAPE. Sentinel 6 demands immediate contact."

Collier adjusted his headset. "Patch him through."

The line connected, and before Collier could even speak, Barrett's voice exploded into his ears.

"TITAN! Where the hell are you?!"

Collier blinked. "Approaching Brussels airspace. What's going on?"

Barrett didn't answer immediately. He took a sharp breath, his rage barely restrained. "I need you in my office 30 minutes ago."

Barrett turned to Captain Julia Reynolds. I want Adjudant-Onderofficier van Dijk and his team in my office when Collier gets here."

He turned to his tactical display monitor without waiting for acknowledgement.

When the fighter touched down at SHAPE's airfield in Brussels, Collier was already unbuckling before the aircraft came to a full stop. He climbed down the ladder and turned to the pilot.

"Refuel and stand by. I might need a quick ride back."

"Yes, sir," the pilot nodded.

Collier strode across the tarmac, flanked by aides, and was immediately ushered into the secure briefing room.

Inside, Sentinel 6, General Victor "Iron" Barrett — a towering Marine with decades of battlefield experience etched into his face — stood at the head of the table.

His fists were clenched, the veins on his forearms bulging. Three others sat at the table.

"Titan," Barrett growled, his voice low and heavy, "we've been outplayed. Meet Adjudant-Onderofficier van Dijk and his intelligence team."

Van Dijk stood to brief. Collier remained silent, grabbing two cups of coffee from a side table.

He handed one to Barrett. "Vic, sit for a moment. Take a breath. Clear your head."

Barrett hesitated, then exhaled and dropped into a chair. "Thanks," he muttered, taking a sip. "But this is a damn mess."

Collier leaned against the table. "Give it to me straight."

Barrett nodded, his voice steadying. "The Russians sold us a deception while they were massing in the south. Moldova's being wiped off the face of the earth as we speak, and our southern flank is wide open."

He took a sip of coffee that was far too hot to drink. But he didn't care. "We don't have the boots to hold them. Adjudant-Onderofficier van Dijk will brief you on everything he has pieced together."

Barrett looked up at Collier, desperation quivering in his eyes. "Titan, I need you to somehow defend your southern border, even after I stripped your assets."

Collier exchanged knowing glances with Jasper van Dijk, who stood motionless, his sharp eyes tracking every flicker on the screens.

Master Corporal Kern and Sersjant Nygaard, both sweating under the weight of the intelligence they had just uncovered, waited for the storm to break.

It did. "Vic, I already know. Thank you Adjudant-Onderofficier, but we don't need to go over it."

Barrett exhaled slowly, but it was a futile attempt to contain his fury.

He turned to van Dijk, hesitating a moment before slamming his open palm against the table so hard that papers scattered.

The room went dead silent. Even the comms officers froze.

"I want a name, van Dijk." His voice was low, controlled, but it carried the weight of impending detonation. "Who the hell is your source?"

Van Dijk met his gaze evenly, and paused. He had to weigh disobedience with preserving the art of spycraft. "Sir, I told you. The source is unverifiable, but the intelligence is absolute."

Barrett's hands curled into fists. "Sir –" Nygaard started, but Collier waved him off.

"DAMN IT, SIR." Nygaard was not going to be silenced.

Nygaard switched to the Moldovan command frequency.

The radio static crackled, momentarily drowned out by the distant thunder of missile impacts. The Moldovan Defense Forces were shattered — what few units remained had no air cover, no reinforcements, and no hope.

The bunker shook violently, dust cascading from the overhead concrete. A nearby impact had hit within a block of their headquarters.

Colonel Ion Brătescu, Commander of Moldova's last standing forces, pressed the transmitter to his lips. His uniform was soaked with sweat and dust, his face streaked with the blood of an aide who hadn't survived the last blast.

The few remaining soldiers in the command center looked at him, faces blank, defeated.

"Sir … we have to go. We —"

Another explosion rocked the ground. Monitors blinked, one going black entirely.

It was over.

Brătescu exhaled slowly, pressing the transmitter down.

His voice was calm, level, but unmistakably seething with grief and betrayal.

"This is Colonel Ion Brătescu, Moldovan Defense Forces. To NATO Headquarters. To every commander watching from your satellites. To every soldier listening to your encrypted

comms."

He paused. The words felt like poison in his throat.

"May God have mercy on your souls for just watching us be exterminated."

There was no plea for help. His voice finally cracked, and the pain of failing his people roared inside him.

There was no request for air support.

There was only judgment. Condemnation.

The transmission cut as the room was swallowed in white light.

The war room at SHAPE Headquarters was deathly silent.

The monitors showed nothing now.

Just a black screen.

No one spoke. No one moved.

Even Sentinel — the man used to issuing orders in the face of catastrophe — looked pale. Tears forming.

Jasper slowly turned away from the monitor, his hands shaking.

"May God have mercy on *your* souls..." he muttered under his breath.

No one corrected him.

No one argued.

Because they all knew.

They had just watched an entire nation be erased.

And they had collectively done nothing.

Barrett stalked to the main screen, jabbing a finger at the projected 4th Guards Tank Brigade movements. "Three days! Three goddamn days of military deception, and SHAPE — this command — my command — just watched it happen!"

His voice dropped, but that only made it more lethal.

"How in the holy hell did I let the Russians outplay me? It will take at least 15 hours to reposition into a hasty defense."

No one dared answer.

Collier took the last sip of his coffee to calm himself, and turned towards Sentinel, his face betraying the fury building inside of him. "I am van Dijk's source, Vic. I've already got a plan in motion."

Barrett's eyes narrowed. "How soon can you execute?"

Collier looked at his watch, checking his smirk. "About 15 hours ago."

Barrett choked on his coffee, sputtering before locking eyes with Collier. Barrett's voice dropped to a whisper, dangerous and edged with disbelief. "You insubordinate son of a bitch. You knew this was coming?"

Collier's lips curled into a smirk. "With all due respect, Sentinel... Let's just say I have some information NATO will need months to sift through. We don't have time to wait. If I hadn't taken initiative, we'd be watching the 4th Guards roll into Romania with nothing in their way but some diplomatic outrage and empty rhetoric."

"But to be clear," Collier gestured to the drone footage over Moldova, "this was not something I saw coming. Only

Russians rolling through their country."

Barrett's nostrils flared, but for the first time in 24 hours, a sliver of relief cracked through his frustration. He ran a hand through his short-cropped hair, exhaling sharply.

"NATO owes you for your initiative, Titan. I will get drone support for eyes out in front of you ASAP."

Collier's smirk faded. "My units are mostly repositioned south, REDCON 1 across the board. The southern border is ready. No drones, please. The Russians are expecting my people to cross into the Baltics at any time. Send drones that way until the fighting starts. Keep them thinking I am not where I am."

Barrett nodded once. "Then get your ass back on the ground. We're about to fight a war."

Collier's voice was quiet but unyielding as he glanced at the monitor no longer displaying anything. "We already are."

At the door, Collier turned, saluting with crisp precision. "Anchor is set. Titan out."

Then, with one final glance, he disappeared into the corridor and mindlessly made a quick stop to drain his bladder before departing... he was already mentally back at the front lines.

He could hear Barrett calling Van Dijk to his personal office.

The Kremlin's secure briefing room was dimly lit, the glow of satellite imagery reflecting off polished mahogany. Minister of Defense Sergei Orlov leaned over the massive digital map, his eyes fixed on the live feeds from Russian reconnaissance satellites.

Captain Viktor Mikhailov, now the GRU's assistant director of operations, stood beside him, arms crossed, his expression one of quiet satisfaction.

Orlov tapped the screen, zooming in on NATO's troop movements. Kaunas. Grodno. Suwałki. The pieces were all moving as expected.

"They're still reinforcing Lithuania," Orlov muttered, a hint of amusement in his voice. "They believe our attack will come from the north."

Mikhailov exhaled, a slow smirk forming. "Our deception is holding. The American commanders are sending more NATO armor toward the Polish border. Their satellites see what we want them to see."

Colonel Oleg Vasilyev, Director of Counterintelligence looked on, always suspicious. "What if these reports are inaccurate? What if NATO knows of our deception and is playing their own deception?"

Mikhailov swiped the screen, shifting to another satellite feed — the eastern borders of Romania, Slovakia, and Hungary. Nothing.

No NATO armored movements, no troop concentrations. Empty.

Mikhailov turned to both Orlov and Vasilyev, "The door is open. They suspect nothing."

Orlov nodded. "Then Army Group South will walk right through it. Moldova has been completely neutralized."

He stared at the screen a moment longer. "Your asset, what are her odds of success?"

"Her odds are 99%." Mikhailov grinned, *"But our odds of success,"* he corrected, "are now 100 percent," pointing back at the Romanian border.

"If she fails in her mission, we accept Europe's surrender. If she succeeds, though highly unlikely, we have our scapegoat."

The Perun Initiative was prepared to double cross General Markov if the invasion failed. They would pull back, to look like the ones who tried to stop him. Not his accomplices.

"Villám get me back, ASAP. Set comms to my command frequency." They were airborne in under 400 meters, taking off with full thrusters.

The war room at SHAPE was eerily quiet despite the storm brewing across NATO's eastern front. A dozen monitors displayed live satellite feeds, intercepted Russian military movements, and the frantic coordination of forces preparing for what seemed inevitable.

General Victor "Iron" Barrett, the Supreme Commander of NATO Forces (Sentinel), stood at the head of the operations table, arms crossed, jaw tight. He didn't like surprises. And right now, everything about this war felt like a damn surprise.

His eyes flicked toward the strategic map, where General Nathan "Titan" Collier's sector was rapidly turning into the most dangerous battlefield on the planet.

Across the table, Air Marshal Pieter Roelofs, the Chief of Air Operations at SHAPE, leaned back in his chair, seemingly unbothered by the rising tension.

Glancing over at Adjudant-Onderofficier van Dijk, he noted the intelligence warrant officer twist his cuff buttons, where cufflinks would be. He let out a breath, casually gesturing toward the air combat readiness charts scrolling on his display.

"You know, Sentinel," he said, voice measured, almost amused, "our entire Southern NATO Air Command is sitting on the sidelines."

The room went still for a half-second.

Barrett's eyes snapped toward him. "Explain."

"Southern NATO Air Command — our forces in Italy, Spain, Greece, and the Adriatic — are completely untouched by current operations." Roelofs rotated his chair slightly, tapping the screen. "Meanwhile, Central NATO Air Command is still postured in a way that, if needed, they could swing north to reinforce Northern NATO Air Command, should the Russians push through Belarus."

Van Dijk, standing near the intelligence board, glanced up at the Air Marshal and caught the slightest smirk curling at the edge of Roelofs' mouth. He knew exactly what was happening.

Barrett exhaled sharply, rubbing his chin. He hated committing too soon, too hard. NATO's entire doctrine was built on flexibility and controlled escalation — not burning through their entire airpower stockpile on one engagement.

But Titan needed more. The Russians had taken Collier's bait, yes, but the war hadn't even started yet.

And if Markov's supporters, or Moscow itself, changed their strategy, Barrett couldn't afford to be caught flat-footed.

The solution was right in front of him.

"Deploy Southern NATO Air Command in full force to reinforce Titan." Barrett's tone was clipped, decisive. "That gives him the firepower to lock down the battlefield. But keep Central Air Command postured to shift north if necessary. If the Russians still come through Belarus, I want them ready to swing back. We cannot overcommit."

Roelofs cautioned. "Have the assets ready for immediate launch. But we must be cautious not to tip our hand too early."

He turned toward Roelofs. "Do it. Now."

Roelofs simply nodded, as if he had expected nothing less.

As the Air Marshal leaned forward to give the operational orders, van Dijk locked eyes with him across the room. The Air Marshal touched his cuff button.

A silent exchange passed between them.

Van Dijk had spent his career watching how decisions were made, not just what decisions were made.

This wasn't about Titan alone. This wasn't just Barrett sending a message.

This was about the Flying Dutchman following through.

Collier was the only commander on the ground seeing the war for what it was.

Now, Sentinel was backing him — without admitting it outright. And Steve Johnson was still in the fight.

Van Dijk smirked, just slightly. Roelofs gave him the smallest nod in return before turning back to his staff.

Orders were going out.

⬦

NATO's Southern Air Command was coming in full force. "Titan 6, this is Skywatch Actual," came a voice over the secure channel. "All southern and central NATO air wings are under your operational control. Airbases from Torrello to Durvani are fully operational, with sortie planning underway to prioritize SEAD missions and ISR support. Over."

Collier exhaled, letting a small amount of tension ease. He has no idea why this just happened, but he has other things to worry about. "Copy that, Skywatch Actual. Keep the tempo high."

"One more update, Titan 6. The Fifteenth Fleet has begun its transit from the Anvalis to the Black Sea. Turkesian air forces are providing additional cover. Initial reports indicate a smooth passage. Over."

"Understood, Skywatch Actual. Keep me in the loop. Titan 6 out." Collier wonders what is going on to be suddenly given these assets.

After a moment's thought, Collier keyed the radio. "Skywatch, Titan 6. I need an AWACS at my disposal. I'm going up. Coordinate with the Fifteenth Fleet to beam all operations to my bird."

The wars are fought was about to change.

In the narrow Anvalis Strait, the fleet moved in a disciplined formation. *NSS Sentinel's Edge*, the lead carrier, cut through the waters, escorted by its destroyers, cruisers, and submarines. Above, Turkesian F-18s roared in tight combat air patrols, their formation sharp against the afternoon sun.

Orbiting high overhead, AW-600 surveillance planes provided a constant stream of intelligence. Below, attack submarines monitored the depths, their sonar pings keeping watch for any threats.

"Admiral, the carrier group is halfway through the strait," the operations officer reported on the bridge of *Sentinel's Edge*.

"Turkesian air cover is steady. No unusual activity detected."

"Maintain formation," the admiral replied. "Ensure all systems are on high alert. We'll be in the Black Sea shortly."

Titan had just been given the firepower to dominate the battlefield.

And yet, NATO still had the flexibility to react — just in case.

The lonely, desolate and quiet hum of the Moldovan border was broken only by the soft whir of NATO reconnaissance drones and the faint rustle of wind over the fields. Reports had been trickling in all morning from the air cavalry patrolling overhead: Russian reconnaissance probes were testing the lines.

At first, it was small groups, cautiously scanning for any defensive positions on the border. Now the reconnaissance was massing in size and becoming bolder.

In Alpha Sector, Captain Morales of C Troop, 3rd Squadron, 17th Armored Cavalry Regiment, monitored the reports with grim focus.

His troopers had dug in, their vehicles camouflaged and ready, but the tension was palpable.

Less than 50 kilometers away, a lone Russian scout vehicle had been observed crossing back into Ukraine earlier and heading toward the southernmost crossing.

A BTR-80, painted in a crude attempt to blend into the muddy terrain, moved like a predator stalking prey.

Overhead, air cavalry drones followed its path, their infrared cameras capturing every detail.

Donovan's voice crackled over the command net: "All Iron Shield elements, tight until contact on our side. Hold the line."

In her tactical operations vehicle, Colonel Sarah Donovan kept one eye on the feeds and another on her map.

The terrain offered some natural choke points, but the open fields south of Alpha made her uneasy.

She keyed her mic. "Titan 6, this is Iron Shield Actual. First probes reported. One vehicle heading for our southernmost line. Weapons tight until it breaches NATO territory."

General Collier's voice came through, calm as ever, despite the roar of his fighter's engines in the background. "Iron Shield, Titan 6. Copy all. Weapons tight. SITREP as the situation develops."

Collier sat in the back seat of the Hungarian Gripen NG, the pilot weaving through the lower atmosphere as the aircraft approached the Black Sea coast.

Collier leaned forward and tapped the pilot on the shoulder. "Can you take us low over Bulgaria, then follow the coastline north? I want a border trace over Alpha."

The pilot glanced back, surprised but compliant. "Yes, General. Adjusting course now."

The BTR-80 crept closer now less than 50 meters from the NATO line. Morales's voice broke over the comms: "Iron Shield Actual, this is Coyote 6. Enemy vehicle approaching Alpha Sector Line. Request weapons free."

Donovan hesitated. The vehicle hadn't crossed the line yet. But before she could respond, Collier's voice cut in, direct and measured. "All Titan elements, Titan Actual. Negative. Weapons tight."

Donovan frowned, confused. The reconnaissance vehicle was inches from breaching NATO territory. Her hand hovered over the button to confirm Titan orders.

High overhead, the Hungarian Gripen NG looped down, its gray body gleaming against the morning sun.

Inside, Collier leaned forward again, gripping the edge of his seat. "Pilot, what's your air-to-ground capability?"

The pilot hesitated. "General, this is an air superiority fighter. Air-to-air configuration only. Besides, this model is a trainer. We only have a 27mm Mauser BK-27 Revolver Cannon with 125 rounds and 2 AIM-9X Sidewinder missiles."

Collier's hand clamped onto the pilot's shoulder, his voice calm but commanding.

"It's the warrior, not the weapon, Captain. Switch to guns.

Son, *YOU* are now this fighter's air-to-ground capability. *Villám,* you are now *Weapons Free.*"

The pilot swallowed hard but complied. The Gripen NG banked sharply, dropped his external fuel tanks before diving low over the Moldovan border, coming in barely a meter off the ground.

As he squeezed the trigger, "For Moldova."

The sky over Moldova was painted in deep blues and purples, the first whispers of dawn still trapped beneath the horizon. The wind carried the damp scent of churned-up earth, mingling with the distant diesel fumes of NATO armor holding the line, burning fields, and thousands of pounds of exploded munitions.

Black smoke settled over the horizon.

The Russian BTR-80 had crept forward under the illusion of silence, its eight wheels grinding softly against the rocky soil.

Inside, the crew moved with trained efficiency, the commander's gloved hand gripping the overhead rail. All he could do was concentrate, forcing himself to focus despite the shock of everything he had just witnessed.

The gunner peered through the sight, fingers wrapped around the controls of the 14.5mm KPVT heavy machine gun, scanning the distant ridgeline.

Though prepared for war, he felt deep pangs of regret for what his leaders had done to people whose only crime had been where they lived.

The driver, a young conscript with sweat dripping down his temple despite the chill, exhaled slowly.

The town they had just gone through looked very much like his own village, and he struggled to drive while crying, imagining that was his family he had just seen broken and riddled with bullets.

They had done border probing before. This felt different. Something gnawed at the back of the commander's mind — a whisper of danger just beyond his perception.

The BTR-80's nose had just crossed the NATO line when a streak of tracer fire tore through the air, the first 27mm round hit.

The Mauser BK-27 cannon shell slammed into the BTR's right rear, punching through the thin armor like a hot knife through butter.

The fuel cell ruptured instantly, a violent spray of diesel misting through the crew compartment.

The explosion that followed was not immediate.

For a split second, the crew felt the heat — not fire, not yet — but a flash of unbearable warmth, a sudden, suffocating wave that seemed to expand outward from the puncture.

The commander's eyes went wide as the warning lights on his panel flickered and died.

Then, the second shell came.

The cannon round tore into the already compromised structure, igniting the atomized fuel in a blast of fire and shrapnel.

The driver was incinerated before he could scream, his body vaporized in a flash of orange light.

The gunner, lungs already filled with superheated air, collapsed against his station as the flames raced across the confined space.

The commander felt nothing. By the time his brain processed the impact, his body was already in pieces.

The BTR-80 detonated violently, its armored hull crumpling outward in a bloom of burning steel.

The concussion rippled across the frozen field, sending shockwaves through the earth.

A black mushroom of oily smoke curled into the sky, the metal skeleton of the vehicle still glowing red-hot from the inside.

About 30 meters away, inside the concealed position of C-33, callsign Coyote Blue 3, the shockwave hit like a hammer. The crew buttoned up, believing it was Russian artillery.

Another 20 meters behind them, Captain Luis Morales had barely raised his binoculars when the blast wave slammed into their position.

A wall of concussive force that rattled every chest cavity sent a cascade of dust spilling from the overhead camouflage netting.

He had felt explosions before, but this one carried an unnatural heat — as if the air itself had been momentarily cooked before returning to the bitter cold.

"SHIT!" Someone shouted.

Staff Sergeant Donahue, crouched behind a Javelin launcher, instinctively ducked, his ears ringing from the blast.

The scent of burning diesel and scorched metal filled the trench, thick and noxious. The heat wave lingered, like a giant hand pressing against their skin.

Through the dissipating smoke, Morales caught a glimpse of the wreckage — a charred, blackened husk where the BTR-80 had once been.

The burning wreckage crackled and popped as rounds inside the vehicle cooked off, sending smaller secondary explosions into the morning air.

"Jesus Christ," whispered Donahue. "That wasn't artillery. That was close air support."

Morales swallowed hard and keyed his mic.

"C-33 to Iron Shield Actual — uh, we have a BTR-80 that just got turned into vapor. Aerial strike. Unconfirmed NATO asset."

There was a long pause on the other end of the line before Colonel Sarah Donovan's voice came through, low and controlled.

"We see it. Hold position. Keep your heads down. I'll get confirmation on that bird."

Morales lowered the radio and exhaled, still feeling the heat against his skin.

Whatever had hit that BTR, it wasn't Russian.

Donovan looked up, stunned, as the Gripen NG roared overhead, tipping its wings in a salute before climbing back into the sky.

Her lips curled into a wry smile as she keyed her mic. "Titan 6, Iron Shield Actual. The bullets hit home."

Above the battlefield, Captain Árpád *"Villám"* Tóth pulled back on the control stick, yanking the Gripen NG into a sharp, almost vertical climb. The G-forces slammed into his chest, his vision narrowing to a gray tunnel as he gritted his teeth and pulled oxygen through his mask.

His entire body felt like lead, pinned to the seat, his arms shaking as he held the maneuver steady.

But beneath the strain, a feral thrill surged through his veins.

He had just fired the first NATO shot of Cold War II.

The Mauser BK-27 had performed perfectly, its rounds finding their target with surgical precision.

Through the HUD, he caught one final glimpse of the

smoldering wreckage below — a black scar against the cold earth.

He had done that.

And he felt no remorse.

His hands trembled slightly from the adrenaline dump, but his voice remained steady as he keyed his mic.

"Target destroyed. Returning to base."

In the rear seat, General Nathan Collier, NATO's Titan Actual, exhaled through his nose, watching the fireball below shrink beneath them. He keyed his mic, voice calm but firm.

"Good work, Árpád. Let's head back to the line, son." Collier reflected on his proximity and role in the first shots fired, his voice steady as ever.

Villám grinned beneath his visor as he adjusted his flight path. Hungary had fired the first shot.

And he had been the one to pull the trigger. The son of a pepper farmer.

The echoes of 27mm cannon fire continued to thunder across the plains.

I Will Get You, Too

Budapest, Hungary — Széchenyi Imperial Hotel

Steve shifted gears, the rumble of his 1971 Pontiac GTO reverberating through the cobblestone streets of Budapest. The city's charm was lost on him tonight; the gleaming Danube and grand architecture served as nothing more than a backdrop to their mission.

He glanced at Anya in the passenger seat. Her expression was focused, eyes scanning the surroundings.

Steve had insisted on her taking the lead this time, leveraging her GRU contacts to locate General Markov.

"This is the place," Anya said, breaking the silence.

She pointed to a building up ahead, a relic of the Soviet era — a grand hotel with its faded prestige etched into the ornate columns and weathered facade.

Steve parked the GTO across the street, its engine growling into a low idle before shutting off. "A former Soviet hotel for communist party elites," he remarked, his tone wry. "How fitting for a Russian hardliner."

Anya smirked. "The kind of place where they toasted their victories and plotted their betrayals. Markov's arrogance would bring him somewhere like this."

As they crossed the street, Steve's eyes swept over the darkened windows, his instincts on edge.

The hotel's exterior still bore the vestiges of its former grandeur, but its glory had long since faded. A few lights switched on from within, hinting at life, or something less innocent.

Just as they reached the entrance, Steve's sat phone vibrated in his jacket. He paused, stepping aside to take the call. "Collier," he said tersely, recognizing the number.

"Susi, the border's secure," Collier's voice came through, calm but firm, using Steve's codename. "First contact with Russian forces was a success. The deception worked like a charm. We caught them off guard."

"That's good to hear," Steve replied, his eyes flicking to Anya, who waited patiently. "But I get the feeling you didn't call just to share the good news."

"You're right," Collier said. "It's time to turn up the heat on your end. Markov is a dangerous loose cannon; his rockets can now reach half of Europe's urban centers. Unless you take him out, every victory we have in this region will still not stop us from losing the war. I need you to push harder. Turn Budapest into a furnace if you have to."

Steve let the words sink in, his jaw tightening. "Understood. Any intel you can feed me?"

"You're running point now, Steve. I trust you to figure it out," Collier said. "But remember — time's not on our side. Make it count. Titan out."

The line went dead. Steve slipped the phone back into his pocket, his mind already turning. He met Anya's gaze. "My plan worked. The Army Group South will be stopped outside Moldova. Looks like it's time to kick this up a notch."

Her eyes glinted with a mix of determination and resolve. "How did you? ... Never mind. Tell me over a celebratory drink. It's time we find Markov and make him regret ever stepping foot in this city and betraying the Russian people."

Together, they pushed through the hotel's heavy wooden doors, stepping into a cavernous lobby.

The air was heavy with the smell of dust and stale cigars, remnants of a bygone era.

Crystal chandeliers dangled overhead, their light dim and uneven. Steve's hand hovered near the holster under his jacket as they approached the front desk.

"Stay close," he whispered to Anya. "This place is more haunted than a cemetery."

She nodded, her own instincts sharp as they began their hunt for General Markov in the labyrinth of the old Soviet stronghold.

To her right, Anya noted four members of her team that had been sent as backup.

But a man sitting in the corner of the lobby had a Russian newspaper on the table beside him, and he did not look like a tourist or businessman.

Anya looked back, nervously and the man was gone. Only the newspaper remained.

The war room at SHAPE was electric with tension. Lines of encrypted communication streamed across massive screens. A holographic projection displayed the eastern Black Sea, highlighting Russian airbases, NATO surveillance flights, and the latest intelligence from Adjudant-Onderofficier Jasper van Dijk.

Seated at the center of the strategy table, Vice Admiral Erik Stiansen, the Norwegian Supreme Naval Commander of NATO Black Sea Operations, folded his hands, his piercing blue eyes scanning the operational map.

The intercepted ELINT data from Sersjant Nygaard was clear — the TU-106s, Russia's next-generation strategic bombers, were preparing to launch cruise missile strikes. If they took off, NATO ground forces in Romania, Moldova, and the Black Sea Fleet would be devastated.

Van Dijk leaned forward, his voice quiet but forceful. "Sir, we don't have time for a prolonged debate. The TU-106s must never reach altitude. If they do, they'll fire from beyond interception range, and we'll be counting the dead in the thousands."

Admiral Stiansen nodded. His voice was grim but decisive. "Then we hit them before they leave the ground. A stealth precision strike from Turkey, coordinated with a naval missile barrage from the Black Sea. We decimate their runways before they can launch."

He turned to Air Marshal Cemal Akçay, Supreme Commander of the Turkish Air Force. The Turkish general had already been preparing for this moment. "Admiral, my F-35 squadrons at Incirlik Air Base have been on alert since Moldova fell. My pilots are ready."

General Barrett leaned forward, "Make it happen. Right now. Titan is deep in his fight and will need his momentum."

As Sentinel began committing the might of NATO, the grand chamber of the European Council building in Brussels was filled with tension. The emergency summit had been called with unprecedented urgency, the air thick with the weight of history.

Leaders from all 27 EU member states sat around the vast circular table, their national flags standing behind them like silent witnesses to the crisis unfolding in Eastern Europe.

Leaders of non EU nations had been invited to participate, as this affected all. Their flags displayed in this sacred chamber, as equals, not guests.

At the head of the room, European Commission President Lukas Neumann stood, his normally measured voice carrying an edge of controlled fury as he addressed the assembly.

"We are all fully aware that the Russian government has launched an unprovoked massacre and annihilation of Moldova, violating every principle of sovereignty, peace, and European security. This is an act of war against the stability of the entire continent, and it shall not go unanswered."

The chamber erupted into murmurs, some voices filled with righteous anger, others with nervous hesitation.

German Chancellor Annalena Weber spoke first, her voice steady and resolute. "Germany stands with our NATO allies. The time for appeasement is long past. Russia has been emboldened by our restraint. We cannot afford further delay."

French President Charles Dutoit nodded in agreement. "We cannot allow another Bucharest Summit failure. Our resolve must be absolute. France will not hesitate to support NATO's defensive actions to ensure that Russian forces are stopped."

Across the table, Polish President Marek Nowak pounded his fist on the table. "My country has lived under Russian boots before. We will not ever live under them again. Poland demands the immediate deployment of additional NATO battlegroups across Eastern Europe."

The Nordic states — Sweden and Finland, new NATO members — echoed Poland's stance.

Prime Minister Eirik Lund of Norway was even more direct. "This is not merely about Moldova. This is about all of us. If Moscow wins here, they will move again. NATO's counteroffensive is a necessity."

However, not all voices were in unison. A murmur spread through the room, particularly among the more neutrality-inclined members.

President Alexandros Petrides of Cyprus nodded in agreement. "The EU INTCEN was designed to coordinate intelligence and security policy at the highest levels. If Russian forces are on the move and this truly is an existential crisis, then why have we not been briefed through our own channels? Why must we rely on NATO's word alone?"

At the head of the room, European Council President Gérard Moreau exhaled sharply, exchanging a look with his aides before responding. "Because the European Union has provided nothing of substance to ESID or NATO. You have not asked for intelligence, nor have you contributed to it."

His gaze swept the room. "Let us not pretend that INTCEN has the same operational capability as NATO's SIGINT, ELINT, and HUMINT networks. It does not. Our intelligence services are fragmented between twenty-seven nations, many of whom hesitate to share what they know."

Moreau's words landed like a hammer. The silence that followed was thick with discomfort.

Polish President Marek Nowak seized the moment, his voice cold and cutting. "You question NATO's intelligence while contributing nothing to European defense. It is the United States — who faces no direct threat here — that is providing the bulk of the ISR, SIGINT, and HUMINT keeping our forces alive. Yet you, President Petrides, demand to know why your agencies are not briefed when they sit idle, waiting for others to act?"

French President Charles Dutoit leaned in, nodding. "France has contributed intelligence–surveillance–reconnaissance (ISR) flights. Germany has committed divisions. Poland has troops on standby. And yes, the United States, despite the Atlantic Ocean separating them from the battlefield, has committed forces, intelligence, and strategic resources. What has Malta contributed? What has Cyprus offered?"

President Petrides of Cyprus bristled, his tone defensive. "We are not NATO members. We are not obligated to —"

Swedish Prime Minister Eirik Lund cut him off. "Then stay out of the way of those who are."

A tense silence followed. The weight of the argument was clear.

Moreau pressed forward. "Europe's security is not a passive observation. It is an active responsibility. You cannot demand intelligence without contributing to its collection. You cannot question NATO's commitment while offering nothing in return. And you cannot accuse the United States of overreach while expecting them to defend Europe in your place."

Moreau's final words silenced the dissenters, leaving the room with only one uncomfortable reality — NATO had stepped up.

Some EU nations had as well. Some nations not affiliated with either had stepped up. Others were merely watching, waiting, and questioning.

Austrian Chancellor Eva Moser leaned forward, her face set in a deep frown. "Austria condemns all military aggression — from both Russia and NATO. The EU's role should be diplomacy, not escalation. Austria cannot support any expansion of the conflict."

Maltese President Franco Debono nodded in agreement. "Malta has always stood for peace, as we have withstood occupation over centuries. We strongly condemn Russia's invasion, but we cannot endorse an open NATO counterattack that risks escalating this into a regional war."

Cypriot President Alexandros Petrides added his voice to the dissent. "The Eastern Mediterranean already suffers from instability. Cyprus cannot support direct military retaliation without further diplomatic avenues being exhausted."

An uncomfortable silence followed.

From across the room, Ireland's Taoiseach, Daniel Hayes, finally spoke. "Ireland will abstain from voting on direct military actions. We stand by Ukraine and Moldova, but we must also prioritize a peaceful resolution."

Several European leaders shook their heads in quiet

frustration.

Spanish Prime Minister Isabel Santiago leaned forward. "Neutrality will not protect you when Russia no longer respects our borders. The time for half-measures has ended."

European Council President Gérard Moreau finally cut in, his voice firm. "Let us be clear: The European Union condemns Russia's actions in the strongest terms possible. The Kremlin has shattered European security. This Union stands behind Moldova and NATO's commitment to defend every inch of its territory. Those who wish to abstain or condemn NATO's response must live with the consequences of their hesitation."

The summit ultimately ended in a majority vote in favor of supporting NATO's defensive actions — though with clear divisions. The EU reaffirmed economic sanctions on Russia, but Austria, Malta, and Cyprus remained vocal in their opposition to NATO's escalation, while Ireland remained noncommittal.

European Commission President Lukas Neumann dreaded the upcoming call with the President of the United States. European Union nations are starting to slowly turn on their most powerful ally.

He hopes the feeling is not mutual.

As the leaders left the chamber, the divide in Europe's response was evident. The resolve of NATO remains unshaken, but within the EU, shadows of Cold War-era division and hesitation had resurfaced.

OPERATION THUNDERSTRIKE
TITAN FRAGMENTARY ORDER 01-015A

Objective: Isolate and destroy the 4th Guards Tank Brigade by forcing them into the open terrain south of Moldova, into Ukraine, while simultaneously driving the remaining elements of Army Group South toward the Black Sea shores. This operation aims to dismantle Russian armored and mechanized units, ensuring NATO gains the strategic initiative in the region.

Phase I: Fix and Distract

Norwegian Armored Brigade (Call Sign: Fjordbreaker) and German 21st Panzer Division (Call Sign: Iron Spear) will engage the 4th Guards Tank Brigade along their entrenched positions at the southern edge of Moldova. Their mission is to hold the line and prevent Russian forces from retreating northward or eastward while minimizing NATO casualties.

Artillery batteries from Task Force Thunder will pound enemy positions to pin the 4th Guards in place, making them reliant on limited maneuverability.

Phase II: Encircle and Isolate

17th Armored Cavalry Regiment (Call Sign: Warhorse) will spearhead the breakthrough in a pincer movement.

B Troop, 3rd Squadron, equipped with M1A2 SEPv4 Abrams tanks, will lead a direct assault southward, tearing through the center of the 4th Guards. Their mission: breach enemy defenses and open a corridor to force the Russian brigade into the open plains.

Pembroke's Royal Albion Armoured Guards Regiment (Call Sign: Lionheart), with their Challenger 3 MBTs, will swing north and flank the Russians at full speed, cutting off escape routes.

AWACS "Eagle Eye 9" will direct NATO air assets to strike Russian logistics and retreating columns.

Phase III: Air Superiority and Ground Support

Air Forces: Every available NATO aircraft from Southern Commands will participate in the assault.

Air Units:

10th Fighter Wing "Blue Knights" (F-35 Lightning II)

52nd Tactical Fighter Group "Hammers" (Eurofighter Typhoons)

99th Bomb Squadron "Reapers" (B-1B Lancers)

Turkish 3rd Air Wing: Provides naval air cover over the Black Sea, targeting Russian ships.

Fifteenth NATO Fleet Air Arm: Harpoon missile strikes from carrier-based F/A-18 Hornets.

Dogfighting: NATO aircraft, controlled by AWACS, will engage Russian MiG-31s and Su-35s in coordinated waves to clear the skies for close air support operations. We will plan for a heavy air to air battle.

Phase IV: Naval Warfare

Fifteenth NATO Fleet:

Submarines, including *USS Hawthorne*, Commander Jack Johnson's former vessel, will hunt and destroy Russian submarines attempting to disrupt the operation.

Turkish frigates and destroyers, under Task Group Trident, will suppress Russian warships near the Odessa coastline.

The Stryker command vehicle rattled as it plowed through the treeline, its eight wheels kicking up frostbitten soil and shattered pine branches. Colonel Sarah Donovan rode with the hatch open, scanning the battlefield with her binoculars pressed tight to her eyes.

Sarah had just finished reviewing her units. They were ready to take this to the Russians.

"The greatest honor a Commander has is walking the line, seeing her troops." Sarah smiled at her life's good fortune, leading soldiers.

Her crew was tense but calm — seasoned professionals, knowing this moment was coming.

"Enemy armor in the open, due north — " Her gunner cut in.

"I see them. Marking targets. Jesus, they've got a whole brigade rolling in."

Through the distant smoke and haunting flames of a ruined Moldovan town, Donovan spotted the Russian lead tank — a T-90M breaking the tree line.

Her stomach twisted.

Across its turret, painted in stark Cyrillic letters, was a single word:

Владивосток

"The Vladivostok." Her voice was calm, but her grip on the Stryker's rail tightened.

Her radio crackled.

"Iron Shield, enemy armor moving fast — battalion strength — looks like the 4th Guards Tank Brigade, call sign confirmed."

She pressed the radio.

"All units — Antenna Tank. The Vladivostok is the lead. I want guns on that bastard now!"

The Stryker's 30mm autocannon fired first, its tracers stitching across the hull of a Russian BMP.

Then the battle exploded.

Colonel Alexei Sorokin adjusted his binoculars, watching his T-90s move into battle formation. The NATO positions had just revealed themselves — and at the front of their line, he saw a single Stryker leading the charge.

Sorokin's smirk widened.

"Ah. There you are."

The vehicle should not be out here without their wingman. Just like the west. Cowboy commanders.

They never learn that there is safety in numbers.

He turned to his tank commanders, voice sharp.

"The lead vehicle. The one that just fired. Find it. Kill it. Make it burn."

His grin showed his pleasure in destroying her vehicle.

"Sabot incoming!"

The Stryker's driver wrenched the wheel, throwing the vehicle sideways as a Russian tank shell streaked through the air.

It missed by meters — slamming into a Norwegian CV90 behind them, tearing through its armor.

Donovan didn't even flinch.

"Gunner, keep firing! Driver, keep moving!"

The Stryker's autocannon spat another burst, punching through a Russian BTR, sending it into flames.

Then the Vladivostok fired.

The T-90M's 125mm shell struck the Stryker square in the side.

"IRON SHIELD. Hold the line." The vehicle lifted off the ground, metal shrieking as it flipped, fire and debris scattering across the battlefield.

Inside, Donovan's world turned into a tumbling vortex of fire, screams, and shrapnel.

Her final thought was one of satisfaction.

She died leading from the front.

The choppers came in low over the battlefield, their rotor wash kicking up dust and smoke. Lt. Colonel "Becky" Carter stepped off, her tanker boots landing on the cold, hard ground of the war she had abandoned.

She had heard the final transmission.

The attack on Moldova revealed General Collier's information was correct. Becky knew her place was back in a tank.

She was returning to battle when this happened.

She had seen the last stand of Colonel Sarah Donovan on their approach.

And now, she stood before the smoldering remains of Donovan's Stryker.

A German medic stepped forward, saluting.

"Es tut mir Leid. Colonel Donovan is gone, Ma'am."

Carter didn't react. She just took a slow breath, then exhaled.

"Where's my tank?"

She marched past the officers waiting outside the command vehicles — past the 17th ACR soldiers who gave her wary, hostile glances.

She knew what they were thinking.

She had abandoned them.

She had walked away from the war before Moldova fell.

Now, she was back — standing where Donovan should have been.

Lt. Colonel Pembroke, commander of the British Challenger 3 battalion, saluted her without hesitation.

"Welcome back, Lt. Colonel Carter. Allions stand ready to fight with."

The Americans of the 17th ACR?

They stayed silent.

She pressed the radio.

"Iron Shield to Titan."

Collier's voice came back immediately.

"Go ahead, Iron Shield."

She closed her eyes for just a second.

Donovan was gone.

She was the shield now.

"Sarah's dead. I have command. We hold the line."

There was a pause. Can she handle it? Will the soldiers follow her orders?

Then Collier's voice, cold, deadly.

"Iron Shield Actual, Titan. We will avenge her." Formally recognizing her call sign legitimized her command authority.

Carter's fingers tightened around the radio.

"With full disrespect, Titan —" she said, her voice sharp. "Not if I get Vladivostok first."

Lt. Colonel Carter looked around at the troops and leaders who were looking back at her.

"I need a tank."

Pembroke stepped forward. "Ma'am, it would be our honour to have you lead in a Challenger 3."

Carter strolled over to her Stryker, now holding Colonel Donovan's remains. She opened the hull stowage box. It was right where she left it, still in its metal case.

It was the sabre her father gave her when she graduated the Basic Armor Officer Course. He had been in the Air Cav during Desert Storm.

"We are going to move as one, in an overwhelming force. We will start as a Wedge formation. I will take point. Allions in the center, 17th ACR had the right flank, Norwegians and Germans on the left flank." Becky let it sink in for a moment during a last munte sand table exercise.

"Excuse me, but are you the right person to lead us?" It came from the back right. A voice Lt. Colonel Rebecca Carter knew instantly.

She turned to face everyone. "As commissioned officers, regardless of our nation, we have a moral obligation... no, we have a duty to listen to our conscience. In the face of illegal orders, we all had a decision to make. Regardless of future circumstances changing their legal basis."

She let this sink in for a moment. "I chose the moral high ground, making the difficult decision in the face of an order which contradicted the orders issued to all of us. I chose not to follow them... just as you chose to follow the same illegal orders. Only the genocide of 2.5 million Moldovans made your decision legal; and gave me cause to return to follow the NOW legal orders of a General we both equally admire."

Turning back, she finished. "If you are still good with your decision, let's carry on with this sand table, Captain Morales. Upon contact, we will come on line. Once we are deeply engaged, Allions will fix the 4th Guards Tank Brigade while the flanks turn it into a Vee formation, using a pincer maneuver to destroy their flanks. It will be like shooting fish in a barrel."

"Questions?" Becky noticed a change in everyone's demeanor. "Mount up. We cross the LD in 30 minutes."

The forest was alive with movement. Tanks lurched forward, their engines roaring, the steel beasts rolling into the firestorm of battle. Carter's Challenger 3 sat at the front of the charge. She gripped the hatch rail, staring at the battlefield ahead.

She pressed the radio, her voice steady.

"Iron Shield, this is Actual."

Her tank rolled faster.

"We are Cavalry. We are Lions. We are Vikings and Huns. Warriors to the core. NATO's finest from every nation."

The tread thunder grew louder.

"It is time we take the fight to the enemy."

The British, American, and Norwegian and German tanks surged from the tree line, roaring toward the Russian 4th Guards Tank Brigade.

Carter raised her sabre — her voice cutting across the radio with absolute clarity.

"CHARGE!"

Her Challenger 3 raced far ahead of the entire strike force and fired the first shot, the round blasting straight into a Russian T-90.

The cavalry charge thundered into battle.

And for the first time, NATO wasn't just defending.

They were hunting.

The roar of Challenger 3s echoed across the plains as Pembroke's Royal Albion Armoured Guards Regiment surged forward.

Their commander, Lt. Colonel James Pembroke, watched

from his turret as his tanks crested a shallow rise, the sun gleaming off their composite armor.

Smoke plumes from Norwegian and German artillery strikes marked the horizon.

"Lionheart Actual to all callsigns. Full throttle. We're cutting off their heads," Pembroke barked into his radio, his voice calm but steely.

Across the field, the 3/17th ACR's B Troop had already punched a hole through the 4th Guards' outer defenses.

Captain Jenna Mills, leading the charge in her Abrams, directed her gunners to prioritize T-90Ms. "I want those turrets popping!" she shouted, the tank shuddering as its 120mm smoothbore cannon fired again and again.

The muddy Moldovan countryside trembled as Captain Mills adjusted her position inside the M1A2 SEPv4 Abrams.

Her crew had been stationary for three hours, hidden in a defilade overlooking a shallow valley. The thermal sights of the Abrams' next-generation FLIR (Forward-Looking Infrared) system scanned the horizon, cutting through the dense fog that rolled in from the Danube River.

"Contact, two o'clock!" her gunner, Sergeant Delgado, called out.

On the advanced IVIS (Inter-Vehicle Information System) display, Mills saw the unmistakable outline of a Russian T-14 Armata tank, its active protection systems shimmering as it crept into range.

"Target acquired," Delgado said, his voice calm despite the

tension crackling over the radio net.

"Load Sabot," Mills ordered, gripping her commander's override. The M829A4 armor-piercing round slid into the breach, designed to pierce even the T-14's cutting-edge reactive armor.

"Fire!"

The Abrams roared, the kinetic energy round streaking through the air.

Mills tracked the projectile on her heads-up display, watching as it slammed into the Armata's turret. The explosion was muffled but deadly, smoke billowing as the Russian tank ground to a halt.

Suddenly, her IVIS lit up with warnings — multiple heat signatures emerging from the woods to her west. "Driver move out!" Infantry with Kornet-EM anti-tank missiles were flanking her position.

Mills keyed her mic. "Apache flight, this is Titan 4-6. Danger close. Request immediate support, grid coordinates zero-niner-eight, seven-six-two. Over."

"Roger, Titan 4-6. Hellfire inbound," came the reply.

Moments later, the sound of AH-64E Apaches filled the air.

The helicopters' Longbow radars locked onto the infantry positions, unleashing Hellfire missiles that streaked down like meteors, obliterating the threat.

Mills exhaled and keyed her radio. "Enemy neutralized. Prepare for a counterattack."

Above, the contrails of NATO aircraft streaked the sky. AWACS "Eagle Eye 9" crackled over the comms. "Blue Knights, you have a dozen bogeys inbound. Hammers, stay on their six and keep them off the bombers."

At 30,000 feet over the Black Sea, Major Ethan Garrison's F-35A Lightning II cruised silently, its stealth profile masking it from enemy radar.

His mission was simple but dangerous: locate and destroy the mobile S-400 missile system guarding the Russian advance.

Garrison's Distributed Aperture System (DAS) painted a holographic view of the battlefield inside his helmet. His eyes flicked to a faint signal — a radar pulse barely detectable against the electromagnetic noise of the battlefield.

"AWACS, I've got a faint lock on the target. Request confirmation."

"This is Titan Actual. Confirmed S-400 battery, 20 clicks northeast of your position. Engage and neutralize."

Garrison banked his F-35, flying low to avoid detection.

His internal weapons bay armed a pair of AGM-88G AARGM-ER missiles — state-of-the-art anti-radiation munitions designed to home in on enemy radar.

The system finally revealed itself — a convoy of vehicles tucked into a wooded area. Garrison's sensors identified the launchers and the accompanying Pantsir-S1 anti-aircraft system.

"Lock acquired," he muttered, pressing the release. The missiles roared free, streaking toward their targets. The AARGMs hit their mark, destroying the radar and rendering the S-400 useless.

But the Pantsir-S1 opened fire, its autocannon sending tracer rounds screaming through the sky.

Garrison banked hard, deploying countermeasures. The rounds missed by inches, but he maintained control, climbing to safety.

"Threat neutralized. Returning to base," Garrison reported, his voice steady despite the pounding of his heart.

"Negative. Prepare to engage inbound fighters."

"Roger, Eagle Eye. Blue Knights, break left and engage," came the response from Major Garrison, whose F-35 banked hard, locking onto an approaching MiG-31.

The ensuing dogfight lit up the skies, missiles streaking between jets.

A Typhoon pilot from the Hammers team managed to tail a Su-35, loosing a Sidewinder that sent the Russian aircraft spiraling in flames.

Below, B-1B bombers, their payloads guided by laser designators from ground troops, obliterated Russian supply convoys and command posts.

As the battle raged on land and in the air, the Black Sea became a theater of its own.

Turkish F-16s strafed Russian corvettes while frigates from the Fifteenth NATO Fleet launched salvos of missiles.

Beneath the waves, the USS Maine silently stalked a Russian Akula-class submarine. "Target acquired," the sonar operator reported.

A torpedo was loosed, its path swift and deadly. Moments later, a deep rumble signaled the Akula's destruction.

The 4th Guards Tank Brigade, now fully exposed on the plains, attempted a desperate counterattack. "Iron Shield 6, this is Lionheart Actual. Northern flank is sealed. They've got nowhere to run but to the sea," Pembroke called over the radio.

Norwegian Leopards and German Panzers held the line, trading fire with advancing T-14 Armatas. The ground shook as tanks exploded and machine gun tracers crisscrossed the battlefield.

"Copy that, Lionheart," Lt. Colonel Carter replied from her Challenger. "Let's finish this. Titan, give me everything you've got."

The skies darkened as Collier sent forth an entire wing of every Southern NATO aircraft, descending and unleashing precision strikes that left the 4th Guards in disarray.

What remained of the Russian brigade broke, fleeing toward the Black Sea where NATO naval forces awaited.

Steve frowned as his satellite phone vibrated again. The screen flashed an encrypted NATO relay code — SHAPE was calling directly.

"This is Susi," Steve answered, stepping away from Anya.

A clipped European accent came through the line. "Susi, this is Van Dijk, SHAPE intelligence. We have an immediate update. The Russians moved faster than anticipated. We are pushing them to the Black Sea."

Steve's jaw tightened. "Meaning?"

"We decrypted new Russian orders. Army Group South accelerated operations. Markov may already be aware of the deception. He's more dangerous now than ever. You need to neutralize him if he discovers the NATO success..."

Steve exhaled sharply. "Copy that. Once the final battle starts, I need electronic jamming of military frequencies on my location. Markov needs to be in the dark. Move the battle to meet our goal. Keep me updated."

"We have assets available. ESID needs Markov alive. I have to go." Van Dijk was walking back to his desk.

Steve looked around, curious. "Be careful at SHAPE. You are ESID first. Do they know?"

The line went dead before van Dijk could respond.

He turned back to Anya, his voice low. "We need to move.

Now."

"Sir," A SIGINT analyst called out. "We intercepted a high-priority transmission from Budapest — Agent Susi just took a classified call from within SHAPE." Van Dijk's gaze sharpened. Steve was running point in Budapest, deep inside Russian-controlled networks.

If Markov knew the deception had played out, the mission could be compromised. But who in SHAPE was watching Susi? Why is SHAPE watching Susi?

He straightened. "Alert Sentinel of the Russian timeline moving up. Get me to the war room. Now."

Silently he thought of Susi trying to catch Markov in the act and bring down the Russian government. Titan's battle is not the major fight.

SHAPE had one more card to play. As Russian forces scrambled to recover from the ferocious NATO counterattack, an entirely different war was about to unfold at 35,000 feet.

Comms flashed at the TOC

Titan, Sentinel Actual. Operation Phantom Talon, time

now.

Under the cold, black waters of the Black Sea, Commander Philip "Ghost" Forrester of HMS *Vengeance* stared at the countdown timer in the dimly lit control room.

"Missile lock confirmed, all targets acquired," the fire control officer reported.

Forrester exhaled sharply. "Launch all tubes. God save the King."

The Astute-class submarine expelled a full salvo — 20 Tomahawk cruise missiles — breaking the ocean's surface in a streak of fire.

The weapons shot toward their pre-designated Russian airbases, flying low and undetected beneath enemy radar, striking airstrips, hangars, and command centers with surgical precision.

Russian fighter squadrons at Mozdok, Engels-2, and Akhtubinsk never got off the ground.

Van Dijk turned sharply toward his operations and intelligence team. "We need satellite and ELINT cross-referencing. Have the Black Sea Fleet made any unannounced movements? Check for deviations in their standard patrol pattern."

Nygaard nodded, keying in the request.

A minute later, a new alert chimed across the intelligence

screen. "Sir... we have something. A Russian carrier, the *Admiral Kirov*, has repositioned further west than expected. Its air wing has increased CAP rotations along the NATO perimeter."

Van Dijk's frown deepened. "They're covering something. Or preparing for a strike."

He glanced at Stiansen, "Admiral, we might have just found our jamming squadron."

"Sir, the Black Sea Fleet is up to something," Nygaard reported.

"The carrier *Admiral Kirov* has launched a full electronic warfare squadron. We're picking up strong broadband jamming along NATO's radar coverage. They're actively suppressing satellite targeting data."

Van Dijk exhaled sharply. "They're trying to blind us before the TU-106s launch."

Stiansen turned to the operations team. "Find me an asset that can take down that carrier's jamming system."

Master Corporal Kern could not suppress his smile. "There is a new Canadian frigate, with the Fifteenth fleet, ready to go, Sir." Canada was joining the fight.

Vice Admiral Stiansen spoke into the encrypted link, his voice measured. "Canadian Task Group, this is SHAPE Command. Execute coordinated strike. Target: *Admiral Kirov's* electronic warfare squadron."

Aboard HMCS *Winnipeg*, Captain Lévesque confirmed

the order. "Firing solution locked. Weapons free."

A bright plume of fire streaked from *Winnipeg's* deck as the twin Tomahawk missiles launched, cutting through the night sky.

The first missile struck amidships, tearing into the carrier's command center. A second impact followed seconds later, detonating near the flight deck — *Kirov* will be limping away.

Across the Black Sea, Russian radar screens went dark. The jamming stopped.

Van Dijk watched the real-time satellite feed, nodding in satisfaction.

"Well done, team. That evens the playing field."

Eighteen F-35A Lightning IIs streaked northward in terrain-hugging formation, flying low through Armenian valleys to evade Russian early warning systems. Inside the lead jet, Wing Commander Alper Demirci of the Turkish Air Force glanced at his HUD.

The Russian bombers were still on the ground. They had to strike now.

"Phantom Leader to all callsigns — switch to strike package. Bombers on the tarmac. Weapons free."

The F-35s ascended just above tree level, lining up their targets.

One by one, they loosed GBU-53/B StormBreaker smart bombs — each guided to TU-106 bombers sitting on their runways.

The TU-106s, massive aircraft nearly the size of a B-2 Spirit, erupted into fireballs, their wings shearing off in the explosions.

Ground crews scattered in panic as Russian SAM operators scrambled to respond.

"Splash three bombers!" Phantom 3 called.

"Two more destroyed. They never saw it coming," Phantom 7 added.

As the last bomb detonated, Russian S-400 systems roared to life, sending surface-to-air missiles streaking toward the F-35s.

"Defensive maneuvering — burners on!" Phantom Leader commanded.

The squadron executed a precision break, deploying decoys and chaff before igniting their afterburners.

Their next challenge lay ahead — escaping through Russian airspace to the Black Sea.

As the Phantom Squadron raced south, Russian MiG-31s and Su-35s from the surviving airfields scrambled to intercept.

Just as the F-35s prepared for deeper evasive maneuvers, another group of fighters entered the battle — coming head on to the Phantom Squadron.

"Phantoms spread now." The F-35s created a gap of 10 meters between them. The Turkish pilots watched in awe as their allies screamed by, barely meters away, taking the fight to the Russians.

Bulgarian MiG-29s and Su-25 Frogfoots screamed into the fight at almost Mach 1, flying between the wings of the F-35s, missiles already locking onto Russian fighters.

Flight Lieutenant Nikolai Stoyanov toggled his weapons selector." Iron Fangs, break and engage. We are in the fight."

Missiles streaked across the sky. A Bulgarian pilot in Fang 5 loosed an R-77 medium-range air-to-air missile, sending a Russian Su-35 tumbling in flames.

But the Russian pilots were veterans, and their numbers were overwhelming. Within minutes, Iron Fangs ran low on missiles.

"Fangs, switch to guns!" Stoyanov barked, pulling into a tight barrel roll.

A Russian MiG-31 flashed past him, and Stoyanov's cannons shredded its fuselage, sending debris raining over the mountains.

Another Bulgarian pilot, Captain Radostin Petrov, executed a high-G scissors maneuver, juking a Russian missile. His MiG-29's fuel warning blared, but he pressed on, guns blazing.

"Bullets it is!" he snarled, tearing into an enemy Su-30 at point-blank range.

As the aerial battle raged behind them, Phantom Squadron received a final order from SHAPE.

"Break south. Do not engage. Priority is mission

completion."

But Wing Commander Demirci hesitated. His men had done their job. The bombers were gone.

But now their Bulgarian allies were outnumbered, fighting for their lives.

Then, a new voice cut through the channel. "This is Valkyrie Flight — USS *William McKinley* strike group. We are inbound. Hold the line."

A squadron of F/A-18 Super Hornets from the NATO Carrier Task Force in the Black Sea was en route. The cavalry was arriving.

With the Bulgarians battered but still in the fight, eight Super Hornets from USS *William McKinley* screamed into the fray, launching AIM-120 AMRAAMs into the heart of the Russian formation.

Master Corporal Kern monitored the battle from the U.S. Space Force satellite feed. The Russian carriers were turning into the wind. Vice Admiral Stiansen wasn't going to let them play. "*Winnipeg*, take out the carrier *Varyag* and its sister carrier, the RFS *Pyotr Velikiy*, too."

Within seconds, four more plumes of flames spread out low over the Black Sea, neutralizing the carrier-based threats to the returning fighters before they could launch more than a handful of fighters.

⁂

Wing Commander Demirci could not let everything they did cost more lives. "Phantoms, break left and switch to guns." The F-35s were joining in the fray. "Air Marshal Cemal Akçay will relieve me of my command..." his thoughts drowned out as he engaged the first MiG.

"If this is my last flight, at least it's the right one." The Phantoms demonstrated their prowess in good old fashioned dogfights, closing with guns and taking the pressure off their Bulgarian neighbors and allies.

Missiles detonated in perfect sequence, obliterating three more Su-35s and forcing the remaining Russian fighters into full retreat.

The battered Bulgarians and victorious Phantom Squadron finally turned south, escaping into the safety of NATO-controlled airspace over the Black Sea.

⁂

The AWACS feeds came across. "Raptor-5, confirm splash with drone overwatch," and another reported, "Drone feed confirms impact on primary bombers."

In SHAPE, Admiral Stiansen smirked. "Operation

Phantom Talon is a success. The TU-106 threat is gone."

Air Marshal Akçay exhaled, shaking his head. "The Bulgarians fought like demons."

Van Dijk nodded. "They bought us time. They will be honored. With Phantom." The fine line between insubordination and bravery had been crossed.

As the F-35s and Super Hornets landed safely back at Incirlik, the war had changed. The TU-106 bombers were no more. But Russia would not take this humiliation lightly.

The operation had been a masterpiece of coordination, a relentless symphony of firepower and precision.

As the dust settled, Lt. Colonel Carter watched the live drone feed, satisfaction tempered by the grim realization of what lay ahead.

The war was far from over, but tonight, NATO had delivered a decisive blow.

General Collier turns to his Chief of Staff. "Get me in an AWACS. NOW!"

"Welcome aboard, sir." The operations center aboard the AWACS Eagle Eye was a hive of activity. The faint hum of electronic equipment provided a backdrop to the voices of technicians and officers locked in an intricate dance of data, intelligence, and command.

The stakes were monumental: Army Group South's destruction or their retreat, and NATO's survival rested on a daring gamble.

Staff Sergeant Elena Brooks, the lead electronic warfare EW technician, sat hunched over her console, her fingers dancing across the keyboard as algorithms streamed across her monitor.

The room felt thick with tension as every officer present watched her work.

"Come on, come on ..." Brooks muttered, her voice barely audible over the chatter. "We're close. I can feel it."

General Collier, standing tall with his arms crossed, loomed behind her, his calm, commanding presence anchoring the team.

He glanced at the mission clock. They were running out of time to turn the tide before the Russians could regroup and unleash their mobile missile systems.

"Brooks," Collier said, his voice low but urgent. "Do you have it?"

Her eyes lit up as a notification popped on her screen. "Got it! Sir, we've cracked their encryption protocol. Frequency 121.7 MHz. It's routed through their local command relay at Army Group South HQ."

The room fell silent as all eyes turned to Collier. He leaned over the comms panel, his hands steady as he adjusted the microphone.

His tone was resolute as he spoke in flawless Russian, a skill he'd picked up in his years of dealing with Eastern adversaries.

"This is Titan Actual," Collier announced. "I am speaking directly to the commander of Army Group South. Respond immediately."

For a few agonizing seconds, static filled the channel. Then, a gruff voice, strained with authority and caution, broke through.

"This is Zmey," the Russian commander replied, his call sign meaning Dragon. "Who am I addressing?"

Collier straightened, his gaze piercing. "Zmey, this is General Collier, Titan Actual, commanding all NATO forces in this theater. Listen carefully. Your air cover is gone. Your forces are pinned, and we have the initiative. But I am offering you a way out."

The silence on the other end of the line was palpable. Everyone in the room waited with bated breath as Collier pressed on.

"You will order the immediate abandonment of all mobile missile launchers under your command. Leave them where they stand and begin your retreat. You have one hour to comply. Once the launchers are abandoned, we will discuss a ceasefire and allow your forces to withdraw. Everything and everyone else may retreat, but those launchers stay. Fail to comply, and I will unleash the full might of NATO's air, sea and ground forces. You will not escape. The choice is yours."

The static returned, followed by a long pause. Then, Zmey's voice returned, his tone laced with defiance but also a hint of resignation.

"General Collier, you are bold, I will give you that. But you should know, the Russian Army does not simply abandon its weapons."

Collier's tone hardened, the steel in his voice unmistakable. "And NATO does not bluff, Zmey. You have one hour. We'll be watching."

Zmey's exhalation was audible over the line. "Very well. One hour."

"Issue my order." Collier pointed towards his communications officer communications officer as he stepped back, his expression unreadable. "Brooks, monitor their comms for any movement. Relay everything to ground command. If they even think about using those launchers, I want our air assets ready to strike."

Brooks nodded. "Yes, sir."

Collier watched the real-time satellite feed overlaying the battlefield in eastern Romania, his tactical display merging drone footage, AWACS radar sweeps, and ground unit telemetry.

His orders were being executed in seconds, his commands relayed through encrypted data-links to air and ground forces spread across thousands of square kilometers.

The sheer scale of it hit him all at once.

He was the first ground commander to ever fight a battle from the skies above the fighting.

Every past general had fought from command bunkers, battlefield HQs, or distant war rooms. But Collier?

He was directing armored movements, airstrikes, and naval operations from the operations cell of a modified Boeing E-4B, linked into NATO's most advanced warfighting network.

And for the first time, an intelligence officer was being granted direct combat authority — not just advising the war, but actively reshaping it.

He was leveraging ESID's intelligence feeds, SIGINT from NATO's cyber units, and real-time data from the U.S. Space Force satellites, all fed through Van Dijk.

He had the entire battlefield at his fingertips, and for the first time in modern warfare, a single real time and confirmed intelligence-driven decision could alter the entire flow of battle.

Collier exhaled slowly.

"Hmmm ... what could Patton have done with all of this at his fingertips?"

If they won this fight, wars would never be fought the same way again.

Collier turned to his staff, his voice ringing with authority.

"They have one hour, people. Let's turn the pressure on now."

"After everything the Russians had endured, how could they just now be turning the pressure on them?" thought Brooks.

The countdown began, and the fate of the battlefield hung on Collier's latest order.

The command-and-control center of Operation Thunderstrike was alive with coordinated chaos as orders flashed across every screen and voice channels buzzed with urgent chatter. General Collier's directive had gone out — every NATO air unit in the theater was now tasked with executing one of the most aggressive combined arms maneuvers of the war.

"All air elements of Thunderstrike, this is Titan 6," the general's voice echoed across frequencies. "You have new mission orders: establish a protective air cap over the operational zone. Watch for any movement of mobile rocket launchers. Ground forces, pull back a minimum of three kilometers and hold your positions. Thunderstrike II is about to commence. Air elements, be advised, Iron Falcons will be joining and together you have fifteen minutes to wreak havoc on every Russian vehicle in the kill zone. After fifteen minutes, break off and refuel.

The Iron Falcons, a heavy strike wing of NATO aircraft, took to the skies like a wrathful storm. Call signs buzzed across the airwaves as the fleet acknowledged their orders:

"Falcon One-One, rolling in hot."

"Viper Two-Three, forming up. Targets sighted."

"Thunder Three-Five, weapons free."

In perfect formation, the Iron Falcons roared over the battlefield. F-16s and Tornados screamed through the air, strafing Russian armor and troop convoys with pinpoint accuracy.

Diving at a high rate of speed, A-10 Warthogs, the unmistakable "hogs" of close air support, descended like avenging angels, their GAU-8 Avenger cannons shredding tanks and armored vehicles.

The unmistakable brrrrrt of their fire filled the battlefield, a death knell for anything in their path.

"Falcon One-One, splash three tanks. Moving to a new vector."

"Viper Two-Four, rocket launchers spotted! Engaging now."

Missiles streaked from wings, tearing through mobile command vehicles and rocket launchers.

Russian forces scrambled in vain to retaliate, their anti-air defenses either obliterated or suppressed by NATO SEAD (Suppression of Enemy Air Defenses) teams.

For fifteen relentless minutes, the combined might of virtually every aircraft of Southern and Central NATO unleashed hell, leaving trails of destruction across the open fields and roads.

Russian armor burned, and their formations crumbled under the unrelenting assault.

Precisely at the 15 minute mark, their squadron leaders called the retreat.

"Falcon One-One, time's up. Breaking off to refuel."

"Viper Two-Three, pulling back. All elements, clear the zone."

One by one, the aircraft pulled back to their designated airbases and refueling tankers orbiting over safe zones.

As they climbed to altitude, the battlefield fell momentarily silent — until the thunderous roar of naval artillery shattered the quiet.

From their positions in the Black Sea, the Fifteenth Fleet unleashed everything in their arsenal.

Guided missile destroyers and cruisers fired volley after volley of Tomahawk cruise missiles, aimed at hardened positions and retreating Russian forces.

The naval guns opened up, their salvos pounding the Russian ground forces with devastating precision.

The fleet's submarines joined the fight, launching torpedoes and cruise missiles to eliminate any lingering Russian command-and-control nodes.

Meanwhile, Turkish F-16s provided overwatch, ensuring no Russian aircraft dared to challenge the naval onslaught.

The battlefield was a cacophony of destruction, with fire

and smoke marking the Russian positions.

Mobile rocket launchers, command vehicles, and supply convoys were systematically destroyed.

Any hope of regrouping was obliterated under the coordinated hammer blows of NATO's combined air and naval forces.

As the naval bombardment subsided, General Collier's voice crackled across the comms.

"All elements, this is Titan 6. Stand by for status updates. Continue monitoring for rocket launcher activity."

Brooks stared in astonishment. "General Collier, Sir." She handed him the mic and turned on the speakers.

"Titan, this is Zemy."

"This is Titan."

"We are abandoning our missile launchers and retreating 10 kilometers east. Out." Zemy couldn't stand the heat.

The battlefield fell into a tense silence, broken only by the distant rumble of burning vehicles and the occasional crack of secondary explosions.

In the skies above and the waters beyond, NATO forces remained poised, ready to strike again at a moment's notice.

Collier turned away from everyone, pulled out his sat phone and dialed the number.

Double Crossed and Alone

Moscow, Russia — GRU Headquarters

The tension inside the GRU Cybersecurity Division was suffocating. Colonel Oleg Vasilyev, Director of Counterintelligence, stood at the front of the war room, his gaze a storm brewing behind dark eyes.

The massive screen behind him displayed cascading lines of code, system logs, and internal GRU data access points.

It all pointed to one terrifying conclusion.

They had been breached.

Vasilyev turned to his lead investigator, Captain Viktor Orlov.

"Tell me we have something," Vasilyev growled.

Orlov's fingers tensed against his keyboard. "We don't."

Vasilyev's jaw tightened. "That's not an answer."

Orlov exhaled sharply, then tapped a key. A series of red alerts scrolled across the screen.

*ACCESS VIOLATION DETECTED —
CLASSIFIED ARCHIVE 021-B
*ACCESS VIOLATION DETECTED —
TARGET DIRECTIVE 37
*ACCESS VIOLATION DETECTED —
OPERATION NIGHT STALKERS

Vasilyev's pulse quickened.

These weren't just random breaches.

Someone had accessed highest-level intelligence directives — classified GRU operations, internal security logs, and even mission orders tied to Markov's Perun Initiative.

A mole.

It had to be.

Orlov hesitated. "Sir... every access attempt originates from within our own network."

Vasilyev's stare hardened. "That means we have a traitor in the building."

Silence.

The room shifted uneasily, agents exchanging wary glances, knowing what was coming next.

Orlov swallowed. "Sir... there's something else."

Vasilyev didn't flinch. "Then say it."

Orlov tapped another command. A log appeared in red, highlighted in flashing text.

*ATTEMPTED FILE TRACE: FAILED

*SOURCE: UNKNOWN

Vasilyev's breath hitched. "What the hell is that?"

Orlov ran a hand through his hair, glancing at his team before answering.

"We attempted to trace the security breach back to its source," he explained. "But every single time, it bounces through a different officer's credentials."

Vasilyev's stomach clenched.

"They're masking their access?"

Orlov nodded. "Yes, sir. And not just once — it changes every few hours. We've flagged thirteen officers so far, but when we interrogate them... nothing."

Vasilyev turned back to the room, his voice cold.

"I want every officer flagged for review," he ordered. "No one leaves until we find this traitor."

A nervous ripple went through the room.

Orlov cleared his throat. "Sir... I don't think we're looking for a mole."

Vasilyev's gaze snapped to him. "Explain."

Orlov tapped a key. Another log appeared.

*NEW ACCESS ATTEMPT DETECTED —
GENERAL STAFF NETWORK
*LOCATION: UNKNOWN

No IP. No access logs. No digital footprint.

Vasilyev's heart pounded.

"Impossible," he muttered.

Orlov's voice lowered. "Sir… this isn't a human leak. This is something else."

Vasilyev's breath slowed.

"You're telling me an AI system has infiltrated our networks?"

"Not exactly, sir." Orlov hesitated. "It's… different."

Vasilyev's hand curled into a fist.

"You need to find this, block this, or disable it immediately. Current operations are going to be compromised within the hour." Vasilyev's words clearly meant to stop this by any means.

Orlov started to activate override protocols. But Cypher's sub routine predicted it and migrated through before the protocols were fully in place.

"It's no good, Sir. We cannot even shutdown or disconnect the system. Whatever this is, it appears to have been programmed in from the start." Orlov looked up. "Could the FSB have done this? They have every file we ever created."

They weren't hunting a traitor.

They were hunting a digital phantom.

Vasilyev fumed. "Delete everything. Wipe it. Format every trace of our files. We can restore from backups later."

As Orlov walked away, he thought out loud, "I'm pretty sure our backups have been compromised already."

"Thanks, Collier. Great work." The first burst of automatic fire shredded a row of century-old Hungarian paintings.

Collier's voice came through calm and measured. "Steve, you're making a lot of noise for an undercover guy."

Steve exhaled. "Yeah, well, not everyone got the memo. Markov's here. So is Anya. And so is every flavor of GRU you can think of."

A brief silence. Then, "Define every flavor."

Steve's muscles tightened as he checked the magazine on his PPS-43C and rolled. "I've got GRU guys in black ops gear, full suppression kits. Those are the Night Stalkers that Jasper learned about."

He paused, scanning the opposing forces beyond the gilded archway of the lobby. "Then I've got GRU agents in leather trench coats, looking like they just stepped out of a 1980s KGB recruitment poster. I assume those are Anya's guys."

Collier's voice was sharper now. "And Markov's?"

Steve cocked the charging handle on his PPS-43C. "They're the ones shooting at both sides."

A dry chuckle came through the line. "Outstanding. Keep me posted. I'll see if NATO has a hand in this yet."

Steve shoved the comm earpiece deeper, switching his focus back to the chaotic lobby.

The opulent hotel bar had turned into a battlefield. A framed work of Mihály Munkácsy — once worth millions — exploded in a cloud of splintered wood and shattered glass.

Steve winced. "Goddammit, that was Munkácsy's *Ecce Homo*. It belonged to the Hungarian National Gallery."

A second burst of gunfire stitched the marble floor, sending a pair of hotel staff diving behind the reception desk.

A CS gas grenade rolled past the wine cellar, hissing toxic vapor into the air.

Steve kicked it into an open corridor just before the thick white cloud erupted.

"Alright, Susi, think. Who the hell is shooting at who?" Steve hoped talking through it would give him an epiphany.

Anya's guys? The ones in leather coats.

The Night Stalkers? No leather — just black assault gear, all silencers.

Markov's guys? Ex-Soviet Spetsnaz, shooting at everyone.

A flashbang detonated near the grand staircase, the deafening concussive wave slamming through Steve's skull.

He blinked past the disorientation, moving through the swirling fog of CS gas.

Another flurry of shots from the mezzanine chewed into the bar's crystal display, sending thousands of dollars of fine Hungarian Tokaji cascading onto the floor in golden rivers.

Steve ducked behind an overturned mahogany dining table, coughing as the CS gas seeped into his lungs.

"I need better cover."

He moved fast, weaving between upturned chairs, before throwing himself through an open side door into a grand banquet hall.

A flash of movement beyond the shattered wine bar.

Markov.

Steve spotted him weaving through the smoke, two of his personal bodyguards covering his retreat.

No time to think. No time to question.

Steve surged forward, emptying half a magazine toward the fleeing Russian general.

The first shot clipped one of Markov's guards, sending the man crashing into a grand piano, blood streaking the ivory keys.

The second shot missed.

Markov was fast — too fast for an old man.

Steve vaulted over a dead GRU officer, rolling as another flashbang detonated to his right.

"Alright, think. Think."

He had Anya. But was she playing him?

He had some GRU on his side. But how many? And which ones?

And then there were the Night Stalkers. The GRU's most ruthless black ops hunters.

A fresh burst of gunfire tore through an antique Zsolnay porcelain display, sending shards of deep blue ceramics scattering like glass rain.

Steve flinched, exhaling.

"GRU guys always wear leather coats. Why the hell didn't Anya tell her guys to leave their coats in the damn cars?!"

The next burst was aimed directly at him.

Steve vaulted over an overturned catering cart, feeling the rounds chew into the silk-draped banquet table he'd just occupied.

His ears rang, eyes blurred — but he kept moving.

Markov was almost at the exit.

"Not this time."

Steve slid to a halt, snapped his PPS-43C to his shoulder, and squeezed the trigger.

Anya dove for cover next to Steve.

"My plan succeeded. NATO has all the mobile rocket launchers. Markov is powerless after they are destroyed."

As he turned back, he saw the GRU agents, too late.

"Get down!" Steve roared, shoving Anya behind a marble column as the first burst of gunfire ripped through the silence.

The beat of his heart matched the cadence of the bullets, each shot echoing like the stanza from a song that refused to leave his mind.

"Markov just ran from the bar to the elevator. He has people with him." Anya had switched to acting in her full GRU major personality. "Let's go."

Anya led with her Makarov, Steve put his Tokarev away, pulled out the PPS-43C and unfolded the stock.

He dropped in a fresh 35 round magazine and flicked off the safety.

"Let's take the stairs." Anya twisted, and looked behind Steve. She nodded.

Steve tried to hurry her, "We have to get to Markov before he can activate the launch codes."

Anya's grip tightened around her Makarov, but her eyes weren't tracking the escape route. They were on him.

Steve saw it then. Something's wrong.

The hesitation. A half-second too long. A fraction of delay in a woman who never hesitated.

His body knew before his brain. The primal instinct screamed — MOVE.

In that split second of reflection, Steve wondered why she would betray him if she had a bounty on her head. Then wondered why he ever trusted her.

Anya opened her mouth –

Steve spun — his only thought is another GRU beating he's going to endure.

The world flashed white-hot.

A sharp, crushing impact exploded across the back of his skull.

Pain.

Falling.

"I'm sorry. I always loved you, Stephan Ivanovich." Were the last words he heard.

Darkness.

Colonel Aleksei Sorokin wiped the soot from his face and pulled himself back into the turret of Vladivostok, his battle-worn T-90M. Smoke clouded the horizon, the remains of logistics vehicles scattered like broken toys along the muddy road behind him.

Shredded BM-27 Uragan rocket launchers smoldered beside overturned KamAZ trucks, victims of NATO's relentless airstrikes.

"Comms are spotty, Colonel," Major Vadim Kolesov said, his voice strained. "We're being jammed. And... Zemyakin is gone. He abandoned us."

Sorokin's knuckles whitened on the turret ring. His fury swelled, but he buried it beneath the hardened resolve of a veteran commander.

Their once-proud Army Group South had become a disorganized rabble.

Every Uragan they'd fired in the opening salvos felt like a cruel irony now.

Through the Sosna-U sight, Sorokin surveyed NATO's defenses — a mixed force of U.S. 17th ACR and British 5th Dragoon Guards, entrenched along a rocky ridge two kilometers away.

The Challengers sat hull-down, their Dorchester armor presenting only their heavily armored turrets. Supporting Abrams tanks shifted slightly, their FLIR optics glinting ominously.

Infantry dug into reverse slopes behind them, their

positions reinforced by portable Javelins and mortars.

"Vadim, patch me into the brigade frequency," Sorokin commanded.

"Sir, the jamming — "

"Do it," Sorokin snapped, his patience frayed but his resolve intact.

Static hissed, then resolved into faint, broken voices. Sorokin keyed the mic.

"4th Guards, this is Sorokin. Forget Zemyakin. Forget the retreat. We are not finished." His voice cut through the static, cold and unyielding. "Before us stands NATO — arrogant Americans and British fools who believe we are beaten. But we are the 4th Guards Tank Brigade! Fulfill your duty. Advance and destroy!"

Acknowledgments crackled hesitantly through the static. Sorokin switched to his company net.

"First Battalion, with me! Drive into their center. Second Battalion, flank left and fix their infantry. Artillery, I want suppressive fire now!"

The T-90Ms lurched forward, their V-92S2F diesel engines growling as they surged toward the NATO lines.

Behind them, older T-72B3s followed, their reactive armor glinting in the fading sunlight. BMP-3 infantry fighting vehicles kept pace, their 30mm autocannons scanning for targets.

Leftenant Mark Taylor crouched behind a berm, his L85A3 rifle resting on the dirt. "Javelin teams, ready!" he barked, his eyes never leaving the advancing Russian armor. The Russians were coming hard, their T-90Ms supported by BMPT Terminator vehicles bristling with ATGMs and autocannons.

The British Challengers behind him stood poised to counter, their 120mm L55A1 smoothbore cannons tracking targets.

"Fire!" Taylor shouted.

The Javelin missiles streaked out, their distinctive top-attack profiles slamming into Russian armor.

Two T-90Ms erupted into flames, their turrets blasted skyward. But the Russians pressed on, BMP-3s disgorging infantry under the cover of suppressive fire.

"Challengers, engage!" Taylor ordered.

The Challenger 3s fired in unison, their shells punching through reactive armor like paper.

Volleys of Excalibur artillery from NATO's M777 howitzers rained down, tearing through the Russian flanks with precision-guided devastation.

Amid the chaos, Captain Ryan "Tex" Collins of the 17th ACR's Echo Troop leaned into his Abrams' CITV. "Gunner, designate lead T-90. Range?"

"Two thousand meters," Staff Sergeant Peterson replied, calm under pressure.

"Send it."

The Abrams' M256 cannon roared, its depleted uranium

sabot round obliterating the lead T-90M in a fireball.

Collins surveyed the battlefield through his optics, his stomach tightening as more Russian armor emerged from the smoke.

"They're not stopping," Collins muttered. "All units, weapons free."

Soroking gritted his teeth as NATO artillery pounded his flanks. Inside Vladivostok, the air reeked of cordite and sweat. His gunner, Lieutenant Igor Markov, called out targets, but Sorokin's focus was already ahead.

"On the Abrams! Range, one-point-eight kilometers!" Markov barked.

"Load sabot!" Sorokin ordered.

The autoloader slammed a 125mm APFSDS round into the breech. The T-90's gun recoiled violently, the sabot streaking toward its target.

The round hit low on the Abrams' glacis plate, deflecting with a shower of sparks.

"Damn it!" Sorokin growled. "Reload and fire again!"

Before they could, an Apache Longbow swooped in, its Hellfire missile turning a nearby T-72 into a fireball.

Sorokin's driver veered sharply, narrowly avoiding the wreckage.

From high above, General Collier watched the Russian advance unfold on his command screen aboard Overlord 1. The humming of the E-7 Wedgetail's massive radar arrays filled the cockpit, a constant reminder that their airborne fortress was watching the entire battlefield unfold beneath them.

At 12 kilometers above the fighting, they were untouchable. Their power wasn't in firepower, but in absolute battlefield control.

Major Jakub "Ski" Wojcik, the Polish Air Force pilot, tilted his head as the latest real-time battle updates scrolled across his HUD.

He glanced at his co-pilot, Captain Mateusz "Matty" Radzinski, who smirked.

"So tell me, Major — how long before the U.S. Air Force starts asking us to teach them how to fly?" Radzinski joked, his accent thick with Polish pride.

The two American officers in the rear command section of the cockpit, Major Evan Cartwright and Captain Jake Daniels, rolled their eyes.

"Oh, come on, Matty — just because we let you drive the bus doesn't mean you run the airline." Daniels shot back, adjusting his headset.

Cartwright, the electronic warfare specialist, let out a chuckle. "Besides, you're flying an American airframe, using an American battle network, and running a war led by an American general."

"Yeah, yeah." Radzinski grinned, adjusting the throttle. "But it's a Polish pilot keeping this thing in the air. And your general? He's about to go down in history."

From the command station behind them, Colonel Hannah Larson, the mission coordinator, was watching the live war map update in real-time.

The screen flickered as JSTARS, satellite feeds, and forward drone ISR all converged into a single tactical view of the battlefield.

At the center of it all, General Collier's orders were being executed like a grandmaster's final chess moves.

The USS *Mount Whitney*, the NATO flagship operating in the Black Sea broadcast the imagery to Overlord, fed from Reaper drones and JSTARS aircraft, painted a grim picture.

—◆—

THE 4th Guards Tank Brigade wasn't retreating anymore — they were charging headlong into the teeth of the 17th ACR's defenses. Brooks turned as she hit the speakers. "Sir, you need to hear this."

Sorokin's defiant voice crackled through the static.

"No retreat. We are the 4th Guards Tank Brigade."

Collier stared at the screen.

Then, at the radio.

"Sir?"

Collier closed his eyes. "That's bold," Collier muttered, leaning forward. "He's willing to die here."

As he contemplated the last stand of the 4th Guards Tank Brigade, he debated on using air power, naval batteries, artillery, or ground forces to bring about Sorokin's demise.

General Collier stood ramrod straight, with full respect. "He deserves everything we have."

The tactical display inside the AWACS Forward Command flashed with the updated ISR data from JSTARS, AWACS, and SIGINT intercepts. General Nate Collier scanned the real-time battlefield feed, taking in the carnage unfolding across the plains of Moldova.

The 4th Guards Tank Brigade, one of the last true elite Russian formations, was the only thing left standing.

He toggled his radio. "Air Cavalry, this is Titan Actual. Paint the 4th Guard Tank Brigade elements and bring the hammer down."

Turning back to his impromptu, newly formed command module, "I need eyes. Give me every RQ-21 Blackjack and

RQ-170 Sentinel drone the Navy has available. And some MQ-9 Reapers from the US Air Force."

Collier's voice came over every command net. "All Thunderstrike units; execute. End this. I say again, ALL THUNDERSTRIKE ELEMENTS. Give everything we've got."

Apache Longbows descended, their laser designators illuminating Russian tanks.

Every NATO gun erupted.

The 72-ton Challenger 3 tank rumbled across the torn battlefield, its massive L55A1 smoothbore gun lowering toward its next kill.

Inside, the crew of Lancaster 2-1 braced for their final engagement of the afternoon.

They had been expecting the Russians to fully retreat.

"Steady lads, let's finish this. We are going to be in the history books."

The voice of Sergeant Owen "Oz" Mitchell, the tank commander, was calm — almost casual. Years of combat experience had hardened him, but tonight felt different.

This was history in motion — the final death throes of a once-unstoppable Russian tank formation.

"Driver, slow ahead. Gunner, contact front, T-90M, 1,200 meters — give 'em a bloody good send-off."

"On the way!" shouted Corporal Jamie Tate, the gunner, as he squeezed the trigger.

The 120mm CHARM 3 APFSDS round left the barrel at

hypersonic speed, slamming into the T-90M's glacis plate.

The Russian tank shuddered, its ERA panels blowing off in a flash — but it wasn't enough.

"Bastard's still up!" Tate cursed, loading another round.

"Loader, put a finisher in him."

Private Sean "Benny" Bennett, the loader, rammed another armor-piercing round into the breach.

"Up!"

"Send it!"

The Challenger fired again. This time, the sabot penetrated clean through the turret, detonating the T-90M's autoloader ammunition carousel.

The Russian tank exploded violently, its turret catapulting 50 feet into the air, a fitting end to a once-feared machine.

"Great shooting, Jimmy. Your Mum will be proud of you." Oz knew it was a moment for Tate. His grandfather was killed in action.

Mitchell watched through his optics, nodding with satisfaction.

"That's for the Desert Rats, you miserable sods."

All at once every ground, air, and naval system swung into action.

B-1B Lancers unleashed AGM-158C LRASMs, targeting Russian supply convoys attempting to retreat toward Transnistria.

F-35B Lightning IIs from HMS *Queen Victoria* dropped GBU-53/B StormBreaker smart munitions, vaporizing

Russian command vehicles.

AH-64E Apache Longbows hunted fleeing Russian infantry, firing AGM-114L Longbow Hellfires with deadly precision.

M270 MLRS units unleashed a final GMLRS saturation strike, flattening the last Russian artillery positions.

U.S. Army M1A2 SEPv3 Abrams lined up their final shots, firing M829A4 depleted uranium sabots into the remaining Russian armor, cutting through reactive armor like paper.

USS *Roosevelt* (DDG-80) launched a final volley of RGM-109E Tomahawk cruise missiles, obliterating a GRU command post outside Odessa.

Colonel Larson exhaled slowly, watching the final Russian positions vanish from the battlefield display.

"Damn," she murmured. "Reapers are reporting the destruction faster than we can receive the data. Collier's actually doing it. "

"Doing what?" Wojcik asked, glancing back at her.

Larson didn't take her eyes off the screen. "Changing the face of modern warfare."

For a moment, the cockpit was silent. The crew of Overlord-1 had spent their careers training, preparing, and running exercises that simulated this exact kind of war.

But this wasn't an exercise.

For the first time in history, a war wasn't being commanded from a ground-based HQ or an aircraft carrier – it was being run instantaneously, using integrated AI battle networks, electronic warfare, and precision coordination across all branches of NATO.

This wasn't just a battle.

This was a new way to fight wars.

Radizinski exhaled, rubbing his jaw. "Huh. Guess we better start writing the manuals then."

Daniels smirked. "Yeah. And don't be surprised if we make you Polish guys honorary U.S. Air Force pilots after this."

"Not a chance, Jake. We'll let you train with us, though." Wojcik rolled his eyes, grinned and added, "Maybe."

The laughter was lighthearted, but the reality was clear — this moment, this night, this war — was a turning point in history.

And they were flying right at the heart of it.

A deep hum of electronics filled the air as the White House Situation Room remained locked onto the live battlefield feed of NATO's engagement in Moldova. At the head of the oval-shaped conference table, President David R. Killian sat, his face set in stone, eyes locked on the monitors streaming real-time ISR footage.

To his right, Vice President Ethan Marshall watched silently, arms crossed.

Across the table, the Joint Chiefs, National Security

Advisor, Secretary of Defense, Secretary of State, and key Senate and House leaders sat in grim silence, the glow of digital war maps reflecting off their tense faces.

On screen, General Nathan Collier's voice cut through the command net.

""All Thunderstrike units; execute. End this. I say again, ALL THUNDERSTRIKE ELEMENTS. Give everything we've got."

A moment later, aerial footage showed NATO Apaches diving in, targeting Russian T-90Ms with precision laser-guided munitions.

Hellfire missiles slammed into their targets, naval batteries devastating the battlefield, Multiple Launch Rocket Systems, 155mm artillery pieces, every air-to-surface missile, and A-10 35mm guns — all roaring at once, leaving behind only burning wreckage and smoke curling into the afternoon sky.

Chairman of the Joint Chiefs, General William Hargrove, leaned forward, adjusting the live tactical feed with a touchpad. "Mr. President, you're witnessing something unprecedented. Collier isn't just commanding the battle — he's controlling the war. This is real-time intelligence, air support, and force deployment at a level we've never attempted before."

On screen, a Hellfire missile slammed into a BMP-3, its turret flipping end-over-end.

Senator Mark Ridge, a former Marine and member of the Senate Armed Services Committee, let out a slow whistle.

"You're telling me the entire war effort in Eastern Europe is being run by one general 40,000 feet in the air, coordinating real-time ISR, JSTARS feeds, and battlefield AI?"

National Security Advisor Daniel Monroe nodded. "That's the future of warfare. A single command node, processing live intelligence and striking before the enemy even realizes it."

Senate Majority Leader Christine Walker folded her hands. "That's incredible. But let's talk about the bigger issue. Why the hell is it always American boots on the ground?"

Vice President Ethan Marshall exhaled sharply. "Because NATO still functions on American money and American firepower. The European Union should be leading this defense effort, but we all know who's really holding the line."

The President leaned forward. "That's a problem. If this war drags on, we're footing the bill. We're losing American soldiers. And for what? To protect Europe's borders while they sit back?"

Monroe scrolled through his tablet, then turned to the room. "At last assessment, European NATO forces are at 63% readiness. The Germans, French, and Poles are engaged, but the bulk of frontline combat strength is the U.S. Army and Air Force."

Walker scoffed. "That's unacceptable. This is their damn backyard."

Senator Ridge leaned in. "And if we don't hold the line here, then what? We fight the next war on American soil? NATO isn't just about helping Europe — it's about keeping war off our doorstep."

A few heads nodded at that, but the tension in the room remained.

Inside Vladivostok, Sorokin felt the end. Climbing out of his burning tank, he stood amidst the chaos, watching his brigade disintegrate. Yet, even in defeat, he felt a grim pride.

"To all remaining units," he radioed, his voice resolute, "no retreat. We are the 4th Guards Tank Brigade."

The first Hellfire missile struck a T-72, sending a fireball curling into the sky.

Sorokin braced as the shockwave rocked Vladivostok.

His men were still fighting.

Even now.

"No retreat."

"Vadim," he said softly, glancing at Kolesov. The younger officer stood beside him, eyes locked on the advancing NATO forces.

Sorokin closed his eyes.

"We did our duty. That is all a soldier can do."

He climbed out of the turret, pistol in hand.

A final salute.

One shot.

A warrior's death.

Then, he advanced on foot, firing at the nearest Challenger.

A flash.

Darkness.

The Challenger's wingman finished the job, not knowing who their loader had just shot.

The wingman's commander climbs out. Lt. Colonel Rebecca Carter confirms her loader has killed Vladivostok's commander.

For you, Sarah."

Inside Collier's AWACS Forward Command, the battlefield map winked — and just like that, the entire Russian 4th Guards Tank Brigade had ceased to exist. Collier watched the final reports come in. His voice was calm.

"It's done. We own the battlefield. They were caught by surprise."

4th Guards Tank Brigade neutralized; NATO maintains full dominance in Eastern Europe; Russia's last elite armored force has been vanquished.

Collier leaned back, staring at the holographic map.

Markov had bet everything on this battle.

Deep in the Slovak mountains, beneath layers of concrete and encrypted firewalls, Emil "Cypher" Kovács leaned back in his chair, watching the algorithmic data threads pulse across the dark monitors. His custom-coded deep subroutine, embedded in GRU's network, had been running autonomously for weeks — digesting thousands of terabytes of intercepted transmissions, decoding them on the fly.

A low chuckle echoed through the bunker.

Cypher leaned back, boots propped against a stack of outdated servers, watching the GRU's intelligence feeds update in real time.

They were running in circles.

"They think I'm one of them," he muttered, taking a sip of cold coffee.

The monitors in front of him flickered, showing new interrogation records. Another GRU officer dragged into a holding room, his credentials flagged as suspicious.

Cypher smirked. Perfect.

His subroutine — Doppelgänger — was working exactly as designed.

Instead of just stealing intelligence, Doppelgänger had embedded itself inside the GRU's security infrastructure, creating false access trails, redirecting blame, and making it appear as if multiple officers had compromised intelligence.

Now, the GRU was hunting its own men.

Cypher scrolled through the live security feed, watching Vasilyev interrogate his own agents, demanding to know who leaked information.

They had no idea.

It wasn't one of their own.

It was their own system.

A new alert flashed red on Cypher's screen.

His smirk faded.

    *NEW GRU DIRECTIVE — THREAT
ELIMINATION ORDER
*PRIORITY TARGET: WOJTEK

His fingers stilled over the keyboard.

They had issued the kill order.

And they weren't using regular operators.

Cypher scanned the execution order.

    *ASSIGNMENT: NIGHT   STALKERS
OPERATIONS TEAM
*MISSION STATUS: ACTIVATED

He exhaled sharply.

Steve wasn't just being hunted.

The GRU's elite kill unit had been deployed.

Cypher reached for his comms, opening a secure encrypted
transmission to Jasper.

He didn't bother with greetings.

Cypher stared at the screen, watching the GRU's own security forces unravel.

Cypher's fingers danced across the keys, rapidly injecting false updates into GRU kill order communications, delaying the team's movement. It wasn't much — but it might buy Steve a few hours.

"They don't know his exact location yet," Cypher messaged Davy Jones. "But the moment they do…"

He let the sentence hang.

Cypher's grin returned. "I won't let them find out."

He cracked his knuckles and went back to work.

Cypher frowned, adjusting his black-rimmed glasses as the decryption finalized.

"GRU Directive: Wojtek has been captured. Markov has what he needs. After the launch, execute as planned. Terminate the subject."

"Shit."

Cypher snapped upright, hands flying across his mechanical keyboard. He routed another emergency ping to Jasper van Dijk — The Flying Dutchman's Davy Jones.

At SHAPE headquarters, Brussels, Jasper van Dijk's secure comms unit vibrated violently against his desk. One look at the incoming transmission from Cypher, and his normally composed expression hardened.

He immediately dialed into Jansen.

The intelligence director at SHAPE didn't waste time with pleasantries.

"Titan's deep in it. Final push succeeded in Moldova. No NATO assets are coming for Steve. We don't have the authority."

Jasper's fingers tightened on his phone. "Then I'm making my own authority."

Jansen sighed. "Jasper —"

But the line was already cut.

At Frankfurt's Special Operations Base, the alert came through. The GSG 9 tactical operators in the Passau barracks moved with precision, donning their gear in synchronized movements.

Black ballistic vests, marked "GSG 9 — Bundespolizei."

Helmet-mounted NVG units flipped down in readiness for night operations.

HK416 rifles locked and loaded, silencers screwed on.

G36K compact assault rifles slung tight for urban combat.

The commander, Oberstleutnant Lukas Heidenreich, checked his HK45 sidearm before striding into the ready bay where the team's specialized Mercedes-Benz G-Class and Vito vans waited, matte black, stripped of luxury — built for war.

The Vito lead vehicle was modified for rapid breach-and-extraction operations.

Bulletproof plating capable of stopping 7.62mm rounds.

Tactical breach system installed beneath the chassis, able to punch through reinforced barriers.

A comms suite wired to SHAPE intelligence and satellite feeds.

The Mercedes G-Class SUVs followed as tactical response units, their twin-turbocharged V8s purring like caged panthers.

Inside the convoy, GSG 9 operators clipped gear onto their tactical rigs:

CS gas grenades and flashbangs lined their belts.

Infrared laser sighting systems on every rifle.

Encrypted short-range comms with adaptive frequency-hopping to counter GRU jamming.

Oberstleutnant Heidenreich climbed into the lead Vito, grabbing the secure tablet.

A single image flashed on screen — Steve Johnson's file.

A voice crackled through his earpiece. Jasper van Dijk.

"Find him. Bring him home."

The convoy roared out of the hangar.

At a remote RAF base in Lithuania, the SAS Quick Reaction Team was already preparing.

Major Gareth "Reaper" Mercer leaned against the open cargo ramp of a waiting RAF C-17, watching as his troop of eight SAS commandos checked their equipment.

Sig Sauer MCX carbines, loaded with armor-piercing rounds.

L119A2 short-barrel rifles for close-quarters combat.

Breaching tools and compact explosives in case Steve was locked down hard.

Jansen's direct call to British Intelligence had sealed the deal.

They were going in as backup.

No negotiations. If Markov's men didn't surrender, they wouldn't get the chance.

Secretary of State James Kendall tapped the table. "While we're focused on Europe, China is watching. And frankly, I don't like what I see."

National Security Advisor Monroe nodded. "Australia and Taiwan are vulnerable right now. We've had to shift naval assets to Europe, and Beijing knows it. They're waiting for us to overcommit here."

President Killian turned to the Chief of Naval Operations, Admiral John Raines. "Admiral, how much of a problem are we looking at?"

Raines leaned forward, his expression unreadable. "A very serious one, Mr. President." He tapped a holographic map, bringing up China's modern naval footprint.

"Twenty years ago, the People's Liberation Army Navy (PLAN) was a regional force. Today, it's the largest navy in the world. Their shipbuilding rate outpaces the United States by 4 to 1."

He pointed to the updated fleet assessments.

Four active aircraft carriers (two more under construction).

Twelve Type 055 Renhai-class guided missile destroyers (comparable to U.S. Aegis destroyers).

Dozens of Type 052D and Type 054A warships, all missile-heavy platforms.

At least 80 modern submarines, including new nuclear-powered attack subs.

An estimated 700 naval aircraft.

The numbers were staggering.

A heavy silence settled over the room.

President Killian tapped a pen against the table, deep in thought.

"Let's assume we win this fight. What then? Is Russia really our greatest threat? Or are we bankrupting ourselves in a European war when the real danger is in the Pacific?"

The room was silent.

Vice President Marshall glanced at Monroe. "If we stay in Europe too long, we may not have the resources to fight China when the time comes."

Senator Ridge shook his head. "Mr. President, if we pull out of NATO, we signal weakness. We keep the fight in Europe so it never reaches our shores."

Senator Ridge continued. "If we so much as suggest NATO is weakening, Moscow will move. Period."

His fist came down on the table, rattling coffee cups as the other officials tensed.

The Secretary of State, James Kendall, rubbed his temples. "Mark — "

"No. You listen to me." Ridge's blue eyes burned with intensity as he swept a glare across the room. "I fought in the Gulf. I commanded troops in Iraq and Afghanistan. I've seen what happens when the U.S. shows hesitation."

His voice lowered, deadly calm.

"Weakness breeds opportunists. And right now, we are staring down two of them — Russia and China."

Daniel Monroe, the National Security Advisor, leaned forward, shaking his head.

"Senator, nobody here is suggesting we just walk out the door tomorrow. But we have to be real about this. The U.S. has been the backbone of NATO for over seventy years. We're spending close to a trillion dollars annually on global defense."

He gestured toward the live tactical map on the screen.

"This war is burning through resources at an unsustainable rate. And while we're holding the line in Europe, we're leaving our flanks open."

He tapped a new intelligence report on the table.

"We have satellite confirmation of increased naval activity in the South China Sea. Beijing knows we're overcommitted, and they're taking notes."

Chief of Naval Operations Admiral John Raines cleared his throat, his voice grave.

"I can confirm that assessment." He adjusted the digital map, pulling up the Pacific theater.

The screen filled with blinking red markers — Chinese warships in the Taiwan Strait.

Admiral Raines exhaled. "Twenty years ago, the U.S. Navy outgunned China ten to one. Today? They have more surface combatants than we do. And they aren't stopping. If they decide to take Taiwan, we'll be playing catch-up in our own backyard."

Senator Ridge scoffed, shaking his head.

"You're all looking at this backward."

He stood, placing both hands on the table, looming over the policymakers.

"Russia is watching. They know if we start pulling back, NATO will fracture. And if NATO fractures, they roll into the Baltics next. We're not preventing war by debating this. We're inviting it."

His gaze locked onto Killian. "You think withdrawing means we avoid a two-front war? You're wrong. You pull out of NATO, you don't get one war. You get two."

The room tensed.

Vice President Marshall exchanged a glance with Monroe.

Killian said nothing.

Ridge pressed forward.

"Moscow will see it as weakness. Putin saw it in 2008 when

he took Georgia. He saw it in 2014 when he took Crimea. And if you think he won't see it now, you're a fool."

Silence.

Then Ridge turned to Raines.

"Admiral, you just told us China has the biggest navy in the world. But do they have the experience?"

Raines hesitated.

Ridge slammed his fist down again.

"No. They don't. You know who does? The United States Navy."

His voice rose, sharp with conviction.

"We are the only reason the world order still exists. We are the only reason Moscow hasn't sent tanks rolling into Estonia. You walk away from NATO, and you give them a green light."

He took a deep breath, then looked Killian dead in the eye.

"Mr. President, you want to protect American interests? Then you don't just keep us in NATO. You make damn sure NATO knows the United States is its spine."

President Killian exhaled slowly, folding his hands.

For a long moment, he didn't speak.

The room watched, waiting.

Killian's gaze drifted back to the live battlefield footage of Moldova, where NATO tanks were still rolling through the ruins of the Russian counteroffensive.

Killian studied the battle footage on the screen.

On the tactical map, the last remnants of the 4th Guards Tank Brigade collapsed under NATO's final assault.

Collier's voice came through over the command net.

"Thunderstrike, engage."

The final Russian T-90M erupted in flames.

His voice, when it came, was quiet.

"I want a full classified report on what an American NATO withdrawal would look like. I want the numbers. I want the consequences. I want to know what happens next."

The room stayed dead still.

Senator Ridge's jaw tensed, his fists tightening.

But he said nothing.

Killian glanced at Monroe.

"At the same time, I want a real-world analysis of our China-Pacific readiness. No Pentagon PR bullshit. I want the truth."

His gaze swept the room.

"Because I'm going to make a decision very soon."

The silence became deafening.

Steve came to, bound to a chair, looking at Anya having dinner with Markov, in the general's room. Feelings of rage and betrayal flow through his veins as he clenched his fists.

Markov watched him, waiting for a reaction.

Anya said nothing. A subtle nod lent to deeper confusion.

Outside, the city hummed on.

Markov swirled his glass. "Funny thing about war, Wotjek. NATO thinks it's winning. They know nothing of what comes next."

Steve didn't respond.

Because he couldn't. One look at Anya and Steve was defeated.

"Double-crossed. Alone." His heart pounded while also thinking, "Where are you, Collier?"

The convoy of black Mercedes-Benz tactical vehicles tore through the German-Austrian border, their headlights flashing a warning to other drivers. Inside the Vito command van, Oberstleutnant Lukas Heidenreich gripped the steering wheel, his gloved fingers steady despite the speedometer needle hovering at 190 km/h (118 mph).

The modified Mercedes-Benz fleet had been stripped down and rebuilt for war. GSG9 chose speed and firepower for their shock and awe.

The Vito Command & Extraction Vehicle leading the convoy has a 4.0L Biturbo V8 engine, tuned for 700 horsepower; run-flat tires capable of absorbing 9mm and 7.62mm small-arms fire; and a custom suspension to maintain stability at extreme speeds.

The Brembo performance brakes are to handle emergency

stops in live-fire situations.

But rarely used.

The Mercedes G-Class Interceptor Vehicles boasted a 5.5L AMG-tuned V8, supercharged to 730 horsepower.

The custom bulletproof armor without excessive weight, allowing full pursuit speeds.

In front, reinforced push bars for high-speed ramming with thermal and infrared sensors installed into the front grille to detect ambushes.

Each driver knew the mission parameters.

This wasn't a high-speed police pursuit.

It was a combat insertion at over 220 km/h.

"ETA to Budapest?" Heidenreich called out.

"Five hours at normal speed, but we're not doing normal."

The G-Class in the rear radioed in.

"If we hold 220 kilometers per hour, we reach Vienna in 1 hour 20 minutes. That puts us in Budapest by 3 hours, max."

A deep breath. Then Heidenreich gave the order.

"Push it. Everything you've got."

They reached the Autobahn — No Speed Limits, No Room for Error.

The convoy unleashed its full power.

The turbos screamed under full boost.

Tires gripped the road like talons, hugging curves at breakneck angles.

Suspensions flexed under the stress of long-range sprinting, keeping the vehicles stable.

The GSG 9 operators inside barely moved despite the sheer velocity — they were strapped into custom-molded seats, their tactical vests compressed against the harnesses.

200 km/h. 210. 220.

The Austrian border passed in a blur.

"Vienna in fifty minutes."

A moment of silence.

Then the radio crackled.

"Correction — Vienna in thirty-five."

Traffic Evacuates on Sight

Local law enforcement had already been notified.

Every civilian car veered off the road as the black GSG 9 column roared past, blue lights flashing.

On the highway message boards, drivers saw the alerts:

HIGH-SPEED MILITARY CONVOY —
DO NOT BLOCK ROADWAY

They moved aside instinctively.

Exactly 1 hour 35 minutes after leaving Passau, the GSG 9 convoy blew past Vienna's outer ring road.

"Halfway."

Three more hours cut down to ninety minutes.

Inside the lead Vito, Heidenreich pressed his tactical earpiece.

"Davy, we're past Vienna. We've cut the clock down. We'll

be in Budapest in 90 minutes. Tell your guy to hold on."

Jasper's voice came through, tight. "Susi doesn't know we're coming."

Heidenreich shifted gears, pressing the accelerator further.

"Then let's make sure he finds out before it's too late."

The engine howled, the G-Class growling like a pack of wolves chasing their prey.

They had already cut the impossible journey in half.

The SAS unit was taxiing down the runway. Estimated time to drop zone: 95 minutes.

Kicked Me When I Was Down

Casteau, Belgium — Supreme Headquarters Allied Powers Europe

Jasper Van Dijk paced inside the darkened command center of The Flying Dutchman, his eyes locked onto multiple monitors. The situation was deteriorating fast. NATO's diplomatic corps was still untangling the political fallout, but Jasper had no patience for bureaucracy.

Steve Johnson was missing.

A secure line was already open. Emil Kovács — Cypher — was on the other end, working his magic from his underground bunker, his fingers flying across multiple keyboards.

"You're sure his phone was activated?" Jasper pressed.

"Ja, I'm sure," Cypher muttered, his Slovakian accent thick with annoyance. "Steve's satellite phone doesn't have accurate tracking, but the secure SIM that I gave him — that's another story."

Jasper inhaled sharply, knowing what was coming next.

"I cracked the GRU network again," Cypher continued. "They're scrambling all over the city, looking for their own leaks. But our boy? He's locked in a heavily secured building, and — you're gonna love this — guess where?"

The screen refreshed, a red dot pulsing on Budapest's inner ring road, just outside the central district.

"The Széchenyi Imperial, coincidentally, across from the Aranykor Palace Hotel and only a few miles from the United States Embassy," Jasper whispered.

Cypher's voice was smug. "They chose a location near the Americans. Bastards are predictable. My 3D model shows the phone is in the main room of the three-bedroom Presidential Suite, top floor, west wing, center, Erzsébet Krt." Cypher whistled. "€ 4,750 a night."

Jasper wasted no time. He patched the coordinates on his encrypted NATO ops channel.

"Get this to GSG9 and SAS," he ordered. "This is going down now."

Major Tom Richards of 22nd Special Air Service Regiment (SAS) crouched on the open cargo ramp of a German CH-53 Sea Stallion, feeling the wind whip against his face, preparing to lift off again. His team — eight of the most elite special forces operators in the world — were prepped for HALO insertion.

"Markov's HQ is on the upper floors, west wing center," Richards shouted over the comms. "The Night Stalkers are guarding it. We neutralize the hostiles, get the elevators and stairwells under our control. GSG9 will move from the ground up. Once they have our package, we extract."

"No room for error," Sergeant Callum Fraser muttered, locking his HK416 against his chest.

"Wouldn't be fun otherwise," Richards smirked.

The jump light turned green.

The SAS team stepped into the night.

Their HALO parachutes deployed flawlessly, guiding them onto the neighboring rooftop adjacent to the Széchenyi Imperial. Their landing was silent, precise, lethal.

The mission was on.

GSG9's vehicles that had roared through Vienna's outer ring, moving at breakneck speed, were cresting the hills outside Budapest.

The lead vehicle — a highly modified Mercedes G-Wagon, packed with operators in full tactical kit — took point.

Adjutant Sebastian Krüger, the team operations, flicked through the data feed as van Dijk's coordinates locked onto their in-vehicle HUD.

"Thirty seconds out," the team leader Oberstleutnant Lukas Heidenreich announced.

"Hit them hard and fast," Krüger commanded. "We go for

the package first. The SAS will clear our way."

Their convoy screeched to a halt just outside the hotel's underground parking entrance.

Two blacked-out SUVs sat idling. GRU security. The guards barely had time to react before suppressed fire cut them down where they stood.

Krüger led his team forward, moving like a shadow. The elevators were disabled. They'd have to breach and clear every floor up to the top.

They were more than ready.

Steve's head throbbed as he blinked back to consciousness, his vision slowly sharpening. The room was cold, dimly lit, and smelled faintly of vodka and cigarettes. He was bound to a heavy chair, his wrists aching from the tight cords.

Across the room, Anya sat at a table with General Markov, her back straight, her demeanor as poised as ever.

They were still eating dinner, an intimate scene painted against the backdrop of treachery. Steve's satellite phone was on the table, between them.

"Is he awake?" Markov asked casually, his gaze flicking toward Steve without much interest.

Anya stood gracefully, her expression hardening as she approached him.

Without warning, she slapped Steve's face so hard that his head snapped to the side, and the force sent him and the chair crashing to the ground.

Pain flared through his cheek and ribs as he struggled to catch his breath.

"Pick him up," she ordered the guards coldly.

The two men stepped forward, setting Steve and the chair upright. Before he could fully regain his bearings, Anya drove her boot into his midriff.

The air left his lungs in a sharp gasp, and he doubled over as much as the restraints allowed.

"You should've stayed in America, Stefan Ivanovich" she hissed, her voice trembling with barely restrained fury.

She leaned down, her face close to his, her eyes blazing. "But no, you had to chase some art curator in St. Petersburg, didn't you? You used me, Steve. I believed in you. I —"

Her voice cracked, and she stood, turning away to collect herself.

Markov chuckled from the table, pouring himself another drink. "So much passion, Major. It's almost admirable."

Anya whirled back to Steve, her composure fraying. "Do you know what you did to me? You broke my heart, you traitor! And now, you'll pay for it. My face will be the last thing you see."

Her voice softened, dangerously tender. "But I'll make it quick. One last kiss before I end it."

She leaned in, her lips brushing his lightly, mockingly. The gesture was chilling, filled with a cruel intimacy.

She straightened and turned back to Markov, her mask of professionalism slipping back into place.

Markov laughed again, standing from the table. "Enough theatrics, Major. Let's finish this."

He moved to the secure briefcase on the side table. It appeared to be an unassuming matte black case with a textured surface to prevent slipping.

Steve noted its edges are reinforced with titanium alloy, and it features a biometric lock screen in the center, glowing faintly green.

Markov placed both thumbs on the screen. The latches popped open to reveal a recessed screen sitting at the center, flanked by a retinal reader.

Markov looks in the reader and a cyrillic keyboard appears on the screen.

Steve's stomach sank as Markov began the sequence, his fingers flying across the keypad punching in his code.

He waited. The system ready light flashed.

Anya stood beside him, her presence as cold as the vodka she poured into a crystal glass.

"You'll be remembered as the man who reshaped Russia's destiny," she said, her voice smooth, calm, unwavering.

Markov exhaled, his breath shallow. "History is written by the victors, Anya."

She smiled, but it didn't reach her eyes.

"You should give the order."

Markov inhaled deeply, then pressed the command key. The encrypted signal flashed on the screen — missile launch protocol activated.

Markov pushed the button. He waited.

And waited

Nothing.

The screen flashed green, then red, displaying the words "Launch Incomplete."

The room remained eerily silent, except for the faint hum of electronic static.

The GRU officers around the table looked at each other, confusion turning into dread.

Markov's face darkened. He turned to Anya, his voice low, dangerous.

"What have you done?"

Anya tilted her head slightly, the weight of her deception settling in with practiced ease.

"Your missiles no longer exist, General," she said, in English this time. "Your nuclear capability was destroyed before you even knew it. NATO saw to that."

Markov's nostrils flared, rage boiling beneath his skin. "Impossible. I would have known — "

"NATO kept the electronic jamming up, isolating you. You were blind. You still are." Anya stepped closer, her voice softer, deadlier.

The realization hit Markov like a gut punch. His empire, his grand plan — nothing more than a mirage.

Anya turned toward the stunned officers in the war room and raised her voice in Russian.

"General Markov, you are under arrest for war crimes against the Russian Federation."

Major Richards' team stacked up against the rooftop access door. Fraser planted a small breaching charge, giving Richards a nod.

"On three," Richards whispered. "One... two... three —"

The charge detonated with a muffled thump, and the SAS operators rushed in like phantoms.

The first Night Stalker sentry barely turned his head before Fraser's suppressed rifle spat a single round into his skull.

They moved fast — room by room, clearing threats in quick succession.

One Night Stalker fought back, managing to fire a burst from his AK-12, but Richards snapped his Glock 19 into position and dropped him with two rounds to the chest.

The rooftop was secured in ninety seconds.

Now they controlled the high ground.

The firefight inside the Széchenyi Imperial's stairwell was pure chaos.

GSG9 operators moved floor by floor, their MP7s barking in rapid succession as they engaged heavily armed GRU operatives.

A Night Stalker lobbed a grenade down the stairwell, giving Heidenreich barely time to react — he shoved his point man aside, grabbing the grenade midair, hurling it back up.

Boom!

The explosion rocked the upper floors, raining debris down the stairwell.

Krüger grimaced. "Move faster."

The team pressed forward, relentless.

Inside the hotel war room, Markov was still frozen in disbelief. Steve hung in the chair, barely conscious, his head lolling forward, blood dripping from his split lip. He heard the words, but they were distant, a muffled echo in a world drowning in pain.

Then — gunfire. Close. Controlled.

Steve blinked hard, forcing his vision to focus. He caught the briefest flash of movement through the crack in the steel door — a silhouette, weapon raised.

SAS.

Then the explosion hit.

A shaped charge blew the hinges off, the door slamming inward as smoke filled the hallway. A single grenade bounced inside — flashbang.

Boom!

The detonation shook the room, disorienting the guards. Before they could react, black-clad operators stormed in. GSG9 — clean, methodical, lethal.

"Contact front!" one of the GRU guards shouted, raising his weapon.

Too late.

Three rounds from a suppressed MP7 stitched his chest, sending him crumpling backward. Another GRU operator tried to retreat, only to be cut down by the SAS team clearing the corridor.

The fight was brutal. The Night Stalkers, elite assassins, fought viciously, knowing this was their last stand. GSG9's precision met Russian brutality in a battle of sheer skill and endurance.

The hallway turned into a kill zone — short bursts of fire, grenades, close-quarters combat with knives and pistols. Steve's restraints were cut. He coughed, sucked in air, and looked up to see a black-clad operator standing over him.

"Time to go, Herr Johnson," the GSG9 operator said, handing him a pistol. "You still in the fight?"

Steve grinned through the blood on his teeth. "Wouldn't miss it."

Anya smiled coldly as she removed the last of his restraints. "I never betrayed you Steve," she whispered. "I used you to get to him."

Steve, now unchained, glanced at her with a reassuring smile and moved fast, lunging to tackle Markov to the floor as the first gunshots echoed from the stairwell.

Some GRU guards had recovered — but Steve was already grabbing the sidearm from Markov's holster.

Two shots — center mass.

The first GRU officer crumpled.

Anya spun, snatching a pistol from a fallen guard.

She and Steve moved back-to-back, firing as GRU reinforcements stormed in.

Suddenly — the door burst open.

Krüger and his GSG9 team also poured in, weapons raised.

"Clear!" Krüger shouted.

Steve exhaled heavily, lowering his gun.

A GSG9 operative secured Markov, zip-tying his wrists. "You're under arrest for war crimes against the EU."

Major Anya Kuznetsova protested. "Oberstleutnant, he has been arrested by the GRU. The Main Directorate of the General Staff of the Armed Forces of the Russian Federation has charged General Markov for war crimes, over 250 million counts of attempted murder..."

"Ja. But the GRU has no jurisdiction here. GSG9 has the power to arrest throughout the European Union." Oberstleutnant Lukas Heidenreich and his team continued to extract General Markov.

Anya smirked. "Looks like you lost, General."

As the extraction team led Markov out into the cool night, Steve felt the weight of the moment settle over him. Whatever came next, it would be written in the shadows of betrayal, sacrifice, and hard choices.

They watched Markov be driven away. Steve glanced at her. "You never stopped loving me, huh?"

She didn't answer, but the faintest hint of a smile played on her lips.

The air in the NATO command center was thick with anticipation. Sentinel stood at the center of the briefing room, flanked by high-ranking officers and intelligence officials. The war had effectively ended, but the formalities of peace required a strong hand.

"The European Union President and the President of the United States have agreed," Sentinel announced. "General Collier, you will represent NATO in the Moscow negotiations. You will accept the treaty on behalf of NATO, Supreme Headquarters, and myself."

Silence followed.

Collier exhaled. He had led armies into battle. He had won wars. But diplomacy?

"Understood," Collier finally said. "Let's finish this."

Live from Brussels, Sentinel's voice echoed across the world.

"This conflict has cost too much — too many lives lost, too many nations scarred. But as of this moment, hostilities will cease. NATO forces will hold their positions. Russian forces will do the same. A diplomatic agreement will be finalized in Moscow. And let me be clear — this treaty is not a suggestion. It is the cost of war."

The message played across every major network. Moscow, Washington, London, Berlin, Paris, Beijing.

The war was over.

Now, Collier would go to Moscow to make it official.

The jet engines of Overlord 1 were still turning as Collier exited, only to go to the steps of a NATO command C-21A Learjet.

It hummed as it waited to taxi on the Romanian tarmac. Lt. Colonel Rebecca Carter and Lt. Colonel James Pembroke stood at the air stairs, waiting.

A second aircraft — a Hungarian Gripen NG — circled above, its sleek delta wings slicing through the early morning sky.

Inside the cockpit, Captain Árpád "Villám" Tóth grinned, rolling inverted as he throttled past the speed of sound. His radio crackled.

"Adjudant-Onderofficier van Dijk, you good back there?"

Jasper van Dijk, strapped into the Gripen's backseat, clenched the harness tightly. "Flying Mach 2 was not on my to-do list."

Villám laughed. "I take that as a compliment! No offense, but General Collier was much more fun to fly with."

Below, exchanged a crisp salute with Carter and Pembroke.

"Lieutenant Colonel Carter. Lieutenant Colonel Pembroke," Collier greeted. "Report."

Carter nodded, eyes sharp. "All NATO forces are maintaining positions. GSG9 completed Markov's extradition. Sentinel's ceasefire held."

Pembroke added, "It's all down to diplomacy now."

A whoosh overhead made Carter flinch. Villám's Gripen came in for landing. Van Dijk stumbled out of the cockpit, his face pale.

"I'd rather be in a firefight," he muttered.

Collier chuckled before turning back to Villám, who had already removed his flight helmet.

"Captain," Collier said, "I want you to command our escort fighter squadron. There will be one fighter from each NATO nation. You'll fly lead."

Villám's grin widened. "Consider it done, General."

A formation of NATO's finest jets taxied onto the runway beside the C-21.

A pair of JAS 39 Gripen NG flown by pilots of Hungary

and Sweden were first in line. Germany and Italy in a pair of Typhoons; F-35As from Norway and Netherlands; Hornets from Canada and Spain; a French Rafale and Polish F-16 rounded out the squadron.

Flying vanguard were an F-22 Raptor flying wingman for an RAF F-35A.

Collier sat in the luxurious command seat aboard the C-21, his fingers steepled. Carter, in a nearby chair, tightened her harness.

"I don't like being airborne," she muttered.

Pembroke smirked from his comfortable leather seat. "Personally, I could get used to this."

Carter shot him a look. "Easy for you to say. I feel vulnerable as hell up here."

"You are vulnerable," Villám's voice cut in over the radio. "That's why we're here."

The formation took off, climbing in a wide arc over Romania.

Van Dijk watched the impressive takeoff of their NATO escort.

As the NATO formation pushed toward Moscow, sensors lit up across every cockpit.

Russian Sukhoi Su-35S Flanker-E fighters — four of them — raced to intercept.

Collier's comms crackled. Villám's voice was calm, but firm.

"General, we have a Russian fighter patrol approaching. Callsigns unknown. They are holding formation but making radar sweeps on our flight."

Carter stiffened. "And?"

"They're shadowing us," Villám said. "I have a radar lock ready if needed."

Pembroke laughed. "Diplomacy, right?"

Villám ignored him, addressing his NATO pilots.

"All escorts — stay in tight formation. No aggressive moves. If the Russians make a mistake, we hold air superiority."

The Su-35s drifted closer, maintaining a 200-meter distance from the escort squadron.

A tense minute passed.

Then, the Russian leader's voice crackled over the radio.

"This is Russian Air Force escort flight. We will guide you to Moscow. Any deviation from course will be seen as hostile."

Villám clicked his mic.

"This is NATO Escort Squadron, call sign Iron Falcons. We're bringing our General in to accept your surrender."

Silence.

Then, the Russian pilot's voice returned.

"Understood. Maintain formation."

Collier exhaled. The last hurdle was cleared.

Now, he just had to end the war for good.

***

Russia's president sat at the grand table of the Kremlin, his expression blank, his advisors shifting uncomfortably in their seats.

Across from him, General Nathan "Titan" Collier, flanked by Lt. Colonel Rebecca Carter and Lt. Colonel James Pembroke, sat like war gods descending upon the ruined empire.

Sentinel's ceasefire had been received. Russia had no options left.

Collier leaned forward. "The conditions are non-negotiable."

The President exhaled sharply. "A full withdrawal from Ukraine, including Crimea?"

Collier nodded. "Plus repatriations."

President Andrei Pavlovich stared at the delegates. "Russia does not have that in reserve. We will not become a Weimar Republic or be bullied. This was a rogue General, with his agents."

"We understand," Collier paused for a drink of water. He did not relish what he must say next. "President Pavlovich, you ordered the invasion of Ukraine. Personally. You are also the duly elected leader of your nation."

Collier leaned in, "Everything in Russia that happens, or fails to happen, is your responsibility."

"We will not be bankrupted. We have until the trial ends to establish these were crimes." President Pavlovich was reaching, trying to buy time.

Pavlovich needed more time before his country would be

on the brink of financial ruin. "We are also arresting all agents associated with the Perun Initiative. We will turn them over to be tried as war criminals. Until judgment is passed, we will not be required to make repatriations."

Jasper van Dijk, sitting quietly at the table, finally spoke.

"We know where the money is," he said coolly. "We have frozen billions in cryptocurrency. Money siphoned through your own oligarchs."

The President's jaw clenched. Collier spun in his chair. Both were equally stunned.

Jasper smiled. "You can argue about war reparations, or you can take the gift we're offering and make General Markov's war chest pay it all back."

Silence. Lieutenant Colonel Pembroke spoke up, "There are also the matters of the recognition of Moldova' and Ukraine's sovereignty; security agreements to provide a divided defense of Ukraine and Moldova, as Germany had been divided after World War II. We propose Russia and Belarus have the northern 1/3rd; NATO the southern 1/3rd to include Moldova; and the remaining 1/3rd as a demilitarized neutral zone."

Lieutenant Colonel Carter added, "These are for defense purposes only. Not for acquisition or administration. We will not have a repeat of the iron curtain. Ukraine and Moldova will be allowed to rebuild in peace, as sovereign nations."

Then, the President exhaled and nodded.

"There will be... a unilateral nuclear disarmament of all

mobile launch platforms," he said finally. "To prevent this from ever happening again. It is my only demand."

Van Dijk whispered to Collier, "Don't forget Susi."

Collier smiled for the first time in days. "One last thing. We need immediate border reopening and resumption of travel between all nations."

"I understand that the resumption of trade and travel is a priority, but I do not understand why this is an immediate requirement. But of course, the moment we have wet signatures, travel can resume." The President looked puzzled, but was very agreeable.

Collier stood. "Then we're done here."

They shook hands, agreeing to meet back tomorrow at noon to sign the formal treaty.

Markov's arraignment will occur in The Hague at the same time.

The Hague tribunal had been a formality. Markov refused to speak. Refused to plead. Now, he was being transported to the maximum-security prison where he would spend the rest of his life. Or so he thought.

The convoy moved through the misty back roads outside The Hague, security tight, armored vehicles at every turn. But not tight enough.

A single explosion — precision-placed — sent the lead vehicle careening into a ditch. The second armored car skidded, tires shredding as Russian Spetsnaz operatives swarmed the convoy.

Markov, yanked from the vehicle, stumbled in confusion as his supposed rescuers moved swiftly, neutralizing NATO guards with suppressed shots.

Then a man stepped forward.

A Spetsnaz lieutenant, his uniform immaculate despite the blood splattered across his gloves.

Markov's eyes widened as he recognized the name tag: *Petrov.*

The lieutenant leaned in, his voice barely above a whisper.

"For my uncle, Colonel Ivan Petrov," he murmured, his breath hot against Markov's ear. "And for Russia."

The blade was swift, slicing through Markov's throat in a single practiced motion.

Blood gurgled, Markov's hands clutching his own neck, gasping as his body betrayed him.

The last thing he saw was Petrov's cold, expressionless stare.

As the convoy burned behind them, the Spetsnaz team faded into the darkness.

Markov was dead.

Russia had closed its own chapter.

The sun hung low in the sky, casting a golden haze over the countryside as Steve leaned against the hood of his 1971 Pontiac GTO. The war was over. For now. But that didn't mean his fight was.

His satellite phone vibrated in his pocket.

Collier's voice came through, relaxed but firm.

"Hey buddy, great news. How fast can you get to the border?"

Steve frowned, rubbing his temples. "Which border?"

"Latvia. The moment we sign, travel resumes. There's a certain lady in St. Petersburg who is dying to hug you. Give her an extra hug from Uncle Nate."

Steve's breath caught. Katya.

"That's a 24-hour drive," he muttered, glancing at the GTO.

Collier chuckled. "Why are you still talking to me? Make dinner reservations at that little restaurant you love. Jasper said 'It's on the Flying Dutchman,' whatever that means."

Steve sighed, shaking his head. "You're probably going to find out sooner than you want to."

The line went dead. Time to move.

The Pontiac's engine roared to life, its deep growl a sound of defiance against the quiet European roads.

Steve downshifted, peeling onto the highway, the speedometer creeping past 180 kilometers per hour.

Crossing into Poland was nostalgic for Steve. The vast fields, old Soviet-era roadside markers, and villages blurred past. He remembered the days of ripping across the farmers' fields in late fall, his Abrams helping to till the fields for spring.

The Polish farmers enjoyed the nice check from NATO, helping them get through the winter and the holidays.

Steve had to stop at a gas station in Lithuania. The bored attendant gave him an odd look as he paid in cash.

A gentleman was sitting in a parked car, facing the highway.

A GRU tail? Or just paranoia? Steve had been in fight or flight mode for too long.

The early morning sun was coming through the windshield. It felt great to be heading east again. Steve tuned in the 24 hour news radio channel.

" ... will never answer for the genocide of 2.5 million Moldovans, money laundering, the assassination of hundreds of FSB and ministry officials, inciting a war with Ukraine and other charges. Witnesses believed it was a Russian special operations rescue mission, but the late Russian General Markov was found with his throat sliced open, with surgical precision. No traces have been found of who they were, and there were no other casualties. Two German prisoner escort officers are hospitalized, but in stable condition."

The reports started to buzz about the ceasefire. The journalists were speculating what the terms of the treaty would be.

"Russia has formally signed the treaty and a withdrawal

agreement. NATO announces travel and trade are immediately reestablished."

Steve's thoughts took over as the road opened in front of him. "Was it really over? Could he actually go back to Katya and be something more than a ghost in the shadows? Would the GRU or FSB stop him?"

Night fell over the Baltic forests as he neared the border. One more stretch.

The border control checkpoint with Russia loomed ahead — dim floodlights illuminating the worn concrete barriers.

The line of cars was short. Most travelers were still waiting to see if the ceasefire would hold.

Steve eased the GTO to a stop at the inspection point. A GRU officer in a black uniform stepped forward, his cold eyes scanning Steve's face before glancing at the documents.

The officer studied the papers for an uncomfortably long time, before returning to his vehicle with Steve following him.

As they approached, from the cheap speakers of the Lada, a familiar guitar riff kicked in, followed by the unmistakable pulse of KISS's *"I Was Made for Lovin' You."*

Steve smirked. "Seriously? Didn't peg you for a disco rock guy."

The GRU agent didn't respond. He was a professional — unflappable, unreadable — but Steve caught the tiniest flicker of discomfort.

Steve nodded to the beat, tapping his fingers against the armrest. "You know, Paul Stanley recorded this in one take.

The guy just walked into the studio and nailed it. No warm-ups, no do-overs. Some people just have it."

Still, silence.

Steve turned his head slightly, watching the driver. "You one of those guys who pretends to hate Western music but secretly loves it?"

The agent exhaled through his nose. "It was on the radio."

The agent scowled but said nothing more to Steve. He made a radio call from his Lada, speaking quickly in Russian.

Steve waited. That was the thing about music — it had a way of twisting a moment into something absurd, humanizing even the most rigid situations.

The guitar solo kicked in, and Steve did a little air-drumming on his knee.

The agent turned the volume down.

Steve just laughed.

A tense pause as he ended the call and deliberately walked back over slowly.

Finally, he leaned in through the window.

"You're clear. But Colonel Kuznetsova has provided you with an escort to St. Petersburg."

Steve exhaled. "Colonel? An escort?"

The officer smirked. "She also said to tell you..."

A pause. Then, the words came with dry amusement:

"She's too skinny."

Steve chuckled, shaking his head. Same old Anya. He never stopped loving her, either.

But it was a different love.

As the barrier lifted, he accelerated forward, the black Lada pulling in front of him, emergency lights clearing the way as they reached 190 kmh.

The black Lada was holding a steady speed on the Russian highway.

Steve exhaled, gripping the wheel of his GTO, his knuckles flexing against the leather.

The old V8 rumbled beneath him, each throaty growl bringing him closer to something he hadn't let himself feel in too long.

He scrolled through his playlist. The GRU agent did actually have good taste in music. A familiar guitar riff came through the speakers.

Steve smirked. KISS. He hadn't thought much of it when it was playing in the Lada, but now? It hit differently.

Ahead, St. Petersburg awaited.

And so did Katya.

The evening air in St. Petersburg carried the last remnants of summer, warm yet with the faintest hint of the autumn chill that would soon claim the city.

The streetlights blinked on, sending a golden hue over the cobblestone plaza as Steve walked slowly toward the apartment

Katya shared with her father.

The war was over. The chaos of the past few years had finally quieted. But his heart pounded harder now than it had on any battlefield.

But this was Katya, not war.

Halfway across the plaza, a small flower stand caught his eye. An elderly woman, bundled in layers despite the warmth, carefully arranged fresh bouquets on a wooden crate.

Her silver hair peeked out from beneath a scarf, her sharp eyes observing the world with quiet wisdom.

Steve paused, inhaling the scent of freshly cut roses.

"Good evening, Babushka," he greeted in fluent Russian, his accent still carrying the weight of his years abroad.

The old woman peered up at him, her gaze lingering for a moment too long, as if she already knew who he was.

"Ah," she smiled knowingly, "you are bringing flowers to a woman you love."

Steve chuckled. "Am I that obvious?"

She waved a wrinkled hand dismissively. "Only a fool returns from war without bringing flowers."

Steve selected a bouquet — white lilies mixed with deep red roses. As he handed over the rubles, the old woman gently patted his hand.

"Take care of her," she said softly. "Some men fight wars. Others fight for love. The second battle is harder."

Steve nodded, tucking the words away like a lesson meant just for him.

He walked on, grabbing a bottle of fine Georgian red wine and two cigars from a nearby shop.

Tonight wasn't just about him and Katya — he would share a drink and smoke a cigar with Sergey, the man who raised her.

The wind carried the scent of the Neva River, its coolness brushing against Steve's face as he stood before the heavy wooden door. Katya's apartment.

His fingers hovered over the buzzer. Just press it.

But his hand trembled.

Not out of fear — he had faced death more times than he could count. But this? This was different.

What if she changed? What if I changed?

What if she resents me for being gone?

What if she found someone else?

That last thought cut the deepest.

His mind raced back to St. Petersburg, years ago.

Her voice in the morning, teasing him in French.

Her laughter as she stole his hat, dancing through the rain.

The way she held him, whispering secrets meant for no one else.

And then — the silence that followed.

The letters he didn't send. The calls he didn't make.

Not because he didn't love her.

But because loving her meant putting her in danger.

Still, he had to know.

He exhaled, a single, shaky breath.

Then, he pressed the buzzer.

A few seconds passed. Then, footsteps.

The sound of a lock turning.

The door creaked open.

And there she was.

Katya.

She was exactly as he remembered and yet completely different.

Her hair was slightly shorter, loose curls falling past her shoulders.

Her green eyes — those impossibly deep eyes — searched his face, wide with disbelief.

She wasn't wearing makeup, but she was still the most beautiful woman he had ever seen.

Steve opened his mouth — but nothing came out.

Then — her lip quivered.

"Steve," she whispered, voice cracking.

That was it.

She threw herself at him, arms wrapping around his neck, holding him so tight it hurt.

Steve gasped — not from pain, but from the overwhelming flood of emotion that crushed him all at once.

Every moment of loneliness.

Every sleepless night wondering if she was safe.

Every doubt that he would ever see her again.

It all broke.

He crushed her against him, arms locked around her as if letting go would kill him.

She sobbed into his chest, fingers gripping his jacket like she was afraid he'd disappear again.

And then she pulled back just enough to look at him.

She touched his face – her thumb brushing the scar above his brow.

"You're really here?" she whispered.

Steve didn't trust his voice.

So, he kissed her.

It was deep, desperate, and full of a particular hunger Steve never knew before.

A kiss that wasn't just love, but years of longing, regret, and pain — melted away in an instant.

She kissed him back just as fiercely, like she had been holding her breath all this time, waiting for him to come home.

Steve felt something warm slide down his cheek.

Tears.

His own. Surprisingly.

She pulled away, resting her forehead against his.

"I thought I lost you," she whispered, her breath shaky.

Steve swallowed the lump in his throat.

"No," he rasped. "You were the only thing that kept me alive."

He held her tightly, breathing in her scent, feeling warmth in a way he hadn't in years.

They kissed — deeply, desperately — the kind of kiss that erased distance and time.

Behind them, a deep voice rumbled.

"Are you going to keep her in the hallway all night, or can an old man get a hug too?"

Steve pulled back, grinning. Sergey stood at the threshold, arms crossed, his gruff face softened by emotion.

Steve stepped forward and hugged the old tank commander, feeling a weight lift from his shoulders. "It's good to see you, Sergey."

Sergey patted him on the back, his voice thick with approval. "About damn time, son."

The small restaurant glowed with candlelight, tucked into a quiet street corner where Steve and Katya had shared many evenings before. The food was warm, the wine smooth, and for the first time in years, Steve felt like he was home.

As they finished their meal, his sat phone vibrated once.

He pulled it out — nothing. No message.

Before he could dwell on it, a courier entered the restaurant, his eyes scanning the room. Spotting Steve, he approached with a small, unmarked box in hand.

"Delivery for you."

Steve exchanged a glance with Katya before taking it, setting it on the table. It was heavier than expected.

Carefully, he lifted the lid.

Inside, two small jewelry boxes and a single envelope.

Steve picked up the note first, recognizing the careful yet informal handwriting.

"*The square box is for you. Compliments of Cypher.*"

Steve smirked, opening it to find a pair of gold cufflinks.

"Of course," he muttered. "Tracking device. Probably a listening bug too."

Katya raised an eyebrow. "Why are you smiling like this?"

"Because it means someone cares."

He turned back to the letter.

"*The other box... well, it's not for you. It's time to stop being the Lone Wolf. Hand it to Katya before you read any further.*"

Steve hesitated for only a second. Then, he handed her the second box.

Katya blinked, her hands trembling slightly as she lifted the lid.

Inside, a beautifully sculpted 2-carat diamond ring gleamed in the dim light.

Her breath caught, eyes filling with fresh tears as she looked back at Steve.

"Steve —" Her voice broke.

He barely had time to react before she launched herself into his arms, kissing him fiercely.

Through her tears, she blurted out, "Da, ya lyublyu!" (Yes. I love you!)

Steve just held her tighter, letting the moment wash over him.

Then, he looked back at the letter, grinning.

"Someone had to ask her for you. Don't waste any time. Your flight leaves in 10 days for an all-expenses-paid honeymoon in the Cayman Islands. You earned it."

Signed, The Crew of The Flying Dutchman.

Steve laughed, shaking his head.

"Jasper," he muttered. "You magnificent bastard."

Katya wiped her tears, still overwhelmed. "What is it?"

Steve smirked, folding the letter and tucking it away.

"Just a reminder that I don't work alone anymore."

She cupped his face. "You never did. You just had to find your way home."

Steve kissed her again, knowing she was right.

For the first time in years, he wasn't running. He was home.

Where Do We Go From Here

Grand Cayman, Cayman Islands — Smith Barcadere

Steve Johnson was a man who had learned to cherish his rare moments of peace. The Caribbean sun painted the sky in warm hues, and the sound of the gentle waves at Smith Barcadere made it easy to forget the weight of the world.

The water wrapped around them like glass warmed by the sun. Katya swam ahead, arms cutting clean through the shallows. Beyond the reef, waves broke gently — more rhythm than force.

She turned, hair slicked back, laughing as two boys scrambled up the rocks again, daring each other to jump.

"They're braver than you," she called.

Steve raised a brow. "They're ten."

"Then you've got no excuse." She winked, dove, and disappeared beneath the surface.

Steve stepped forward, letting the warm water rise to his

waist. A moment later, she emerged beside him, blinking water from her lashes, face lit with delight.

"I saw a barracuda. Long as my arm. He looked bored."

"You weren't wearing jewelry, were you?"

"Just my smile," she said, sticking her tongue at Steve. "That's all I need to wear."

She floated beside him, watching the reef. A thin cloud passed over the sun, then cleared. The cove brightened again, light bending through the water like silk.

"I'd like to learn to dive," she said. "Not tourist-dive. Really dive. Past the reefs. Into the blue."

Steve studied her expression. "You sure?"

She nodded, smiling. "You'll take me?"

"We'll find the right place. Get you trained properly." Steve always loved how adventurous she was.

"I already bought a snorkel set. Pink. Naturally." Katya laughed as she splashed water on Steve.

Steve rolled his eyes, "I'll act surprised."

She kicked back, drifting. The wind carried the faint scent of coconut oil and grilled spices — the nearby beach bar was starting lunch early.

She breathed it in, eyes closed.

"This place," she said. "It feels like music."

Steve said nothing.

"Do you ever think about it?" she asked. "Letting go of everything. Staying somewhere like this. Just... living."

He looked at her, then out toward the reef. "What would

you paint?"

She laughed. "Oh, everything. Light on water. Stingrays. Starfish. Sea grapes. Bare feet. I'd open a studio and pretend I knew what I was doing."

"You'd get bored." He knew it was a lie.

"Not here. Not with you." The look she gave Steve melted him to the core.

He met her eyes. "You really believe that?"

"I do." She moved closer, brushing his shoulder with her fingertips. "You never ask me what I'm running from."

"Because you're not." Steve knew she had spent years running to him.

"Exactly." She smiled again, softer this time. "You're the one who's quiet."

"I like listening." Steve wondered why it had to be so difficult to love and keep his worlds apart.

"Then listen to this," she laughed. "I'm starving. Someone told me about a place — Pepper's, I think? For the jerk barbecue."

"It's real," he said. "Locals eat there. Jerk chicken that makes you cry for more."

"Perfect. You're driving." She laughed as she sprinted toward the rental car.

"Always," he hollered ahead to her, stopping long enough to gather their towels and bags.

They walked across the parking lot, hands brushing, into the tiki hut restaurant. Her laughter drifted ahead of them, carried by salt air and sunlight.

His satellite phone buzzed. He sighed. He wiped the barbecue jerk sauce off his mouth to answer. Peace never lasted.

"Susi."

"Steve, it's Anya." Her voice was calm, but he could tell she wasn't calling for small talk.

He turned away from Katya, walking towards the restrooms. "Talk to me."

"I'm supposed to be dismantling what's left of Markov's Night Stalkers, but they're phantoms. Too good at disappearing. I can't track them — some of them may have even changed identities." She hesitated, which wasn't like her. "I need help."

Steve exhaled. "I know a guy."

"I don't trust most people, Steve."

"You'll trust him."

Anya paused. "Fine, but no promises. I'll only meet him."

Steve smirked. "You already have. I'll set it up."

He hung up, washed his hands and returned to Katya. She knew he never truly had a vacation, with whatever his corporate career demanded of him.

Buckingham Palace's grandeur was unmatched, its golden chandeliers casting a warm glow across the assembled dignitaries, generals, and service members standing in quiet anticipation. The ceremony was formal — a recognition of battlefield leadership that had secured victory in Europe's darkest hours.

At the center of it all stood Lieutenant Colonel William Pembroke, back straight, eyes steady, the weight of history pressing against his chest as he faced His Majesty the King.

A hush fell over the grand hall.

"Lieutenant Colonel William Pembroke," the King's voice carried through the chamber, "for your outstanding leadership in the face of overwhelming adversity, for your decisive command during the Battle of the Bălți Steppe, and for your strategic acumen that saved untold lives, I am honored to bestow upon you the Distinguished Service Order."

A polished silver medal, gleaming with the emblem of valor, was pinned onto Pembroke's uniform.

The King took a step closer, regarding the officer with the respect reserved for men who had changed the course of history.

"Your actions ensured victory without unnecessary loss of life. For that, you have the gratitude of this nation and the honor of its highest recognition. A commendation alone is not sufficient. Kneel."

Pembroke obeyed, lowering himself onto one knee.

A ceremonial sword was placed in the King's hands. The

sword tapped once on each of his shoulders.

"For services rendered to the Crown and to the defense of freedom. Rise, Sir William Pembroke."

Pembroke rose, now a recipient of the Grand Knight Cross.

The applause was thunderous, a rare moment where the stoic discipline of the British Armed Forces gave way to unfiltered pride.

Every servicemember from the United Kingdom present in the European Contingency War was then recognized as His Majesty announced the awarding of the Conspicuous Gallantry Cross.

"To every British soldier, airman, and sailor who fought in the European Contingency War, you are the embodiment of courage. The sacrifices you made ensured victory, and today, you stand recognised among the bravest in our nation's history. For the first time in our history, every single one of our countrymen were on the frontline with you. You did your duty to ensure the enemy never would achieve victory. A momentous occasion."

A wave of Conspicuous Gallantry Crosses were distributed, every rank represented, from hardened veterans to those who had fought their first war and lived to tell the tale.

As Pembroke saluted, now a knight and commander of his own armored brigade, he caught the eye of General Nathaniel Collier, who stood at the back of the room, standing at attention, nodding in quiet approval.

Pembroke smirked slightly. Now the real work begins.

The bar in Lviv, Ukraine, was small, dimly lit, and completely unremarkable — the kind of place the espionage world loved because no one paid attention to anything. Jasper van Dijk sat with his usual Dutch gin, swirling the glass lazily as Anya walked in. She took a moment to glance around, nodding in approval.

"Nice place," she said. "Just the kind of bar that spy novels are set in."

Jasper smirked. "Now that you mention it ..." His mind was in motion.

"Major —" Jasper started.

"Colonel now," Anya corrected.

Jasper lifted his glass. "Colonel. Congratulations. Well earned."

She tilted her head, studying him. "I was taught that you don't usually buy people a drink unless you want something."

"That means you are buying the next round, Colonel?" Jasper joked in a rare moment.

Anya toasted back.

Jasper leaned back. "We would love to help with your problem, since we're on the same team now."

Anya narrowed her eyes. "We?"

Jasper exhaled and took a slow sip. "Ever heard of The Flying

Dutchman?"

She frowned. "As in the ghost ship that sails the seas and strikes terror in the hearts of sailors?"

"Something like that." He smiled. Van Dijk filled her in on their operations.

"Why are you telling a Colonel in the Russian GRU about your off-the-books intelligence service?"

Jasper chuckled, raising his glass again. "Because you're on the team now. Welcome, our Siberian Tiger."

Anya hesitated. "I never agreed to work with you."

"You want what is best for your people and your country," Jasper said. "Just like us. You need to be free of corruption to work independently when needed. We give you that freedom."

Anya considered it. "No governments? No misplaced loyalties?"

"No. Just the truth. However ugly it may be."

Another woman approached the table. Claire Rousseau.

"Tiger, meet the Queen of Diamonds," Jasper said. Claire smiled, taking a seat. "Anya needs to track every recipient of Markov's Night Stalker crypto payments."

Claire sipped her wine before adding, "Would you like their service numbers, office locations, and electronic footprints?"

Anya's eyes widened slightly. They already had everything.

Claire smirked. "I'll have it to you before dinner. I'll also throw in every Russian who has received payments. Even the ones you don't suspect yet."

Anya took a deep breath, sipping her vodka faster than she

normally would.

Jasper saw the shift. Small, but there. She was in.

For the first time in her career, Anya felt something unexpected — like she belonged to an actual team.

That was all he needed.

It was never about pawns and knights. It was about who set the board.

The Caribbean was paradise, but the world didn't care. Paradise interrupted had become the new norm. The next morning, Steve and Katya stepped off a private jet to be immediately whisked by motorcade to the White House. Collier had called while they were packing up their picnic.

"Report to the Oval Office at 1000 hours," Collier had said. No details, no explanations. Just orders.

Now, standing in the most powerful room in the world, Steve received the Presidential Medal of Freedom in a closed-door ceremony. No press. Just the President, the Secretary of Defense, the Joint Chiefs, General Nathaniel Collier, and Katya.

"I hate to sound cliche, but you did save the world, son," the President said.

Katya stepped closer, her voice barely audible. "What is this? What did you do?"

Before Steve could answer, Collier spoke. His voice was level, but not cold.

"He stopped the fire before it spread. Markov had control of nuclear warheads, crypto-funded operations across four continents, and half the Russian war council blackmailed. Steve collapsed the entire network in thirty-six hours."

One of the Joint Chiefs leaned forward, fingers laced. "There's no parade for ghosts. But you're looking at the man who put history back on its rails."

The Secretary of Defense let out a slow exhale. "We'll be digging out of his work for a decade. Intel cleanup, alliance management, diplomatic blowback — all of it. He bought us time."

Katya's hand found Steve's. "And you never said a word."

"I never wanted you caught in that world," Steve said softly. "But it came anyway."

Katya's gaze lingered on the medal. "You stopped a world war."

Steve nodded once.

She held his hand tighter. "I don't know if I can watch you do this again. I could not stand being apart like that, not knowing."

Steve didn't believe in heroism. You did the job, or you didn't. But even he had to admit — stopping Markov had mattered.

Steve looked toward Katya. It wasn't the weight of a medal that would disappear in a drawer that was weighing on his mind — and heart.

The job was never the problem. It was what it cost. He heard it in her words.

He squeezed her hand. "Then stay close enough to stop me."

He leaned slightly toward the President — just enough to draw an instant shift in posture from two Secret Service agents.

"Sir, there's one more favor."

The President smirked like he already knew. "She here legally?"

"On a marriage visa. Six months left."

The President turned to Katya. "Ma'am, would you step forward?"

She blinked. "I... what?"

"Raise your right hand."

She did.

"Repeat after me: I hereby declare, on oath..."

Steve took her hand as she recited the Oath of Citizenship in a trembling voice.

The President clapped her shoulder when it was done. "Welcome aboard, citizen. Sometimes the good guys get to win."

Steve didn't believe in happily-ever-after. But he did believe in standing your ground.

And right now, with Katya beside him, it felt like he'd found solid earth again.

In a sideways glance towards Katya, Steve smiled. The world

might never settle. But she did something even harder — she steadied him. And that was enough.

As she began to sign the oath paperwork rushed in by an aide, Katya looked up at the President.

"No politics between us, you said."

He smiled. "That promise stands."

She glanced at Steve. "Then I guess I'm staying." He smiled as Katya Sergeyevna Belikova signed her name, *Katya Sergeyevna Johnson* for the first time.

—

Anya Kuznetsova — Tiger — glanced at her phone as it vibrated against the lacquered wood of her hotel room desk. A number with no origin flashed across the screen. She hesitated, then answered.

"Tiger. Welcome to the team." The voice was smooth, confident — one she had never heard before. "I'm Cypher."

Anya straightened. Cypher. The name had surfaced in whispers, but no one in Moscow had ever managed to trace him. He was a phantom.

"I just sent you a high-level, eyes-only message," Cypher continued. "It will connect the dots with the information Claire is supplying."

Anya checked her encrypted inbox. A single message blinked into existence.

"Thank you, I guess." She tapped the file open, scanning the contents. Her breath caught. "Are you seriously sending me full evidence that our so-called open elections are already decided? That the outcome is rigged?"

Cypher's voice remained detached, analytical. "Markov's last act of defiance."

Anya gripped the phone tighter. Markov. Even in death, his influence

Anya scrolled the dossier slowly. Ministers. Military advisors. Presidential candidates. All tethered to Markov's accounts.

She'd buried too many friends for the flag. Now the flag looked foreign.

This wasn't about catching traitors anymore. It was about what came after.

Suddenly, she no longer wanted another mission from them. She wanted control — of her own conscience.

"We are glad to have you on the team," Cypher continued. "You will need my files after the election to make the necessary arrests."

Anya exhaled, staring at the screen, as if searching for a hidden escape route.

She whispered, almost to herself. "These are very high level names, even names in the Duma. I need someone I can trust in the FSB."

Cypher didn't reply.

He knew she wouldn't find one.

The White House's East Room was silent, filled with the weight of history as the President of the United States stepped to the podium. The European Contingency War had tested NATO, but more than that, it had tested the warriors who stood on the front lines, who had fought and bled to ensure freedom did not falter.

Medal ceremonies were always solemn affairs, but this one carried an even heavier burden.

And today, two of the Army's finest would receive the highest honors for their service.

"Lieutenant Colonel Rebecca Carter, front and center."

Carter stepped forward, her dress uniform impeccable, her posture rigid, but her eyes betrayed the emotions raging beneath the surface.

The Battle of the Bălți Steppe was already being called one of the greatest defensive battles in modern history, and she had been at its heart.

The President lifted the Distinguished Service Cross, the second highest military honor awarded to an Army officer.

"Lieutenant Colonel Carter, for extraordinary heroism in combat while leading the defense of NATO's eastern flank at the Battle of the Bălți Steppe, for refusing to break even when the odds were insurmountable, and for leading an armored counteroffensive that turned the tide of battle — your name will be recorded in the annals of history next to the Battle of Little Round Top."

The Distinguished Service Cross was pinned on her uniform, and the room erupted into applause.

Carter inhaled sharply, held her salute, and stepped back into formation.

But then came the moment everyone had been waiting for.

"It is with great sadness and the utmost honor that we recognize one more warrior today."

A folded flag was placed on the table beside the podium, a reminder of the price paid for victory.

"Colonel Sarah Donovan, through her final acts, ensured NATO's forces could rally. She refused to abandon her post. She refused to retreat. She stood until the very end. The 4th Guards Tank Brigade could not take an inch of NATO soil, because she did not let them."

A hush fell over the room.

The President turned to the Congressional Medal of Honor, encased in velvet, the nation's highest award for valor.

"Colonel Sarah Donovan is posthumously awarded the Congressional Medal of Honor for her unwavering bravery, for standing against impossible odds, and for making the ultimate sacrifice to defend freedom. She did not falter. She did not fail. And because of her, Europe stands free today."

A General of the United States Army Personnel Command stepped forward to accept the medal on behalf of her family.

The flag beside it would be presented to them in a private ceremony.

The room rose to their feet in a silent ovation.

The war had changed the world, but for those who stood here today, it had also changed them.

"We will reconvene at 11 A.M. on the South Lawn," from the press secretary.

he massive hall of the United Nations General Assembly was packed with world leaders, diplomats, and press from every corner of the globe. The air was thick with tension, but the grief was heavier.

At the podium stood President Andrei Pavlovich, flanked by his advisors. His expression was grave, his movements measured, but as he adjusted the microphone, his eyes betrayed a deep sadness.

He exhaled and began.

"Today, the world mourns the genocidal massacre of the Moldovan people. This was the work of one man."

A murmur spread through the assembly. Heads nodded in silent agreement. No one denied the scale of the atrocity, the unimaginable horror that had unfolded in Moldova. But the fact that a Russian President stood here acknowledging it was almost unprecedented.

Pavlovich let the silence settle before he spoke again, his gaze sweeping across the room.

"I was recently reminded of something. As President, everything that happens or fails to happen in Russia is my responsibility. This will never bring back the two and a half million lives taken needlessly. But Russia will not hide behind silence or excuses. We stand before you, not with words of deflection, but with action."

The murmuring ceased. He had their attention.

"Russia is paying full restitution to Ukraine, for our invasion, and we stand with NATO in the reconstruction of their great nation."

Gasps rippled through the assembly. Several diplomats exchanged glances, others whispered in hurried tones.

"Moldovans," Pavlovich continued, his voice breaking slightly, "there are simply no words. I refuse to insult you by even trying. Russia is making full restitution for your nation. Any Moldovan who wishes to enter Russia will do so without restriction. We are opening our borders. Temporary relocation centers are being built to house you while we rebuild your homeland — brick by brick, road by road, farm by farm."

He wiped his face, his tears visible on the massive screens projecting his speech to the world.

"Russia will fully arm and train your new military. Each Moldovan citizen, every single one, regardless of age, will receive €100,000 to help rebuild their lives. This can never bring back your loved ones, and for that, I can only offer my personal apology."

The room was silent now, stunned, watching as one of the most powerful men in the world stood before them, broken, grieving.

Never before had a world leader shed tears in such a meaningful, powerful way. His own tears, and the tears of those leaders in the room.

"I do not expect you to accept it."

Pavlovich's voice dropped lower, more personal.

"I do not expect your forgiveness."

He exhaled again and looked away, trying to gather himself, before forcing himself to meet the cameras again.

"I deserve neither. I failed your nation — not just my own."

The assembly remained frozen, absorbing what had just been said. It was the most public admission of failure by a Russian leader in modern history.

Seated at the back of the Russian delegation, two GRU agents watched the speech unfold with cold calculation.

One leaned in slightly to the other, keeping his voice low. "Does he realize what he just did?"

The second agent smirked, shifting in his chair. "He's digging his own grave."

The first agent studied Pavlovich for a moment before speaking again. "You think he's on the list?"

A pause. Then a slow nod.

"Soon."

The Night Stalkers are still out there.

The White House South Lawn was filled with military personnel, world leaders, and diplomats. As the President stood at the podium, the global tension was undeniable. Every ally and adversary watched.

Steve, seated in the front row, scanned the crowd. Jasper van Dijk sat two rows behind him, nodding knowingly.

Claire Rousseau, "Queen of Diamonds," watched from the French delegation. And Anya, ever the enigma, stood near the Russian observers — her loyalty still a question mark.

Collier stood in full dress uniform. He already knew what came next.

The President's voice hardened. "In order to meet the challenges of the future, the United States will spearhead a new military alliance. A treaty of Pacific nations, modeled after NATO, built to deter threats in an increasingly hostile world. It will be known as the Pacific Rim Treaty Organization."

A new alliance meant a new warfront. A ripple of murmurs spread through the audience.

Collier's name was next. Supreme Allied Commander RimPac.

Steve exhaled. Collier had fought an entire war, directing NATO from the sky.

Collier not only received The Presidential Medal of

Freedom, he was also awarded the Air Medal, with the President crediting him with redefining modern warfare — the citation read, "fighting an entire war from the sky, coordinating global battlefields in real-time, commanding at 40,000 feet".

Now, he was shifting his battlefield.

The President stepped back up to the podium.

"The United States has always stood for freedom. But the world has changed. New threats emerge. New alliances must be forged."

A ripple of murmurs spread. A new alliance meant a new warfront.

And then came the moment that shattered the world order.

The President's voice hardened.

"As of this moment, the United States of America is formally withdrawing from NATO."

Silence. Absolute, crushing silence.

Then, chaos.

The European delegation erupted into whispered arguments. Russian officials remained still, unreadable.

Steve closed his eyes. It was happening.

NATO had been built to hold the line. Now, it was crumbling before the eyes of the world.

The world had questions.

Nobody could answer them.

In Brussels, NATO Supreme Commander General Barrett — Sentinel — watched the live feed. His knuckles were white.

In New York, President Pavlovich sipped his tea, eyes fixed on the array of flags billowing in the wind through the frosted window. He exhaled slowly. "This changes everything."

A few kilometers away, deep within an upscale Moscow high-rise, Candidate Rodion Dragunov poured himself another glass of vodka. The campaign was merely a formality now. He smiled inwardly.

In Beijing, General Secretary Wei folded his hands. The dragon was waking.

In Jakarta, encrypted communiques flickered through naval command terminals. In Darwin, a late-night call rerouted three destroyers.

And in the shadows, Jasper van Dijk smiled.

Because The Flying Dutchman had already seen this coming. Anya was the start. The others — the quiet ones in Perth, Taipei, and Tokyo — were just waiting for a reason. His team would grow, by necessity.

After the ceremony, Collier caught Steve's arm. For thirty years, he'd held the line with words, warnings, and the weight of history — fighting wars, standing guard when others slept. Now it was breaking. And all he could do was make sure the right men were standing when it fell.

"Enjoy your honeymoon while you can. This world doesn't

let guys like us rest for long."

Steve nodded. He already knew that.

The war to end all wars — was beginning. Again.

Leave A Review

Books Thrive On Reviews By The Readers

Books live on reviews.

If you enjoyed this book,

please visit the website for links to leave reviews:

https://markwilderauthor.com/2-am

Preview Flashpoint Zero – The Aftershock
Washington, D.C. – Rose Garden

The President's voice rang out, with the cameras capturing every angle of the historic moment.

"The United States of America is leaving NATO."

Shockwaves rippled across the global stage as world leaders processed what they had just heard.

The assembled journalists began with frantic questioning.

Across the Atlantic, in the heart of Europe, a new power structure was forming.

SHAPE Headquarters, Casteau, Belgium – The War Room

The conference room, deep within Supreme Headquarters Allied Powers Europe, had seen more than its share of bad news.

Today, it was witness to one of history's worst moments.

"The United States of America is officially leaving NATO."

Silence.

Not the normal kind of silence. The absolute kind.

A silence that settles. The disbelief felt by men who spent their lives serving an alliance, suddenly realize it has just ended — had just watched it all vanish with a single sentence.

The words weren't just spoken. They had detonated.

At the head of the table, United States Marine Corps General Victor Barrett — Supreme Allied Commander Europe (SACEUR) — Call sign Sentinel — stared at the massive LCD screen.

The live news feed showed the President of the United States standing at a podium, flanked by the Secretaries of State and Defense.

The Rose Garden was a chaotic, shouting mess of reporters, all yelling at once.

These words immediately haunted each professional seated in the room:

> *"As of this moment, the United States of America is officially withdrawing from NATO. We will*

honor our commitments through the transition period, but as of today, our military will focus entirely on the Pacific."

Someone in the room muttered, "Jesus Christ."

Someone else whispered, "No. Worse."

Barrett didn't move. His fingers were laced together, knuckles turning white.

His career, his command — his entire existence — had been built on NATO.

He'd fought battles in its name and buried men in its defense.

And now, with a single decision made by men in suits, rather than uniforms, it was over.

His voice, when it came, was low and deliberate. "Is this real?"

At the other end of the table, Jasper van Dijk, his personal intelligence chief, nudged his laptop forward. "It's real."

The video feed was being watched all over the world now, on every major network and social media platforms.

Every government office from Brussels to Beijing was watching NATO dissolve before their eyes.

A British admiral finally spoke, his tone was thick with disbelief. "This is madness. NATO is a deterrence. Without this deterrence —"

"Russia will move."

The words didn't come from the admiral. They came from General Victor Barrett.

The war room stayed silent for another moment. Then all hell broke loose.

"Get me the European Council — now!" Barrett barked, snapping out of his shock. Aides sprinted from the room, cell phones and headsets to their ears.

A French general threw his hands up. "Merde! The Americans have lost their minds! Do they think Russia is just going to sit still?"

"Russia doesn't have to move immediately. We're doing their work for them. The Baltics are exposed. Moldova has been exterminated. " Van Dijk, ever the cool-headed pragmatist, exhaled through his nose, adjusting his tie. "We still have forces in Ukraine that aren't ready to stand on their own. And as of right now, there's no unified command to stop Russia from deciding which piece to take next."

"I want a direct line to Berlin." Barrett snapped his fingers at his aide. "Now."

Another officer, a German colonel, spoke up. "Sir, the Bundestag has already convened an emergency session."

"Then they can answer the damn phone." Barrett's jaw tightened. "And get me London!"

The LCD screen changed. The White House press conference was spiraling into chaos. Reporters screamed over each other, demanding answers. A correspondent stood up. *"Does this mean war?"*

Barrett leaned back, arms crossed, eyes cold.

"Not yet," he answered from thousands of miles away. Then, almost as an afterthought, he added, "But it will."

"Sir, you have an urgent call." NATO's Communications Officer added, quite puzzled, "It's from the Mexican President."

Brussels – European Council Chambers

Brussels didn't take the time to catch its breath. The live feed from SHAPE had barely gone black when the chamber erupted.

France's President Charles Dutoit spoke first, and it wasn't about diplomacy.

"I warned you," he said, eyes hard as flint. "Washington only looks after Washington. Now look at us."

German Chancellor Annalena Weber didn't look up from the notes she'd been making through the entire address. "This isn't the hour for victory laps, Charles."

Poland's President, Marek Nowak, leaned into his microphone. "It's the hour to assume we're alone."

Spain's defense minister tried to slow the stampede. "NATO still exists."

Nowak snapped his head toward him. "For how long? Without American deterrence, what are we? A flag and a logo."

Austria's Chancellor, Eva Moser, stood and waited until the murmurs thinned enough for her to be heard.

When she spoke, her voice carried the clean caution of a country that had survived conflict, wars, and unrest.

"The Americans have made their position clear," she said. "NATO is fractured, whether we like the word or not. And Europe can no longer subcontract its survival."

A few heads lifted.

"The last time I raised it, I was mocked," Moser continued, looking from face to face. "A unified European Defense Force. Today, I'm not asking for permission to discuss it. I'm proposing we formalize it — now. Eurocorps. EU Battlegroups. Common Security and Defence Policy structures. Put them under one command and stop pretending time and nations will wait."

Voices overlapped — some demanding immediate deployments, others clinging to diplomacy with Moscow as if history hadn't already forced the consequences.

Neutral nations pushed back on the very idea of a unified European army.

Smaller states worried about being swallowed by the larger ones.

The room wasn't negotiating yet.

It was panicking.

Nowak leaned forward, eyes sharp. "Who commands it?"

Weber didn't hesitate. "Germany carries the industrial base and the weight. Berlin is the logical headquarters."

Dutoit gave a short, contemptuous laugh. "Berlin? France bleeds and pays too. Paris is the only choice with the political gravity to hold it."

Nowak's answer came like a slap. "Warsaw. Frontline states don't get to be ruled by capitals that mistake distance for safety."

Italy's President, Giancarlo Bellini, lifted a hand as if he were calling a meeting to order instead of trying to prevent a continent from splintering. "Then we'll spend three weeks arguing about whose city gets to be the symbol while Russian armor moves."

The room surged again.

Portugal spoke about being ignored. Finland about the border. Ireland and Malta about neutrality. Iceland spoke plainly: "We have police, not an army. What does 'contribution' mean for nations like ours?"

One question hung over the room:

If NATO's strongest ally is gone, what replaces it?

The United Kingdom's Prime Minister, Malcolm Carroway, waited until the debate hit that familiar European crescendo — everyone talking, nothing moving — then spoke without standing.

"The UK will join," he said.

A few heads turned. A few brows lifted.

"We're outside the Union," he continued, "not outside Europe. We bring lift, ISR, and maritime eyes. And we bring one condition — this cannot become another committee. This has to fight and be allowed to win."

Dutoit's chin rose. "And who do you suggest the orders come from?"

Carroway didn't blink. "A single commander. One chain. Unity of command — orders, not requests."

That was the line that landed. Not because it was poetic. Because it was military truth.

Then Luxembourg's Prime Minister, Jean Gallesen, spoke for the first time.

"Enough."

It wasn't loud. It didn't need to be.

The room stalled mid-motion. The translators went still.

Gallesen removed his glasses, folded them, and set them on the table like he was putting an end to something that had already wasted a century.

"This," he said, "is why Europe never finishes anything. We don't need more speeches. We need a decision."

Bellini's mouth curved with the faintest hint of humor — dangerous humor. "Then perhaps Luxembourg should host it, if you're so tired of hearing us."

For a moment it hung there — half joke, half dare.

Spain's Prime Minister, Isabel Santiago, didn't smile. "Seconded."

It was no longer a joke.

Cyprus's President, Nikos Demetriou, turned toward the chamber and the assembled military chiefs behind them. "Vote now on the motion: the European Defense Force is formalized immediately — with or without unanimity — command headquarters in Luxembourg. Those who join, raise your hand."

Hesitation.

Then one.

Then another.

Then half the room.

Hands went up in clusters as governments made decisions they had avoided for decades.

Some lifted slowly, like they were signing their names into history. Others snapped up like relief.

It was happening.

Santiago looked to Gallesen. "Who commands your forces?"

Gallesen didn't answer immediately. He glanced toward the military advisors, then back to the chamber. "The Grand Duke is the head of our armed forces."

It was not lost on anyone that nobility would once again lead the armies of Europe.

Carroway didn't. "Fine," he said evenly. "We have put a single commander in the chair. He answers to NATO's Military Committee. Not to twenty-seven capitals. Deputies from France and Germany. Polish Chief of Staff. Rotate by performance, not calendar."

Dutoit held Carroway's gaze as if searching for leverage. "And if we disagree?"

Carroway's reply was flat. "Then we lose."

Silence followed — the room had finally stopped thinking like individual nations.

Gallesen put his glasses back on. "We reconvene in one hour with our defense chiefs. You will give them authority, and then we will get out of the way."

Chairs moved and papers gathered. Phones were turned on again.

As they stood to leave, Demetriou's voice cut through one last time, filled with equal parts exhaustion and warning.

"This is a reminder of how quickly we can move," he said, "when we stop performing separately."

The Kremlin — Situation Room

The doors to the Situation Room slammed open. An aide snapped out of the way as President Andrei Pavlovich strode in, coat still on and expressionless.

No signs of joy or anger. Just a controlled satisfaction behind the man's eyes.

At the far end of the table, newly promoted General Dmitry Sorokin was patiently leaning forward, untethered.

His face was awash in the pale light from the monitors, reflecting off his eyes like ice.

He had just buried his little brother only three days ago.

Colonel Alexei Sorokin, Fourth Guards Tank Brigade who

had been killed in the European Contingency War by a British Challenger.

A live feed from Brussels was displayed on the wall. European leaders were arguing over procedure while the world moved without them.

Too many hands in the air with too many words.

Sorokin didn't look away.

"This is an opportunity," he said in a calm voice.

It was the calm of a man who had already made the decisions and was just waiting for permission.

Minister of Foreign Affairs Oleg Petrov shifted in his chair. "We must tread carefully. NATO still exists in name. Europe has not fully rearmed. If we move too soon —"

"Too soon?" Sorokin's head tilted a fraction, hand gesturing toward the feed. "Look at them. Leaderless and scattered. Their alliances are broken, and you want to give them time to remember how to become dangerous again."

Defense Minister Alexei Bondarenko cleared his throat. "Then what are you proposing, General?"

"Leverage." Sorokin was direct. "The world believes Russia is weak. Let them keep believing it. Then we will remind them what they have forgotten."

He touched the console and the Brussels feed collapsed into a map.

Europe filled the wall, bright with borders that could easily transition to anti tank trenches.

North America sat beyond it, distant and arrogant.

Sorokin's finger traced the first move.

"Europe first," he said. "Fast, loud, and decisive."

A pulse of markers appeared over Poland.

"Poland is the hinge," Sorokin continued. "Break it, and the rest of the door swings."

Icons flared across the Baltics, then further south. Arrows, airfields, rail, and hubs that fed armies and cities alike.

"Missile strikes would create command paralysis while airborne drops occur where they cannot afford to lose roads. Special teams will be sent to blind their coordination. Massed drone attacks to reduce air defense capabilities."

He didn't need to call it a war plan.

He tapped again and the map widened.

Alaska lit up, then western Canada.

The room changed.

Even men who built careers imagining war reacted when the war moved somewhere it should not exist.

Bondarenko's eyebrows rose before his discipline caught up. "North America."

Sorokin nodded once. "From the north. While they stare at the actions in Europe."

Petrov started to speak and stopped.

Sorokin's voice stayed steady. "Europe will fall. North America will burn. And Russia will prove itself."

Silence settled over the table. Not from fear, but calculations.

Across from Sorokin, Pavlovich watched without

expression, hands folded like a man attending his own trial.

He did not flinch at the scale of the plan's ambition.

He tapped once on the table. A soft sound that carried anyway.

"Ambitious."

Bondarenko found his footing. "Logistics. Rail transport. Fuel. Ammunition. Sustainment."

Sorokin didn't look offended.

He looked amused that someone still believed wars could be won by simply asking the right questions.

"I will brief the full support plan," he said. "The deception plan as well. It will detail movements, cover stories, and training rotations. The parts that will make it look routine."

Pavlovich's finger tapped again, then stopped.

"Not yet."

Sorokin blinked. The first genuine surprise to cross his face. "Sir —"

Pavlovich raised his hand to restore order.

"We do not strike when the enemy expects it," Pavlovich said. His voice was quieter than Sorokin's and it held more weight. "We let them fight among themselves first. We let them waste resources and we let them fracture further, while we give them something they will want to believe."

Sorokin's eyes narrowed. "Peace."

Pavlovich held his gaze. "I will offer it. They will call it progress and stability and they will trust us enough to stop preparing for the worst."

A chill moved through the room, subtle as a draft through stone.

Sorokin's mouth finally curved. This time it was real.

"Then we let them burn."

Pavlovich exhaled slowly. Not with feelings of relief or doubt. He felt like a man balancing a knife on his finger, by its tip.

"First I must offer peace," he said, gesturing to the screens. "They must believe it before any of this becomes possible."

Sorokin leaned back, his confidence returning like blood after a tourniquet was released.

"We have free elections in ten days," he said, voice low, almost conversational. "You are weak. Dragunov will immediately execute my plan. Your peace will serve as my cover."

Pavlovich did not react.

Saint Petersburg

Steve watched the words crawl across the bottom of the screen, repeating until they lost all meaning

BREAKING: U.S. EXIT FROM NATO FINALIZED — EUROPE IN CRISIS.

BREAKING: RUSSIA CALLS FOR "NEW ERA OF PEACE" FOLLOWING U.S. WITHDRAWAL.

Peace.

He didn't touch the whiskey. The glass sat in his hand anyway, cold against his palm, having found something solid to hold onto while the rest of the world shifted.

Across the room Sergey stood at the kitchen counter with his own drink, turning it with the amber liquid catching the light.

He looked like a man listening to a weather forecast. He was neither surprised, nor impressed. He was just taking note of which way the wind was blowing.

Katya sat close enough that Steve could feel her before he looked at her. Her fingers threaded through his. Firm, not pleading. Claiming him.

Steve exhaled through his nose and stared at the headline again. "I don't know what I am right now."

Sergey's eyes flicked over. "You're tired."

"I'm serious." Steve kept his voice down. "I'm an American and a NATO officer." He nodded at the screen. "Except now I'm not. They just pulled the pin. So who do I answer to? Who do I belong to?"

Katya tightened her grip. "You belong with me."

He turned his head and met her eyes. She held herself the way she always did when she was afraid and refused to show it. Chin up. Shoulders square. Stubborn.

A hug wouldn't fix this. He knew it and she knew it.

"I felt as you do when the Soviet Union collapsed." Sergey set his glass down. The clink wasn't loud, but it cut through the room. "This was coming," he said. "The West spent years tearing itself apart. Today they just did it in public."

"That's not what's eating me," Steve said.

Sergey's eyes turned to his daughter. "It's her."

Silence settled in. The kind that meant the truth had finally been spoken.

Sergey moved to the window and lifted the curtain a fraction.

Streetlights washed the pavement below. St. Petersburg sat calm, almost gentle, the first hints of autumn in the trees.

People down there still had places to go, errands to run, and dinners to make.

Steve knew Sergey wasn't watching the leaves as he leaned forward, elbows on his knees. "She's not safe here."

Katya's fingers dug into his hand. "I'm not leaving."

He looked at her again, really looked.

Not the woman in the chair, but to the years behind her eyes. He saw the years that war had taken from them.

"You have to," he said.

"No." Her response was both flat and immediate.

Sergey turned from the window. "You could both leave."

Steve let out a breath that almost became a laugh. "To where? The U.S. just has lit the fuse, Europe's going to turn into a locked bunker, and Russia..." He nodded at the screen. "Russia is waiting for the smoke to cover the move."

Sergey lifted his glass. "Tahiti."

Steve huffed once. "Only if you're coming with us."

Katya shook her head. "I'm not running, Steve. My work is here. My father's life is here. We stay."

Steve's expression tightened. He looked to Sergey, not for permission, but for an idea that didn't end in blood.

Sergey took a sip and set the glass down again. "She's right."

Steve stared at him. "Dammit, Sergey."

"You love her," Sergey said. "That means you don't get to order her around. Not if you respect her."

It landed harder than Steve wanted.

His gaze dropped to Katya's hand resting in his. The rings caught the firelight.

Not merely jewelry.

Not symbols.

They are proof that a life had finally started to exist between them, fragile and real.

He didn't want to lose her to distance again.

He looked up. "If we stay, we're careful. Every step. No routines. No patterns."

Katya arched an eyebrow. "We?"

Steve let out a slow breath. She had him and she knew it. He nodded once. "We."

Sergey's hand came down on Steve's shoulder, a brief squeeze with more meaning than words. "Then it's settled."

Steve didn't answer. His eyes went back to the television.

A Russian commentator was already explaining, with rehearsed patience, why Moscow was now the only adult left in the room. Why "peace" required obedience. Why history had simply corrected itself.

Steve felt something cold move in his gut. Not fear, but recognition.

He stood and set the whiskey down untouched.

"I need to meet with someone," he said.

Katya started to ask who, but he was already reaching for the secure satellite phone.

Guam – General Collier's Arrival

Overlord One was his aircraft's call sign now.

The converted jet settled onto the runway at Davis Air Force Base and rolled out into the heat, tires gliding over concrete that felt a world away from Europe.

This was supposed to be a stop to stand up the Pacific command structure, direct facilities, and set the rhythm.

Then he'd go back to Hungary long enough to collect his life.

He had left without even packing.

Collier stepped down the stairs into a tight honor cordon with U.S. Marines in dress and Australian officers in service greens.

He returned the salute without breaking stride. The pageantry didn't matter.

"The perk of being a regional commander," he told himself,

quiet enough that only he could hear it, "is having an aircraft when you need one."

Tomorrow he would be drinking coffee from a different mug. He always noticed how coffee tasted different from any other mug but his own.

Inside the operations space they had built for him, the map was already laid out. Not decorative, but working, with pins, overlays, air routes, shipping lanes, and refuel tracks.

Collier didn't waste a minute.

He put a finger on northern Australia.

"Seventeenth Armored Cavalry," he said. "Broome, Darwin, and Cairns. Headquarters to be co-located in Darwin with the joint naval base. Immediate readiness protocols."

The staff around him moved with their pens, tablets, and headsets. No questions yet.

He shifted to the maritime overlays.

"All former European Fleet elements deploy across Taiwan and the Philippines upon arrival. Show of force first. Port rotations after. I want the message sent before the paperwork catches up."

Another tap — air power.

"Theater Air assets re-base as follows," he said, and let the list land clean, one line at a time. "Philippines for rapid response. Northern Australia for bomber presence. Northern New Zealand for southern Pacific reconnaissance. Singapore forward strike. Japan for northern Pacific reconnaissance."

He glanced to the right-hand side of the map where the

Indian Ocean bled into Africa.

"The Marine contingent out of Böblingen will relocate to Diego Garcia," Collier said. "It gives us control over African-based Marine units and flexibility for the Fifteenth Fleet once it's operating in the Philippines."

An aide stepped forward with the political update.

Neutrality had been declared by Vietnam, Papua New Guinea, Tahiti, and Fiji. No permanent installations would be allowed.

Collier read it once, then set it down as if it weighed nothing. "Noted," he said, which was as close to approval as it was going to get. "We'll work around them."

He stared at the map for another minute, letting the new geometry settle.

The Pacific wasn't heating up. It was already hot.

He just hadn't been there long enough to feel it.

He turned back to the planners.

"Get the ships loaded with Seventeenth ACR," he said. "Vehicles, stores, support. I want them through Suez by close of business on 1 November. Every aircraft except fighter support goes to new bases. Cargo birds move everything out of the old airfields. As many trips as it takes."

He looked at the schedule board. Europe was already shrinking behind them.

"Our former bases need to be ghost towns by next Wednesday. We're a mobile military," he reminded them. "Start acting like it. Refuel tanker wings operate around the clock."

He didn't say what he was already calculating — that he needed to be on the first air convoy heading back if he wanted a chance to move his own gear and his command center before things kicked off.

—

Lviv, Ukraine — The Flying Dutchman – A New Era

With General Markov's crypto assets officially seized, Claire Rousseau completed the reallocation in one final pass.

Ukraine and Moldova were paid in full. No delays. No bargaining. No excuses.

What remained went offshore, distributed into accounts designed to survive courts, governments, and headlines.

Untouchable to everyone else. Fully usable by The Flying Dutchman.

Across from her, Cypher scanned the new ledger and let a small grin show.

"So I finally get a salary," he said. "What's next?"

Jasper van Dijk leaned back, took a slow sip of his drink, and didn't bother dressing it up.

"From here on out, any future financial crimes we uncover follow a process," he said. "Asset forfeiture first. Reparations second. Then we fund ourselves and the network."

He glanced at Cypher over the rim of his glass.

"Consider the paycheck an incentive."

Cypher's grin widened. "Sounds fair. Time to start digging."

"It's time for me to process my military retirement, we are going to be busy." Jasper's secure phone buzzed in his hand as he added, "We need Susi."

St. Petersburg

Steve stood at the window, the city spread out below him in clean lines and old stone.

Early October light hit the glass and caught on the new wedding band on his finger. It flashed once, a small bright thing in a world that had stopped promising anything.

He knew what had to be done.

Katya came up behind him and wrapped her arms around his waist. Her cheek pressed between his shoulder blades.

"You don't have to leave," she said.

He let out a breath and turned, brushing a curl away from her face with his thumb. "I do," he said. "But I'll be right back."

It sounded like a lie even when he said it carefully.

He looked at her and felt the familiar weight settle behind his ribs.

In Russia, the only constant was instability.

Behind them, Sergey Belikov watched from his chair, quiet

in the way old men become when they are measuring risk.

Katya's father didn't intervene. He just observed, as if he'd been watching this storm form for decades.

Steve nodded toward him. "Come on, Sergey. We retire somewhere warm together. Tahiti is beautiful all year."

Sergey gave a low chuckle and shook his head. "Russia is my home, son."

His eyes flicked, barely noticeable, toward Katya. "And someone needs to stay. Watch over things."

Steve stepped closer and clapped him on the shoulder. A man-to-man touch that meant more than advice. "Then promise me you'll keep a low profile."

Sergey smirked, the expression thin but real. "I never make promises I can't keep."

Steve hugged her once more. Quick, tight, final in the way goodbyes try not to be. He held Katya a second longer, then let go before he could change his mind.

One last look, and he walked away. Not because he wanted distance.

Because if he was going to build roots, he had to stop the loose ends that kept pulling him back.

Lviv, Ukraine

It was a dimly lit bar in the narrow demilitarized zone of

Lviv, Ukraine.

Jasper van Dijk sat in a corner booth, a fresh glass of Dutch gin and tonic in front of him.

Across from him, Steve leaned back after three days on the road, watching the bartender pour another round.

Lviv had become the cantina of espionage and the underworld.

Not lawless — just self-regulated. Filled with arms dealers and clandestine agents, as well as smugglers of art, precious metals, and gemstones.

"So," Jasper said, tapping his glass to Steve's whiskey, "we've got funding, no bureaucracy, and more enemies than I can count. But what we don't have… is you."

Before Steve could answer, soft fingers traced across his back. A familiar voice, low and teasing.

"I'm one of the perks of the job."

Steve turned, locking eyes with Anya Kuznetsova.

She smirked, leaning close, her breath warm against his ear. "Didn't think you could get rid of me that easily, did you?"

Jasper chuckled and raised his glass. "Steve, Anya is now one of us. Tiger."

He signaled the bartender. "Your best vodka. Chilled glass. We have a lot to celebrate."

They had no headquarters. No single safe haven — only safehouses scattered across continents. Places to disappear, plan, and strike without warning.

The Flying Dutchman was untethered now. Bound by no

government. Answerable only to themselves.

Exactly where Steve belonged.

SHAPE Headquarters, Casteau, Belgium – The War Room

"Buenos dias, Presidente. Generale Barrett hablando." Sentinel's eyes continued to grow. He forgot to breathe.

General Barrett transferred the call to a secure bridge for Brussels. "Patch the Summit. Keep him on the line."

He was already moving toward the exit for the flight line, grabbing his communications officer by the sleeve, explaining along the way.

Brussels – European Defense Summit

The summit of flag officers had already descended into chaos when General Barrett burst in.

"You can leave, AMERICAN," a voice from across the room said — echoing what everyone was thinking.

"Until I am properly relieved, I am still the Commander of all NATO forces," Barrett snapped back. "You will respect the position, regardless of who sits in the chair."

Sentinel had everyone's attention. "My allegiance is to my posting, not a flag."

He regained his composure and nodded once. "My apologies for interrupting. This is of the utmost importance."

He opened the call on the chamber speakers.

The transmission from Mexico came through.

Silence fell as the Mexican President's face appeared on the monitors.

"*Honored members of NATO and the European Union,*" he began, voice firm. "*Mexico formally requests entry into NATO.*"

The room erupted in whispers and side conversations.

Portugal's Prime Minister leaned toward France's President Charles Dutoit. "Did you expect this?"

"Not in a hundred years," Dutoit muttered.

Poland's Marek Nowak cut through first. "Why?"

The Mexican President didn't hesitate. "*Because we see what is happening. If Russia opens a front in North America, we will be next. We do not trust the United States anymore. But we trust NATO.*"

The chamber went still.

"*We offer our military, our bases, and our commitment to defend the Atlantic Alliance.*"

Barrett leaned forward, already working the implications. "This changes everything," he said under his breath.

Then, louder, "If the Council concurs, we stand up a Mexico cell at SHAPE tonight — planning, basing, intelligence liaison. Article Four consultations immediately. Protocol work begins in capitals."

Nowak answered without delay. "Draft the protocols later. Move the planning now."

German Chancellor Annalena Weber voiced what everyone else had swallowed. "Can we truly do this? Process matters. Can we act today in law? *Ist das überhaupt möglich?*"

***

Beijing, China

General Secretary and Central Military Commission Chairman Lì Xíng and the Central Committee quietly watched the world slide toward disarray — the U.S. withdrawal from NATO, elections approaching in Russia, Ukraine rebuilding, refugees fleeing Moldova.

Lì Xíng leaned forward, his voice smooth but commanding.

"The world was once ruled by order," he said. "And it will be again. By our hand."

The dragon waits.

***

To order Flashpoint Zero, or to learn more, please visit:
https://markwilderauthor.com/flashpoint-zero/

About the Author

Mark Wilder is a retired U.S. Army First Sergeant and Abrams Tank Commander who spent part of his military career patrolling the border traces of the inner German frontier during the Cold War. His boots have touched ground across Germany, Japan, the U.S., and Australia — but today he writes while he also pursues his passion for gardening.

An enthusiast of modern warfare fiction, geopolitics, and the spycraft that shaped a generation, Wilder draws inspiration from the sharp realism of Clancy, Coyle, Ludlum, and DeMille. *2 A.M.* marks the explosive beginning of *The Flying Dutchman* series — born from Cold War memory, battlefield precision, and the soundtrack of a world that never truly stood down.

Also by Mark Wilder

<u>Standalone Novellas</u>

I Was Never Supposed To Exist — But I Do

Memoir — Chantelle

<u>Flying Dutchman Series</u>

2 A.M.

Flashpoint Zero

<u>Love and War Collection</u>

The Witches of the Red Sky

Nonfiction / Reference

<u>The Wilder Way to Getting Things Done</u>

<u>Reference Books to Improve Your Life</u>

Publishing Isn't Marketing

&

The Publishing Isn't Marketing Companion Workbook

Is Your Novel "Just Another Can Of Beans" On The Shelf?

COMING IN 2026

Nonfiction / Reference
<u>The Wilder Way to Getting Things Done</u>
<u>Reference Books to Improve Your Life</u>
The 96-Hour Rule

&

The 96-Hour Rule Quarterly Workbook
Keep Projects Moving, Hit Your Deadlines, Finish What You
Start

<u>Historical Collections</u>
History's Greatest Battle Poems
*A Collection of the World's Greatest Battle Poems Through
1930*

Fiction
<u>Flying Dutchman Series</u>
The Architect — Cathedral of the World

<u>The Guardian Chronicles</u>
The Crimson Petal and the Blade

COMING IN 2027

<u>The Viking Queens — A Three-Era Saga</u>
<u>Era I — Rise & Consolidation</u>

Åsa of Agder (Norway)

Thyra "Danebod" (Denmark)

Ragnhild Sigurdsdotter (Norway)

Gyda Eiriksdottir (Norway)

<u>Stories of the Heart</u>

Still, I Choose You

— A Story of Three Hearts

Please visit:

MarkWilderAuthor.com